REUNION

EDEN WINTERS

ROCKY RIDGE BOOKS

Reunion © Eden Winters 2017

Cover art by LC Chase
Interior Layout by P.D. Singer

ISBN-13   978-1-62622-055-3

Published by:

Rocky Ridge Books
PO Box 6922
Broomfield, CO 80021
www.RockyRidgeBooks.com

Other titles by Eden Winters:

The Diversion Series

Diversion (Diversion #1)
Collusion (Diversion #2)
Corruption (Diversion #3)
Manipulation (Diversion #4)
Redemption (Diversion #5)
Suspicion (Diversion #7)

Novels

A Matter of When
The Angel of Thirteenth Street
Fallen Angel
Settling the Score
The Telling
The Wish
Duet
Naked Tails

Novellas and other shorts

The Match Before Christmas (Match #1)
Fanning the Flames (Match #2)
A Lie I Can Live With (Match #3)
Galen and the Forest Lord
Summer Boys
Tinsel and Frost
Highway Man
Almost Mine
The Pirate's Gamble

Many thanks to T.D. O'Malley, Z. Allora, P.D. Singer, and Doug Starr, for priceless critique, handholding, and the precious gift of their friendship, Nurse Sarah for answering thousands of questions and pointing me towards research material, David O'Sullivan for sharing his law enforcement knowledge, L.C. Chase for an amazing cover, my family for unwavering support, and my editor, Jerry L. Wheeler.

Also, many thanks to readers who've followed Bo and Lucky from the very beginning of their tale, and wanted more.

REUNION

EDEN WINTERS

CHAPTER ONE

Another stinking alley. One of many in the bad part of Atlanta, reeking of trash and piss. Either rats or big-assed palmetto bugs scuttled along the ground. Lucky's shiver wasn't all due to a nippy spring evening.

Light mist chilled his face. He stuck close to the shadows, inching away from safety and closer to who the fuck knew. The nasty fug crept into his mouth and took up residence on his tongue. His throbbing ankle worked overtime to convince him he'd gotten too old for this shit.

Damned gimpy-assed leg. Lucky's heart pounded, and sucking air like a vacuum didn't fill his lungs with enough oxygen.

After this case, he'd have to put in more time running, to hell with the bitching ankle. And working out. And doing whatever else came to mind so a mere two-mile run didn't leave him huffing and puffing.

The alleyway ended. He flattened his back against the wall, whipped his head far enough to the left to peer around the corner, and pulled back. Yup. The white panel van. Though the van hid the perps from view, the bumps and bangs gave their whereabouts away.

Six-feet-plus of pissed off fellow agent faced him in all her muscled glory, pressed against the far wall and scarcely breathing hard. Showoff. One look at Loretta Johnson and the perps might shit their pants.

They might laugh at him—for a minute. Small dogs bit hard.

Gun held close to his face, Lucky made a crisscross sign to his partner with his free hand. Johnson nodded. Nice having her play for the good guys. If not for the matching SNB logo on their shirts, he'd be scared of her too.

In a few seconds, some two-bit drug dealers were going to get hit with a whole lot of what they had coming. "If they make me late getting home..." Johnson muttered.

Oh no. Don't ever keep Mama Bear out too late to feed her kid.

Lucky unlocked his knees and bounced out a count. On three, he darted to the left and around the back of the van. Johnson took the front. The van's headlights projected her shadow to giant proportions on the wall behind her.

"Southeastern Narcotics Bureau. Hands on your head!" she barked.

One of the suspects smiled the slick, oily smile of a slime ball. He turned to Johnson with his hands out to his sides. "What have we here?"

His buddy, in the middle of picking up a big blue tote, did as told. Smart man. Making Slime Ball Dumbass the boss, and the flunky with his hands on his head, too much gut, and not enough hair, Idiot Number One.

Idiot Number Two jumped out of the van. From this angle, the asshole couldn't see the red dot on his back. Yup. As much as Lucky hated teamwork, having a weapon trained on an enemy's back worked for him.

And they hadn't yet spotted Lucky, adding "Stupid" to their job titles.

Dumbass took a step forward. "You wouldn't shoot an unarmed man, would you?"

Johnson's evil grin didn't faze the guy, but it scared the shit out of Lucky.

Lucky's musclebound protégé had once knocked his sorry ass to the ground. This guy, who'd probably never lifted anything heavier than a case of beer, wouldn't be a problem.

Shit-for-brains took another step. "I don't believe you'll shoot."

Johnson kept an eye on Dumbass, leaving Lucky free to watch Idiot One and Idiot Two. The first, not given to fighting,

2

now lay stretched out on the ground. "Stop, Ramon. He means business," the guy shouted. Repeated arrests left a man well trained, and twenty bucks said his record beat Lucky's. And how nice of him to provide a name.

"Shut the fuck up!" Dumbass shot back.

"Smile, you're on my body cam..." Hell, the sound of Johnson's booming voice alone ought to put the fear of God into all three targets.

Idiot Number Two reached into the van and pulled out a gun.

Go on, you sonofabitch. Aim at her. Give us a reason to take you down. Body cams came in handy for proving the need for use of force.

And still Dumbass approached, sporting his red back dot. The dot, shuffling from the alleyway, and heavy breathing announced the arrival of the cavalry—slow asses.

Okay, Lucky and Johnson secured the scene, with a man on a balcony above and another in plain sight across the street. The boss could ream Lucky out later for not waiting until backup arrived to approach their marks.

Johnson put extra snarl into her words. "Your buddy there has three seconds to drop the gun, or I'll drop you both." Dumbass hadn't yet realized the danger. The woman standing before him didn't need a gun to put him down.

And call her a helpless female at your own risk. Right before your ass hit the ground.

The asshole walked up and snatched the gun from her hand. She let him.

He scowled. "Hey, no bullets."

Johnson smiled and folded her arms across her body-armor-covered chest. "You're right. I won't shoot you. But my partner might." She nodded toward Lucky.

The guy spun, his face a perfect visual of *Oh shit!* "Get him!"

Idiot Two raised his gun while Idiot One cowered on the pavement, and Dumbass made the biggest target he possibly could.

3

Three shots. Three men lying twitching on the ground. Not as permanent as a gun, but a Taser had its place in the great scheme of things.

And didn't require nearly as much red tape.

Whether the case ended successful or a total fuckup, Lucky still hated all the damned paperwork. But typing up reports gave him a good excuse to stay in his cube, or rather, his side of the cube. He flicked a glance to the unlived-in looking desk across the way. A closed laptop, a pen holder with four matching, department-issued black ink pens, and a Christmas cactus trailing shoots down the side of a filing cabinet. No human.

Lucky's desk stayed piled high with papers, files, and mostly-empty Starbucks cups. Five cups meant Friday. His current brew sat closest to his laptop. Several times in the past, he'd grabbed the wrong one. Brrr... Week old coffee.

He leaned back in the chair he alone in the department managed to tame, one hand on the desk to steady himself lest the Hell Bitch throw him. She'd tried before. Lordy, she'd tried. Succeeded a time or two. But if a chair threw him without video evidence on social media, it never really happened in his book.

He shifted his gaze back to the clean side of the cube. Where was Bo anyway? He'd better not have snuck back to spring a surprise. Only twenty minutes left to be home free, if no one called Lucky into the boss's office to ambush him with cake and off-key singing. Officially, he'd grow a year older tomorrow, but the department never seemed to care. They'd celebrate whenever they felt like.

So far this year, no one had embarrassed him with cake and ice cream, expecting him to play along and act cheerful. People going all out on birthdays. Why? He'd counted the days until he'd turned sixteen and got his driver's license. Then he marked the calendar pages until eighteen, when he was deemed legally, if somewhat inaccurately, an adult.

Then he couldn't wait until twenty-one to go clubbing and survive getting carded. Then he'd counted days until he'd done his time and become a free man.

Now, years rolled around faster and faster. He'd never expected to reach thirty-eight. Yeah, birthdays. Screw 'em.

"Look, I need a favor." A Loretta Johnson-shaped shadow fell on Lucky's desk. No one else dared come here but Walter and Bo, and Walter didn't scare easily no matter how hard Lucky tried. Bo simply rolled his eyes and growled.

Loretta? She ignored Lucky's bluster. Lucky whooshed out a breath and gave his latest trainee his best evil eye. "What do you want?"

She either didn't know or didn't care what kind of violence awaited when Lucky wanted privacy, one of many reasons he'd set up shop in an out of the way cubicle rather than share space with a bunch of perfectly trained lapdogs.

"I'm supposed to see a contact tonight and need backup." She used the one argument guaranteed to sway Lucky every time: "Walter said you were the best man for the job."

"And he's right. Where and when?"

The corner of her mouth twitched, but she didn't smile or gloat. "Tonight, nine o'clock at The Raging Stallion."

Lucky's frown shifted to a scowl. "A gay bar?" Besides being the best man for the job, he'd probably be the only one in the department besides Bo who'd make it five feet past the front door without someone figuring out they didn't belong.

Johnson folded her arms over her chest. "You got a problem?"

Of course not, and he'd been out to Johnson for a while, but still, a gay bar? He'd not gone to The Stallion in years. "Nope, no problem." No problem but going to one of the South's hottest pickup joints without his off-the-clock partner.

He'd probably get hit on, since his lack of socially redeeming qualities didn't show until he started talking. Not like he wanted the attention. A man hotter than any club boy waited at home... or rather, lurked somewhere. Bo's first undercover

5

assignment since he'd gotten out of rehab hadn't left him much time to call home.

Lucky ought to be with Bo, should anything go wrong. Asshole Keith better not let anything happen to him, or he'd answer to Lucky's fist.

"I'm waiting," Johnson said, bringing Lucky back to the here and now. She stood at the entrance to his cube, tapping her foot.

"Oh, all right." He powered down his laptop, stuck it into his case, and stopped himself. Taking work home from the office? Oh, the horrors. The bag fit perfectly beneath his desk, where no one ever cared to look, not even housekeeping. They'd learned to stay away from his desk a long time ago.

He followed Johnson to the parking garage, stopping by her Jeep to see her safely inside. She smiled. "Better watch it or the rumor might get 'round that you're one of them there Southern gentlemen." She cawed at her joke and wiped a tear from her eye. "Meet me at my place in an hour." She looked him from head to feet. "And put on something club-worthy, okay?"

What? His normal jeans and an only-slightly-wrinkled button down weren't good enough? He'd at least worn an official SNB shirt last night for the bust—mostly because he hadn't gotten around to doing laundry. Still grumbling, he stumbled over to his restored Camaro and joined the masses leaving Atlanta during rush hour.

Finally he arrived at his and Bo's front yard, straw spread over the lawn to keep seed in place until grass started growing. No matter how hard they worked, the Harrison-Schollenberger residence made a poor cousin next to the better kept neighborhood houses.

Paint peeled from the shutters, and weeds came up through cracks in the driveway. Fix one thing and two more broke. Their smart investment turned into a never-ending work in progress.

He eased into the driveway and tried the clicker to raise the garage door. Nada. Crap. When he'd paid to have the thing fixed, it should've stayed fixed.

Fluttering curtains in the front window of the house next door gave away the neighbor's nosiness. Lucky sauntered up three steps to the front door. Screw 'em if they wanted a show.

Cat Lucky stared back from the living room window, likely planning evil for the neighbor's dog.

Lucky unlocked and pushed the front door. The door pushed back. He tried again. The door slammed before he could wriggle through.

"Damn it, Moose! Let me in!" Once more he pushed... and crashed to the floor. He sealed his lips into a tight line a split second before the world's biggest puppy swiped its tongue across his face. Yuck! Dog drool!

He jumped up and entered the code before the alarm went off.

A bucket of dog food kept Moose happy in the backyard while Lucky showered and shimmied into a pair of jeans. Hey, they weren't nearly so tight the last time he'd tried them on. Not "I can hit high notes" tight, but body-hugging to the point of revealing his assets.

Next came a T-shirt snug enough to show off all the time put in working on his upper body. Shit-kicker boots completed the outfit, along with a light jacket. The nights still managed to be a bit cool this early in the year, giving him a perfect place to hide his gun.

He squirmed a bit in his car to get comfy with the seam of his Levi's cramping his junk, and readjusted himself several times on his way to Johnson's apartment.

She wriggled her way out of the building to a chorus of catcalls from a group of twenty-something guys milling around the doorway. Wearing a skin-tight dress wouldn't slow her down much if she decided to make one of them an example for respecting women.

One particularly stupid bastard grabbed his crotch. "Oh, baby. Come see what I got for you."

Quicker than Lucky could open his door to come to her defense, Johnson had the jerkoff dangling by his shirt collar. She slowly lowered him back down. "Learn how to talk to a lady and maybe you won't always have to use your right hand for company."

The guy brushed himself off and slunk away, the hoots and hollers from his friends a warning to all.

She finished her strut to the car in peace, the now much wiser punks leaving at high speed.

"You were too easy on him." Lucky would've pounded some heads.

Johnson buckled herself into the passenger seat. "If he tries his bullshit again, I'll dislocate his shoulder. Let's get going."

He hadn't gone hunting at The Stallion since setting up house with Bo, long enough for the overaggressive horn dogs he'd taken swings at to forget him in a fog of alcohol and other rejections.

"So, what's the deal?" No cases involving The Stallion had come across his desk, but Johnson acted more as Lucky's assistant now than a trainee. Walter could have given her something.

"If anyone asks," Johnson said, "we're coworkers, and I'm taking you out for your birthday."

Lucky cut his eyes in her direction. "And?" Surely Walter and the work crew wouldn't go this far to embarrass him with cake and singing.

"And, I'm treating you to a private dance from my contact. You go into the back with him, he dances, you tip him, and he'll give you a list of names. Easy enough, right?"

Lucky had his share of private dances back in the day, and none compared to music played from his ancient stereo and Bo shaking his moneymaker for an audience of one.

But having another man half-naked and rubbing against him? On company time? Well, he'd keep telling himself it was all part of the job. He didn't have to touch except to tip the guy.

8

At the club, Johnson slid him a few bills. "For the tip. Let's go have some fun." He caught her at the door. "My treat," she said, yanking Lucky closer and flashing the bouncer a toothy grin. "It's my friend's birthday!"

If the bouncer stared any harder, Lucky might have to charge the guy fifty bucks, then arrest himself for prostitution.

The musclebound guard brushed Lucky's ass when he passed. "Happy Birthday!"

Asshole. Lucky glared, the bouncer laughed.

Hand between Lucky's shoulder blades, Johnson steered him inside the converted cotton mill and toward the bar. "Two Coors Lights, please."

The place hadn't changed much. Same blend of stale booze and a hundred competing colognes. Same dirty floor he'd never walk barefoot across. Same low light so you couldn't see what your dance partner looked like until you woke up the next morning and tried chew your arm off and escape.

Johnson handed him a glass. "Act like you're here for a good time."

Lucky took a sip and sputtered. She'd certainly learned well about ordering drinks to blend in, like she'd been taught while training in undercover ops, but... "Light beer?"

Blending in wasn't happening with a woman whose fluffy hair and heels put her close to seven feet tall. Did she ever get mistaken for a drag queen? And would Lucky survive asking the question? Even in jest?

The baddest woman in the club meandered through the crowd, Lucky in tow. Lesser beings parted to give her room. One glower and two twinks backed away from the table she'd set sights on and scurried off.

She pulled out a chair. "Wait here. I'll be right back."

Lucky claimed the seat facing the door. Whatever came his way better look out. No sneaking up. He idly patted the gun hidden beneath his jacket.

Johnson took off before he could stop her, leaving him with his beer for company. At one time, he'd have scoped out a likely fuck buddy, someone to share a few meaningless but sweaty moments and then part company with a smile and no names exchanged. How times had changed.

Now he'd trade all the bodies thrashing on the dance floor for an evening with one particular man. He pulsed fuck-off vibes at a couple of men who dared make eye contact. Not interested. Wasn't a single one of 'em could hold a candle to Bo.

Where was Bo tonight? What was he doing? Had he remembered Lucky's birthday? He hadn't sent a card or gift, but his undercover assignment limited contact with the real world. And Lucky had growled enough at him in the past for making a big deal of the day.

But maybe the whole birthday thing wasn't so bad. Especially not when Bo went to great lengths to make Lucky feel special. Breakfast in bed, with bacon. Followed by hot sex. Oh well, maybe next year.

Crap! The overly-groomed moron who ignored a perfectly aimed scowl and slid into Johnson's chair might have been the same persistent bastard Lucky'd punched out during his last visit to the club.

Shit-for-Brains had the nerve to smile. "Mind if I join you?"

Wow. Teeth bleached to blinding whiteness needed a "sunglasses required" warning. "Would saying 'go the hell away' make you leave?" Oh, geez. The guy reeked of some kind of hoity-toity imported beer, cigarettes, and over-inflated ego.

"Oh, don't be like that." The shithead wasn't planning to take no for an answer, and settled more fully in the chair.

Lucky sighed. "I guess not."

The world's most unwanted pest grinned and leaned over the table. "What? You think I'm an ax murderer or something?"

He liked living dangerously, huh? Lucky turned on his best evil leer. "Of course not. What's the chance of *two* ax murders meeting up at the same table, in the same club, on the same night?"

The grin vanished off the man's face for a moment. Then he

laughed and shook a finger in Lucky's direction. If he did that again he'd pull back a nub. "Oh, you are a kidder, aren't you?"

Now to employ his best serious face, saved for important lies. "Not really. But the way I see it, he had it coming. See, he approached me in a bar and wouldn't leave me alone." Lucky leaned in, putting himself nose to nose with the pain in the ass. "I got off on a technicality."

The chair flew backwards. Wow! Someone pull the guy over for speeding. He nearly knocked Johnson over getting away.

Johnson grabbed the chair before it hit the floor. "What's his problem?"

Lucky shrugged. "I dunno. I told him I'm with you, and you're the jealous type. Then he hauled ass."

She narrowed her eyes, silently calling bullshit, but she let the matter drop and sat down across from Lucky, wriggling a bit to bend in her form-fitting dress. "I've got you all set up. Go down that hallway," she said, pointing with a red talon, "and turn left."

"I know where the back rooms are." Let her figure out for herself how he knew.

"Okay. Room seven." Johnson's smirk grew frightening. "Have fun with Rex!"

Rex, huh? Why'd Lucky need to know the guy's name? Get in, let him do his thing, shove a tip in a thong, get the list, and get out. Be home by ten.

And do what? Watch the cat and dog chase each other around the living room? Go to bed alone, or rather with only four-legged company?

Lucky sighed, killed his beer, and slammed his glass down on the table. Time to go to work. He found room seven easily enough, slipped inside, and parked his ass in a comfy chair at the back of the closet-sized space. The indirect lighting might even raise a dancer's looks from a possible six to an eight, or maybe an eight and a half.

The door opened. His heart rate kicked into overdrive. His eyes adjusted, allowing him to make out a man's shape in the gloom. The scent of leather hit his nose the moment the music started. The lights rose enough to paint the dancer's body in shadows and light.

What the fuck? Who the hell danced to *Achy Breaky Heart*?

Leather cap, chaps, thong, and boots.

The dancer kept perfect time, swaying and stepping to the beat, head down, with the hat hiding most of his face.

Oil and a smattering of dark hair glimmered on his muscular chest. He wasn't too bulky, didn't worship at the altar of barbells, but his sleek body fit right in with Lucky's ideal. A swimmer or runner's build.

Something about the movements... Nah, couldn't be.

But yet, the curve of his biceps, the neatly trimmed chest hair. Lucky's heartbeat sped up.

The first verse of the song wound down and the chorus began. Holding his hat in place with one hand, the guy spun, putting the world's finest bubble butt, framed by black leather, up close and personal with Lucky's face.

It didn't matter how or why. Questions could come later. Lucky raised his hands to caress Bo's taut flesh.

"No touching," Rex hissed over his shoulder.

Okay, maybe only no touching for the customer, because the biker's wet dream come to life whirled and straddled Lucky's thigh, thrusting his hips and grinding. He brought his chest within kissing distance of Lucky's lips and backed off.

Lucky shifted in the chair. Damn his tight-assed blue jeans, choking the life out of his bound-up cock. His cock wanted out of the jeans, out of the chair, and into "Rex".

Bo added fuel to the fire by rubbing his hand over Lucky's crotch. A few more rubs would solve the problem.

"How long's it been?" Bo nipped Lucky's earlobe.

"Five weeks, three days, fourteen hours."

"Liar."

"Seems like longer." More like forever since Lucky had

rolled over in the night to find Bo beside him. Forever and a whole lot of sleepless nights.

Bo nuzzled Lucky's neck. "Agreed."

Lucky owed Johnson dinner. His car. His firstborn. Whatever she wanted for giving him the perfect gift.

Bo. Even if he only looked, couldn't touch, and definitely wouldn't get to take the man home.

The song ended. Bo unwound himself from Lucky, sweat sheened, and waited by the chair. Waited for what?

Oh. Lucky tucked the money from Johnson into Bo's thong, adding extra contact with his fingers. No touching, hell!

Bo bent at the waist and barely skimmed his lips over Lucky's cheek while slipping a piece of paper into his hand. What?

Oh. The list. So, Bo wasn't only a birthday gift, but Johnson's contact. Lucky stood, so close he could bring Bo to his chest with little effort.

"Meet me out back in thirty minutes." Like putting on a shirt, Bo rearranged his thong, donned his "Rex the Stripper" persona and swaggered out of the room.

Lucky uncramped his dick, waited a few minutes for his raging hard-on to subside, and made his way back into the bar. Johnson shooed away a few barflies and handed him another beer. "You get the list?"

Lucky nodded.

"Did you enjoy your birthday present?" She grinned.

What should he say? While he loved seeing his partner, even if for a few minutes, it wouldn't do to make too much of her efforts. Lucky was the woman's boss after all. "It was okay." Better than okay. Fan-damn-tastic.

Johnson stood. "Good. Now, let's have some fun while we're here. Dance with me."

Lucky stared at her outstretched hand. Dance? Him? And her? When she could pick him up and twirl him like he weighed nothing?

13

"I'll take that dance." A woman nearly as tall and sturdy as Johnson clasped her hand.

Johnson shrugged, pooched her lip out at Lucky, and settled on the dance floor with her new admirer—an admirer who'd be disappointed if she expected more than a dance.

As far as Lucky knew, Johnson liked men who didn't deserve her, preferably small and blond, with Mama and Daddy issues.

Lucky pulled his cellphone out every few minutes to check the time. Bo strutted onto the tightly-packed dance floor and wriggled out some dancing room.

He'd added chains to his outfit and a fake dragon tattoo trailing down his arm. Folks gave him space and turned to stare. Other Stallion dancers mingled, a young one sashaying his way over to Lucky.

Lucky peered around the guy to get a better look at Bo. Who wanted a young'un when a full-grown man danced so provocatively a few feet away?

The way-too-young dancer pouted and skulked off. Bo commanded attention, dancing with Johnson and her partner, then traipsing off to light up someone else's world.

Someone's "Woot!" snapped Lucky's attention to Bo grabbing the back of a chair and lowering himself down over a laughing man's lap. Totally in his element. Owning the moment. Had he lied to Lucky about hating stripping while earning his way through college?

Bo glanced up and winked, his smile falling for a moment.

Still his Bo. Holy shit! Lucky's lover, turning on other men on while making eye contact with him nearly got him off.

Thirty minutes finally ended. He shot down the hall. The timeclock by the backdoor held a few dozen cards, one for "Rex, T." Hardy har har. Trust Bo to use the nickname he'd hung on Lucky for his stripper name.

Lucky slipped out the back into an alley. Heh. Seemed like old times. Him, Bo, an alley, the scent of barbecue from the restaurant across the street, and a heavy bass beat.

The door screeched open. "I don't have long. Sooner or later, someone will figure out I lied about cops staking out this alley." Bo smashed his lips down and invaded Lucky's mouth with his tongue.

Lucky's "Mppph" of surprise melted into a satisfied hum. He rubbed his hardening cock on Bo through a layer of denim. The black leather thong barely kept Bo's bulge in check.

Both his hands full of firm ass, Lucky finally got to hold his man the way he'd wanted to.

Bo slammed Lucky against the wall, dropped to his knees and fumbled with the zipper on Lucky's jeans. Moist heat. Bo's tongue. The familiar rhythm of two lovers with years of practice. And yet every tongue stroke, every little bit of suction, every moan, seemed sweet and wonderful and new.

Lucky plopped Bo's hat on his own head and worked his fingers through Bo's hair.

Bo here, sucking him off, working undercover, and doing all right.

It had been a long time. Too long. "I'm gonna blow." Lucky gritted his teeth.

Bo pulled off and rose to his feet. "Not yet, you're not."

Oh. Commanding. Yes.

Bo grasped Lucky's wrists and pinned them against the rough brick wall. Oh damn. The heat in his eyes...

And the Bo Lucky knew whispered, "Is this okay?"

"Oh hell, yeah." Mouth to mouth, body to body. Held in place, like Lucky often wished for.

He registered the snick of cuffs a moment before the metal grasped his wrists. What the fuck? Bo grinned, raised Lucky's arms up high, and hooked the chain on something, freeing his hands so he could stroke Lucky's straining flesh.

Bo grabbed Lucky's shoulder and spun him around. Lucky kissed the wall, and night air brushed his bare ass. How had Bo gotten his jeans down so fast? The hat tumbled to the ground.

The club's *thumpa, thumpa* beat pounded the wall pressed

so tightly against Lucky's chest. The muscles in his arms strained, and the cuffs tightened on his wrists.

Restrained. Completely at Bo's mercy.

Fucking A.

Cellophane ripped, a sound Lucky never wanted to hear again. But when Bo sank into a character, he sank deep, like he now sank his slick fingers into Lucky. Hell yeah!

Lucky pushed back as much as possible, but the handcuffs and unyielding brick kept him upright when Bo slid inside.

He closed his eyes. Nothing gentle, nothing sweet. Brutal. Honest. Two men completely caught up in the moment and each other.

The whole department suddenly showing up wouldn't change a thing. No way to stop. Too amazing to end.

Bo wrapped his mouth around Lucky's shoulder muscle. Snapping his hips faster, he moaned low, a familiar sound sending shock waves through Lucky.

Lucky bucked back, urging his partner on. Hard, fast, rough.

Sex.

With the hottest man on the planet.

Perfect.

Bo stiffened and jerked. Nothing else existed. Lucky. Bo. The throbbing of Bo's release deep within.

And the wondrous pressure inside vanished.

Bo turned him and knelt. Lucky stood with his back to the wall once more, his cock engulfed in heat, Bo gripping his thighs and making good use of the leverage. Oh, God yes! Lucky let go with a shout. Pulse after pulse, straight into Bo's mouth. Who cared who heard his cries?

Bo rose, wrapped his arms around Lucky, and held on. Lucky collapsed against the solid comfort of Bo's chest, the steady *ka-thump, ka-thump* of Bo's heart keeping time with the thumping from the club.

He swayed a bit while Bo tucked his sensitized cock back into his now-way-too-tight jeans.

Without a word, Bo retrieved and returned his fallen hat to his head. "I know it's not until tomorrow, but Happy Birthday. I'm sorry I'm not home to spoil you." A few clicks and the cuffs dropped free.

Lucky rubbed circulation back into his wrists. "What about..."

Bo placed a finger over Lucky's lips, gave him a sad smile, and disappeared into the club, twirling his handcuffs and whistling.

Time to go, folks. Show's over. Lucky crumpled back against the wall, rubbing his abused wrists and still feeling the rasp of bricks against his chest.

Gradually, his racing heartbeat slowed, and he recovered a few of his senses. Too cold to stand in a dark alley wishing Bo would come back.

He plodded to the car. Alone.

Damn it.

Johnson leaned against the Camaro. Her smile fell when he approached. "Did I do a bad thing?"

He couldn't blame her for arranging his few minutes with his lover. She'd never understand how badly leaving without Bo hurt. Unlocking the car and sliding behind the steering wheel kept Lucky from having to answer.

Johnson settled in beside him and glanced out the side window. "Clear on my side."

Lucky pulled out of the parking lot and aimed the car downtown.

For too many years he and Bo had slaved away for the Southeastern Narcotics Bureau, going undercover, putting themselves at risk for the greater good. The job started as a death wish. Lucky wouldn't have cared if a drug dealer's bullet put him out of his misery. Why did he deserve to live?

After a while he got his thrills from taking down the bad guys. Being smarter. Proving his worth to himself, if no one else. Then he'd met Bo. Let his guard down. Let Bo in. Now his former adrenaline rush kept him up at night. What if

17

something happened to him? To Bo? They'd made a life together. Bought a house.

Hell, they were as good as married.

Married. Crap. A few years ago, such a commitment wouldn't even have crossed his mind. Who would've thought marriage equality would ever come to the South and open doors for men like him to get all legal?

Marriage. Lucky's parents' marriage had lasted over forty years, and they seemed to be happy. At least they'd been the last time Lucky laid eyes on them. Walter and his wife married fifty years ago and still doted on each other. His sister's marriage crashed and burned, but she'd married young, while still gullible enough to believe a lowlife shithead's promises.

But Bo and Lucky. Married?

Johnson broke the quiet. "You okay?"

Not at the moment. "I'm not sure."

"Well, if I did wrong by bringing you, I'm sorry."

"Was he really your contact all along?" How far had she gone to bring Lucky and Bo together?

"No. I originally met with a guy named Ricky, but he worried he'd been made, so we brought Bo in."

"What the fuck?" Lucky whipped his head to the right at a red light. "You put Bo in danger?"

Johnson snorted. "He may have gone through a rough patch with the whole Mangiardi case, but you know as well as I do there's no better undercover agent in the bureau. Besides, he's been tending bar here for weeks as part of his own case."

Yeah, Lucky did know. He'd been the best undercover agent not so long ago. Not anymore. Bo became one with whomever he pretended to be, and barely managed to separate the two after assignment. Which made him good at his job, but might wind up taking his sanity. "You didn't see him after Stephan shot him up with drugs for weeks." The vision of a broken Bo still haunted Lucky's dreams on occasion. "I worry he went back undercover too soon."

Johnson patted Lucky's thigh. "Of course you do. You love him. But Walter's not the type to send someone out who's not ready."

Yeah. Lucky loved Bo, and Walter never deliberately endangered his team. And he wouldn't have sent Bo out against his will. "You didn't see him, Rett. What it did to him." The image never strayed far from Lucky's mind. Bo, a defeated man, doubting himself and all he'd tried to accomplish.

"It's not like he took drugs on his own. Motherfuckers made him. And remember, I saw the bastard who hurt him, Lucky. Took all my self-control not to tase his sorry ass right then and there. Or worse."

Damned Stephan Fucking Mangiardi! Lucky used to want to bring him back from the dead to kill him all over again. Now he'd bring the bastard back and let Johnson go all South Texas on him. "What mattered to Bo was starting over on his sobriety."

"He still in therapy?"

If Lucky gripped the steering wheel any tighter it would have bent. "Last I heard. Not sure how that works with him on assignment."

Johnson patted him again. "Trust him, okay?"

Lucky snorted. "I'm the one shouldn't be trusted, remember?"

The air grew ten degrees colder. "You're sitting here talk-ing about a man who won't forgive himself, and you bring up your own past? It's gone. For both of you. You see yourselves as you used to be. No one else does."

"Maybe not you." Asshole Keith never let Lucky forget about starting with the SNB as a felon working off a ten-year sentence. Or being a drug lord's plaything. What a difference time made. Back then Lucky lived his life unapologetically lawless, cruising for the next thrill. Now he watched his back every moment for the past to creep up on him.

Thirty-eight years old, almost a third of that time spent with the bureau, equaled one hundred and dead in dealer years. A combination of sheer dumb luck and stubbornness kept him alive this long. The time would soon come for him to hang up the badge.

And do what? His life didn't suit him for many other jobs. He used to dream of driving a cross-country rig. Now, every moment away from Bo tore at his soul. Bo could always join him on the road.

No, since fulfilling his probation obligations in service to the SNB, Bo worked his ass off to prove himself, to be more than a waste of skin like his dad.

"Lucky, the light's green," Johnson said, pulling him out of his musings at the exact moment a horn blasted behind him.

Uh-oh. Better watch out. In his line of work, distracted could mean an obituary on the bureau's memorial page. What if he went to work one morning and never came home? Or for that matter, if Bo never came home?

His chest ached. He couldn't lose Bo. Life wouldn't be worth living.

"Whatever weird shit you've got going on in that brain of yours needs to stop." Johnson clutched Lucky's shoulder, one of the few people who didn't get growled at for touching him. "Pull over."

Lucky wasn't prone to following other people's orders, but he pulled into the parking lot of an all-night grocery store and faced his passenger. "What?"

Her eyes glimmered in the low light. "What's eating you?"

"Nothing."

He attempted to pull his arm away, but she tightened her grip. "You know, whatever it is, you can tell me, right?"

Yes, he did. Loretta Johnson might be a coworker, he might currently be her boss, but she'd become the closest thing to a friend he'd made in years. "I'm letting my age get to me," he said.

"Happens to us all. Let me guess, you're wondering what will happen if you go to work one day and never come home."

"How'd you know?"

Johnson gave him a weak smile. "I do the same thing every

birthday. And I promise myself by my next birthday I'll have made changes, gotten myself a less dangerous job. But every time I seriously consider doing something else, I remember what would happen if people like us suddenly stopped doing what we do."

She released his shoulder. "For what it's worth, you're one of the good ones. I've been around good cops, mediocre cops, bad cops." After a moment's pause, she murmured, "I've even sent a few to prison."

No need for her to name names. "It wasn't easy sending your child's father to prison, was it?"

"Was it easy for you to testify against your lover?"

Lucky didn't talk to many people about Victor Mangiardi. "Like to have killed me."

"But Victor didn't threaten to hurt your kid. Tyrone's daddy knew the first time he stepped out of line, did a favor for an old friend, that he did wrong. Every night when he left home to make some extra money, he knew the cost. When he started using, I stopped seeing him. Told him to stay the hell away from my boy."

Lucky heard this part of the story before. She'd shot a man she'd once loved. Might still love. Had a child with.

He'd never met anyone tougher, and he'd grown up with hard-living redneck types.

"Remember the good you're doing. Few people know the shit we're up against every day. Will never know how many times we kiss our asses goodbye, believing we're about to die." Johnson made a kissing noise. "They might call us narcs or pigs, but at the end of the day, we make the world a safer place."

A safer place. One day Lucky might get blown away, and the only thing he'd have to show for his life would be a blip on the local news, like he'd gotten the last time he died on the job.

Only next time, he probably wouldn't get a new life and a new name.

Wait a minute! She'd wished him a happy birthday earlier, without acting. "You knew it was my birthday all along, didn't you?"

Johnson snorted. "What kind of friend would I be if I didn't?"

If she didn't do or say something soon, he might give in to the urge to hug her and never let go. Or say something stupid.

She saved him from himself. "Now c'mon and get me home. I need to get out of this dress and actually breathe."

They didn't speak for the few short blocks to her apartment until he pulled up to the curb. What could he say? "Thanks."

"Don't mention it." She held her hand out. "List, please."

Oh. That. Lucky dug the scrap of paper out of his pocket and placed it on her palm.

He didn't acknowledge her kissing his cheek or her soft, "Good night, and happy birthday." She slogged up the sidewalk to her building, high heels in hand.

Somewhere in all his screw ups, Lucky must've done something right, because the good Lord had given him Bo, Walter, Charlotte, his nephews, and Johnson.

And damned if he'd let anything bad happen to any of them.

CHAPTER TWO

Lucky punched the clicker clipped to the visor of his Camaro eight times. Nothing happened. He'd put new batteries in the remote, so the fault lay with the gate. How bad to have to ask permission from an unreliable-assed gate to get home? After a grueling workout, taking his frustrations out on the gate with a motherfucking sledgehammer might be the perfect cooldown.

Of course, having Bo here would've sure kept his ass home.

The beautiful, cloudless day mocked his stormy mood. He rolled down his window, punched in a code, and the gate pulled back, barely enough to squeeze the car through. Okay, no rash actions today. Maybe tomorrow.Empty driveway. Again. He hit another visor switch to open the garage. Nothing. Again. Like the damned thing might magically repair itself. Something else on a long list of things to fix on his and Bo's money pit.

One day they might have a house worthy of the mortgage payments, if they could stay off assignment long enough to get the ever-growing to-do list done.

They couldn't win.

Well, at least no unexpected cars sat parked in the front yard. No well-meaning coworkers barging into his life, demanding he celebrate a worthless-assed birthday.

But a neighbor's grill scented the neighborhood with cooking meat, making his mouth water. Ah, what he wouldn't give for a good, juicy, homecooked burger.

He checked the mailbox by the curb. Bill, bill, junk mail, a "Welcome to the Neighborhood" flyer. Jeez, they'd only been living here four months.

The expected envelope lay at the bottom of the pile, postmarked Spokane, Washington. He tore the envelope open and yanked out a card, with some mushy sentiment on the front about him being a great big brother. Lies! His sister signed like she always did: Love, Charlotte, Ty, and Todd. At the bottom she'd added: *Can I tell the boys you're still alive now?*

No. Because they might tell Mama and Daddy, and Lucky wasn't ready to deal with their cold shoulders all over again. Better off for them to believe him dead.

The envelope contained the annual picture of Charlotte and the boys. She'd dyed her hair auburn, but otherwise she hadn't changed much since last year. Both sons towered over her. They'd gotten their height from their dad, their one gift from the abusive bastard. Maybe Lucky should finally change out the picture on his work desk, taken while she'd been pregnant with Ty.

The water bill came to William Patrick Schollenberger III, while the electric bill came to Simon Harrison. One day soon, Lucky'd change his name back to Richmond Eugene Lucklighter, since everyone he hid from knew exactly where to find him.

He trudged up the steps and opened the lock. At least the keypad worked. He listened at the door. Nothing. The hair on the back of his neck rose. Something wasn't right. No alarm. He'd set the damned thing when he'd left for the gym.

Having a dog didn't help much. The only threat Moose posed was knocking a thief to the floor and drooling on them. But still, the beast usually ran to the front door the moment a car pulled up.

Using his body to hide his gun from the nosy neighbors, he pulled his .38 from his gym bag and crept inside. Never leave home without firepower.

Nothing out of place. Footsteps approached fast, a blur speeding across the floor. Oh shit! He braced.

The shape hit him full on. Down he went. The gun landed out of reach, and the mail scattered across the floor. Lucky struggled, but couldn't avoid the big beast's tongue swiping half his face.

"Damn it, Moose. Haven't we told you not to jump on people?" A long string of drool inched dangerously close to his eye. Lucky turned his head in the nick of time.

Moose whined and snuffled Lucky's hair.

"All right, all right, you win!" He scratched Moose's furry ear.

On the couch a few feet away, Cat Lucky watched the show.

Lucky struggled out from under roughly ninety pounds of half-grown dog. He hauled himself to his feet and did his best to amble into the kitchen without tripping over a meowing cat or getting knocked over by an energetic bundle of white fur.

He opened a can of the cat food Bo insisted was better for Lucky Cat than tuna, and poured enough dog food into a bowl to feed a young elephant—or a Great Pyrenees. Moose ran across the kitchen floor and slammed into the bowl, sending brown bits skittering across the tile.

By the time Lucky got the broom, the problem would solve itself. If only other problems went away if ignored.

Crunch, crunch, crunch, came from Moose, while *Grwwmmmm...* came from Cat Lucky.

With the pets fed, it was time to find some human dinner. Lucky rambled through the freezer, sorting through plastic containers of spaghetti and hash. Down to four. Bo better come back from undercover soon before Lucky resorted to eating his own cooking. His frozen pizza and outdoor grilling skills were okay. The rest, not so much.

Taking a container of spaghetti to the microwave, he dodged the four-legged vacuum cleaner hoovering up Purina. With the last crunch, his whining began.

"Okay, okay. I'll let you out."

The fluffy plume of Moose's tail swatted Lucky all the way to the door. How uncomplicated his life had been before acquiring a partner and two, as Bo put it, fur kids.

But he'd been lonely too, even if he hadn't admitted his loneliness at the time. While he didn't normally celebrate birthdays, Bo had spoiled him for not wanting to be alone. Johnson hadn't even wanted to go a few rounds at the gym, saying she had shopping to do. Instead, Lucky pumped iron with a skinny little weasel of a man eyeing his backside.

Well, at least he had a dog and cat for company, and a load of chores to occupy his time. Like fixing the garage door. He opened the new sliding glass door he'd installed shortly after buying the place. Both cat and dog barreled out into the backyard.

"Surprise!"

Shit! Lucky grabbed the deck rail with one hand and his chest with the other.

His work partner better lay off the lies. Loretta Johnson stood at the grill, flipping burgers. Walter and Mrs. Smith sat in lounge chairs. Mrs. Griggs, Lucky's former landlady, loaded food from a box onto the picnic table Bo insisted on buying and Lucky argued they'd never use.

Moose, the traitor who hadn't barked, made a beeline for Johnson's kid.

"The dog will be big enough for him to ride soon," Johnson commented.

Yeah. Fully grown, Moose might weigh in around one-twenty. Better get him some obedience training soon, or he'd destroy the house.

The man responsible for this little surprise approached, his wide grin revealing The Dimple. No point in complaining once The Dimple appeared. If Lucky had his way, he'd make it a permanent fixture on his lover's face. He almost flinched when Bo wrapped him in a hug—almost but not quite.

Everyone smiled. He'd have to get used to acceptance after so many years of hiding his and Bo's relationship. Of course, these folks wouldn't pop off at the mouth with any homophobic comments. They were family. Maybe not a God-given family, but one he'd chosen for himself. Or rather, they hadn't taken no for an answer when they'd chosen him.

Even SNB receptionist Lisa and her husband, but only because they'd visited twice with no sneering yet. They were doing good so far, and if they kept up being sociable but not in his face about the whole friendship and *feelings* thing, they'd be considered second-cousins-once-removed in no time at all.

Lucky yanked Bo to his chest and hid his relief in the crook of his lover's neck. Lover. His lover. And no more hiding from Walter or anyone else. "When did you end your case?"

"This morning. Even if I hadn't, I would've managed to get here somehow. Can't miss your birthday now, can I?"

Lucky kept squeezing until Bo pulled away. If not for a yard full of people, and possibly giving the neighbors an X-rated show, Lucky might be tempted to throw Bo on the picnic table and do everything he'd been dreaming about since their encounter in the alley.

The memory of being cuffed and at Bo's mercy... Just wait until everyone went home.

"Wow! You're awfully friendly." Bo side-eyed their guests and turned his attention back to Lucky. "You mean you're not pissed off because I invited folks over for a cookout for your birthday?"

"It ain't my birthday." No, not today. Everybody got birth-*days*—he'd take a whole week. *Happy birthweek to me!* Especially with Bo home to spoil him.

"Of course it's not your birthday." Walter ambled over. "That's why we went through all this trouble. Any excuse for cake and ice cream." This from a man who drank liquid doughnuts from a mug instead of coffee. He raised his hand.

Even though Lucky braced himself, Walter's playful shoulder swat nearly knocked him off his feet. The man didn't know his own strength.

Johnson flipped a burger, and the grill flared. She never even flinched. Did anything rile the woman?

Lisa waited off to the side, kid in her arms and husband at her back. She looked ready to run if Lucky turned into the asshole he used to be.

Was. Not used to be. She got a free pass for making friends with Bo. And the cute kid. Background checks hadn't turned up anything on the husband.

27

Yet.

Mrs. Griggs came traipsing across the grass, wearing a loose dress and slip-on shoes that weren't a far cry from her usual bathrobe and slippers. She'd accessorized with a black and white tuxedo cat, getting reacquainted with the traitorous feline who'd deserted her in favor of Lucky.

Leave it to Lucky to find a cat addled enough to prefer him over the woman who pampered every cat in the neighborhood silly.

She waved a cat-laden hand toward his house. "Sure you're not gonna change your mind and move back into the duplex? The new tenants are awful. And they hate cats! What kind of rational human hates cats?" Her kissing Lucky Cat's nose and cooing, "It's okay, snookum. Mommy loves you," didn't exactly make her an expert on rational.

Mrs. Smith motioned from the picnic table. "Come. Sit. It's time to eat."

Johnson brought over a platter full of burgers. Two patties with bits of green and red showing sat off to themselves on a saucer. Veggie burgers. How could anyone...

Bo elbowed Lucky's ribs. "They're mine, not yours, so you don't have to get grossed out. I won't make you eat one."

They must've been together too long if Bo read him so easily. Lucky attempted an innocent expression.

Bo narrowed his eyes. "Don't start nothing and there won't be nothing. Snark and I'll snark back."

Bo did know him too well.

Johnson's son hopped up to the picnic table. He couldn't be more than six or seven. What was his name again?

"Tyrone, what you want to drink?" Johnson asked the boy. No, not Johnson. Out of work she wanted Lucky to call her Rett. He still struggled with the idea of having an actual friend and using her nickname.

Tyrone widened his eyes at the candles. "Whoa! That's a lot of candles. How old are you?"

"Tyrone!" Loretta glared at her son. "You don't ask people their age."

"Why not? Everybody asks how old I am." He held up six fingers. "I'm this many."

Lucky sighed. Two hands' worth of fingers wouldn't show his age. "I'm thirty-eight."

Tyrone glanced up at his mother but kept his mouth shut.

"That's okay, kid. When I was your age, thirty-eight seemed old to me too." And what had Lucky accomplished in all those years? Not a whole hell of a lot.

Bo put his elbow in Lucky's ribs again, and this time he didn't growl. "You've got a rut between your eyebrows. Whatever's bothering you, it'll be all right." He wrapped Lucky in a brief one-armed embrace. "Now, let's eat. These folks have come all the way across town to embarrass you by singing Happy Birthday. And I have it on good authority that none of them can carry a tune in a bucket."

Oh God, no. "You did tell 'em they didn't have to do that, right?" One could hope, anyway.

"Lucky, look at these people. Do you know a single one of them who'd do what I said?"

Lucky eyeballed the people gathering around the burgers. "Maybe Lisa."

Bo let out a snort. "Not outside of work. I've tried. Now c'mon and take a seat."

Lucky focused on his burger so he didn't have to involve himself in the idle chitchat folks engaged in at cookouts. Every now and then, he'd glance up and catch Tyrone watching him. The boy always scooted back behind his mom, out of sight. Johnson, no, Rett didn't appear to notice, but she probably did. She didn't miss much.

Maybe Lucky reminded the kid of his father. He was small and blond with blue eyes, just like Rett's ex, the guy she'd had the son with. And later shot. Lucky wasn't fit to be anyone's father. But the toddler squirming in Lisa's arms brought back memories of him holding his nephews Todd and Ty, and wondering if he'd ever have a kid of his own. So long ago.

At last, dinner ended and the moment he dreaded arrived. Walter stood up and started them off. "Happy Birthday..." The others joined in with his off-key singing.

Hellfire. Sounded like someone stepping on cats. Bo kept Lucky seated with a death grip on his knee under the table. Lucky deliberately brought his hand up and ran his fingers over the cuff marks on his wrist.

What a lovely blush Bo had.

Lucky leered and whispered, "Remember the birthday cake I got you?" Which they'd eaten from each other's skin. Oh, man! Who knew someone's face could get such a deep shade of red?

But this cake hadn't come from any bakery. Someone baked for him?

"Aren't you going to blow out the candles?" Bo pasted on his best possum-eating-briars grin.

Rett's son eyed the cake with rapt attention.

Ah, time to get out of something he didn't want to do and foist the responsibility off on someone honored by the hand-off. "Hey, Tyrone. How about blowing out the candles for me?"

"Wow! Can I?" It took Tyrone four tries to blow out all too-damned-many candles.

And that folks, is how you get out of doing something you don't wanna do.

Bo glared, Lucky shrugged, and Mrs. Smith doled out cake. Tasted familiar. "What's this?"

"Mocha," Walter said around a mouthful.

"It's coffee flavored," Rett said. She turned to Bo. "You sure can cook. You can come on over to my apartment and fix me a cake anytime."

Bo had made Lucky a cake. And left zero evidence behind in the kitchen. Lucky couldn't boil eggs without turning the kitchen into a battle zone.

But cake. He used to get homemade birthday cakes every year, until...

Daddy giving half-playful, half-for real birthday swats. Mama baking a cake from scratch, either orange or vanilla. His brothers and Charlotte arm-wrestling for the honor of cleaning the frosting bowl and beaters with a finger, sucking down every last bit of sweet.

Grandma and Grandpa always came over and gave him twenty bucks in a card.

And Lucky, the birthday boy, got the biggest slab of cake.

He hadn't had orange cake in twenty years. He'd never let his mother know, even if they were still talking, but mocha might be his new favorite.

"Presents!" Rett handed him a package the moment Lucky laid his fork down, derailing his side trip to Never-Will-Be-Again-Land. Tyrone ducked behind Mrs. Griggs when his mother stood up.

Eager faces all around. Opening a gift from her in public might not be such a good idea. No telling what she got him. Then again, it couldn't be too bad with her kid present.

Mama used to make him open presents carefully to save the wrapping paper. He ripped into the package, leaving only shreds. The aroma hit his nose a moment before he registered the bag sitting in front of him. "Two pounds of Starbucks decaf." Bo elbowed him into good manners. "Thanks." That elbow had gotten a good workout lately.

But Rett sure knew how the gift-giving thing worked.

"Ours next." Walter slid an envelope down the table. Braves tickets.

"Now you gotta make sure me and Bo are in town to watch the game." And Lucky damned sure would pay Walter back for his part in the surprise party with a B-flat serenade.

Oh! Maybe a rousing rendition of *Achy Breaky Heart*. In the car. Where the boss couldn't escape.

Walter scrubbed icing off his face with a napkin. "Duly noted."

The present from Lisa and her husband didn't shake worth a damn. Gift cards. And good luck getting Mrs. Griggs's hand-knitted cat sweater on the little fur ball currently batting paper through the grass. Overall, not exactly the kind of gifts he'd gotten back in his drug lord's boy-toy days.

Thank God.

Lucky dug his buzzing cellphone out of his pocket. The only people who ever called him after working hours were all here. He checked the caller ID and froze.

Oh shit.

Charlotte.

What the hell? She never called. They texted each other or e-mailed, but they never, ever spoke. And he'd already gotten her birthday card.

Hearing her voice would only hammer home what a shitty brother he'd been, getting involved with the wrong people and going to jail. No matter what, she stood by him, God bless her misguided heart.

Bo peered over Lucky's arm. "Aren't you going to answer?"

"Huh?"

"The phone. Aren't you going to answer your phone?"

Whatever made her break their normal pattern had to be bad news. Lucky shook his head and dropped his phone on the table. She wouldn't call in birthday wishes.

Bo reached for the phone. "Someone really should answer."

"You answer."

The phone stopped buzzing. Good. Maybe she'd leave a message.

The buzzing started again.

Bo sighed and picked up the phone. "Hello? No, it's Bo. That's all right. I completely understand. He's here." The smile fled Bo's face and his voice. He held out the phone with a shaky hand. "Lucky, you need to take this."

CHAPTER THREE

Hard to tell whose hand trembled more, Lucky's or Bo's. Their fingers connected when Lucky took the phone. Bo held Lucky's hand a moment before letting go. Holy hell. Must be something awful.

"Let's all go inside." Bo herded their guests out of earshot.

"Richie? Richie!" came from the tiny speaker.

Staring didn't make the phone disappear. Lucky braced for the worst. "Hello?"

"Richie? Thank God!"

No one had ever thanked anyone for Lucky. Years disappeared, his sister's voice as familiar as if they'd talked yesterday. Tears sprang to his eyes unbidden. Throughout the bad years, she'd been his lifeline. The only one who never gave up on him.

He schooled the tremble out of his voice. "What's wrong?"

She'd never sugar-coated the truth. "I really hate to call with bad news like this, especially on your birthday, but it's Dad."

An invisible fist slammed Lucky's gut. If he hadn't been sitting, his suddenly weak knees would have dumped him on his ass. "What about him?"

"You know he's been on the list for a liver transplant for a while now, right?"

"Yeah."

The following pause didn't bode well. "He's running out of time."

Well, damn. Lucky might not have spoken to his folks since his arrest, and they might believe him dead, but at the end of the day, they were still his parents. They'd always been

33

there before, and he'd figured they always would be. "Is there anything can be done? Doesn't someone have to die and give him their liver?" Most of the people Lucky'd seen die over the years hadn't had enough liver left to donate.

"Not necessarily. We're hoping to match him with a living donor. They can give part of their liver."

"Then we gotta find a donor. Um... how do we go about finding one?" As kids, Charlotte always dreamed of nursing, while Lucky dreamed of driving trucks. Lucky, find a usable organ? No chance in hell. Know how to wreck one with booze and drugs? Oh, yeah, buddy.

"It's best if they can find a family member. They're more likely to match. But Uncle Ben's in too bad of health, and he's the only one of Dad's brothers still alive."

"Uncle Ned passed? When?"

"Ten or eleven years ago."

"And you didn't tell me?"

"You didn't like him much, as I recall."

Lucky liked Uncle Ned fine until he'd started preaching fire and brimstone and gays going to Hell. "What about Day?"

"Daytona's going through rehab again, Dallas's diabetes means he wouldn't work, and I'm not a match."

Which left two sons. "Bristol?"

Charlotte snorted, the sound bringing back memories of a teenaged version of her. "He says it's in God's hands, and if God wants Dad to live, then he will."

How had their sweet mother given birth to such a useless shithead as Bristol? "That leaves me."

Her sigh wafted over the phone. "That leaves you."

Lucky drew in a deep breath and exhaled slowly. "I can't even give blood 'cause I'm gay. What makes you think they'll let me donate body parts?" If such a thing were even possible. But Lucky's knowledge of medical stuff ended where the drugs began. Still, squirming started in his guts.

His sister dropped her voice to a mere whisper. "I wouldn't ask if you weren't our last chance—his last chance."

Double damn. "If the old man knew it came from me, do you reckon he'd even take it?" Not likely. Stubborn-assed Lucklighters. "He'll take it."

"You sound awfully sure."

"I am."

Lucky jumped when a hand landed on his shoulder, then he leaned back into Bo's embrace. Bo didn't say a word, merely held on tight, exactly what Lucky needed. As much as he'd love to say he'd do anything to save his old man, he wasn't alone anymore. He'd have to talk things over with his partner.

Using Bo for an anchor, Lucky replied. "When do you need an answer?"

"Soon."

"I gotta think about this thing." And discuss the matter with Bo.

"I understand. And I wouldn't blame you if you said no, but Richie, I had to ask." Her voice took on a hopeful note.

"I know." She'd do anything for anybody. Of course she asked.

"So, you decide what's best for you, but don't take too long, okay?"

Time. Dad must not have much left. "I won't. And Charlotte?"

"Yeah."

"It's... it's good to hear your voice again."

"Yours too. I love you, Richie."

He started to answer, "Back atcha" like he used to. No. After so long, those words wouldn't do. Eyes closed, picturing his sister's face, he clearly spoke each well-deserved word. "I love you too, Char." The truth needed saying, even if his heart threatened to break.

"Happy Birthday, big brother."

Bo took the phone from Lucky's numb fingers, plopped down beside him, and held on. How did he always know exactly what Lucky needed?

Dad. The man he'd looked up to, used to want to be like. The man he'd tried so hard to impress. In Lucky's mind, Clarence Lucklighter lifted hay bales and slung them into the truck bed like they weighed nothing, or wrestled goats to the ground single-handedly for shots or hoof trimming.

No way could Dad be dying.

But he was. And he'd grown older since Lucky last laid eyes on him, might not be as robust. Lucky clung to Bo like a lifeline. "Did she tell you?"

"A bit."

"Should I do it?"

"I can't tell you. You have to make this decision."

"You're no help." Bo should say yes or no and keep Lucky from having to decide.

"I'll be here for you either way. You know that."

Yes, he did. All the shit they'd gone through together ought to count for something. "Will you at least help me figure out what to do?"

"If you need me to." Bo tightened his arms around Lucky.

Lucky drew back enough to make eye contact. "In spite of one of us being so pigheaded it almost didn't happen, we're partners, right? Didn't you say after I bought a house without your input that we needed to share major decisions?"

Bo rolled his eyes heavenward. "*Now* he listens." His forced smile took the sting from the words. "Let's go inside. Sleep on it. You don't have to decide tonight."

No, but judging from Charlotte's urgency, Dad needed an answer soon. "If I said yes, and I ain't saying yes yet, mind you, what would I have to do?"

"First, you need to have some tests run to determine if you're even eligible to donate."

Oh. Yeah. A few tests might take the choice out of Lucky's hands. Maybe doctors might get him off the hook, but then again, the little boy in him still needed his father to always be there. Even if it meant giving of himself to a man who'd cut him out.

Bo stood and took a step toward the house. "Let's go to bed."

Wait. What? Where'd their guests go? "What about Walter and everybody? And by the way, how'd they get here? Their cars aren't here."

"They walked down the street to the clubhouse where they parked. I baked the cake there so you wouldn't know I'd come home yet. C'mon, help me clean up."

Next time Lucky would be sure to check the clubhouse.

They got everything back into the house in a few trips, though Moose had to sniff every inch of the backyard before charging back inside, tongue lolling. He gave Lucky a wet swipe on the hand. Lucky jerked away.

Lucky Cat didn't evade fast enough. He arched and spat. Moose licked him again.

"That cat is so like you." Bo snickered and led Lucky out of the kitchen, through the living room, and to their bedroom. The pets trundled in behind them. Moose collapsed onto the rug at the foot of their bed.

Cat Lucky perched in the bedroom window, staring out at the night and likely planning evil for the beagle next door. Bo drew the blinds.

Lucky flumped down on the bed and kicked off his shoes. "I thought your assignment would never end." *I missed you. I love you. Never leave me alone again.* If so many thoughts weren't churning up his mind, they'd both be naked by now.

"I was only gone a few weeks."

A few weeks Lucky's ass. Seemed like a lifetime.

Bo peeled off Lucky's T-shirt. "Don't tell me you missed me."

Lucky shifted, letting Bo yank his jeans down and off. "Okay, I won't." Snuggling up to Bo tonight might mean a good night's sleep, after a sleeping tonic of getting his brains screwed out.

An hour ago he'd planned to give his lover a proper sexual homecoming the moment their coworkers left. Now, Lucky's cock wasn't much of a concern.

He lay on his back, staring at the ceiling fan lazily turning. Moose pounded the footboard with his paw while scratching an itch.

Cat Lucky curled beside Lucky while Bo stepped into the bathroom and turned on the shower.

One little piece of Lucky might save his father. A father who'd disowned him. Wait a minute! Charlotte said Dad would agree even if he knew where the offering came from, but could Lucky possibly give part of his liver without his parents finding out the donor?

The people who used to care about him didn't know where he was or what he called himself. Or even that he lived. He'd ask Charlotte later. She'd called and broken their text and e-mail only routine; they might as well start talking from now on.

About damned time.

On autopilot, he trudged into the bathroom and stood beneath the shower's spray, barely helping while Bo scrubbed him down. All day long he'd planned what to do when Bo finally came home: take him on every flat surface and attempt the vertical ones.

Now his mind kept returning to the kind of things he visualized when trying not to get hard. Hospitals, doctors, needles... drugs.

And yet Bo dried him off, put him to bed, and held him without using the stiffie occasionally brushing Lucky's thigh.

Safe in Bo's arms, he didn't have to worry about the right thing to do.

And yet he did.

CHAPTER FOUR

Lucky sat at his desk, but his mind hadn't made the trip to work yet. Sipping cold coffee and staring off into space hadn't accomplished much.

His father needed him, but would his father accept his help if he knew where it came from?

Charlotte said yes, but back home folks didn't say "stubborn as a mule" like they did in other parts of the South. Nope. The folks in their little farming community said, "Stubborn as a Lucklighter."

Down to the last one.

On Lucky's computer screen, the image of a young man smiled at him—a man who'd lost his life in the line of duty before Lucky joined the SNB. No guarantees. Lucky or any other agent could go out today and get gunned down, or have a wreck in rush hour Atlanta traffic.

Or live to a decent age and suffer liver failure. Dad had been twenty-one when Lucky came squalling into the world. He hadn't reached sixty yet.

Too young to die.

Way too young.

Lucky scrolled down the bureau's fallen agent page. If he died today, what good had he done, selflessly, for someone else, expecting nothing in return?

Not a thing, regardless of what Richmond "Lucky" Lucklighter's online obituary said about dying in the line of duty while protecting a fellow agent. Now came a chance to do something good for his family. No one had to know. But if his sister wasn't a match, who said Lucky would be?

Bastard Bristol probably matched perfectly. And the sorry sonofabitch was unwilling to give up a chunk of liver to save their old man's life. Heh. For once in his life, Lucky got to be something other than the black sheep of the family. Pretty weird. Not like him at all.

He closed the memorial page went back to his internet surfing.

Each reference to "liver transplant surgery" and "living donor" confused him more and more with all the doctor talk. And damn, get a load of the possible side effects. He didn't even realize he'd been squeezing the life out of a pencil until it snapped.

"Hey! You okay?" Bo traipsed into their shared cubicle, took the broken pencil pieces from Lucky's hand, and tossed them in the trash.

Anybody else, and Lucky would have either growled or grinned and said, "Fuck, yeah!" Bo saw through his lies. "I'm not sure." He slammed his laptop closed on a way-too-graphic surgery picture.

Bo sat down and rolled his chair over to face Lucky, taking Lucky's hands into his own. "You're driving yourself crazy. If you have doubts, maybe you should listen to yourself."

"But if I don't do it, my dad could die. Why do I have to be his only chance?" What had Dad done to end up with this life resting in Lucky's unreliable-as-all-shit hands?

"I hate watching you beating yourself up like this."

"I'm not—"

Bo lowered his chin and raised one eyebrow.

"Okay. Maybe a little." Or a lot. "What if I get tested and I'm not a match? Then what?"

Bo put his nose inches away from Lucky's. "I'll go with you. Get tested too."

All those possible side effects? Did Bo truly know what he offered? "You don't have to do that. He's *my* dad."

"Yes, he's your dad. Which makes him important to me. Because you are." Bo dropped a kiss on Lucky's nose.

Just when it hadn't seemed possible to love the guy more. The warmth in Lucky's chest wasn't all due to heartburn from too much coffee. "You'd do that for me?"

Bo squeezed Lucky's hands. "Don't you know by now I'd do anything for you? I'll have to tell the doctors about Stephan Mangiardi's magic elixir and the time I spent in rehab for hydrocodone dependence. But if they'll let me donate, and I'm a match, I'll help."

Not many people wandered by Lucky's cube without being court ordered. They'd learned to avoid the resident ill-tempered sonofabitch about his second week on the job. And the old timers warned the newbies.

Still, there came a time when a man had to do what a man had to do, no matter who might happen by. Lucky wrapped a hand around the back of Bo's head and yanked him into a whole-hearted, can-feel-it-clear-down-to-my-toes-gotta-do-it-now-or-die kiss.

And he didn't jerk away once their lips touched. When Bo couldn't possibly get any better, he got better.

Bo pulled away first. "Call Charlotte and get instructions."

Charlotte. *Call Charlotte.* Seemed so weird after all this time to pick up the phone and call, but right now Lucky couldn't rightly remember why he'd avoided talking to her in the first place.

She answered on the first ring. "Hello? Richie?"

Oh yeah. A whole lot of hurt and shame from a million broken promises. He'd sworn to always be there for her. Yet in her worst moments, he'd been somewhere else, breaking a few dozen laws.

"Richie?"

"Oh, hey, Charlotte. I was... um... wondering..." Lucky shrugged and sought help from Bo, who might not have suddenly lost the connection between brain and mouth.

"...wondering what you have to do to find out if you're an eligible donor," Bo said quietly enough for Lucky to repeat the phrase to Charlotte and make the words sound like his. Sort of.

Charlotte's gloomy tone brightened. "I'll e-mail you all the details. And Richie?"

"Yeah?"

"Thanks. I know this is hard for you."

What kind of person did she take him for if she honestly believed he'd say no? Oh, the kind of guy who got arrested and hadn't been there for her like he'd said he'd be.

Now came the words he longed to say for so long, and couldn't stop saying. Making up for the bad years might take a lifetime. "I love you, girl."

"Love you too, Rich. I've missed you more than you'll ever know."

He'd barely ended the call when her e-mail arrived, giving instructions for his doctors.

After being poked, prodded, needle-stuck about a dozen times and every test possible run on him, Lucky stumbled out of the doctor's office in a daze. First hurdle cleared. He and Dad both had A negative blood, and were roughly the same size, or rather, were now after Dad's illness cost him some pounds. He'd always been a stocky-built guy, mostly muscles from honest days' work.

People back home used to call Lucky "Junior" because he looked so much like his old man.

Umpteen years ago.

Lucky spent time in the gym and working out at home for what used to come naturally. What did his dad look like now? He'd never had guts enough to ask Charlotte for a picture, and she'd never offered.

Bo staggered out of the door and into the parking lot, running his fingers repeatedly through the hair sticking up every which way. At some point, he must've taken off his shirt, for now a few buttons were mismatched to the wrong buttonholes. "Sorry, Lucky, but my medical history puts me out of the running as an organ donor. I'd never pass the psych test anyway."

Psych test? "You can't know that." Lucky's stomach gave a lurch. Because he might be able to donate, or because he might *not* be able? And no denying he breathed easier knowing Bo wouldn't have to endure surgery and the accompanying risks.

"I'm still in therapy for PTSD and substance abuse." Bo yanked at the shirt hanging unevenly on his body "It's been less than a year since my overdose." He frowned down at his shirt and corrected the buttoning.

"I'm in therapy too!" Hopefully, Lucky unloading his mind on a therapist once a week wouldn't hold him back. "Hell, half of Atlanta is probably going to some kind of head doctor." Or should, judging by the lunatics Lucky avoided on the roads every day.

Bo sighed. "Not because of drug addiction. And I'm doing better with the emotional outbursts, but I'm not exactly the most stable person around."

"Not your fault." Lucky would gladly accept life in prison to bring Stephan back and kill him in the most gruesome and painful manner possible. He slid behind his Camaro's steering wheel while Bo took the passenger seat.

Lucky's stomach rumbled. Time for food, and soon.

"Lucky? What are you doing?"

"What? Huh?" The tailgate smack dab in front of his car needed painting.

"What're we doing at a burger joint?"

The truck inched forward and the menu and speaker came into view. Pre-Mr. Healthy coming into his life, Lucky regularly drowned his sorrows in greasy burgers and salt-laden French fries. Now he munched grilled mushrooms and salads, saving burger fixes for special occasions, or when Bo wasn't around.

"I'm sorry. I kinda zoned out there for a minute. Maybe the car remembered the way." Yeah. Good story.

"May I take your order, please?" a voice crackled from the speaker.

Lucky shot Bo his best hopeful expression. Warm burger, grease dripping down his chin, a smear of ketchup to lick off his lips. His stomach rumbled agreement. Comfort food. He needed comfort food.

"I'll have a house salad, no meat, vinaigrette dressing," Bo mumbled.

A test. This had to be a test. Lucky didn't dare order what he truly wanted and get away without a lecture.

Bo placed his hand over Lucky's. "Look, you've got a lot on your mind and you've had a hard day. One splurge isn't likely to kill you."

Really? "I'll have a triple burger, extra pickles, large fries, peach milk shake." He side-eyed Bo. "And apple pie." Bo raised an eyebrow but didn't say anything. Okay. Relationships thrived on compromise, or so he'd read on the cover of a magazine he'd flipped through in the grocery store checkout line to avoid talking to the chatterbox behind him. "Hold the onions on the burger? Oh, and a sweet tea. The bigger the better."

There. Compromise. He hadn't gotten *all* he wanted.

"I'll have water," Bo said.

They ate on the way home, in silence except for the occasional moany-eating-good-food sounds, a slurp, or a world class belch from Lucky. That's right, he belched like a boss, but only because Charlotte wasn't around to challenge him.

The woman could burp.

And he went back down memory lane, his brothers huddled around, watching in awe as Lucky and Charlotte guzzled soft drinks and fought to belch the loudest. She usually won. Sounded like a fog horn.

Mama would fuss. Daddy would laugh and say, "Aww, leave 'em alone. Let them kids be kids."

How Lucky would love to be a kid again, with a bad test grade his worst problem. He'd grown up safe and secure. Other kids at school talked about divorced parents or a drunk daddy. Lucky's family might've been poor redneck farmers, but they'd been close, and they might give each other shit from time to time, but nobody outside better mess with a Lucklighter.

"You okay?"

Bo's words broke through his brain fog long enough for Lucky to click the button nine times. Nothing.

"Here, let me." Bo pressed the visor button once. The neighborhood gate swung back.

Okay, so the gate took things personal against Lucky. One day. Or night. Lucky. A sledgehammer. The gate. Oh, yeah.

Lucky drove to their house. Their house. What a concept. And he still hadn't fixed the broken-assed garage door.

Barking sounded from inside.

Bo leaned over the console and brushed his lips against Lucky's. "You've got a lot on your mind, so go in and get comfortable. I'll feed the kids." The finest bubble butt in all of Georgia flexed beneath a layer of denim up the steps to their front door.

Their front door. Their house. Their life. Lucky had security here, with Bo, without the Lucklighters.

But damn, he'd love to introduce them all.

He wandered into the house, puttered around a bit. Bo stayed close but not underfoot. Lucky got the message. *I'm giving you space, but I'm still here.*

The back deck called, as always when Lucky felt out of sorts. The doctor laid a whole bunch on him today, and not just health issues.

If he donated part of his liver, not only would he miss work, he might wind up responsible for whatever bills the recipient's insurance didn't pay, like follow-up appointments. According to Charlotte's e-mail, Dad's insurance wouldn't cover the full cost of both surgeries. Their parents would be in debt for years.

Hell, he and Bo hadn't owned the house but a few months, with decades left on the mortgage. Even with the GI Bill helping out, Bo's college loan repayments ate a chunk of their budget, as did his truck payment, the electric company, water, trash pickup.

The neighbor with too much belly and not enough hair waved through the crack in the privacy fence and went back to his hedge trimming. Lucky put fixing the fence higher on his to-do list. At least the crack wasn't big enough to let Moose through.

Though the cat might take advantage to taunt the neighbor's beagle. As if on cue the mutt stuck his head through the fence and gave a bark.

"He's not outside," Lucky told the dog.

Lucky rested his hands on the deck railing. When had he become so concerned with bills? When had he settled down and started acting like everyone else in the neighborhood?

Well, maybe not everyone else. Chances were the balding guy next door didn't get shot at on a regular basis and wasn't living under an assumed name.

Then again, how well did he really know those people? He should've done a background check *before* moving in.

The guy went inside, the *chick, chick, chick* of his lawn sprinklers guilting Lucky into adding a mental note to water his and Bo's newly planted grass.

Damn it! How could he worry about grass when Dad lay dying? What would happen to Mom?

Maybe he shouldn't have faked his death. Maybe in time they'd have come around, welcomed him back into the fold. Too late now. And too bad. They'd have loved Bo. And Moose. And Cat Lucky. Probably the closest things to grandkids they'd get from their eldest son.

The sun set, the sprinklers stopped. Crickets, frogs, and birds made for one hell of a flashback.

Back on the farm, he'd have slept with the windows open on a night like tonight, whether or not he planned on sneaking out to do some fishing, or lie on his back and look up at the stars. Good Friday was coming up, when Dad did most of his planting. Then the family got together for Easter dinner, the one day of the year Mama dragged him by his ear to church.

Summer would be here soon, when he'd have headed down to the river with all the other farm kids to swim after they'd finished chores. And where he'd first realized he found a shirtless Billy Tucker far more interesting than the guy's bikini-clad sister.The door opened behind him. "It's getting late. You coming in?"

Damn. He'd been out here brooding and probably worrying poor Bo half to death. Things were a whole lot easier when he hadn't given a shit about other people's opinions.

A whole lot lonelier too.

"Yeah, I'm a-coming."

He held the door open to let Moose out and followed Bo in the house and into their darkened room. Flickering came from the bathroom. A sweet scent teased his nose, and light from a dozen candles caught the mirror, all shiny surfaces, and the half-filled Jacuzzi tub.

Bo said nothing, but he tugged at Lucky's shirt until Lucky raised his arms and let his partner undress him. Lucky reached for his jeans zipper.

Bo lightly tapped his hand away. "Allow me."

Lucky raised his feet, first one, then the other, for shoe and sock removal, nothing playful or sexual about Bo getting him naked.

"Get in," Bo ordered.

Lucky avoided the candles on the tub rim and sank into warm water to watch the show. Bo opened his shirt one button at a time, but his movements weren't sultry like a trained stripper. The pain in his eyes grew nearly unbearable—not pain for himself, but the pain of not knowing how to help someone.

When Bo finally unveiled his amazing body and slid into the tub, Lucky was half hard, and content to stay that way for now. Instead of sitting opposite, Bo settled by Lucky's side.

He mapped Lucky's face with lips and fingers, exploring every feature. Lucky savored the tracing and arched into the soothing touch of the scrubber and bath gel.

Water sluiced from Bo's body and candlelight glinted on the droplets clinging to his skin as he rose and held out a hand to Lucky. He pulled two fluffy towels from the cabinet and toweled them both dry.

Lucky's semi-erection withered, and if Bo expected sex, he gave no sign. He pulled the covers over them and held Lucky close. "You want to talk about it?"

"I don't know where to start."

Bo raked his lips over Lucky's forehead. "Why not start in the middle and work your way from there? I know you're worried about donating for your father, but what else is eating at you? Maybe I can help you figure things out."

"It's just... so much to take into account, and you know making serious decisions ain't my strong suit. I'm a doer, but this time I can't run in, guns blazing, take out some two-bit drug dealer, and save the day."

Bo pulled Lucky's head more firmly to his chest. "No. And I know it has to hurt. I remember when my mother died. I wondered if she'd have done something different if I'd been with her. Some kind of motherly instinct to protect me might have saved her."

Lucky shook off unpleasant images of a young Bo being thrown from a car. "Or maybe you'd have died too."

"But at least I'd know if I could've changed things."

Lucky stayed quiet, soaking in the comfort of Bo's arms around him, the gentle thudding of Bo's heart pounding against his ear. "I hate to say this, but I'm glad you don't know. I need you here."

"Yeah. I might not have ever met you."

Lucky forced a chuckle. "Might've been a good thing for you."

Bo didn't join in the laugh. "No, not meeting you would have been the worst thing to ever happen to me."

Now wasn't the time to get mushy, not with Lucky's heart already hurting. "The doctor says the operation is fairly safe, but there's still a chance I could die."

"Yeah, mine told me the same thing, if I'd been eligible to donate. But there's a chance I could choke on my morning tea too. Until then, I plan to keep on living."

Taking a deep breath to buy time didn't soften Lucky's bad news. "And then there's the financial part. Charlotte tells me Dad's 'bout maxed out his insurance, and like hell am I gonna let Mama have to worry about selling the farm to pay his bills, but this could cost us one helluva lot of money. Money we ain't got."

Bo turned Lucky until their eyes met. "We're talking about your father. Isn't he worth any amount?"

Lucky shrugged as best he could, pressed tightly to Bo. "Yeah, but he's my responsibility, not yours."

"What would you do if my brother needed a liver, and I wanted to save him? Or my aunt? Can you honestly say you'd let me face it alone?" Bo jostled Lucky for emphasis.

"No. But—"

"No buts. We'll get by, tighten our belts a bit. Dan down at the club said I can work any weekends I want to."

Lucky jumped back. "He said what?"

"He said I could tend bar or dance at the club if I wanted for extra money." Bo shrugged. "I made pretty good tips, after all, though dancing got me a whole lot more than pouring drinks."

Other men, seeing Bo nearly naked on a regular basis? "You said you didn't like stripping in public, feeling like a piece of meat."

"Yeah, but if it's for a worthy cause." Bo's strained smile wouldn't fool anyone. "Besides, lots goes on in the club we should know about, and me working a night here and there would keep old T-Rex alive and well for when I need him. Undercover operatives need to maintain personas we can resume if we have to."

Lucky gave Bo a free pass on the textbook-speak. "I couldn't ask you to do that." Not to mention how bad it'd tear Lucky up inside for a bunch of no-account drunks to drool over Bo, fantasize taking him home. "Lots of hot men and temptation at a place like The Stallion. You might find someone... taller." Richer. Less of a lowlife. Not an ex-con. Someone Bo could be proud of.

"We've gone over this. I wasn't a virgin by a long shot when we met. I've been around enough to know my own mind." Bo patted his chest and Lucky settled back into his favorite spot. "If you don't know by now how much I love you, and that I'd do anything for you, then I reckon I'll have to take the time to convince you."

Time to lighten this heavy-assed conversation. "I'm real stubborn. Could take a lot of convincing."

Bo's chuckle rumbled in Lucky's ear. "Oh, I know it will. Might even take the rest of my life."

"You got that kind of time?"

"For you, I'll make that kind of time." Bo squirmed, getting comfortable. The hard-on Lucky hadn't even noticed he'd sprung nudged against Bo's thigh. And out came The Dimple. Hallelujah! "What say I take your mind off things?"

"I don't know, Bo. Distracting me won't be easy."

"Want me to put my chaps on?"

Oh, hell yes.

CHAPTER FIVE

Bo tugged and pushed, positioning Lucky on his back with Bo half on and half off him, their erections sandwiched in between.

Oh yeah. Nice position. "That's a good enough start." No telling who moved first, and it didn't really matter. Lips sealed together, they explored each other's mouths, an adventure Lucky'd been deprived of for a few hours too long.

Tongue to tongue, body to body. The sweet music of desperate moans. Bo's cock, his beautiful, perfect in every way cock, sliding against Lucky's thigh. Heaven.

Bo wrapped his hand around Lucky's answering hardness, broke the kiss, slithered down the bed to put his mouth to better use—and stopped.

"What's the matter?" Lucky threaded his fingers through Bo's hair. Not pushing. No. Thinking about it, but not pushing.

Bo placed his lips against Lucky's belly and kissed his way back up to join their mouths.

"What the hell?" Lucky griped into the kiss.

"Tell you later."

"Tell me now."

"Not the time." Bo's kiss shut Lucky up.

Lucky's cock seemed fine with a hand job, and when Bo squeezed and slid his hand up and down... Oh yeah. Now what was he disappointed about a minute ago?

And wasn't he rude to lie back and let his lover do all the work? If tonight was hand job night, so be it. The extra skin on Bo's erection made for some nice sliding, and judging by Bo's quick gasp, he liked hand job night too.

Good Lord, could the man kiss. Deep and demanding one moment, then softening to a gentle tugging of teeth on Lucky's lower lip the next, and abandoning Lucky's mouth to swipe lips over Lucky's cheek, his forehead, eyelids, nose.

Every time Lucky tried to repay the favor, Bo retreated and restarted his mission to drive Lucky insane.

Okay, time to join the game. Lucky made a mad dive for Bo's neck, sucking the tender skin where shoulder met neck.

"Oh yeah," Bo choked out, arching into the attention. He gasped and yanked back. "Tonight's about you."

No, the years before they met had been all about Lucky. "Selfish" didn't come close to how he'd treated the men bold enough to follow him home.

If he couldn't get Bo off, he wasn't coming either. The concentration on Bo's face, eyelashes sweeping his cheeks as he threw back his head, shuddering. What a gorgeous sight. And he'd open his eyes, stare straight into Lucky's and let go. More often than not, Lucky sailed over the edge close behind, the image of Bo burned into his brain.

The memory added to the sweet torture of Bo's stroking, joined by other memories—Bo sinking down, taking Lucky into his body, free of barriers, free of work stress—just two men, loving each other.

The moment raged closer, Lucky's muscles tightening as he arched off the bed. "Oh damn!" He tugged harder and faster on Bo. Closer, closer. The wonderful tension built within, fogging his brain. On a long groan, he let loose, his body jerking in time with his spurts.

Through the lust-filled haze, he fought to keep his hand moving—a nearly impossible task now. His own spasms lessened and Bo tensed, wrapping his hand around Lucky's to help keep the faltering rhythm.

Bo bucked, pushing his cock through Lucky's fist, his foreskin bunching and relaxing. Finally, he braced his hands on the headboard above Lucky's head and fucked Lucky's fist.

The bed creaked and groaned. Lucky took Bo's balls in his free hand. Oh, to pull him higher so Lucky could use his mouth.

Nah, took too much effort and functioning cells from a sex-fried brain.

Bo cried out, his thrusts growing erratic. This time Lucky maintained the beat, keeping the friction going so Bo's approaching climax didn't fizzle out.

"Ah..." Bo closed his eyes.

Wait for it... He reopened his eyes, the fiery heat of his gaze coming close to sending Lucky off and running again. His cock throbbed in Lucky's hand, sending thick droplets raining down.

Bo shuddered and collapsed onto the bed, his and Lucky's come pooling on Lucky's stomach.

They returned to the Jacuzzi. Lucky put a foot in barely warm water. "Wait!" Bo hadn't drained the tub. "You'd planned for us to need the water again."

Bo's lopsided smile ought to be illegal. "You said you wanted distracting. You're hard to distract if you've got your mind on something." And yet he'd succeeded.

Lucky folded his arms over his chest and mock-glared. "You fight dirty."

"Clean is for wusses." Bo grinned, showing a flash of The Dimple. An appearance of The Dimple could win any argument. So could an eyeful of his perfect bubble butt.

Or just him being Bo.

A man who'd strip, a job he'd hated, to help pay for the operation to save Lucky's dad.

When Bo strutted and showed off his assets to strangers, was he dancing on stage or was it the Rex guy he'd played at the club? Would Rex ever take Bo over like Cyrus had on their last big case? The darkness could have Bo over Lucky's dead body. But who'd save Bo from himself with Lucky gone?

"Um... Lucky? You still with me here?" Bo waved his hands in front of Lucky's eyes.

Lucky startled out of the horror story his mind insisted on writing. "Lost in thought, I guess."

One side of Bo's mouth lifted. "That's because—"

"Don't you dare say 'because it's unfamiliar territory'."

Bo lifted his hands. "Wasn't gonna."

"Then what were you going to say?"

"That it's because I screwed your brains out."

Well, they hadn't exactly screwed, but one lesson Lucky learned from his partner was to pick his battles. If he didn't, he'd be fighting every minute of every day. Of course, baiting coworkers didn't count as fighting, did it?

"Lucky? Silence isn't a comforting thing right now."

"Oh, what?"

"I said you couldn't think because I'd screwed your brains out."

Not the best save in the world, but better than poking fun at Lucky's lack of higher education. "I didn't have much upstairs to begin with."

Bo scooted across the tub and cradled Lucky's cheeks in his hands. "Who said that to you?"

Where had those words come from? Oh, yeah, right. "My asshole of a brother, Bristol." Not to mention Victor's assorted kin. Them Lucky learned to ignore. His brother had been more vocal. And while he'd never bested Lucky in a fist fight, the weasel learned to use words as weapons.

Bo peered into Lucky's eyes clear down to his soul and snarled, "If and when I ever meet him, I'm opening the biggest can of whoop-ass the South's ever seen. Got that?"

"No need to humor me. I know I'm not as smart as you." Or Bristol, with his college education, big house, and fancy bank job.

Bo gave Lucky's head a little shake. "A stupid man wouldn't have survived years working for a drug trafficker as ruthless as Victor Mangiardi. And he wouldn't have tracked down more traffickers to avenge a sick girl. And he wouldn't have survived the bullshit in Mexico to bring down Stephan."

But a smart man wouldn't have gotten involved with the likes of Victor and Stephan in the first place. "C'mon. Let's get clean and go to bed since my brain's no longer working."

Lucky locked up while Bo fought to convince their pony-sized dog the bed belonged to the humans, finally tossing a chew toy on the rug to help Moose understand.

Cat Lucky settled between Lucky and Bo. Cats did as they pleased. If they locked him out of the room, he'd yowl all night and keep them awake. Picking battles. Yeah. And picking cat and dog hair off everything they owned.

Lucky spooned against Bo's back in their bed as much as the cat allowed. "What did you mean when you said you'd tell me later?"

No answer, huh? The squirmy worms feeling began in Lucky's stomach. Bo let out a sigh and rolled onto his back. "We've made it through our six-month window after the needles and blood exposure, but sometime soon a doctor might start asking you some very personal questions, if he hasn't already. I don't want you to have come this far to be turned down as a donor for having had unprotected sex with another man. Now I'm glad I stayed in character and used a condom that night at The Stallion."

"We have to wait even longer?" No, no, no, no, no! "What damned business is it of the doctor's?"

"Charlotte may have some pull since she's representing the family, but the doctor might make a big deal out of you being gay as it is."

Good point. A sore one, based on the opinions of idiots. "And we can't let anything stop us, right?"

"Who else is there if not you?"

Who else, indeed? Being someone's only hope put a lot of pressure on a man. "So, we're back to gloving for the loving?" Damn it. They'd come so far, gotten over Lucky's weird-assed hang-up about barriers between them, only to have to use condoms again. The waiting period was over! Now they'd have to wait again?

Bo nodded. "I'm afraid so. We could both take PrEP, but I'm not so sure if the doctor will accept that. We won't give him any reason to turn you down."

Once more, Bo talked sense when Lucky didn't really want him to. Parts of his body might not be his much longer. It wasn't just himself he made decisions for. "Okay, but when this is over, I don't want to find another damned condom in this house."

"Yes, sir." Bo snickered. "Now, get some sleep. You need your rest."

Easier said than done.

The clock read eleven, then twelve, then one... Lucky wrapped a towel around his waist and headed back out to the deck.

No use keeping Bo awake. He needed his sleep too.

CHAPTER SIX

What a long day, especially running on three hours' sleep. Lucky got off the elevator and staggered down the SNB hall toward the gym. Couldn't let Bo know he hadn't slept last night.

Lisa sat at the reception desk, typing on her laptop. She stopped and glanced up with wide eyes. Well, he'd spent years cultivating his asshole reputation, even if she'd been to his house and witnessed his softer side.

Oh, who was he kidding? He didn't have a softer side unless one counted Bo. Best to keep up appearances, at least while asshole Keith leaned against the wall by the reception desk.

Keith frowned at Lucky and barked at Lisa. "Are you finished with my report?"

Do what? Lucky growled. "Agents are required to type their own reports." Because if they didn't, he'd have Lisa work on all of his.

The department's resident jerk turned a sneer on Lucky. "She's helping me work through a backlog. When you handle as many cases as I do—"

"Blow as many cases as you do, don't you mean?"

Lisa shoved a manila folder between Lucky and Keith's ever-closening noses. "As promised." She sat back, wringing her hands.

Keith brandished his folder and stalked off without so much as a word of thanks.

"Thank you," Lisa whispered.

Lucky kept watch until Keith vanished around a corner. "For what?"

57

"For sticking up for me. I get so tired of doing his work for him, but what can I do? He's a senior agent, and I'm only a receptionist."

She didn't need to know Lucky defended her by accident while trying to get a rise out of his mortal enemy. "Anytime. He gets you to do all his reports?"

Lisa's sigh sent her bangs flying. "Yes. For some reason, he considers me his personal assistant."

If the SNB started handing out personal assistants, they'd better give Lucky one first. Only, who in their right mind would want to work for him? He barely registered approaching footsteps.

"Is there a problem?" Bo gave Lisa concerned eyes, and narrowed those eyes Lucky's way.

"Oh hi, Bo!" Lisa's attitude suddenly changed from gloom and doom to sunny. "Lucky here was saving me from doing Keith's job."

Bo's wide-eyed disbelief might be worth a hit to Lucky's asshole character. He looked from Lisa to Lucky and back again in a quick whiplash. "You're doing his work?"

Lisa nodded. "For the last year."

"And Lucky told him off?" Bo arched a brow in Lucky's direction.

Nobody did smug like Lucky. "Sure did."

A furrow appeared between Bo's eyebrows. "Is your counselor giving you meds?"

"Hey! I resent that. Why's it so hard to believe I done a good thing?" Ha! Let Mr. Politically Correct answer without putting his foot in his mouth.

"It's not. You do good all the time. You just won't admit it in public."

Oh, fuck. Lucky better get a grip before he ruined his hard-earned asshole reputation all on his own.

Bo brightened and slapped Lucky on the back. "Good job. You seem to have this under control. Lisa, why don't you tell Walter about Keith?"

"Keith's a senior agent. I'm entry level." The receptionist who took way too much shit off a major asswipe swung her chair back and forth.

"Doesn't give him the right to dump work on you. If it happens again, I want you to let me know." A world of hurt for Keith flashed in Bo's eyes.

Lisa darted a glance from Bo to Lucky and back again. "Okay. But I don't want to start any trouble."

No way Lucky couldn't add his opinion. "Someone told me 'don't start nothing and there won't be nothing.' Keith started it." How many times had Lucky spoken those three words over the years?

"If you're sure." She stopped biting her bottom lip long enough to smile. "Thanks, guys."

"Anytime." Bo strolled down the hall, clutching his gym bag, pausing to take a barely perceptible glance over his shoulder.

Lucky followed, grin widening with each step. Nothing worked better than showing up an enemy while impressing a lover to renew a man's strength.

Lucky stared in the direction of the bedroom ceiling. Occasionally a car passed on the road outside, and the open blinds let in enough of the backyard security light to watch the ceiling fan spin for a turn or two. Working his ass off and spending an hour at the gym hadn't helped him relax. Nor had the spaghetti dinner Bo fixed for him.

Beside him Bo let out a snuffle, rolled onto his back, and snored. Let him sleep. Lord knew he'd lost enough shuteye in the past few years.

Moving as little as possible to avoid waking him, Lucky rose and felt his way out of the bedroom and into the living room, where he collapsed onto the couch. The fake leather cushion stuck to his naked butt. Moose padded in behind him and dropped down on the rug by his feet. After a few more moments, Cat Lucky wriggled his way into Human Lucky's lap. Lucky pushed the feline to one side. The varmint wasn't going to knead and sink a claw into Lucky's tender bits.

That the animals came with him meant they knew, of him and Bo, he most needed a close watch these days. Or they hoped he'd wander into the kitchen for a late-night snack and share the wealth.

If he didn't give his dad a hunk of liver, the old man might die. If he did give a hunk of liver, he could die. The doctor said severe complications didn't happen often, but karma owed Lucky a few dozen bitch slaps.

Not too long ago, death would have been a relief. No one gave a rat's ass about him back then. Okay, Charlotte had. And maybe Walter. No one else but possibly Victor, and at the time Lucky believed the man dead and himself to blame.

Nope, not going there. No amount of logic could make sense of Lucky's old life. Now? Now he had a life worth living. Someone he loved. And someone who loved him back. Thank God for the man's bad judgement if he found Lucky interesting enough to keep around.

Dying didn't scare Lucky. Much. What might happen to Bo? Well, more than a heavy dinner kept him awake tonight. When he'd bought the house without Bo's knowledge, Charlotte shook enough sense into Lucky to put Bo's name on the paperwork to protect him from greedy vultures like Bristol.

Bristol never cared for Lucky. Without Lucky, he'd have been the oldest of the Lucklighter boys, and for some unknown reason, the guy never could stand having two older siblings. Who was Lucky fooling? Bristol never gave a happy damn about anyone but Bristol. He sure didn't seem to care enough about their father to try to save the man's life.

And while Bristol probably crowed with glee when the folks gave up on the family black sheep, not a chance in Hell he'd pass on a chance to get at any assets Lucky might leave behind.

Adding Bo's name to the mortgage ought to help some. But what about insurance? And did Bo even know he'd been added as beneficiary?

Was there any way for Bristol to make life rough for Bo? Waste money in court fighting? What if something happened and Lucky wasn't dead, but not in any shape to make decisions for himself? Bristol would tell the docs to pull the life support if Lucky slept too hard.

No. Way. In. Hell.

Bo dreamed of the house with the white picket fence and kids. Lucky wanted to stay out of prison and free to be his own man.

Bo didn't stop him from being his own man. He made Lucky a better one. Lucky scrubbed a hand down his face, stubble scraping against his palm.

Time to do the right thing. What he should have done the moment Bo got out of rehab. Or the second they got back from Mexico. Or when Bo rescued him when he'd hobbled around the woods with a busted ankle.

The moment he'd met the guy he should have shocked Walter, got down on one knee, and begged Bo to be a part of his life forever.

Well, better late than never.

Instead of slipping into the bedroom and risking disturbing Bo, Lucky showered and shaved in the guest bath and padded through the kitchen to the laundry room. Those jeans weren't too dirty. Nope, not reusing underwear. Commando, then.

His faded black Pink Floyd T-shirt passed the sniff test, and he shoved his feet into the amazingly unchewed boots he'd left by the back door. Moose must be slipping to miss accidental leather chew toys.

The better stores weren't open, but one shining beacon of whatever he wanted whenever he wanted stayed open twenty-four seven. Maybe he'd luck out and find something decent and act fast before nerves or self-doubt talked him out of his chosen course of action.

Only having to drive four miles helped him keep his resolve.

Except for the occasional earrings or necklace for his sister, he'd never approached the jewelry counter in this store, and he damned well couldn't afford the place he'd shopped back when he'd used someone else's credit card.

Something not too tacky. Somewhat tasteful. Should he buy two alike or contrasting ones? Did Bo like white gold or yellow? What if he preferred silver?

Lucky circled the jewelry counter a few times. Maybe if he prowled around enough times, other choices might miraculously appear. It never worked when he stalked the fridge, but, hey, who knew? After a few minutes, a clerk strolled down the aisle and behind the counter, in time to catch Lucky on his knees with his nose pressed to the glass display case. A man on a mission didn't have time for embarrassment.

The clerk bent over the counter. "Oh, sorry! I was on my break. Can I help you?"

Lucky owned socks older than this girl. In fact, most of his socks were older than this girl. "I'm looking for wedding bands."

The kid grinned, showing a full set of braces. "Aww... isn't that sweet?" She unlocked the case from the inside and pulled out a tray of diamond engagement rings.

"Um... Nothing like that. I need bands."

"Okay. What size ring does she wear?"

Why did everyone always assume he meant a woman? Girl needed to catch up with the times. "This is *his*." Lucky placed Bo's high school ring on the counter.

The clerk's smile faltered, then bloomed into a grin. "Too cool! Do you want a matching band?"

Did he? Decisions, decisions. He'd not worn rings in years. But if making a leap, might as well go whole hog. "Yeah."

The clerk dropped Bo's ring on some kind of measuring stick. "Do you know your size or need me to measure?"

"Do what?"

"Do you know your size?" She held up a bunch of rings, tied to another stick by tiny chains.

His what? Oh. His ring size. He must be tired. For a moment there... He stuck out his left hand and tried to hold still while being fitted.

The girl dropped to her knees on the other side of the counter, leaving Lucky to study the cotton candy colored streaks on the top of her head until she stood up again. Why was everyone in the whole damned world taller than him?

The traditional-looking bands she offered weren't eye catching, but they'd do the trick.

While Lucky whipped out his credit card, the woman rang up his purchases, smiling so hard her face had to ache. And not the phony "let my sell you something" smile he expected. Once or twice, she even did a little wriggling thing. He'd backed away from the counter, gearing up to fight back against some kind of homophobic slur. He was still in Georgia, right?

She handed him the tiny bag holding two boxed rings. "If you need a cake or anything and don't want to deal with the 'we don't serve your kind here' bullshit, go to the Sugar is Sweet but Our Cakes Are Sweeter bakery on Peach Tree Street. They'll hook you right up."

Cake? Oh, crap. Weddings. Cake. Guests. Churches. Someone willing to marry two men. Thank God the laws had changed, making his cockamamie scheme even somewhat doable.

He paid for a pack of Oreos at the front of the store on his way out the door. When the going got tough, the tough resorted to junk food.

Since they'd moved in together, Bo'd learned all of Lucky's hiding places for cookies and potato chips. And what he didn't find, Moose did. Big furry snack stealer. But if Lucky bought goodies at the store and wolfed them down in the car...

He drove the long way home, taking deep breaths to calm his nerves, and munching cookies. "Look, Bo," he told the dashboard, "I've been thinking..." No, wouldn't work. Bo might say, "I hope you didn't sprain anything." Oh, wait. He'd say that, not Bo.

At the next red light, he tried again. "Bo, you know how you always talked about forever?"

And he sure wasn't going to say, "You should marry me to keep my piece of shit brother from trying to pick your pockets after I take my last breath."

The sky had begun to pink around the edges when Lucky pulled his Camaro into the driveway. He sat for a few minutes, breathing in and out.

No one in their right mind would call him a good catch. Not with his past, total lack of couth, and fly-by-the-seat-of-his-pants method of planning for the future.

Hey, if it wasn't broke, why fix it?

But it was broke if Lucky's actions slopped over on the best man he'd ever met. He didn't deserve Bo, pure and simple. But the guy hadn't run screaming yet.

The kitchen, Bo's domain, quite frankly baffled the hell out of Lucky most days. This morning he managed not make too much of a mess stirring batter from a boxed mix and making pancakes, even if he did have to banish the dog and cat the third time they tried to double-team him and steal a few of the finished product.

The coffee burbling in the coffeemaker might not come close to Bo's, but hey. No such thing as bad coffee unless he counted the horrible shit Keith made at work.

"Oh, something smells good!" Bo strode into the coffee-and-pancake scented kitchen in a pair of nylon running shorts, scratching his belly.

Damn! Lucky hoped to serve him breakfast in bed. But he sure looked fine in next to nothing. Lucky popped a decaf green tea K-cup into Bo's one cup machine.

One quick fall to the floor, a grab and a pull of the waistband, and Lucky'd wrap his mouth around something a whole lot more interesting than the misshapen pancakes he placed on a plate.

Bo did a double take. "You're cooking?"

"You think I can't cook?" It's not like Bo did *all* the cooking.

"Yes, but your idea of cooking usually involves a grill and animal parts drowned in barbeque sauce."

"I'll have you know Southerners make barbeque an art form!" The only art form Lucky practiced. He dropped a dish-towel over the department store bag to hide the evidence and let out a deep breath.

Now wasn't the right moment. Soon. Real soon.

Bo sidled up behind Lucky. "Anything I can do to help?"

Step away from me before I spring wood, haul you off to the bedroom, and say "Screw breakfast?" Lucky managed to keep the words from escaping his mouth. Practice made perfect, and he'd gotten a lot of practice lately in not blurting out the first thing to cross his mind. Kept things more peaceful at home.

"You can get the syrup out and set the table," Lucky finally answered before he lost control and took Bo right on the kitchen floor—again. Good thing he'd put Moose in the back yard. Getting a cold nose on the backside while preoccupied with other things tended to make even the hardest cock wilt in shock.

"Sure." Bo kissed the back of Lucky's neck and ambled off, the slams of cabinet doors and rattle of silverware marking his progress.

Lucky flipped the last pancake onto a plate with the others, dumped a pack of stevia into Bo's cup of tea, and hauled breakfast to the table.

Bo helped himself to a few pancakes and a modest pool of syrup. Lucky, on the other hand, liked a little pancake with his syrup.

Bo patted his middle. "You know we'll have to run at least three miles to work these off, right?"

"I got better ways to burn calories." And Lucky did too. Creative ways. Exhausting ways. Ways to leave them both in a sticky, sweaty, panting mess.

Lucky watched Bo eat and lick his lips clean of syrup, squirming in his chair to adjust his rising stiffie.

Bo moaned. "Oh, this is good. To what do I owe the honor of waking up to breakfast?"

"Hey! You act like it's the first time I've ever gotten up early to fix you breakfast."

One of Bo's brows went upward, the other down. How did he do that?

He made a good point, even with only facial expressions. "Well, okay. So it doesn't happen much. Do I have to have some special reason?"

Bo leaned back in his chair, folded his arms across his chest, and lifted his already gravity-defying brow higher.

This wasn't the way things were supposed to go. Things were supposed to be—Lucky shuddered—romantic. Seemed he'd found another thing he sucked at.

"I'm waiting." Bo activated a tappy toe.

Okay. Now or never. Should Lucky drop to one knee? Ask the question he'd never thought he'd ask and then hand over the ring? Or should he distract Bo with the bling first? He should have asked Charlotte. The way she used to plow through romance novels, she'd likely know eight hundred ways to commit.

So, two knees? One knee? Standing? No, not standing. Lucky's wobbly legs wouldn't hold him. And if he went down to the floor now, Bo would fear he'd passed out and try to resuscitate his unromantic ass.

Blunt. Lucky always came across blunt. Bo either liked him blunt or put up with blunt. But he hadn't bailed yet.

When had the tile gotten unlevel? He stumbled twice on his way to the counter for his bag, and once more on the trip back to the kitchen table.

There, in their own home, a few days after his birthday, with sun streaming in from outside and a dog standing on his hind legs, pressing his face and paws to the glass, Lucky mumbled, "Iwantyoutomarryme."

"What?"

Damned words. They'd never been Lucky's friends. He up-ended the bag and dislodged the two ring boxes. One hit the floor and skittered beneath the dishwasher.

On hands and knees, butt in the air, Lucky fished under the appliance in bad need of a kick plate. Bo turned his chair to face the action. He sat close enough to crawl to. With Lucky crouched on both knees.

And a ring box in his hand.

Heh. Even a blind squirrel found an acorn every now and then.

Words. Who needed 'em? He smacked the box onto Bo's palm, and with both hands curled Bo's fingers around the sides.

"What's this?" Bo unfurled his fingers.

"Open it." The other box lay on the table, untouched. Would be Lucky's luck to have given the wrong ring. He swallowed his nerves and forced himself to watch his partner snap the box open. After a million years, or maybe the longest minute in history, Bo rolled his eyes upward.

Even with all they'd been through, the misery in Bo's eyes set a new record. He stroked the ring with one fingertip, cut his gaze to the other box, and swallowed loudly enough for Lucky to hear. "Why?"

"Why what?" Lucky's heart hammered double-time.

"Why are you giving this to me now?"

Lucky ran his fingers through his hair. Still no perfect words came to mind. "You read the same stuff from the doctor's office I did. You know what could happen."

"Death is a rarity in these kinds of operations."

"But it could happen."

Bo hopped up and paced the room. "It could happen with any operation. Hell, I could walk out in front of a car. Either one of us might catch a bullet one day."

Okay. Not going as planned. "That's why we should make things official. So if anything happens to me you're taken care of."

"I'm on the mortgage. That's what you worried about when we moved in together, right? That if something happened someone would try to take the house."

"It's more than that." How had Lucky managed to screw this up so badly? "What if I'm incapa... incapatitate... whatever!" He threw both hands in the air.

"Incapacitated?"

"Yeah. What if I'm inca... incapate... Oh, hell. What you said. And can't make my own decisions." Bo could be trusted. Bristol? Not a snowball's chance in Hell.

"We don't have to get married. You can give me power of attorney."

"I can?" Gee, why hadn't someone clued Lucky in before? But... Legal mumbo-jumbo without the words "I do" fell short of his plans. He'd bought into Bo's vision of the future. House. Car. Kids. Damn it, he wanted the whole white picket fence thing too. More than he'd ever wanted anything in his life.

With Bo.

It took every ounce of Lucky's courage to throw himself on the sinking ship of dreams. "I still want to marry you. Will you?"

Bo closed his eyes and shut the box. "I'm sorry, Lucky, but I can't."

CHAPTER SEVEN

Somebody catch the motherfucking mule that just kicked the crap out of Lucky's chest. No? Bo said no? "What do you mean you can't? It's legal now, even if some bigoted shitheads don't like it." His hands stopped listening to his commands and shook so hard he gripped the counter by his head to keep from toppling off his knees.

"Being legal's got nothing to do with this." Oh, for an appearance of The Dimple now.

"But you said you loved me. Wanted us to be together. To have a... family. For us to be a family. Together." Family. More than Lucky deserved. He should have known his dreams were too good to be true. He didn't deserve happy. Not after the shit ton of crap he'd done in his life.

Bo placed the ring box on the counter and took his time letting go. He dropped down onto his knees and took Lucky's face between his palms. "Loving you has nothing to do with this." A kiss took a bit of the sting out of rejection, but not much.

"Then what does?"

"Look at me." He pulled Lucky's head up until their eyes met. "If and when we decide to stand in front of our family and friends and pledge our lives to each other, I want it to be because we both want to. Not because one of us feels honor bound or afraid or anything else. Those aren't good enough reasons."

"But—"

"But nothing. When all this is over, if you still feel the same way, then we'll talk. But no ring on my finger can make me love you any more than I already do. And if I have to say words for you to know I'll always, always be here for you, then

I'm not doing something right." The next kiss lingered, Bo rubbing his lips against Lucky's without trying to go farther.

For some reason, the simple contact of skin to skin felt more intimate than sex, cutting Lucky open and letting Bo get to the places inside he usually kept hidden behind a wall of bluster and bad temper.

The kiss gradually deepened. Lucky parted his lips and welcomed his partner's tongue into his mouth, the taste of green tea and syrup. His partner. Not his husband.

One day. One day when Lucky didn't have to search for words or wonder how to say them. When he wanted to marry Bo so badly he could get past his own self-doubts.

Bo loved him. Said he did. Showed he did. Lucky would show the commitment he once ran from. "I want to give you power of attorney. And if something goes wrong, do the right thing. I don't want Charlotte to have to make the decision."

"Why me?"

"She's so softhearted and never gives up. She'd have me on life support for the next fifty years." Lucky shuddered. "I'd like to think you love me enough to let me go." And he trusted Bo to do right by him.

Bo blinked a few times, eyes glimmering. "I do. But we're not going to have to go there. Everything will turn out fine. You'll donate a part of you and come back home. To our home. In two months, you'll be good as new, and your dad will recover."

God, are you listening? "Yeah."

"Sure you don't want to let your parents know you're alive? That it's you doing the donating?"

Oh hell no. "And risk them telling me to fuck off again?"

Bo snorted. "They didn't tell you to fuck off."

Steel bands tightened around Lucky's chest. He wouldn't cry. He wouldn't. "They told me not to call back. If that's not 'fuck off,' I don't know what is."

"One of these days, I want us all to sit down and talk. The man they turned their backs on isn't the man you are today."

The world became a better place when Lucky had Bo's lips against his forehead.

"Maybe one day." When Hell froze over.

"Lucky, I mean it. You talk a good talk, but I know it bothers you not to have your folks in your life. What if we have kids one day? Would it be fair to keep Grandma and Grandpa away from the kiddies?"

"You don't understand..."

"No, I don't. I'll never understand what it's like to have a living mother I can call and talk to. Or a father who taught me to hunt and fish. Gave me useful advice instead of a smack across the mouth. Who smelled of sweat from an honest day's work instead of booze." Bo shook his head. "Sorry. I shouldn't say such things. Sometimes, though, I'm jealous of you. You had a wonderful, close relationship, and I want you to have that again."

Maybe not the words Lucky wanted right now, but the words he needed. Bo still wanted a family with him.

Good enough for now.

And if and when Lucky survived, they'd talk about trying one more time to reach out to his parents. Hadn't he and Bo promised while waiting to die in a tunnel in Mexico? But when he did reconnect, he wanted to introduce the family to his husband.If he used his original name again and they hyphenated, any kids might be in junior high by the time they learned to spell Schollenberger-Lucklighter. Or maybe Schollenberger-Lucklighter-Harrison?

Something else to worry about. Maybe they should throw out all previously used names and pick something simple for a change. Then maybe signing checks wouldn't take so long. Smith. Nah. Walter got there first. Something short, one syllable. Were there any last names with three letters? Two? Or maybe he'd do like famous people who went by one name.

"Stop thinking so hard."

"I'm not!" Lucky snapped, though if he contemplated his future any harder smoke might pour from his ears.

"Yes, you are. You got those 'I'm thinking' wrinkles right here." Bo ran a finger between Lucky's eyebrows.

The bad thing about having someone around who knew him so well was they knew him *too* well. He couldn't get away with shit.

"Now, I believe you have an advantage over me. You have on too many clothes." Bo plucked at Lucky's T-shirt.

Lucky normally wasn't one to do as told. But when told to do what he wanted to do anyway? Yeah, buddy. And he'd even swallow his pride and pretend this wasn't make-up sex to smooth over Bo ripping out his heart.

No. Not fair. Bo wanted the hearts and flowers. Needed hearts and flowers. He wasn't the kind of guy to settle to make things easier.

Not something Lucky would forget again.

He lost himself in the feel of skin on skin and the prickles of Bo's unshaven cheeks. The cold tile on his bare ass when he shimmied out of his jeans added to his awareness of the moment.

Tomorrow could go fuck itself. He had today. He had Bo. The house he'd never even realized he'd wanted until Bo opened his eyes. The dog. The cat who'd chosen him. His life was as close to perfect as it had ever been, with him sliding his body against Bo's.

No time now to worry about condoms or no condoms. With hands and hard thighs to hump and necks to bite and suck, nothing else mattered.

Bo kissed Lucky's eyelids and ran his callused fingertips over Lucky's skin, skating over a nipple, brushing against the straw-colored hair on Lucky's chest.

He wrapped his fingers around Lucky's wrists, raised them over Lucky's head and pinned them to the floor. His gaze smoldering hot enough to melt lead, he descended, forcing his mouth down hard on Lucky's.

What did it cost him to give the roughness Lucky wanted while risking his own triggers?

"You don't have to," Lucky murmured against Bo's mouth.

"I want to." Bo released Lucky's arms to slide a cushioning hand between Lucky's skull and the tile floor. He took both their cocks in the other hand.

Lucky grabbed any bit of Bo his arms could reach. Tugging, holding, never letting go. Not merely sex. Something beyond sex. Something better than a million random back alley encounters with a million random guys. Sex once meant a hurried fuck with some nameless guy. No kisses, no gentle caresses. Just hard, fast, and mean, until they came, zipped up, and slunk away without a backward glance.

With Bo, he'd learned to make sex more than a race to the finish line.

Lucky found friction for his cock against Bo's thigh, and Bo answered in kind. They fell into rhythm, mouths joined, bodies melded together.

The two of them. Nothing to intrude on them here. How had Lucky ever existed without Bo? How had he ever...

"Oh, damn," Bo said. That had to be the most erotic thing ever, especially when he jerked, once, twice, three times, adding slipperiness to Lucky's thigh, all while staring deeply into Lucky's eyes. Too deep. No secrets, no hidden thoughts.

Laid open. Bare. And trusting Bo to never use Lucky's weaknesses against him.

Lucky fought not to come, focusing everything on the sheer bliss on Bo's face, the way he tried to keep pumping Lucky when all his brain cells pooled up in a big puddle of contentment. Where Lucky would be in...

Spasms hit with the force of a bomb. He gave up fighting and let loose, moaning out his passion. Bo grabbed Lucky's cheeks and swallowed the moan in a frantic play of tongue against tongue. The ebbing shockwaves crested again.

For moments the pleasure held him tight, as tightly as Bo's arms. Lucky lay on the floor, half on and half off his lover, each breath, each heartbeat a precious gift.

Reality crashed down. He'd proposed, and Bo had said no. Even sex couldn't dull the pain.

CHAPTER EIGHT

Damned if he did, and damned if he didn't. Lucky stared at the sheet of paper in his hand, mind still reeling from the doctor's words. *"Congratulations. You're a match for the patient."* And not a single homophobic crack. Yet.

A shadow fell over Lucky's desk, too narrow for Walter and not libido-amping, so not Bo. The hand holding a cup of coffee his way sported long red fingernails. "What do you want, Johnson?" He took the peace offering—or bribe, depending on the next words out of her mouth.

"Um... Have you forgotten? We have a distribution center to evaluate today."

"Wha...?" Oh, yeah, right. Work wasn't about to stop because Lucky had his head up his ass. It never had before either. "Yeah. Give me a second." He shoved the doctor's report in his desk drawer and slammed the drawer on his fingers. "Shit! Motherfuck!" He shook his wounded digits. That hurt!

"Hmm... two cuss words in five seconds. Nice. But nowhere near your record. Now get your ass in gear. We're burning daylight."

In a perfect world, Bo would pop in about now, allowing Lucky to rant and rave, whimper and cry, or whatever else might happen when he showed the paper.

Although the last few months had come close, Lucky'd never lived in a perfect world. He tapped out assignments for the rookies under his care and sent them off in an e-mail. Heh. How to spoil a whole lot of people's day with one simple "send".

He tried to pretend he didn't have to rush to keep up with

Johnson's longer strides. At the reception desk, Lisa smiled and waved.

Lucky never should have eased up on his natural growly personality around her. Now she acted like he deserved a good morning smile. Or maybe she'd intended the smile for Johnson and missed.

Either way, Lisa wasn't too bad a person and didn't blab around work about how many times she and her husband had attended cookouts at his house—courtesy of Bo's invitations—bringing along her curtain climbing, drool puddle of a crumb snatcher.

Cute li'l bugger. And if faced with death or saying those words out loud, he'd take death. Hell, he'd survived the grim reaper before.

The moment they stepped in the elevator and the doors closed, Johnson scowled down at Lucky. "Spill."

Lucky cradled his cup to his chest. "Spill good coffee? Sacrilege!"

Johnson tapped to toe of, not her normal uncomfortable-looking uniform shoes, but a pair of sturdy work boots roughly the size of Lucky's car. She'd replaced her SNB golf shirt with a blue button-down, paired with the same type of navy pants hanging in Lucky's closet. Lucky wore faded blue jeans, tennis shoes, and a vintage Molly Hatchet T-shirt.

"You better have a good reason for forgetting our appointment today." Johnson punched the button for the basement parking garage.

Since when did the employee get to call out the boss?

She planted one hand on her hip, holding her coffee cup with the other. "You been walking around here in a daze since your birthday, and I'm not going away so you'd better answer me. What's wrong?"

Oh, yeah. Since the employee topped him by a good six plus inches and came dangerously close to Lucky in the attitude department. And she gave a shit, which entitled her to some slack. Not much, but some.

"I don't want to talk about it." Lucky added enough bark to scare off most coworkers. But not all.

"Did I ask you what you wanted?"

The door opened on two rookies. Spending the day researching illegal websites might keep the young'uns out of Lucky's hair for a while.

Heading out into the city with Johnson saved lives today.

"You're late again." Lucky tried to glare without appearing to look up. Why did everyone have to be taller than him?

But to Lucky's credit, at least he hadn't said, *"You're late again, asswipes."* A few words of prayer from Walter every month or so kept Lucky's tongue somewhat in check. If he'd known getting promoted meant being professional, he might have told Walter to find the nearest bureaucrat and shove the promotion up their ass.

But then the promotion might have gone to the king of all assholes, namely Keith. And his and Bo's money-eating mortgage needed feeding.

Hmmm... Did "King Asswipe" count as unprofessional? He'd have to check. But if he stayed here giving rookies a hard time he didn't have to spill his guts to Johnson.

Johnson grabbed his arm and yanked him off the elevator. "C'mon. You won't talk to me, but you'll growl at the newbies." She pressed a hand to her chest as best she could while still clutching her coffee cup. "I'm so hurt."

Not hurt enough to slow down on the way to her Jeep. Between the poofy hair she wore natural today and legs nearly as long as Lucky's body, Johnson didn't fit too well in Lucky's Camaro, which meant she liked to drive.

He didn't hate her driving, but why let on? So much more entertaining to criticize her sharp turns and sudden braking to keep from plowing some idiot who hadn't left home in time and demanded anyone else get out of the way.

"Try not to trade paint with my car on your way out of here." He hopped into the passenger seat, one hand protecting his precious coffee.

"You'll tell me what's got your panties in a twist eventually, so you might as well go ahead now." Johnson made a big show of buckling in and glowering until Lucky followed suit.

He would tell her. Probably. At some point. Maybe a crumb of truth would hold her off. "I'm still working things out in my head."

She cut a sharp glance his way when she stopped the Jeep to turn left out of the parking garage. "You're not shitting me, are you? You're actually planning to tell me without me having to take you to the gym and punch it out of you?" A quick jerk of the steering wheel and her flooring the gas pedal put them in traffic.

"Sooner or later, I'll have to." Hard not to notice her boss missing for a few weeks, especially a particularly mouthy one. Things might even get quiet without Lucky's daily presence.

"Okay. Take your time. As long as I know by the end of today." She slammed on the brakes to avoid a Toyota cutting into her lane, held her arm out the window, and extended her middle finger. Not fair her not having to behave professionally. Then again, maybe she'd be willing to be unprofessional on Lucky's behalf. Yeah, could work.

He contemplated his cup so long his coffee almost got cold. Not too cold to drink, but cooler than he liked.

Coffee never got too cold to drink. Except for gawd-awful ice coffee. Brrr... Some people had no respect for good caffeine.

Lucky sighed. How he missed caffeine. He didn't miss sleepless nights of tossing and turning, but decaf didn't knock the early morning cobwebs out of his brain.

Johnson parked her car on a side street, about a block and a half from their destination. "You ready?"

"I'm always ready. You go 'round the front, I'll take the back. We meet in the middle." He reached into the back seat, grabbed a Longhorns ball cap, and slapped it on his head.

Longhorns. Someone should tell Johnson she wasn't in Texas anymore. She put on a roomier cap, a peel and press name tag for her shirt, and grabbed a toolbox.

And the part of lowlife thug went to Lucky, a role he'd been born to play.

To the place's credit, the twelve-foot-high, razor wire-topped chain link fence didn't invite trespassers, but why have a fence at all if the two-foot gap in the trucker's gate let Lucky slither right through? Someone had a reaming coming once Lucky took a few pictures and turned in his report.

One lone camera monitored the gate. Hmm. Gravel, right where he needed. Now to test his aim.

Pop, pop, crash! Walter might have something to say about Lucky taking the camera out, but the absentee owners of this warehouse paid good money and did ask for a thorough assessment of their weaknesses.

"Careful what you wish for," his boss often said.

He rounded the corner toward the loading docks. Two guys lounging against a pickup truck nodded his way and went back to smoking and talking. Dumb asses. He'd lay good money it wasn't even their break time.

Climbing onto the loading dock took a little effort, especially when he tried his best to get noticed. And not even a camera to dodge. No challenge at all. He might as well have stayed back at the office. This slack-assed place didn't deserve a man of his skills. He should've sent a rookie.

At least the door required a key card. Rigging the damned thing wasn't worth the effort. He flattened himself against the wall and waited.

Soon enough, a trio of guys stumbled out the door, yelling greetings to the two by the truck. Lucky bumped into the last guy. "Oh, sorry."

"Watch where you're going, asshole." The guy took off after his buddies, minus his access badge.

Three minutes from street to inside the building. Not Lucky's best time, but... oh, who cared anymore if it took three minutes or three years? Too easy. Please! Would someone give him a challenge already? When breaking into buildings got boring, it was time for a more exciting job.

Man, did these people have something against lighting? How did order pickers see in the warehouse? Camera to the left, facing down the first aisle, camera to the right facing the last aisle. Lucky sauntered down the middle with his hands in his pockets, whistling past carton-laden racks filled with everything from headache remedies to cough syrups.

"What took you so long?" Johnson lounged at the far end of the aisle, arms folded over her chest.

Lucky grinned. "Paused to take a break. Meet any resistance?"

"Nah, told 'em I came to fix the warehouse phone, and they let me in. Aren't they supposed to escort visitors?"

"Yup."

"And when I reached the security door, some guy I've never met before in my life winked, stuck his badge in the reader, and opened the door for me." She removed her hat and fluffed out her hair.

"Spot any cameras on the way in?"

"Four. But since the guard waved me in, I'm not expecting company anytime soon."

"Let's do this." Lucky made a beeline toward the good stuff at the center of the building. With any luck, he'd stolen the right employee's badge.

As he'd figured, a heavy steel cage sat in the middle of the floor, filled with cardboard boxes lined up neatly on rows of racks. The cage door popped open at a swipe of the pilfered ID. Yes! Someone trusted Mr. Donald Carson enough to give him access to the restricted area.

The guys had sauntered out back for a morning break, and likely wouldn't return for fifteen minutes or so—more if they lacked time-telling abilities like warehouse workers from past experience.

Boxes labeled "oxycodone" and "hydromorphone" sat on racks. Damn, those belonged in a secured vault, not a flimsy cage.

And only one sweeping camera in here. How stupid. Time it right, duck beneath a rack while the camera panned Lucky's way, then grab a few bottles of evidence. Johnson caught the whole thing on video from right outside the cage.

Five, four, three. He darted from under the rack and raced toward Johnson, who opened her toolbox and placed their bounty inside. He eased the cage door shut. "Meet you back at your Jeep." Lucky didn't bother waiting for an answer, and the only worker he met waved and kept on walking. Moron.

He kind of hoped a guard or someone would search Johnson's toolbox, but didn't hold out much hope.

The guys out back had formed a huddle. The tell-tale scent of burning pot reached Lucky's nose. Oh yeah. Time for the owners of this warehouse to do some major housecleaning.

And he'd send a memo to Atlanta's finest, arrange a possession bust.

He dropped the stolen badge on the dock and left the same way he'd come in, snapping a few pictures and beating Johnson to the Jeep by a good two minutes.

She huffed when she got in. "I would've made it here sooner, but I got cornered by the guy who winked at me. He... uh... got a bit too pushy asking for my phone number."

Crap. "You didn't hit him, did you?" Walter frowned on such. Lucky should know.

"Nah. Told him my girlfriend didn't like me dating other people. He shut his mouth."

Yeah. Good line. "Did they search you?"

"Nope." Johnson reached into her toolbox and extracted a bottle of liquid worth about $250 on the street.

"Don't you hate when they go easy on us? I sort of feel guilty getting paid for so little work." Not really, but hey, sounded good.

"When the worst obstacle is getting 'round a guy who thinks he's a ladies' man, then yeah. Too boring." Johnson yawned for effect. "Now tell me what's got you all preoccupied. That's not boring at all."

He trusted her about as much as he trusted anybody, and more than he trusted most of the human race. "It's about my dad."

"Wait, what? You mean you actually got parents? Yay! I won the bet. The betting pool says you're a demon from the lower hells, sent here to torment rookies."

Oh yeah. "Lower Hell's Demon" was so going on Lucky's next accomplishments list for his annual review. He'd claim the demon's union demanded he get a raise.

Despite her attempt to lighten the mood, the dark cloud over his head settled in. "I haven't seen my folks in about thirteen years, give or take."

"Their choice or yours?" She glanced over her shoulder and steered the Jeep into traffic.

"Theirs."

"Do they know they're missing out on some damned good barbecue?"

"Who do ya think taught me to grill meat?" And raise it, on most occasions.

"Oh. So, now dear old Dad..."

"Needs a chunk of my liver."

Johnson slammed on her brakes even without an errant Toyota to blame. The guy behind her blew his horn and flipped her off. She reciprocated and flashed her SNB badge. He sped away. She gave Lucky a side-wise perusal and flexed her biceps. "So, Dad who wants nothing to do with you comes begging, and you're considering doing what he wants. Why?"

Wow. The woman getting ready to beat some ass over Lucky? Nice. "It's not like that. You came to the department after it happened, but you've probably figured out by now I haven't always been called Simon Harrison."

"Yup." She said nothing more on the way back to the office, and Lucky didn't feel the need to offer info. If she wanted to know something, she'd ask.

Johnson pulled the Jeep under the SNB building, killed the engine, and reclined back in her seat, facing Lucky. "There's probably not one single SNB agent who hasn't heard of Lucky Lucklighter. If you're really trying to lay low, excuse me, but you're doing a piss poor job."

True. "The only folks who don't know I'm still around are mine. They were told I died in the line of duty over two years ago."

"I'm going out on a limb here, but don't you think if they knew you were alive, it might help your chances of seeing them again? Or did you do something boneheaded and deserve their disapproval?"

Ouch. Direct hit. "Oh, I did my share of stupid shit, but being a dumbass on occasion never seemed to bother them before. Then I got arrested and they stopped talking to me. Never said why exactly." Pick a reason, any reason. He'd given them plenty.

"Then I shall torture them until they confess. Where do they live?" Johnson cracked her knuckles.

"They didn't do any more than I deserved."

"Are you feeling guilty about not coughing up your liver?"

"No, I'm feeling scared as shit because I am." There. He'd barfed up his secrets.

"Oh. I suppose you'd shoot me for telling folks at work what a great guy you are, wouldn't you?"

"Yes. And don't even start that rumor." If people got wind of Lucky doing a good deed, he'd never hear the end of it. And the rookies wouldn't be nearly scared enough.

Johnson softened her voice. "What can I do to help?"

"Bo's still dealing with shit from our case in Mexico. He's strong, but some things he can't manage alone. Would you look out for him?"

"You make it sound like you're not coming back.""The doctor says it's a possibility. A small one, but still there." And this time when he died, Walter Smith and his millions of connections couldn't simply pull strings and bring Lucky back to life again.

Johnson yanked the name tag off her shirt and tossed the label onto the back seat. She and Lucky shared the same housekeeping techniques. "Bo knows the risks, right?"

"Yeah. I'm giving him power of attorney and doing anything else I can to take care of him."

"You really love him, don't you?" She relaxed her rigid stance.

Lucky glared. "Let's not get mushy."

Johnson slapped a hand down on the steering wheel. "Oh, my God! You do! The great Lucky Lucklighter done gone got himself totally wrapped around Bo Schollenberger's little finger."

No use denying. "Don't get used to saying my given name."

"Yeah, right, sorry. Lucky *Harrison*. You know, if you married him you could change your name to his and ensure he's taken care of."

She had to go and say the M word. "I... um... tried. He said no." And the word cut as deeply now as when Bo first turned him down.

"What? You're kidding me, right? Mind if I ask why?"

Lucky put extra growl into his reply. "Since when has my minding ever stopped you?"

"Never has, never will."

"He said he didn't want me to ask because I thought I had to." Half the marriages back home were a matter of have to. Rednecks and shotgun weddings went together like pickup trucks and "hold my beer and watch this." With the same bad results more often than not, like in Charlotte's case.

Johnson tossed her hat into the back to join the label. "Not the most romantic proposal in the world. Doesn't he know how much you love him?"

She needed to lay off the L word. Hard enough confessing *feelings* to Bo. To a coworker? Uh-uh. Not happening.

"The fact that Walter hasn't had to rip me a new one for chewing out a rookie since Bo moved in ought to tell him a lot." Not that Lucky hadn't wanted to rip some stupid jerk a new asshole. But like when he'd been a kid, if he got in trouble at school, he'd catch double hell at home.

"Yeah. You're downright mellow lately." Johnson snorted. "Any day now you'll be baking cupcakes and leaving them in the breakroom for everybody—not. You're a hard ass, you've always been a hard ass, and you'll stay a hard ass. It's what you do. And someone's got to call bullshit every now and then or we'll all end up a bunch of mindless cattle, mooing along with the herd."

Do what? "Johnson, is that your backhanded way of telling me you appreciate me?"

She put her nose close to his. "Lucky, no one at work but maybe me and Walter will tell you they appreciate you. They might try to look down on you, some might be afraid of you, but at the end of the day, they know damned good and well they stand a better chance of staying off the SNB's memorial page because you've got their backs. Even that asshole Keith in surveillance knows when you go out on a job, you're bringing his precious equipment back in one piece. Have you even looked at your numbers lately?"

"What numbers?"

"Your bureau ratings. How many assignments versus how many arrests. And how many of those arrests led to convictions because you did your homework?"

No, he hadn't looked. Hadn't needed to. Up until recently, he'd been secure in being the best. Now? Not so much.

Johnson drew back to her side of the Jeep and tapped her fingernail against the steering wheel. "Walter promoted you to training for a reason. We learn law in a classroom, the right way and the wrong way to do things, but you show us how to walk the fine line that'll bring down suspects and get us home at night."

Damn. And every now and then Lucky grumbled about Walter promoting him as punishment. "What're you saying?"

"I'm saying that you're one hella good agent. And with a little more training, I might turn you into a halfway decent friend."

"Don't you dare say that shit to anyone. Understand?" Yeah, people hear Lucky's name and "friend" in the same sentence, and they might start expecting those cupcakes in the breakroom.

"Okay, now you know you're good at those things, you can let it rest a bit. Work on something you might not be so good at." She took on a tone she likely used when instructing her son.

When uncomfortable, revert to habit. "But I'm the best at everything."

"Then why did Bo turn you down?"

Ouch. "I told you why—"

"He turned you down because you weren't asking from your heart. My mama always told me the one and only reason to get married is because the other person makes your life better than it'd ever be without them. Does Bo do that for you?"

Cooking, looking out for his health, offering to strip on weekends to ease Lucky's mind about finances. Holding Lucky when he needed, making his redneck ass see reason. Believing in him when no one else did. Saving him from himself. "Yeah, he does."

"And do you do the same for him?"

An image came to mind of Lucky at the table, waiting for Bo to put dinner out, or Bo making sure Lucky ate after a hard day. Yeah, he'd done his best to be there for Bo during bad times, but what about when times weren't so bad? He'd cooked Bo pancakes, but only to sweeten him to pop the question. "I'm not sure."

"Be sure. Then ask again." She hopped out of the Jeep and headed toward the elevator, never even looking back. Not smart. Lucky could easily take the twenty-dollar bill over her visor, and in his past felon life, one quick snatch and a shove into his pocket and her twenty became his twenty.

But no, he'd never steal from her. She trusted him. And for once in his life, he deserved the trust. He wouldn't do anything to hurt her. And yes, he'd take a bullet for her. Might have to, one day. He'd give her hell if he lived, making sure she heard every groan and whine of pain, felt properly guilty, and catered to his every whim for a while, but he'd take a bullet for her.

As he would for Charlotte, Walter, Bo.

He'd go through nine kinds of hell for Bo. So why couldn't he make the man's life better? What would it take?

Johnson stopped and leaned against the open elevator door. Nothing left to do but go back to work, bury himself in the job and try to tune out the frantic humming of his mind.

Johnson didn't say a word when he stepped on the elevator, nor on the ride up and trip down the hall to the evidence room to turn over the samples. The moment Lucky's ass hit his desk chair back in his cube, she started in. "Figure anything out?"

"I don't want to talk about it anymore right now." Contemplating the fifteen-plus-year-old picture of his sister he kept on his desk didn't give him any answers.

"Okay, but if you need a listening ear, a kind shoulder, or someone to haul your drunk ass home should you decide to drown your sorrows, you know where I am."

Yes. Yes, he did. Only, his liver might not be too happy about getting drowned in booze. Neither would Bo. And he wanted to keep both of them happy.

"What say we get this report written and get out of here?" Her leaning against Bo's desk across the cube only reminded Lucky how badly he wanted to show Bo the paper he'd shoved into his desk drawer.

Nice of her to change the subject. Now for a few cold, hard truths he'd have to tell the warehouse owners, let Walter decide whether to call in FDA and shut the place down, and if/ when to toss them to DEA.

Had Lucky's heart been in his assignment he'd have found tons more to report on, but what he and Johnson found was bad enough. "Do you reckon 'your warehouse ain't secure for shit' is a good enough report?" Typing up four pages wouldn't change the meaning. The security sucked. And not in the good way he'd been missing from Bo lately. Johnson's hip check almost put him off balance.

"Tell you what," she said. "I'll take care of the paperwork and upload the video. You go talk to the boss."

He put up a token resistance before Johnson wrestled him out of his chair. "But I don't need to talk to Walter."

"Yes, you do, to arrange a leave of absence. And I suggest you talk to Human Resources about what expenses our insurance covers for a liver donor, if your father's insurance doesn't foot the bill."

"No." Planning made things too real.

Johnson pointed down the hall. "Go."

"No."

"Yes. If you don't get your ass in Walter's office and take care of business, I'll throw you over my shoulder, haul your scrawny ass in there, get the hell out, and lock the door."

Pick his battles. Yeah. He'd do what she said. Or at least pretend to. Hey, he got out of typing the report.

He'd gone a whole three steps from the cube when his self-appointed conscience called out, "And if you even think about walking past that door, I'll tackle you to the floor, hog tie you like a Texas steer, and drag you kicking and screaming in there anyway."

And so he stood at the boss's door, fist raised to knock.

Johnson shrieked from down the hall. "I called Lisa. She's guarding the elevator in case you try to run."

Damned teamwork. Lucky knocked.

"Come in, Lucky."

Lucky entered the room he'd come to a million times, either to talk shop, ask advice, give a report, or get a well-deserved ass-chewing, and settled into the chair he'd permanently marked with a butt print. "How'd you know it was me?"

"Because your trainee texted me, said you needed to talk, and insisted I keep her informed if you weren't in my office in two minutes." Walter reared back in his chair and rested his hands on his belly.

Where to start? "I need some time off."

"How much time?"

Lucky shrugged. "A few weeks. I'm not sure yet."

"You're off probation, you don't need to ask my permission if you have enough vacation days."

Nope. Getting the house ready for Bo ate all the days Lucky saved. "I need a medical leave of absence."

"I see." Walter sat up straighter in his chair. "You don't have to explain. Fill out the forms with H.R. So why are you really here?"

Because ever since the father given to Lucky by nature disowned him, Walter filled in nicely for the role. "Because I'm trying to do the right thing, and my track record for doing the right thing ain't too good."

"I don't agree, but if you need to talk, you know I'm here for you."

"I haven't seen my Dad since before I got locked up. Now he's dying. Or rather, he might be." Lucky paused and attempted to string words together sensibly. "My sister told me a piece of my liver could save him. Even though the old man'll never find out what I've done, I got to do this."

Walter nodded. "It sounds to me like you're doing the right thing."

Lucky buried his face in his hands. "I miss him. I miss the whole damn family." No. he wouldn't hide from Walter, and he dropped his hands back into his lap. "The doctor says it don't happen often, but sometimes the donor has... complications."

"I've known both organ donors and recipients who've had no problems. It's a relatively safe procedure."

"Yeah, but in my life, if things can go wrong, they do." And horribly so.

"I beg to differ with you. You've made a tremendous impact for the better on this bureau and your fellow agents." Strange how Walter's assurances almost blocked out the doctor's dire warnings. Almost.

One agent in particular he'd had impact on, though maybe not for the better. "I wanted to let you know what was what. They tell me I'll be out of work for about six to eight weeks."

"I appreciate your telling me. I'll reassign your cases and put off field training until you're ready to return. As your department manager, I'll ask that you plan your absence with me, and as a friend I'll ask if I can do anything."

Not much anyone could do. "You're a praying man, right?"

"I am."

"Say one for me." Or one hundred. Lucky needed all the help he could get.

"I always do."

Of course he did. "Thanks, boss."

"Anytime. Might I ask what you'll do with your pets while you're gone?"

"Mrs. Griggs offered to take them. The cat'll be fine there, but I'm afraid she might find Moose a bit of a handful, so we're taking him to a kennel." Poor guy. Cooped up in a kennel, with no room to run and no squirrels to chase.

Walter shook his graying head. "You'll do no such thing! We have a large, fenced-in yard, and I quite like your dog. We'd be honored if you'd let him stay with us." He gave a forced smile. "The local squirrels have become quite complacent, I'm afraid. They could do with a bit of exercise."

Wow. "Really? You don't mind? What about your wife?"

"She'd have my hide if I allowed that sweet creature to go to a kennel." Walter gave Lucky his best boss face. Daring Lucky to say no?

"It'd take a load of my... I mean, Bo's mind." There Lucky went, nearly blowing his hard-assed reputation again.

"Then I'll tell Lucy to expect him. She'll need time to buy the pet shop out of dog toys."

What more could Lucky say? "Thanks, boss. Now I reckon I better get down to H.R. and find out if my insurance will cover the medical costs."

Creases appeared between Walter's eyebrows. "Lucky, have you checked if your father's insurance covers a living donor?"

"It does, but my sister says Dad's nearly maxed out his

benefits." Maybe Bo wouldn't have to spend his weekends dropping trou for tips, though, if Lucky's insurance kicked in.

"Have you discussed financial arrangements with anyone?"

"I can't exactly talk to people who believe I'm dead. My sister is the only one I've talked to. I'll ask H.R. They're probably my best bet." They didn't like him much, but did their job.

"You do that. And Lucky?"

"Yeah?"

"Good luck."

Luck. A man called "Lucky" should have plenty of the stuff. But the world never gave a shit what Lucky wanted.

Lucky sat in his car in the SNB parking lot, staring at a bunch of legalize from his insurance provider, printed out on five pages. *Not included. Maximum allowed: $50. Not included. Not covered. Eighty percent after deductible met. Up to $100.* Dear God! One hundred dollars didn't cover jack shit of what his prescription bill might be.

His stomach sank.

But money meant nothing when compared to his father's life.

Even if Lucky spent the rest of his own life in debt.

CHAPTER NINE

Lucky settled on the couch with his laptop, propped his feet on the conveniently footstool-shaped Moose, and started answering an online questionnaire. How damned many questions were there?

Chigger disease? He'd never heard of half these ailments. Lifestyle questions. Had he had unprotected sex in the past six months? No, damn it. What he wouldn't give to be bare inside of Bo.

Was he healthy and feeling well? How much exercise did he get? Getting personal, weren't they? The front door opened. Lucky's furry footstool shot across the room.

"Yah! Damn it, Moose! Sit!" Bo collapsed on the floor under a mound of fur, twisting and wriggling to evade Moose's tongue.

Lucky stroked his hand over Cat Lucky's head. The cat hopped off the couch and trotted over to Bo. "Traitor."

Still spitting fur out of his mouth, Bo crawled from the floor and plopped down on the couch. "I owe you a kiss when my lips are less fuzzy."

"What's a little dog hair among friends?" Lucky pulled his man in for a proper hello. "How'd your session go?"

"Okay. I'm getting better at keeping my temper. I told the doctor that whenever the pets go running, I know I'm about to lose my shit and need to stop." He snorted. "Or when my partner starts fussing over me too much."

"Do not."

"Do too." Bo exaggerated a nod.

"Do not."

"What 'cha doin'?" Bo craned his neck for a better view of the laptop. "And you do too."

Lucky let him win round one. Especially if it meant help with the nosy-assed questions. "Filling out a form for the doctor. What's en... encept... enceptalikus?"

"Encephalitis?

Lucky squinted at the page. "Close enough. What's that?"

"Swelling of the brain due to viral infection."

Hey, Bo hadn't sounded like a textbook in a few days. Lucky must be losing his mind if he missed Bo's quoting. "Chigger disease?"

"Chagas disease."

"Do I have those?"

"Not to my knowledge."

Good enough for Lucky. He scrolled down the page, clicking boxes. Too bad this wasn't high school. Then he'd make patterns on the paper by filling in the right bubbles and hope for the best. His teachers never commented on the dick picture he'd turned in once—and he'd passed!

"Need help?"

One of the many things to love about having a partner. "Sure." Lucky slid his laptop over to give Bo a better look at the screen, and hopefully make him say, "I got this. You go take a nap."

"No to number seventeen, no to twenty." Bo stroked a finger over the display. "Nope, nope, nope."

"How do you know?" Especially when Lucky didn't.

"The same way you know stuff about me. I hacked your files."

"You didn't." Mr. Honest hacking files? Might give Lucky a stiffie.

"No, I didn't. But those diseases don't exist in the USA, and you've never been to the UK or Central America."

Oh. For a moment there... Lucky squirmed and adjusted his interested cock. He'd still dream. Agent and the computer hacker would add a nice touch to their role playing. If and when he ever got to fuck again without condoms.

He used to insist on gloving for the loving. Now he'd give his left nut to go back in time, find the sonofabitches who invented the damned things, and kick the living shit out of them.

Bo kissed the side of Lucky's neck. "How much more you got to do?"

"Four more pages." Four more pages of hunt and peck typing. "I might be finished this time tomorrow."

Bo hip-bumped him. "Go on, I got this."

Hallelujah.

Lucky stared at his latest e-mail. Surgery, May 15. Wow, they didn't dick around, did they?

He put his signature on Johnson's report, the last paperwork he'd file for a while.

"Did you know you get a furrow between your eyebrows the size of the Grand Canyon when you think too hard?" Johnson placed a steaming coffee cup on Lucky's desk and sipped her own brew while scowling at the half-dozen empty and semi-empty cups littering the surface. "You really should throw those away, you know."

"What do you want?" He gave her his best evil eye.

She'd brought him coffee, been his friend when he didn't deserve her. He opened his mouth to apologize—

"Walter gave me part of your caseload. I came to check if you had anything else to tell me that wasn't in the files."

Okay, maybe he'd give her his full attention. "Who you working with?"

"Landry."

What the fuck? "The king of morons? What about Bo?"

Johnson parked her butt on Bo's empty desk. "What about him?"

"Why aren't you assigned to work with him?" Johnson might be good, real good, but not ready to take over the role of trainer.

"Maybe you'd better ask Walter."

Yeah, maybe he'd better say goodbye to the boss while he had the chance.

"Lucky?" The cockiness left Johnson's voice.

"Uh-huh?"

"Good luck. I'm not much of a praying woman, but I've mentioned your name to a few folks who are."

And Lucky'd changed his name so many times over the years, the man upstairs might scratch his head and ask, "Who?"

Good manners said he should thank her. She saved him from the effort. "I gotta run. Please keep me posted."

He bluffed a bravado he didn't quite make sincere. "Why, Johnson, I didn't know you cared."

She swooped so fast he didn't have time to duck and pressed her lips to his cheek. "Of course I care. Who else's ass am I gonna whoop at the gym?" She nodded toward the bulk of the SNB's Department of Diversion Prevention and Control. "The rest of these guys can't hold their own."

She moseyed off down the hallway.

Lucky swiped at his cheek and wound up with a sticky red mess on his hand. "Yeah, Johnson," he murmured, "I reckon I'll miss you too."

One day a stiff wind might cause a desk avalanche on Mount Paper Pile, aka Walter's desk. He'd carved out enough space for his laptop and coffee cup. Books filled every shelf on a massive cabinet, and motivational posters hung from the walls, spouting the benefits of teamwork.

Lucky still liked working alone. Or with Bo or Johnson. Not that he'd confess.

"Why isn't Bo taking my cases while I'm gone?" He dropped down into his usual chair in front of his boss's desk. "You said something about no field exercises while I was gone."

Walter paused mid-sip of a cup of sugar and whipped cream laden sludge. "And good morning to you too, Lucky." He nudged his boss again. "Johnson tells me you assigned her to my cases. Why?"

"Because I read your reports. She's doing well under your instruction."

"Not good enough to be cut loose with Landry." There wasn't one damned thing Walter could say to make Lucky breathe any easier.

Walter regarded Lucky with too-knowing eyes. "I'll be acting as handler."

Okay, maybe there was. "You? Why you? You haven't been out of the office much in years."

"All the more reason to do so now, wouldn't you agree?"

Disagreeing with the boss might not be the smartest thing to do, but it did make for some lively debates. "You're out of practice." Nothing better happen to Rett Johnson.

"I'll be coordinating with Jameson O'Donoghue."

Brakes squealed in Lucky's mind. "That sonofa..." As much as he'd like to put down the bastard, O'Donoghue knew his stuff. He'd never be as good as Lucky, but then again, who was?

Bo. And in about six months, Loretta Johnson might come in a close third. Who knew? Maybe Lucky might get handed another rookie to train with more than shit for brains, and he'd start mass producing good agents.

"Okay." Lucky blew out a breath. "You and O'Donoghue relive your glory days. Where does that leave Bo?" They'd better not push Bo to the side. He'd worked too hard to get his head back on straight.

"I've got a special task in mind for him."

"Oh?" So, no shoving to the side. But it better not be undercover for months. Lucky might need him.

"I recommended Bo for temporary transfer to the SNB's Richmond, Virginia office as part of our inter-department cooperation." Walter tapped on a few computer keys and settled back in his chair with a smile.

Richmond. Where some as-yet-to-be-seen doctor planned

to whack open Lucky's innards and help himself to an organ. "Does Bo know?"

"Not yet. I plan to discuss the matter with him later today." Walter dropped his business attitude. "I also will remind him of our policies regarding domestic partnerships. He's free to request a medical leave of absence to care for his partner."

And Bo wouldn't. Leave didn't completely match salary, and they might be in over their heads financially in a few days. "I doubt he'll take leave."

"Which is why I've planned his reassignment. The third option would be for him to use up some of those vacation days he keeps racking up." Walter leaned forward, elbows on the desk, and peered over the top of his bifocals. "Have the two of you discussed the matter?"

No. They hadn't. Lucky'd been so stressed out about his own issues he'd neglected Bo. "No, sir."

"Then I suggest you do. And you needn't worry about anything here. Go. Help your father. Work can wait."

"But—"

"No buts. In a way you're still working. Saving a life. And if I were in your place, I'd want my wife by my side." And pity the man who tried to keep Mrs. Smith from Walter's bedside. The tiny Southern belle with the good manners would show her claws.

Words refused to come out of Lucky's mouth, smart-assed or otherwise, and tickling began in the back of his throat. His eyes burned. Subject-change time. "When I see Bo, I'll call him 'the little woman.'"

Walter cracked a smile. "And probably be handed your head. After all, you trained him." He paused for a moment, rose from behind his desk, and took the vacant chair next to Lucky. "If there's anything you need, anything at all, please don't hesitate to ask."

What could he say? "Um... Thanks." Time to leave the boss's office before things turned too mushy.

Bo passed him in the hall and paused to give a tight smile. "Walter wants to see me."

"Then don't keep the man waiting." Oh, to be a fly on the wall for the next ten minutes. Lucky went back to his cube. No Bo to talk to. Rett might do in a pinch. No sign of her either.

Well, time to make good on a few barbeque dinners. He strolled to the reception desk.

"Can I help you, Mr. Harrison?" Lisa glanced up from her typing.

"Nah, just stopped by to say howdy." And because he didn't want to be alone right now. Back home in North Carolina, she'd have caught three bugs by now with her wide-open mouth. Hey! Who knew he could shock people by being nice?

The guilty eyes and flushed cheeks made him round the reception desk and peer over her shoulder.

"Hell no. Tell me Keith isn't still making you do his work for him. What did I tell you?" The no-account asswipe had a comeuppance heading his way. "Tell him to take his report and shove it—"

"Mr. Harrison!" Lisa's eyes got big. "I can't do that. Keith is a senior agent. I'm just a receptionist. He could get me fired for insubordination."

"And I got promoted, so I rank higher than him. If anyone says anything, I'll back you up. Anyone gives you grief, you tell 'em I told you to."

Lisa hung her head. "I don't want to get into trouble."

Okay, time for a better idea. "If he insists on others doing his work for him, why don't I help too?" He wriggled his fingers in an *up-up* motion.

She hesitated a moment before yielding her chair, leaving Keith's report open on her computer.

Lucky sat down and tapped out a few words. Yeah, that'd work. After five minutes, he relinquished her chair. "Now remember, I outrank both you and Keith, so my words stay in, got that? No deleting."

"Oh my!" She slapped a hand over her mouth, cutting off a giggle. "Are you sure about this?"

"Never been surer." He swaggered back to his cube, whistling off-key a song about sexy tractors. Just wait until Walter Smith read Keith's report.

Busy work took about ten minutes, and desk-cleaning took twenty. He didn't want to come back to a bunch of science experiments growing in coffee cups.

If he came back.

After an hour Bo returned and took his place at his desk, saying nothing.

"Long meeting there," Lucky prodded.

"It did go a little long."

So not like Bo to withhold information. "And?"

"And what?" Bo scrunched his brow.

"What did Walter say?"

"Oh!" Tension drained out of Bo. "He offered me a chance to take time off for your surgery or work out of the Richmond office so I can be close."

"What ya planning to do?" Lucky held his breath.

"Discuss it with you first. What would you like me to do?" Bo tilted his chair back, rubbing a bit of five o'clock shadow on his chin.

Come hold my hand? "What do you want to do?"

"I asked you first."

"Yeah, but you'll be the one hanging around a hospital all day." Shit. Hospitals meant drugs. Drugs meant temptation. "Would that be a problem?"

"Not at all. If I take leave or vacation, I'll be underfoot all the time. If I work, I might not be there when you need me."

"Ah, you know me. I'm tougher than a pine knot. I'll be fine." *Please, please come with me!* Lucky's fingernails dug into his palms from the tight fists he made.

Bo studied Lucky, from the top of this head to his feet, not even pausing at the good stuff. "You're scared."

"Am not." Okay. Maybe a little. No need worrying Bo, though.

"Are too. And it's okay to be scared."

"I'm not scared of nothing." The last time Lucky'd said those words they'd been true. Before Bo. Before Mexico. Before he'd had something to lose.

Bo slid his chair across the floor and stroked his fingers across Lucky's cheek. Who gave a happy damn how anyone passing by might react? Those fingers needed to stay. They didn't.

Bo stared into Lucky's eyes. Lucky couldn't have turned away if he'd tried. "Lucky, I've spent some time researching lately. The doctors in Richmond have stellar reputations. These are some of the best transplant surgeons alive. Nothing's going wrong."

"You forget. This is me we're talking about. Life ain't about to pass on a chance to hand me shit." Payback. Karma. Whatever. If a remote chance existed of something going wrong, it would.

"You don't have to do this. You can always say no."

And let Charlotte and her boys down? Let down his parents, though they'd never know. "I can't."

A quick chin dip was all the nod Bo gave. "I know. But it's killing me watching you worry so much. It's going to be fine. Hey, I got you something." He spun around and pulled an object out of his computer bag. "I meant this as your birthday present, but we got, um, distracted."

Bo's being there and baking a cake had been birthday present enough. Bright colors hung before Lucky's eyes, taking a minute to come into focus—a miniature metal dragon on a keychain, scales changing from blue to green and back again in the light.

"My collection is too big for you to take on assignment, so I got you this little guy. He'll watch over you when I'm not there. Sort of like the hummingbird totem you got me." Which now hung from a chain around Bo's neck. "You can take him with you to the hospital, for when I can't be there."

"Bo, I—"

Bo's smile fell, and he dropped the hand holding the dragon into his lap. "I know. Sorry. I have my lame moments sometimes."

Lucky plucked the dragon from Bo's fingers. "Thanks. I'll hang him from the bed rails." He left his hand on Bo's, and after a moment shifted the gift to his other hand and laced their fingers together.

Calm poured through the connection.

"Well, lookie—"

Twin glares of death should've reduced Keith to ashes. Instead, he leaned against the wall of Bo and Lucky's cube, smirk firmly in place.

"Oh, Keith?" Lisa appeared, breathless.

Keith turned. "Yes?"

"Mr. Smith would like to see you in his office. To... discuss your latest report." She sealed her lips in a tight line, but laughter shone in her eyes.

The asshole of the year spun on his heel and trounced off.

Lucky had to ask, "Did Walter really ask for him?"

"Oh yes." Lisa collapsed into giggles, hanging on to the cube wall for support. "Seems Keith's last report contained the words to *Mary Had a Little Lamb*, among other things. The boss is... concerned. Thank you, Lucky. I really appreciate your help." She snickered again and wandered away.

"*Mary Had a Little Lamb*?" Bo asked. "What's she talking about?"

"Oh, nothing." With about three more years of practice, Lucky might master looking innocent.

"Lucky." Bo's tone nearly matched Lucky's mother's when he'd tormented one of his younger brothers as a kid.

Time to fess up. "Keith didn't heed my warning and made Lisa do his work again. I... helped."

Bo winced. "Helped, how?"

"Remember the kid's book *Green Eggs and Ham*?" Lucky used to read the story to his nephews.

"Yes." Bo folded his arms across his chest. "I'm not going to like this, am I?"

Lucky rolled his shoulders. "Maybe. Maybe not. But I rewrote it. Kind of. 'I should not make Lisa do my work, I should

100

not be a stupid jerk, I won't make Lisa type again...' I don't remember all the rest. But the ending is clear enough. 'I do not like you, Keith my man.'"

Bo managed a straight face for all of a half minute and released a cackle. "You didn't!"

"Sure did."

"You know you've just won a valuable ally, right? Lisa knows about as much of what goes on around here as Walter does."

"I'd rather have you bent over my desk." Lucky's attempted leer fell short.

"How about you save that thought?"

"Till when?"

Bo glanced right and left, then brushed his lips over Lucky's. "Till we get home."

Lucky raced Bo up the sidewalk to their house. Neighbors might get an eyeful. Let 'em.

Bo won the race, leaving Lucky to fumble to get the door open while he stood on one foot and yanked his shoe off.

He grabbed Bo and fused their mouths. The door sprung open. Together they fell through the doorway. Lucky tossed the shoe God knew where and slammed Bo against the wall.

"Clothes! Off! Now!" Lucky grabbed either side of Bo's button-down shirt and ripped, buttons pinging off the walls.

"My shirt!" Bo cried.

"I'll get you a new one." Lucky ran his lips down newly exposed skin. "I'll get you a dozen." He slid to his knees, working Bo's belt loose. "I'll get you three dozen."

He slipped the leather from the last loop and let go. The belt vanished before hitting the floor. "Damn, it, Moose!"

The dog wagged his entire body, brandishing his prize in his teeth. Lucky lunged. He could replace shirts, but the belt made one hell of an expensive chew toy.

Bo grabbed Lucky's arm. "Let him have it." He knocked Lucky over onto the floor and climbed on top, wrestling

Lucky's T-shirt off. One moment he straddled Lucky, fumbling to open his blue jeans, the next...

A white blur hit with all the force of a Mack truck.

"Ack!" Over Bo went.

Lucky took advantage of the distraction to grab the belt. "Here, Moose, fetch!" He tossed the belt, which landed in front of the hall, cutting off their escape to the bedroom.

Bo and Lucky faced each other, Lucky on his knees, Bo on his back. As one they exclaimed, "Garage!" and hauled ass through the kitchen and out the door.

Lucky barely got the door shut when a ninety-pound dog missile hit the barrier. "Now, where were we?" He tuned out the insistent whining and the smell of oil and gas, to focus his full attention on Bo.

His partner perused the area, a slow smile spreading across his lips, igniting The Dimple. "Mechanic and Businessman?"

"Sounds good to me!"

Bo wriggled out of his jeans and boxers in record time, and parked his magnificent bubble butt on the weight bench in the corner.

Oh, hell yeah. Lucky strapped on his tool belt. "What seems to be the problem?"

"I'm having a bit of trouble here." Bo leaned back and dropped his legs open. A drop of fluid clung to the tip of his erection.

"Oh, rod trouble."

Bo nodded.

"I can help you out there." Lucky dropped back to his knees, scrabbling to open his jeans and free his cock. "Oh fuck." He'd have to go back into the house after all.

"Check the saddlebags," Bo said, running his hand up and down his shaft.

The saddlebags? Lucky leapt toward the Harley and tore through the saddlebags, in search of... "Got 'em!" He crawled back to Bo, releasing his painfully cramped cock on the way. Apply a condom, slather with lube...

And lock his lips to Bo's. Bo arched, meeting him half-way. Lucky aimed the tip of one hell of a hard-on at where he'd most like it to be, sliding up and down, slicking the way. Damned tool belt stopped him. Lucky did some rearranging and tried again.

Wearing nothing but socks, Bo slid farther down the bench, giving Lucky more access.

Best gift Lucky'd ever gotten. He slipped in a mere inch, only to pull back and push in a tiny bit more. Advance, retreat, advance, retreat.

"Stop teasing and fuck me like you mean it." Bo wrapped his legs around Lucky's thighs and pulled.

The man getting all forceful? Yeah, buddy! "This here's Lucklighter's Garage. I call the shots."

"Ever hear of 'the customer is always right'?" Bo forced out between grunts as Lucky worked his way farther inside.

Lucky's rhythm never faltered. "Pushy businessman, ain't ya?"

"The pushiest. Now shut up and fuck."

Sounded like a plan. Lucky buried his cock in a smooth glide.

Bo sucked air through his teeth, eyes scrunched closed.

Lucky stilled.

Bo cracked open one eye. "I thought I told you..."

Lucky grasped Bo's thighs and pulled him back, angling high and using his leverage to full advantage. "Oh, God, yeah!"

Deep inside his lover, the tight squeeze of muscles and heat from Bo's body felt so fucking perfect.

"I think I can get this rod loosened up for you. Just needs some grease." He released one of Bo's thighs and took matters in hand, stroking Bo from outside and within.

Bo stretched out on the bench, hair mussed, grasping the barbell over his head and forcing himself back, meeting Lucky's every lunge. God, what a gorgeous man.

Faster, harder, deeper. Bo's moans mixed with the squeaks from the bench and Lucky's harsh breaths.

Sweat dripped down Lucky's face. He'd wipe the drops away later. Bo lifted up, joining their mouths. His moan vibrated against Lucky's tongue.

Lucky answered with his own moan. *Oh, yeah. Oh, yeah. Oh, hell yeah.* Ecstasy slammed into him. His muscles seized. Staring into Bo's eyes, he plunged in once more, twice more, held and let go.

"Ahhh..." Lucky arched back, shuddering through his climax.

Bo grabbed his hand, keeping the tempo going while Lucky's brain turned to mush. Eyes unfocused and mouth open, he jerked and splattered his stomach and their hands. Again and again he lurched and shot.

Finally, he collapsed back on the bench, laughing. "I'll never look at getting the Durango's oil changed the same way again."

"I'll change your oil." Lucky leered. He leaned over Bo, catching his breath.

"Anytime."

Lucky eyed the Harley. "How about a ride?"

Bo laughed. "You just had one."

Lucky didn't bother fighting about driving when they wrangled the garage door open by hand and got out the Harley. Instead he hopped on the back and snugged himself up against Bo's ass.

They rode out of the already-open complex gate, the purr of the engine balm for Lucky's soul. The vibration and his dick pressed between Bo's ass cheeks didn't hurt. No need for talk, no need for thought. Out here nothing existed but him, Bo, the bike, and a hell of a lot of scenery.

Subdivisions gave way to abandoned buildings on the outskirts of town, which gave way to farmland.

They passed a freshly manured field. Lucky held his breath. The stench triggered memories of his dad fertilizing the tobacco fields. A few miles down the road, the air held traces of freshly mown hay, honeysuckle, and other things he couldn't name.

And under it all, the scent of Bo's cologne. His soap. His shampoo. The scent of sex clinging to him. Bo. Lucky's entire world. Sun on his arms, his cares disappeared. Easy to cast them off out here. Pretend he and Bo could keep driving and never have to face facts again.

They'd go to the mountains, maybe find a place to camp. Love each other on the ground with nothing but stars overhead. How many times had he promised to take Bo hiking? How many times had something else gotten in the way?

If he made it out of this, he'd take Bo hiking. Hell, he'd go anywhere the man wanted—even a vegetarian restaurant.

If he made it out.

All too soon, the fantasy ended where it'd started—back at the house. Bo ran his fingers over a worn Mr. Pizza flyer posted to the refrigerator door. "We could order pizza. What kind do you want?"

What? Mr. Healthy eating carbs, and fat, and whatever else? "Why?"

"Why what?"

"Why pizza?"

"We gotta eat, and I don't feel like cooking. We'd have to go grocery shopping first anyway." Bo planted a kiss on Lucky's nose. "I'd rather stay here with you."

The condemned man's last meal: pizza. Well, maybe not last meal, but close.

"Besides," Bo said, "we got a visitor coming."

Lucky's heart dropped to his stomach. If Bo warned him first, probably not Walter or Rett. "Who?" And should he hop in his car and haul ass?

The long pause didn't bode well. "Your sister."

Charlotte? Oh, God. "Why?"

Bo dragged his fingers through his hair. "You need to see her. Talk to her. She misses you."

And Lucky missed her. But what could he say? What could he do? "I don't know if I can. I promised to always be there for her... for the boys. And I ain't been shit." Rubbing the back of his neck didn't stop his fast-approaching headache.

Bo wrapped his fingers around Lucky's free hand. "That was a long time ago. You were different then. You're a good man now, whether you believe it or not."

Johnson's words came back to him: *"You show us how to walk the fine line that'll bring down the bad guys and get us home at night."* Had to count for something, right?

Without knowing quite how he got there, Lucky sat on the couch, getting a shoulder rub. More of Johnson's words got to him. *"And do you do that for him?"*

Tonight. He'd pay the man back tonight.

After he faced his demons, or more accurately, the sister he'd let down.

CHAPTER TEN

The warning buzz from the front gate gave Lucky a few minutes to try to compose himself.

"Breathe, Lucky, breathe." Bo patted his back. "She's your sister, not an Uzi-welding crime boss."

"Uh-huh." Of the two, Charlotte might be the deadlier.

"It's not like she's one of Nestor's people, come to take you out."

"No. She'd eat those wannabes for breakfast. You haven't met my family." And Lucky wouldn't blame him for running once he had.

"What are you expecting her to do? Kill you?" "You don't know her like I do. She can get riled sometimes." Lucky shivered at a particularly vivid memory, involving a well-placed bucket of hog slop and a vengeful sibling.

"Don't I know it! She... Oh, dear God! She pulled a gun on me. She's vicious. Let's hide!" Bo patted his foot, scowl firmly in place.

"You're making fun of me."

Bo's scowl softened. "Sorry. But for years I've heard how much you miss her. And I've never quite gotten why you wouldn't even talk to her."

"You wouldn't understand."

"Try me."

"I made promises I didn't keep. I'm a bad example for her kids. I'm not the kind of guy anyone in their right mind would want for a brother." There, he'd confessed—and got a mock punch to the shoulder for his efforts. "What'ya do that for?"

107

"In the tunnel in Mexico we promised once all the shit passed, we'd reconnect with our families. Have we? Huh?"

God, did Bo always have to be right? "I told you you wouldn't understand."

"The hell I don't. Why do you think I haven't laid eyes on my brother in years? Huh?"

"If you feel the same way about your brother, why're you being so hard on me?" Lucky rubbed his shoulder.

"Because you need to tell me these things. How are we supposed to work out issues if we don't communicate?" And there Bo went being right again.

"*You* coulda told *me*, you know." Lucky glowered.

Bo blew out a sigh. "Yeah. Maybe—"

They both froze at the sound of the doorbell.

"Aren't you going to get the door?" Bo whispered.

"I thought you were." For some reason, Lucky's feet wouldn't do his bidding.

The doorbell rang again. Neither moved. The knob twisted. Lucky held his breath. Hundreds of drug busts, hundreds of times facing drugs dealers and other dangerous types, and his heart had never pounded harder at what he'd soon face.

The door creaked open. A woman who looked too much like Lucky's mother stood in the doorway clutching her handbag like a weapon. "Oh! Hey, y'all!"

Older, maybe, her smile more hesitant. She'd filled out since being the scrawny runt of a girl who used to dog Lucky's footsteps and run when he'd chased her with frogs—only to find a bigger frog and chase back.

After he got into bed with a four-foot blacksnake, Lucky checked the sheets for years.

"Richmond Eugene Lucklighter. Are ya just gonna stand there looking purty, or are you gonna invite me in?"

Still as sassy as a jaybird.

Bo unfroze first. "I'm so sorry. Charlotte, it's wonderful to see you again. Please, come in." He glowered at Lucky. Yeah, right. Like she hadn't threatened to shoot Bo the last time they came face to face.

One step, two... Lucky grabbed his sister, burying his damp face in her hair, and held on for dear life. Oh God. Charlotte. He squeezed tighter lest she suddenly disappear.

The scent of familiar perfume surrounded him, a gift he'd sent her one Christmas.

Charlotte, his best friend growing up, his partner in misadventures, and one of the few people to ever best him in a wrestling match.

She'd learned to fight dirty while still in grade school.

"Ack! Rich! Let's go! You're choking me!" Charlotte wrenched away from his grasp and stared him in the eyes.

She grabbed him back. Her purse connected with his kidney. Ow! "Oh, dear God, Richie. I've missed you so much!"

Lucky held on tight, opening his eyes to watch Bo quietly retreating. He opened his mouth to tell Bo to stay, but the pizza delivery guy buzzed from the gate and gave him an excuse to back off.

The pizza guy came and went, and still Lucky and Charlotte clung to each other, like she'd once clung to him as a child after a nightmare.

In the background, Bo clanked dishes as he set the kitchen table. Once they finally broke apart, Lucky and Charlotte both scrubbed their faces with the backs of their hands. Bo traipsed out of the kitchen and handed them each a paper towel, but said nothing about their tears.

At least Lucky's hadn't formed black streaks down his face like Charlotte's.

"Pizza's getting cold." Bo vanished into the kitchen.

"Hungry?" Lucky asked between sniffles. The lovely aroma of pizza managed to get through his stuffed-up nose.

"I could eat." Charlotte wiped her eyes, tossed her suspiciously heavy pocketbook onto the couch, and let out a whistle. "Day-um, boy! Nice house. You done good for yourself. I want a tour later."

"Okay. Let's eat first." That would buy Lucky time to pull himself together. Charlotte. Here. Now.

Suddenly not talking to her all those years except for texts and e-mails seemed like a dumb idea. Who'd come up with such nonsense anyway? Oh. He had.

"So, how've you—" Lame, lame, lame. First time face to face in years and nothing better came to Lucky's mind?

"I got so much to tell—"

They stopped in the kitchen doorway and stared at each other. No telling who started first, but laughter burst from them both.

In a moment of déjà vu from days gone by, Charlotte smacked Lucky on the back of the head. "That's for not talking to me for all these years!"

What could he say? Talking to her made things too real, brought down the ton of guilt he'd earned for being a jerk, an asshole, and getting himself locked up so he couldn't watch over her anymore.

And her boys grew up without Uncle Richie. "I deserved that."

Bo piped in from the table. "If you don't sit down and eat, I'll smack you too."

Charlotte winked. "Better do what the man says and sit your ass down. I like him. He's feisty."

Lucky started to sit next to Bo, but he stopped himself and took the opposite chair at the four-topper table.

Charlotte smacked him again. "If that's where you usually sit, then sit. It's not like I don't know y'all are together." She grabbed the chair from Lucky and parked herself in front of Bo. Stubborn woman.

Wow! Bo had gone all out, even serving the pizza from a plate and not the cardboard box as Lucky would have. He'd ordered one veggie, one meat. Bacon! Lucky might have to kiss the smug little smirk off Bo's face when his sister wasn't looking.

"Lucky, since y'all invited me to stay the night, I reckon you better loosen up a bit. Go on. Kiss Bo if you want to. Matter of fact, if you don't, I might. Pizza!" Charlotte yanked a piece of meat pizza onto her plate.

Spend the night? Lucky glared at Bo. Bo had the good graces to blush. Not that Lucky minded her staying, but Bo could've said something—and allowed Lucky even more time to worry his ass off. He eyeballed his pizza-munching sister. "Dang, woman! Don't they have pizza in Spokane?"

"Yup," she managed between bites, "but I try to fix the boys healthy meals. Gives them more incentive to move out when they're eighteen."

Liar. She'd be torn to pieces when her boys left home. Lucky wouldn't put it past her to finally go to college like she'd been planning for years in order to keep an eye on her kids.

"How was the drive down?" Leave it to Bo to swallow down enough nerves to play host.

"Southern drivers ain't got no better since I moved away." She grinned. "I had to flip off a couple hundred, I reckon."

"Where are the boys?" Charlotte's arrival should come equipped with two nephews for Uncle Richie to get reacquainted with.

"They're staying with a friend while I go tend the folks. They'll be joining me when the school year ends." She paused, took a sip of iced tea, closed her eyes, and smiled. "Now this is something I've missed living in Washington. Sweet tea. Bo, this is really good."

Lucky mock-glowered. "How do you know I didn't make the tea?"

She swallowed her mouthful. "Um... because I've met you? If it weren't for Bo, you'd probably have bought a house without a kitchen, if you could find one."

True. Lucky sipped his tea. At least she still appreciated the Southern nectar of the gods after being away so long. He had millions of questions he wanted to ask, but they'd been raised not to talk business, or talk much at all, at the table. With four other kids to compete with, the slowest eater might not get seconds.

They polished off the last crust and Charlotte rose first. "Y'all bought dinner, I'll clean up."

Maybe Lucky wasn't the only one who needed a few moments to get his act together. Of course, she might run screaming for soap and water if she got a load of the mess she'd made of her makeup.

Bo stood and picked up his plate.

"I said, 'shoo!'" Charlotte flipped a hand in the general direction of the living room. "Go talk about me before I get in there and you have to hush."

"Yes, ma'am." Bo put the plate back on the table.

Charlotte slapped a hand to her chest. "Be still my beating heart. A Southern gentleman. Richie, you got a well-trained one there. You better be good to him or I'll haul him back up north with me. Folks would buy him drinks all night to hear him talk."

Funny, she'd spent years in the Northwest, but if anything, her Southern accent had only grown thicker. But then again, he'd not heard her in years.

And whose fault is that? echoed in his head—in Charlotte's voice.

The moment he stepped into the living room, Lucky grabbed Bo as hard as he'd grabbed his sister earlier. Right now, without an anchor, he'd surely fall.

"Shh... It's okay." Bo held him, rocking a bit.

Lucky sobbed, tears soaking Bo's T-shirt. Family. He'd lost his family. And no matter how hard he pretended otherwise, they'd left a big, unhealed hole in his heart.

Charlotte alone stood by him. Had always been there. Had even come to his trial and heard him get a ten-year sentence. And cried.

Like she'd cried tonight. Sooner or later, he'd have to stop causing the woman tears. Bo pulled him down onto the couch and held him till his heart stopped breaking.

His fault. His own damned fault.

When Charlotte bustled out of the kitchen a few moments

later, the red nose and additional mascara streaks down her cheeks said she'd spent her time the same way Lucky had.

Sniff. "How about the tour now?" She wiped her hand across her face but only smeared her makeup even more.

Yeah. Stay busy. Best thing to do to keep from thinking and regretting too hard.

She turned around in the living room, sauntered over to the backdoor, and screamed. A wall of white hit the glass. The scream turned into a giggle. "Richie, your horse wants in." She squatted down by the door, tapping the glass and cooing at Moose. "You raising goats now, or what?"

"Found him at the pound. Couldn't leave him behind." Not when Moose wriggled his way into Lucky's heart, reminding him of the Great Pyrenees he'd grown up with as herd dogs for the family's goats.

Charlotte shot him a "who are you and what have you done with my brother" look. "Can we let him in?"

"Not if you want to stay upright. He's a bit of a handful right now." The drool pit of doom whined through the glass, turning adoring eyes on Lucky.

"A handful. Ha! Takes after you then, don't he?" After a bit of circling, and stopping by the bookcase to admire Bo's dragon statue collection, Charlotte marched to the hall and waited.

Bo took the hint and shot to his feet. "The bedrooms and bathrooms are back this way. Here's your room." He opened the door to the guest bedroom, furnished with Rett's hand-me-down air mattress and a half dozen boxes waiting to be unpacked. "We're still moving in."

Charlotte flipped on the light switch. "This is nice. And bigger than my bedroom back home."

"The bathroom's this way." Bo strolled off down the hall.

Their voices faded. Oh crap. Getting quiet must mean they'd started talking about him. Lucky dashed down the hall and into his and Bo's bedroom, too late to stop Charlotte from opening the door to the room he and Bo didn't speak about.

"What a cute nursery!" Charlotte winked at Lucky. "When y'all planning on using it?"

Lucky turned to stare at Bo, who stared back with the same dumbfounded, wide-eyed silence.

Charlotte's smile fell. "Oops, hit a nerve there, did I? Sorry. Don't mind me. I'll just be over here prying my foot out of my mouth."

Lucky opened the bathroom door, getting a chance to change the subject. "We've still got a lot of work to do on the house, but this room's pretty much finished."

"Lordy, what a bathroom." Charlotte poked her head into the walk-in closet. "I got closet envy like all get out."

Her mouth dropped open again in the garage while circling the Harley. "When'd you get a bike?" She managed to hike her leg high enough to hop onto the seat, and sat gripping the handlebars. "Wroom! Wroom!"

Again Lucky exchanged looks with Bo. How much should they tell?

Bo saved Lucky from lying. "I went undercover in a biker gang, and got a sweet deal when the case ended."

What a relief. Lucky had never been able to lie to his sister—she knew him too well. And Bo hadn't outright lied. Having a former drug lord hand over the keys to one hell of a ride counted as a sweet deal, didn't it?

But one day soon, the "drug lord" might call in the favor.

Damn. Lucky might still have reasons to keep Charlotte and her boys at a distance.

CHAPTER ELEVEN

"Sure you got enough covers?" Lucky searched the closet for another blanket while Bo trekked out to Charlotte's car for her suitcase.

Charlotte stopped Lucky's digging with a hand on his arm. "Any more and I'd never find my way out of the bed."

"Need another pillow? We got extra pillows." If not, he'd have more in twenty minutes or so after a trip to the local Wal-Mart.

"Richie?"

"Need a glass of water?"

"Rich!"

Lucky snapped around to face his sister. "What?"

"Would you please stop twirling? You're freaking me out."

"I'm not twirling." Whatever the hell twirling meant.

"Yes, you are." She cupped Lucky's face between her palms. Her high boot heels put her right at eye to eye. Finally, someone shorter than him! "This is me. No matter how long it's been, I'm still Char, you're still Rich." Her peck on his cheek brought back a thousand memories.

"But so much has changed."

Her evil grin didn't bode well for him. "I can still kick your ass."

One minute he stood upright, the next she had him in a headlock, rubbing her knuckles over his scalp.

"What the..." Bo dropped the suitcase just inside the door. "Lucky? Charlotte? What are you doing?"

Charlotte let Lucky go. "Reliving old times. A day didn't go by when we didn't give each other grief as kids."

"When we weren't teaming up on Dover." The fourth Lucklighter kid learned slow that if he picked on one of the older young'uns, the other wasn't far away.

Charlotte rounded on Lucky. "You still calling him his old childhood nickname?"

Lucky inched to the side and a clear shot at the door. "Old habits die hard... Talladega." He squeezed past Bo in the doorway, Charlotte hot on his heels.

"You'll pay dearly for that, *Eugene!*" Giggling took the heat out of her threat.

He grabbed the back of the couch, swung himself over, hid a flinch when his bad ankle hit the floor, and crouched, ready to haul ass.

Charlotte's grin matched his own as she paced him on the other side of the couch. She feinted left and back right.

Nope. Not falling for her ruse. Lucky stood his ground midway of his protective not-leather shield.

Charlotte sprung. *Wham!* "Gotcha!" Lucky and Charlotte tumbled to the floor in fits of laughter.

Bo muttered, "Kids," and dropped down onto the couch.

Leave it to his sister to take Lucky from tears to laughs in no time flat. She hopped up first and offered her hand. One of her favorite ploys.

"Aww...C'mon." Charlotte wriggled her fingers. "Don't you trust me?"

Lucky folded his arms across his chest. "Nope."

"Then I'll do it." Bo hauled Lucky off the floor. "Tell you what. Why don't I go polish the bike or something and leave you two alone?"

What? "Stay. You don't have to go." In Lucky's excitement of his sister's visit he'd totally left Bo out.

Bo and Charlotte shared a look. Oh. They must have already talked this out.

"I'll be out in the garage working on the door opener if you need me." Bo brushed his lips over Lucky's. This time Lucky managed not to flinch. As much as he loved Bo's kisses, hiding

116

their relationship had become a habit he needed to break. It wasn't like Charlotte hadn't witnessed him kissing men before, starting with a summer field hand she'd caught him in the hay barn with way back when and used as blackmail to get him to do her chores for a week.

Charlotte sat down and patted the cushion beside her. Lucky eased down, wary for an ambush. Instead she dragged his arm over her shoulder and settled in. "Oh, God, I've missed you some kind of fierce."

Lucky kissed the top of her head. Sometimes words weren't enough.

She jostled him with her elbow. "Don't think for a minute you're gonna shut me out again when this is all over."

"I won't." No. Never again. His own half-truths came back to him. Sure, he hadn't spoken with her on the phone or talked to her in person because his own failure stared him in the face. But his biggest fear? Asking a question he'd stuffed down inside for so long.

"Charlotte, I need the truth. Why did the family turn their backs on me?" Or rather, why in particular? He'd certainly given them plenty of reasons.

His sister pushed a few strands of hair out of her eyes. Stalling.

"C'mon. Whatever you got to say can't be any tougher than losing my family."

Charlotte took a deep breath and blew it out slowly. "I honestly don't know. Once Daddy made up his mind, he refused to explain. And you know Mama. Whether he's right or whether he's wrong, she goes along."

Yeah, Mom had always stood by Dad. Dad did the same for her.

And Bo did the same for Lucky.

Still, he had to know. "It's important. Anybody you can ask besides the folks who might have some idea?"

Charlotte's snort reminded Lucky of many other snorts over the years, a sure sign of his sister putting her foot down.

And no Mama around to give her what for. "Bristol wouldn't tell me for love nor money. Dallas can't keep a secret for shit. If he knew, he'd've told me by now."

"That leaves Daytona." They both winced. Daytona hadn't been the most reliable of sources back before Lucky's life went to hell. No telling what another decade worth of drugs had done to the kid. "I don't suppose he's gotten any better. You told me he couldn't donate his liver because of his drug abuse."

"Poor kid. He's tried." Charlotte wriggled, settling closer to Lucky's side. "Lord knows he's tried. Been in and out of rehab since high school, but he's never quite gotten his act together."

"But if he knew something, would he tell you?"

"Remember how scared he used to be of the Noogie Monster?" She cracked her knuckles. "He never quite got over his fear of us."

"And we never touched him." Much.

"Well, you were the one giving him noogies three times a day. I just short-sheeted his bed."

"...put a dead rat in his sock drawer, tossed a handful of corn on his plate whenever Grandma brought over a pot of chitlins."

They both made a face. Many more chitlin ordeals in his youth, and Lucky might've joined Bo in being a dedicated weed eater, especially as he'd believed he saw the pig's last meal when someone hid corn on his plate. Who the hell decided, *"Hey! Let's eat pig innards!"* "We gave our brothers hell, didn't we?"

"Yeah, but remember on the bus, those guys tried to pick on Day?"

Boy, did Lucky remember. He and Charlotte both got kicked off the bus. She'd come home with scratches and bruises, and Lucky sported a black eye.

The other guys came out worse. All five of them. Bigger, heavier, and only half as mean as two pissed off redneck farm kids defending the baby of the family.

And the bastards never even looked crosswise at Daytona again.

"I could call him. He's living with Mama and Daddy now." Charlotte dug her cellphone out of her purse. "If you're sure you want to do this."

Good thing Lucky wasn't in the hospital hooked to a monitor yet. Nurses might come running for all the energetic bumps and thumps his heart made.

One phone call might solve years of pain. But what if whatever Daytona said carved Lucky's heart out again? Or what if Day didn't know jack shit? Bo. Lucky needed Bo here. But Bo wasn't here. He'd given Lucky space. Lucky took a deep breath. "Call him."

Charlotte hit a few buttons so the ringing came through the speaker, and set her phone down on the coffee table.One ring, two rings, three rings...

"Hello?" came a groggy-sounding voice. Lucky's heart lurched.

"Hey, Day." Charlotte leaned over the coffee table and probably spoke louder than necessary. "It's me. Did I wake you?"

"No," the voice from Lucky's past said through a yawn. Daytona Jerome Lucklighter, his pest of a little brother who'd once idolized Lucky. How he'd followed along like a puppy.

And yet he'd wasted years of his life to drugs. While Lucky wouldn't trade his life for anything, being law-abiding meant he'd grown a conscience over the years. He'd failed Daytona, like he'd failed Charlotte. And his parents. And Dallas.

A band of angels couldn't have helped Bristol.

Even after all these years, Daytona made an awful liar. Wouldn't have surprised Lucky a bit to hear snores.

"Why you got me on speaker?" Had the kid always sounded so suspicious?

"'Cause painting my toenails takes two hands." Charlotte? Now there was one dyed in the wool liar. Lucky never had been able to beat her in poker.

"I take it there's a reason for you to call me this late," came over the speaker.

Nine P.M. was late?

"As a matter of fact, there is. You know I'll be staying there while daddy's in the hospital and while he's recovering." For the past sixteen years she'd lived in the great Northwest, yet sounded more Southern than Lucky, who rarely strayed north of Tennessee without a warrant.

"Yeah. Need something?"

"Just information." Charlotte hardened her face into a mask of determination. Daytona might run if he saw her.

The suspicion returned to Daytona's voice. "What kind of information?"

"Mama got to crying, talking about what a shame it was 'bout Richmond and all. And she started to say something but stopped when Dad called her. So, I'm hoping you can fill in the blanks. What happened to make them stop talking to him?"

Silence. Then, "Daddy said we weren't never supposed to mention that asshole ever again."

Wow! Even Lucky didn't growl so low unless really pissed. Whatever had he done to deserve his brother's anger?

Charlotte mouthed to Lucky, "What the hell?" To Daytona she said, "Well, now I'm asking. I need to know, and you're gonna tell me."

She probably used the same no-nonsense tone on her boys to keep them in line.

Daytona muttered, "Fuck" too low to have intended Charlotte to hear. "It's over and done with. That's what Daddy said. Besides, Rich is dead. Mama always told us not to speak ill of the dead."

Charlotte turned down her demanding tone, sweet talking like she'd once done to Lucky to get him to share candy. "I wouldn't ask if it weren't important. Please, Daytona, he's... he was my brother too."

Lucky mouthed back, "Nice save!"

"Oh, alright. I don't s'pose it'll hurt nobody now."

Charlotte grinned and fist bumped Lucky. "I want anything you can tell me."

Another silence followed. At last Daytona said, "Remember when I overdosed my first week at college and nearly died?"

"Yes."

He'd nearly died?

Lucky opened his mouth but Charlotte shushed him. "Go on."

The silence stretched, nothing to hear but the air conditioner's soft whirring and Moose barking in the back yard.

Cue the dramatic music and they could be on an episode of Lucky's favorite soap opera, *South Bend Springs*.

After a small eternity, Daytona said, "It was all Richmond's fault."

CHAPTER TWELVE

"Do what?" Folks three states away probably heard Lucky yell.

Charlotte slapped a hand over his mouth. "It was Richmond's fault? How could it be his fault?"

Daytona sounded small and lost. "It was right around my birthday. I'd only been in college for a couple days, and I got a present from Rich—ten grams of heroin. Purer than any shit I'd ever had before."

"Ten fucking grams?" Lucky yelled and yanked Charlotte's hand back over his mouth.

"Ten grams? That happened a long time ago, but are you sure it came from Rich?" Charlotte made an "I'm sorry" face and squeezed Lucky's hand until he no longer felt like screaming.

But wait! She hadn't whapped him, so she must not believe Daytona.

"I'm sure. It was addressed to my dorm and had his return address. The card was in his handwriting, and he told me to have myself a party."

"Are you sure that's what he said?" Charlotte asked in hopeful tones.

"Positive. In fact, I still got the card. Hold on a minute while I go get it."

Charlotte narrowed her eyes at Lucky and hit the mute button. "Brother, I love you, but I'll kill you myself if you sent the kid drugs. He nearly died!"

Lucky knew better than most the effects of a heroin overdose. He'd rounded up enough bodies in his time with the SNB. But he hadn't dealt with anything as base as heroin during his own drug trafficking days, only pharmaceuticals.

"Think about it. Would I spend close to a thousand dollars on the twerp's birthday?"

Her scowl eased up. "Not saying you're cheap or nothin', but no, you wouldn't."

Daytona came back on the line. "Got it." Was that a sniffle? "It says, 'I know I shouldn't encourage your vices, but here, knock yourself out.'"

What the fuck?

Lucky lay back on the couch, vision going a little black. Sure, he'd sent his brother birthday presents. He'd sent them to all his family members. But not drugs. Never drugs. His cheap nature might be the only thing keeping him from dying for real at his sister's hands—that and Victor's unwillingness to hand over large amounts of cash.

Addressed to Daytona, at school, Lucky's handwriting on the card. Lucky whispered, "Ask if he still has the package, showing his address."

"You didn't keep the package, but any chance, did you?" Charlotte nibbled her lower lip.

"No, I'm afraid not."

Damn.

"Thanks, Daytona. I appreciate you telling me. Now I gotta go. Love you, kiddo." Charlotte snatched her phone off the coffee table and gave Lucky the evil eye. "Start talking."

"I didn't do it. I mighta sent him a gift, like I did the rest of you. But it sure the hell wasn't heroin." Not even if he could have afforded the price.

"What did you send him then?"

"I don't remember offhand. Jeez, woman. You expect me to recollect something happened over ten years ago?" He wasn't getting old. Nope, surely not. He just—had a lot on his mind. Yeah, sounded good.

Charlotte's shoulders sagged and she unballed her fists. Maybe Lucky wouldn't get punched after all. The minutes of head scratching and staring out into space grated on Lucky's nerves.

"You're creeping me out here. Say something." Anything'd do right now.

She slammed a hand down on her thigh hard enough to make Lucky jump. "Someone at the college must've switched your package."

"College? Fuck! He said it came to his dorm room, right? That proves I didn't send it. I knew how suspicious Mom and Dad were of Daytona's friends, so I always mailed stuff to the farm where they'd know about it."

"But how would it get from the farm to his dorm, and who switched it and framed you?" Charlotte nibbled at a fingernail. "And why?"

Lucky had a good idea, but he wasn't going to say until he got a chance to check out his suspicions. Would his shady past ever leave him alone? Right around the time Daytona received the package the buzzards had circled, waiting to swoop down on Victor's operation. Two tickets. To Rio.

The Lucky of fourteen years ago wouldn't have left his family.

Unless his family forced his hand. And Victor sure had access to about any kind of drug he wanted.

But why would Victor pay for the kid's college and try to kill him?

Lucky lay alone in bed, without even a cat or dog for company. Darned traitors preferred Charlotte's company apparently.

Bo stepped out of the bathroom, naked and damp from a shower.

"Sorry 'bout that." Lucky lifted the covers for his man to slide beneath.

"Did you two have a good talk?" Bo slipped beneath the covers, skin warm from his shower.

Staring at the ceiling didn't make the words come any easier. Bo might not believe Lucky hadn't supplied his brother's drug habit. Especially when Lucky couldn't remember exactly what he'd sent. "My folks disowned me for sending my kid brother enough heroin to OD the whole damned family."

"You what?"

Lucky held Bo close in case he tried to run. Averting his gaze made confession easier, and hid any disappointment or accusation in Bo's eyes. "Someone delivered a birthday present to his dorm. He said I'd signed the card. He'd know my writing. But, Bo. I swear to God I'da never hurt him."

Bo's reply came instantly. "Any idea who did?"

"Victor wanted me to leave the county with him before we got busted. No way would I have left my family. Maybe he arranged things so I had no reason to stay." Victor might have been a drug trafficker, running one of the biggest pharmaceutical drug rings in the country, but drugging a teenager wasn't his style. No matter the reason.

"You don't believe it was him."

"No. But who else could it be?" If only he could pick up the phone and call Victor, ask him. But now, talking to him again wasn't on Lucky's to-do list. Ever.

"Someone who wanted you out of your folks' life?"

"My family liked Victor, or his money at any rate."

"Any spare homophobes hanging from the family tree?" Bo turned off the bedside lamp and spooned against Lucky's side.

"Dad didn't quite get it, and Bristol preached about me going to hell, but he still took Victor's money for college."

"And you don't remember what you actually sent?"

"No. I've slept a lot since then." He barely remembered breakfast, let alone what he'd bought for his brother's birthday umpteen years ago.

"We could always ask Nestor."

Nestor. Code for asking a man who'd supposedly died but might possibly be in France living the good life with a former Mexican drug lord. Maybe if Lucky didn't have to talk to Victor directly...

"I don't know how to get in touch with him. And Victor's

memory might not be much better than mine." If Victor even agreed to answer.

"He'd remember drugging your brother."

Damn. If Lucky's head didn't quit spinning it might twist right off his neck. "Maybe."

"At least talk to Walter."

Yeah. Walter knew things he shouldn't. He might be able to track down two international narcotics agents.

Bo drew the covers back and pressed his hand against Lucky's shoulder until he lay flat on this stomach. "I know I'm asking the impossible, but try to put it out of your mind for now. You need to get some sleep."

Sleep. Helluva lot easier said than done. "What did you do out in the garage?"

"Worked on the door. It still doesn't lift right. I'm afraid we need a new door opener."

One more thing on an already ungodly to-do list.

Bo worked his knuckles against the knotted muscles in Lucky shoulders. The man had him some skillful hands.

Lucky groaned, shifting around to put the worst tension in the line of fire.

"Oh." Bo stopped rubbing. "I downloaded a new game on my cell phone."

Lucky growled until the rubbing resumed. "You what?"

"I got a new game on my phone. It's pretty cool. There's all these things in the backyard to catch..."

"A game?"

"Yes, a game. I can download it onto your phone too, if you'd like."

Lucky shot out of bed. "That's it!"

Bo grabbed the comforter and barely missed hitting the floor. "What's it?"

"My brother loved video games, and Victor had some connections, so I managed to get a copy of something he wanted before it hit the stores. I can't for the life of me tell you the name, but I swear to God, all I sent was a video game."

I know I shouldn't encourage your vices, but here, knock yourself out.

A game. Only a game.

Lucky's guts untwisted, only to twist up again. Someone had switched the game for heroin. Daytona wasn't a good enough liar to make up such a story.

So. Victor must have sent the drugs.

Who else could it be?

Being in the boss's office without the boss freaked Lucky out, but he'd crept in twenty minutes early to lie in wait and avoid coworkers, or most particularly, Bo.

And getting up and walking out meant losing his nerve. Nope. Not happening. He needed answers, answers only Walter Smith stood a chance of getting. Had the clock on the wall always been so loud ticking off the seconds?

The boss shuffled into his office, Starbucks cup in hand. Normally Starbucks cups set Lucky to drooling, but anything in Walter's cup had to be covered in whipped cream with lots of caramel or whatever. Eww... One accidental sip had Lucky in the bathroom scraping his tongue once.

Lucky slunk down in the chair, his ankle crossed over the opposite knee. Walter didn't notice him until letting out a groan and sinking into his own chair—which also groaned.

"Lucky? My goodness! What are you doing here this early?" Walter glanced at his watch.

"I found out something last night, and I need to ask our mutual friends a question."

"And which mutual friends are you referring to?" Walter didn't have to make so much noise sipping his cup of pure sugar, did he?

"The ones who offered me a job."

Walter stopped sipping in mid slurp. "What kind of question? While I'd never hold you back, I'd hate to lose you here."

127

Oh. Damn. Charlotte would be slapping Lucky upside the head for his poor choice of words. "Nah, I haven't changed my mind. But you remember me telling you about my family disowning me? Not speaking to me?"

"Yes, I recall. It happened right after your arrest, correct?"

"Thereabouts."

"And?"

"And last night I had a long talk with my sister. Turns out what pissed my parents off is me sending heroin to my kid brother, the one with the drug problems." If Lucky hadn't been studying Walter closely, he might have missed the narrowing around the man's eyes, his pursed lips, the harsh breathing.

Lucky returned the scowl with one of his own. "Do you honestly believe I'd do that to anyone, let alone my own brother? I might have helped Victor ship a lot of drugs back in the day, but only pharmaceuticals, not any schedule 1 drugs. And even if I lost my fucking mind and tried, Victor would've found out and stopped me if I so much as talked to a heroin dealer. Too much of a chance of leading cops to his door."

And just as subtly, Walter's puffed-up hostility deflated. He lifted his bifocals and scrubbed a hand over his face. "Forgive me, Lucky. I know how much your family means to you. You'd give your life for theirs. But if he received such a package, why did they suspect you as the sender?"

"Because it came with a birthday card I'd actually sent him. Only someone replaced the video game I'd bought with drugs." He pushed the next part out around a boulder lodged in his throat. Victor Mangiardi knew about the gift. Hell, even used his pull to get a pre-release copy of the game. "Victor wanted me to go with him out of the country when the Feds started getting too close."

"But you'd never have abandoned your family." A statement, not a question. Of all the folks Lucky knew in this bureau, only Bo and Walter ever noticed the Lucklighter clan-shaped hole in his heart.

"No, I wouldn't. He'd have had to convince me to leave them behind."

"And your family disowning you would have been a suitable reason." Walter's expression gave away nothing of his feelings. "You believe Victor sent the drugs to your brother."

"Who else would have spent that much money?" Lucky dropped his head against the chair back.

"An enemy, perhaps?"

"All my enemies at the time would've taken a direct approach." How in the world had Lucky survived so long without someone putting a bullet through his brain? Pure, dumb luck.

"Did your brother use the drugs?"

Oh yeah. Lucky never had been able to tell a story right without leaving shit out. "He OD'd. Damn near died." Counting ceiling tiles made a better pastime than watching Walter blank face, hoping for a hint of emotion.

Not many folks' opinions mattered to Lucky. Walter's did.

Walter twirled an ink pen against his desk blotter, drawing Lucky's attention from the ceiling. "Do you believe Victor would have put your brother in such danger? Remember, I knew him once upon a time. He might have been an opportunist when it came to making money, and skirted laws for longer than most traffickers without getting caught, but nothing I've heard of him would lead me to believe he'd risk your brother."

Victor paid for all three of Lucky's brothers to go to college, and when Charlotte fled her abusive husband, Victor bought her a house across country and paid a 'little visit' to the loser. Not to mention all the times he'd bailed the Lucklighter farm out during hard times. Why go to so much trouble then try to kill Daytona? "Good point."

"Plus, as you said before about enemies, he'd take a more direct approach."

"Yeah, he would, but I can't be sure till I ask. While I don't expect to run into any of the family but Charlotte while I'm in the hospital, I still gotta know if Victor screwed me over, and why." Plus, even if Daytona never found out, Lucky had to prove his innocence, for himself and for Charlotte.

"I understand. And while I can't promise anything, and I have no direct contact with him, I'll do my best to pass your message along." Walter-speak for "consider it done". "Is there anything else you want to say?"

Was there? The boulder in Lucky's throat grew to twice its size, dropped down, and wedged in his heart. While he'd never completely figured out his feelings for the man who'd shown him the finer points of drug trafficking and had shared his bed, he'd never once hated Victor.

If Victor gave Daytona drugs, years of hate were coming on. "That's all I can ask." And it'd be nice to have an answer before going under the surgeon's knife. Minutes ticked away, and still so much to be done before taking an extended leave. "I appreciate all you can do." Lucky rose from his chair, shaking his foot to restore circulation. Rookie evaluations called, and he must answer. He'd made it halfway to the door when Walter spoke again.

"I take it you're still leaving tomorrow?"

"Yeah."

"Don't worry about Moose. Lucy and I will take good care of him."

"Thanks, boss."

"Well, good luck to you. If you need anything else, anything at all, please let me know."

"I will." An imagined elbowing from Bo on one side and Charlotte on the other prompted, "Thanks."

"Don't mention it. You're my best agent. I wish you Godspeed and safe return."

Lucky stood frozen. Should he say more? Tell Walter how much he admired him and how much he appreciated having someone believe in him, give him a chance, when no one else would? And who apparently believed he hadn't send a heroin gift pack.

Walter struggled to his feet and moved faster than Lucky'd

ever seen. One moment he came barreling down like a freight train, the next...

"Acck! Boss! I can't breathe!"

"Oh, so sorry." Walter relaxed his bear hug slightly. He held on and on, and whispered, "If you tell anyone I said this, I'll deny it with my last breath, because I really shouldn't play favorites, but Lucky, you're the son my wife and I always wished we'd had." He stepped back, pushing a thumb and forefinger beneath his glasses to wipe his eyes. "Safe travels."

He turned and took his time going back to his desk. Crying, maybe?

Which worked out fine. Better off nobody glimpsed the tears in Lucky's eyes either.

Nobody seemed to notice the world's impending doom. They went about their typing, gossiping, coffee-sipping, like always, in the SNB cube farm.

But if Lisa wrung her hands and said, "Good morning, Mr. Harrison," one more time... Then again, maybe Lucky should quit passing by her desk while stalking the boardroom, waiting for Bo to appear.

What kind of meeting lasted—he checked the clock on the wall—two hours? Oh. Only two hours? Jeez, seemed like ten.

Johnson caught him mid-pace. "Bo's meeting went over. I'm taking you to lunch."

No asking, just telling. "And if I say no?"

The woman Lucky probably *wouldn't* say no to shrugged. "Then I sling you over my shoulder, slap you on the ass, and drag you kicking and screaming to Bucky's."

The glint in her eyes said she'd do it too. One more glance toward the closed conference room door didn't make Bo suddenly appear.

Lucky's stomach rumbled.

Johnson grinned. Winning didn't mean she had to gloat.

Lucky marched toward the elevator. "Fine. But wipe the smile off your face, or we take my car." Watching her try to fold herself into his tiny Camaro ought to be good for a few laughs. Amazing she'd managed to squeeze in the night they went clubbing, especially in her high heels and painted-on dress. She stopped smiling when they reached her Jeep. "If you need anything—" Her attention on opening the door meant Lucky wasted a perfectly good eye roll.

"Why do people keep telling me that?"

"I don't know. Maybe because we *fucking care*." She never raised her voice and didn't have to. What an impressive amount of sarcasm she'd manage to put into those two words. She climbed into the Jeep and drummed her fingernails on the steering wheel while Lucky got in and buckled his seat belt. "My cat is kind of territorial, but you got a place for the cat and dog? I can come over and feed 'em if you need me to."

"Walter's taking Moose, Mrs. Griggs is taking the cat."

"Good. How long you reckon you'll be gone?" Johnson fired up the vehicle and drove out of the underground parking garage, straight into Peachtree Street traffic.

A few weeks? Forever. Lucky shuddered. Nope. Not going there. "I dunno. I'll be back as soon as I can."

She dropped her voice to a murmur. "You need me, I'll be here."

No tears. No way, no how. "Keep the rookies in line while I'm gone, would ya? Don't let 'em burn the place down."

"Sure thing, boss. And you keep an eye out for hot doctors or orderlies."

"Does Bo know you talk like this to me?"

"I'm not asking you to look for you, I'm asking you to look for me."

"What about Philip?" Had she finally seen the light? She deserved so much better than the loser she dated.

"I'm dating, not dead. And watching hot doctors will keep you occupied and your head out of your ass."

Rett shouldn't get so mushy on him at work.

But yeah, he'd miss her too.

Lucky turned a blind eye to the front lawn in need of, well, more lawn and less bare spots. His sister hadn't commented on the tons of work the house needed, or the crack in the driveway determined to snag her boot heels as she traipsed from the front door out to her car. Lucky trailed behind her, lugging her suitcase, while Bo kept both hands on Moose's leash.

Excited mutt wanted to go for a ride.

"I've gotta get to the farm before anyone misses me." Her boots lifted Charlotte enough to plant a kiss on Lucky's cheek without rising up on her toes.

Lucky forced his gaze to meet hers. "You don't really believe Daytona, do you?"

"I believe that he believes." She placed a hand against Lucky's cheek. "But I also believe you. You wouldn't hurt him or the rest of the family. Besides, like you said, you're too cheap to spend so much money on something you can't drive."

Truth there. Plus, Victor's generosity knew no bounds as far as possessions went, but he'd doled out only modest amounts of cash.

Still, what happened to Daytona couldn't be erased. The truth needed to be found out and told. Even if it did piss off a few people he'd have to be crazy to mess with. No one ever accused Lucky of sanity.

Not even the counselor he met with weekly.

Charlotte tapped a fingertip against her cheek. "Now, gimme some sugar."

God, how long since Lucky last heard those words? He planted a kiss where she pointed.

A hug for Bo, head scratches for Moose, and Charlotte got into her car.

Lucky watched her drive away, the warm day suddenly much colder until Bo dropped an arm around his shoulders.

He trudged back into the house and sagged down onto the couch. Bo never said a word, just held him. Moose laid his head on Lucky's knee, rolled his big, brown eyes upward, and gave a bit of a whine.

Lucky laughed despite his heavy heart and gave the petting whore a nice ear rubbing. A black and white fur ball squeezed into his lap and began to rumble.

If the critters and Bo felt the need to be close to him, he'd let them for a while.

Maybe forever if he got that long.

The gloomy gray morning and light drizzle matched Lucky's mood.

Bo loaded his computer bag into the car. "Got everything?"

No. Not really. But taking the house with them wasn't an option. "I reckon." He handed Cat Lucky to Mrs. Griggs under her umbrella big enough for six people. He wouldn't say, "Take good care of him," but settled for a good chin scratching for Cat Lucky.

Moose sat beside Lucky, whining and tugging at his leash. "Is there room in there for this beast?"

Bo eyed his loaded-down Durango and the ninety-plus pound, slightly damp dog. "We'll get him in there somehow."

"Don't worry about a thing. I'll take very good care of your kitty." Mrs. Griggs touched noses with Cat Lucky. "Won't I, snookums?" With the expert motions of long practice, she secured the spoiled critter in a cat carrier and lugged him to her car. One down, one to go.

"Ready to do this?" Bo threaded the leash through the vehicle and out the other side. "On the count of three, I'll pull, you push."

Five minutes later Lucky still had his back to the truck, pushing with his legs to get Moose inside. Funny how they'd had to restrain the beast to keep him out of Charlotte's car, and now couldn't get him in their own.

The neighbor stopped by with his beagle on a leash. "Try this. It's what I do when my dog won't get in the car." The man reached into his pocket, pulled out a brownish lump, and strolled around to Bo's side of the car. "Here, boy! Want this?" He waved the offering.

Lucky staggered from having the unmoveable object behind him suddenly move. He whirled around. Moose sat in the backseat, chomping the treat.

"Thanks," Bo said.

The neighbor bobbed his head and waddled on down the sidewalk, tugging the leash to get the beagle moving.

"Let's go." Bo jumped into the driver's seat. "It's about ten hours, give or take, allowing gas and lunch stops and dropping Moose by the Smiths."

Moose stuck his head between the seats, licked Lucky's ear, and proceeded to drool all over his T-shirt.

At this rate, he'd have to shower and change clothes once he reached the Smiths.

Lucky flipped the radio off on the third depressing song in a row. He should've brought his iPod. Too late now. And why did traffic have to cooperate today of all days? They crossed town in record time.

He idly rubbed Moose's head.

"It's going to be okay," Bo said for maybe the millionth time.

Easy for him to say. He got to keep all his innards. No, not fair. Lucky's predicament wasn't Bo's fault. Bo had been nothing but awesome. "Thanks." Words often spoken in the past days.

"Third house on the left?" Bo turned on the blinker and slowed.

"Yeah."

"Wow!" Bo let out a whistle. "What a house. And just the two of them?"

"Yeah. I think Walter's nephew lived with them a while once, but otherwise, just them." In a house three times the size of the seven-member Lucklighter homestead, and in much better repair.

135

Walter's wife came out the front door of the stately old home the moment Bo pulled into the driveway.

Moose yanked on the leash the moment Bo let him out, straining to reach more admirers.

"Oh my! He's bigger every time I see him!" Mrs. Smith patted Moose on the head, setting his tail to wagging. She moved her hand and Moose whined and leaned against her leg. What an attention slut.

Such a dainty lady, but Moose stopped tugging at the leash and dropped his butt to the ground at her, "Moose, sit!"

Nice. The moment Lucky got back, he needed to find out her secret.

Even the rain let up for Mrs. Smith. She waved. "Good luck. And when you get back, come by one evening and have dinner with me and Walt."

"Yes, ma'am, we will." Bo climbed back into the SUV. "Ready?"

Ready to face fate?

No.

CHAPTER THIRTEEN

Bo played soft music on the radio, thankfully not *Achy Breaky Heart* or *Pachelbel's Canon*. Too many memories, good and bad, clung to both. Too many to deal with right now.

All too soon the ride ended in Richmond. Quickest ten hours in Lucky's life. He stayed in the Durango while Bo retrieved the keys for his new, hopefully short-term abode.

Bo's smile didn't produce The Dimple when he opened the door of the small frame house, one of many in a long row of lookalikes on a tree-lined street. "Not too bad."

Lucky dragged in one of his suitcases, containing a go-to-court suit Bo hadn't seen him pack—clothes they might bury him in. Hope for the best, but plan for the worst. Yeah, right. Who was he kidding?

"I've seen worse." Lucky'd lived in worse, with neighbors from Hell and palmetto bugs lying in wait outside the front door. Palmetto bugs. The vilest creatures on earth. Lucky eyed the baseboards for evidence of unwanted guests.

Doors opened and closed in the kitchen area. "Kitchen is a bit small, but then again, I've gotten spoiled." Bo took the bag slung over Lucky's shoulder and dropped the twenty-pound weight to the floor. "Someone went and bought me a house with a big-assed kitchen. Puts this one to shame."

Tiny living room, tiny bedroom, tiny bathroom. And a tub too short to fit one of them comfortably, let alone two. Yeah, their house had Lucky spoiled too.

They brought in the remainder of their things, Lucky trying and failing to keep his mind in the moment and not race on ahead to tomorrow. He'd deal with tomorrow in the morning and not a moment before.

Bo hauled the cooler out of his SUV.

Oh, right. Lucky'd promised to be a better partner. He tried to take the cooler. "You drove most of the way. Take a nap while I unpack."

"No. I'll get this." Not even cut open and already Bo treated him like the wounded.

"I'm not in the hospital yet. I can help."

They stood, facing each other, each trying to carry the cooler. Bo released a harsh breath. "Fine. Ruin the surprise." He let Lucky carry the cooler into the house and place the burden on the table, but opened the lid himself.

Inside, along with the things Lucky'd help pack, were a few items he hadn't, like a pack of Portobello mushrooms.

For the condemned man's last meal.

No eating or drinking after midnight. He'd make the most of the hours until then.

Lucky lay awake, staring at the ceiling. Outside traffic rolled up and down the street, and a neighbor liked TV loud.

Too damned noisy here. Not like the house. Bo's attempt at snoring couldn't match Moose's, and no Cat Lucky perched on the end of the bed, waiting to attack his toes if Lucky dared move his foot.

This wasn't home.

Bo rolled over and slung an arm over Lucky's waist.

Then again, maybe home wasn't a house.

They'd told him he wouldn't run into his family, but still Lucky crept through the parking lot and into the hospital with his sunglasses on, his body language suitable for a major walk of shame he hadn't even earned.

Bo didn't hold his hand while Lucky checked into the

hospital, but he stayed close. Nice, modern building, with lots of glass and shiny surfaces. Must be hell to keep clean.

"You can have a seat in here and fill these out." A yawning nurse handed him a clipboard full of papers and showed them into a deserted office. He plopped down on a butt-ugly red leather couch. Bo sat more gracefully next to him, close enough to place a hand on Lucky's back or knee every time he tensed to run.

He completed stacks and stacks of paperwork, asking everything from his medical history to what he'd had for breakfast: nothing. Then came the yes/no questions. Hadn't he answered all these before, except for the food part, online? Forget his eyes—Lucky's whole body began to glaze over.

Check, check, check. They'd already picked out split-tailed gowns for him, so a bit late to be asking. Half of these diseases he couldn't even pronounce. "Here. Put your college education to use." He handed the papers to Bo, tilted his head back, and closed his eyes. A trained pharmacist ought to be able to figure things out.

"Family history of diabetes? I can't remember from when we did this before."

"My younger brother." Lucky should've printed out the online questionnaire.

"This part is marked 'optional', but do you have any religious preference?"

Lucky opened one eye. "Any that say 'whatever you do is fine by us'? What's yours?" Funny, he'd never asked about religion in all their time together.

Bo answered without looking up. "Catholic mom, heathen dad."

Oh really? "What's that make you?

"A Cathen. Now, do you want to answer this question? You don't have to." Bo's tensed jaw didn't mean angry this time. More like worried or scared shitless.

Lucky's snark—his own method of dealing with scared shitless—should've at least gotten a rise out of Bo. Anything beat him being so stressed out. "Mama raised us Baptist. Dad raised us redneck."

No smile. No raised brow. "That makes you a Baptneck. I'll check 'other.'"

They sat quietly for a few minutes, except for the scratching of Bo's pen on the paper and the occasion person passing by in the hallway.

And overall, the freaky-assed, nose-searing antiseptic stench of hospital cleaner.

After a while a man in a white coat entered, smile too wide to be the angel of death he might turn out to be. He marched straight to Bo. "Mr. Harrison? I'm Dr. Wheeler."

At a nudge from Bo, Lucky took the doctor's hand. "I'm Harrison." Right now. No telling who he'd be next week—if he still ranked among the living.

The man spewed out doctor jargon for the next five minutes, Lucky nodding and throwing out an "uh-huh" or "you don't say" whenever the doctor paused to let him get a word in.

Bo stopped scribbling to ask a question here and there, leaving Lucky free to tune out. He'd gotten the important stuff. Best case? Him and Dad both lived. Worse case? Some programmer at SNB added yet another profile to the company's website.

Maybe they'd use a picture this time, for some agent ten years from now to look at and worry about job hazards.

Poked, prodded, blood drawn, weighed. Blood pressure checked.

All the while Lucky let his mind go anywhere but a few hours into the future. Hard to do while lying on a gurney with his ass hanging out of a thin cotton gown.

Bo smoothed the blanket covering Lucky. "I wish the doctor wasn't so nice."

"Why?"

"So I won't feel so bad about whipping his ass if he doesn't treat you right." It came out like, *"If you die, the doctor's toast."* Lucky wasn't the only one who'd been raised redneck. "I'll be right here waiting for you." Must be a trick of the light, the extra sheen in Bo's eyes.

To hell with anyone else's opinion. Lucky brought Bo's hand to his mouth and kissed the knuckles. The closest nurse giggled and busied herself elsewhere. Lucky sucked a finger.

"Lucky!" Bo yanked back.

Yup. Shocked beat worried. Fear and pity didn't belong in Bo's eyes, especially if Lucky might never see Bo's eyes again.

Stop being such a wuss! Even Walter said this wasn't a dangerous procedure.

"I love you," Lucky said. "You really should've married me. You look so good in black." Though hopefully, Bo wouldn't wear funeral black anytime soon. "Especially leather. Especially leather assless chaps."

"I'll only wear those for you." Bo mouthed, "I love you." The gurney moved, and Bo stood in the middle of the hallway, arms wrapped around himself, until a pair of double doors closed, shutting him off.

Tight bands wound around Lucky's chest. Air. Oh, God. He needed air!

"Mr. Harrison? Is something wrong?" a masked man asked.

Losing his shit in front of people couldn't happen. Lucky willed his wildly pounding heart to calm. Curtains cut the room in half. "What's behind the curtains?" And did he really want to know?

"Someone who's going to owe you his life." The man wrapped tubes over Lucky's ears and inserted two prongs on the joined middle into Lucky's nostrils. Oxygen flowed into his nose.

Lucky stared at the curtain, straining for any sound over the whooshes and beeps coming from his side of the room.

Dad. Damn, how his heart still ached for the man who'd thrown him up in the air and caught him as a child, who'd taught him how to drive: first a four-wheeler, and later a dirt bike, tractor, and farm truck.

Dad, who'd sit in front of the TV every Sunday afternoon during racing season to watch NASCAR, one of the few times he took a break from work during daylight hours.

The man who'd taught Lucky the value of a hard day's work, and inspired him to find an easier way to make a living, even if illegal. And now that rock of a man needed Lucky. About time Lucky stepped up to the plate, even anonymously.

He barely noticed the IV hookup shoved into his hand, all the monitors now pulsing with his heartbeat, recording his blood pressure. This was the closest he'd physically been to family in years, except for Charlotte.

No. Not true. Bo waited somewhere outside the room, probably pacing or checking in with the boss. More than likely he ran his fingers through his hair, frown lines bunched on his forehead.

That's not how Lucky chose to picture him. Better memories filled his head. Him and Bo lying in bed on a lazy Sunday morning, sunlight streaming through the window while they sipped coffee or tea and talked. In the brightness Bo's freckles stood out, and The Dimple formed on his cheek when he smiled at some ridiculous thing Lucky said.

How Lucky loved The Dimple. And every single freckle.

"Mr. Harrison? It's time to go to sleep. This will take about a minute to work." The man behind the mask inserted a needle into a tube in the IV bag and pushed the plunger. "Count backwards from one hundred.

"One hundred, ninety-nine, ninety-eight, nin..." The world tilted.

Beeps, blips, footsteps. Lucky let out a moan.

"Mr. Harrison? Mr. Harrison, you're in recovery and doing well. I'll be back to take you to ICU." Same voice. More face without the mask. Young guy, mid to late twenties. Copper hair.

"How... How'd it go?" Who'd set fire to Lucky's throat?

"You did great, and now your liver is hard at work regenerating."

"My d... The other guy?"

"He's still in surgery. Doing fine last I heard."

Not "the patient will make a full recovery", but good enough for now.

Another smiling face. "Hi, Mr. Harrison we're going to ICU. Ready?"

Ready to get out of recovery, yes, but not bouncing over every bump along the way. Holy Mother of God! He grabbed his midsection.

"Sorry. We'll give you something more for pain once we settle you in your room." The orderly jostled him a few more times getting him on and off the elevator.

Finally the gurney ride from hell ended.

No windows to the outside, but the windows to the hallway offered a fine view of Bo, with his nose practically pressed against the glass.

So close her shoulder touched Bo's, Charlotte dabbed at her eyes with a tissue and gave Lucky the happiest cry face in history. Yeah. He still had family. And for unknown reasons, they loved him, and he survived surgery.

But Daddy wasn't out of the woods yet.

Lucky and Charlotte lay on their backs on the hilltop overlooking the farm, sun warming their cheeks. How many times had they lain there, telling each other their dreams?

His sister's voice. Why had he missed it? She'd been here the whole time, hadn't she? But instead of talking about being a nurse one day like she normally did, she rambled on and on about other things.

"Todd's been accepted at Clemson and the University of North Carolina at Chapel Hill. Remember how I used to want to go there? Anyways, I wanted him to stay in Spokane, but you know how kids are. Spend half their lives trying to get away from home and the other half trying to get back. Do you ever miss the farm?"

Why would Lucky miss the farm? They were still here, right?

"Anyway, at UNC he'll be closer to Mama and Daddy. Clemson would put him closer to you. Either way he can go help them out when he doesn't have classes." She paused, staring up at puffy clouds. "Don't be mad, Richie, but I told the boys about you. They were upset at first that we didn't trust them, but now they're happy to have Uncle Richie back. Which explains why Todd applied to Clemson. He wants to get to know you again. Says you're the closest thing to a father he's ever had."

What Todd? Oh. An image came to mind of Charlotte, a few years older, holding a squirming, crying bundle, and the bundle wrapping Uncle Richie around its little finger.

She turned and put her lips to his forehead. "I love you, big brother. And I'm so proud of you. You've turned out to be one helluva man."

Strange. Who in their right mind would consider Lucky a father figure? He shifted into a more comfortable position and faded back to sleep.***

A hand. Holding his. Quiet humming. The comforting scent of Bo's cologne. Bo's thumb stroking the back of Lucky's hand.

Gentle kisses across this forehead. A soft, "Told you you'd be all right and wouldn't die."

Not dying. A good thing. The man holding Lucky's hand made life worth living.

He lived. No more making decisions under the gun. "Have you changed your mind yet about marrying me, since I'm still alive and all?" Sleep dragged him down without an answer.

Sleep, wake up, feel like shit, get meds, go back to sleep. At times Lucky awoke to Bo's face, sometimes to a nurse's. Several times to Charlotte's. They talked, smiled, whatever, but Lucky faded out without really hearing.

He woke to a darkened room and froze. Every instinct pinged of danger. The lights from the monitors cast a faint glow over the face of a man who couldn't possibly be there.

This better be a dream brought on by mighty good drugs.

If he had to dream about drug lords, at least Nestor Sauceda might not kill him outright. If he'd wanted Lucky dead, he'd had a million chances.

"What chu doin' here?" Lucky managed to get out.

"Would you believe I was in the neighborhood and stopped by?" Nestor stood ramrod straight by the bed, the faint light catching the white in his hair.

"No."

Nestor laughed. "Still the same cynical Lucky. I'm here because you asked a question, and although our mutual friend couldn't answer directly, we both know you. If you didn't hear straight from us, you'd pick any answer apart and not believe. So here I am."

Conscious thought tried to crawl through the murky, drug-induced fuzz in Lucky's head. "Wha?"

"You asked if Victor delivered drugs to your younger brother."

Oh, yeah.

"He's quite displeased you even had to ask, but I reminded him who you are. He said, and I quote, 'Tell the suspicious sonofabitch he should know I'd never harm his family.'"

"If he didn't, who did?" Lucky forced out.

"It happened a long time ago, so other than the card your brother saved, the evidence is gone. However, as a favor to you, I'll use our resources to help find out."

"Happened years ago. How'll you do that?"

Lucky barely felt the hand on his shoulder through his opioid-induced haze. "You have your sources, we have ours."

"Have I ever told you you're scary as hell?" Oh, crap. Drugs made Lucky's uncouth mouth even worse.

Nestor laughed. "Coming from you, I'll take that as a compliment."

What the fuck ever.

"I won't stay long, you're recovering, but even without the question I wanted to check in on you. I'm sure you expect me to say I'm surprised at your selfless act, but I'm not in the least. You try so hard not to be, but you're a good man, Richmond Lucklighter."

Lucky managed enough energy to shoot back, "Don't even start that rumor."

Nestor's laugh became a snort. "Don't worry. Your secret's safe with me, and I've made a career out of keeping secrets."

"How'd Walter get in touch with you?"

"He has his ways, though I'd not expected him to use them this soon, and not for this reason."

"Huh?"

Nestor patted Lucky's hand—the one not sporting a needle. "The job offer still holds, if ever you decide to take it. We can use a man like you."

International drug task force. A chance to kick drug trafficker ass on a global scale—without Bo. "Not hap'nin. I'm where I belong."

"For now. But if you ever reconsider..." Nestor shrugged and slipped out the door.

Lucky's eyelids grew heavy. Sleep, glorious sleep, called to him.

"How are you feeling?" Bo sat at Lucky's bedside, cellphone in hand. Probably hunting down pokies or pookies or whatthehellevers.

"Like someone cut me in half and forgot to put me back together." And if Lucky could move now, he'd kick the ass of the nurse who'd made him get out of bed and shuffle ten miles uphill to the bathroom. Of course, the jury hadn't yet decided the worst of two evils: having to walk to the bathroom to pee or having a tube shoved up his dick. He coughed. Oh, dear God!

And may he please live the rest of his life without crossing paths with another drainage tube.

Bo shot to his feet. "Are you okay? Want me to get the nurse?"

"Nah," Lucky choked out. "I'll be okay." Maybe. One day. A million years from now.

"Can I get you anything?"

Bo's eager puppy act wore Lucky out. "No. But I gotta tell ya, I had the strangest dream."

"What kind of dream?"

"I dreamed Nestor showed up and told me Victor didn't send those drugs to Daytona."

All the color left Bo's face. He nodded toward the side table. Rett's sunflowers sat next to Charlotte's whatever-they-were, and a long-stemmed red rose from Bo with the dragon keychain hanging beneath.

All were dwarfed but a huge arrangement of orange blossoms. Orange blossoms? Where had Nestor gotten orange blossoms? The scent filled Lucky's nostrils, taking him back in time to a house in Florida, surrounded by orange trees.

Victor's vacation home, where Lucky opened the windows to let the sweetness perfume the house.

Oh shit. Not a dream.

CHAPTER FOURTEEN

Lucky understood the need for an assigned nurse experienced with transplants, but was stalking in the guy's job description?

Every few minutes, Nurse Andy insisted on fluffing Lucky's pillow, taking his blood pressure, or otherwise hanging around trailing the scent of Eau de Hospital in his wake. What'd the guy do? Marinate in peroxide? There'd been a time when Lucky simply hung his own monikers on people. Now, learning names worked better to keep track so he'd know who to chew out later.

Andy rearranged the water pitcher on the table.

Lucky tried for a scowl known to send rookies screaming from the room. "Don't you have other patients?"

"Now, Mr. Harrison, until we're done here, no one else matters but you, the patient I'm with now." Andy fluttered his fingers. Creepy much?

Pressure cuff on one arm and an IV in the other, Lucky counted ceiling tiles. Sooner or later the overly attentive nurse would wander off and allow some privacy. An itch, right *there*, demanded attention.

Pressure good, pressure cuff off. Andy leaving in five, four, three, two...

Andy fluffed Lucky's pillow again and rearranged the chair by the bed. "You'll be going to a private room soon and won't feel so much like a zoo exhibit."

Zoo exhibit?

The perk of having a window into the hall to do some people watching took an evil spin. Good ole Andy had to go and remind Lucky the window worked both ways.

Asshole.

The discomfort grew fiercer. Lucky squirmed, trying to scratch the itch behind his balls with a little thigh rubbing. The itching kicked up a notch.

Why did Lucky even care? The him of two or three years ago would've reached down and had a good scratch no matter who saw what. Damn. Bo's good manners done rubbed off on him again.

Nurse Andy stayed. And stayed. And stayed.

What the hell. Lucky reached his unencumbered hand beneath the sheet and attacked the itch. Ah, much better.

Andy's lips twitched.

One laugh and Lucky'd share his pain. "Well, what am I supposed to do when nobody'll leave me alone long enough to scratch my balls in peace?" A passing nurse whipped her head around and quickly averted her eyes from the bit of sheet rising up and down with the motions of Lucky's hand.

He stopped mid-scratch. In about five minutes, she'd be running her mouth about the patient in ICU she'd caught jacking off.

He resumed scratching. From what Charlotte told him, some days hospital work got boring. Public service. Adding something to talk about to someone else's day.

Andy snickered. "I have some ointment we can use if you've developed a rash, which can happen sometimes with the medications you're on."

Um... Yeah. Private room. No hall windows.

And no Nurse Andy.

Attila the Orderly hit every motherfucking bump on the way from ICU to the private room.

**

"Let's get this over with." Lucky glared until Nurse Andy backed off to let Lucky crawl out of bed by himself. The man in hospital scrubs stuck to a target better than the SNB's finest. A new floor should've meant a new nurse, but no.

Lucky wriggled to the edge of the mattress. Oh dear God! Kill him now! Who snuck in while he slept and fucking sawed him in half again?

The nurse did a piss-poor job of hiding a smirk while helping Lucky to the bathroom. Keeping an eye on the clock and his comments to himself, Lucky finished up what he had to do, shuffled back to bed and glared. "Meds. Now." No please necessary until Bo arrived, and his shift ended at five, so...

The nurse hummed what might have been *Bad, Bad Leroy Brown* while dosing him up, but he didn't talk. Good. Kept Lucky from having to say things he'd have to apologize for if Bo walked in at the wrong moment.

Maybe he should've said please after all, in exchange for information. "How's my d... the guy I gave my liver to?" Pain meds disabled Lucky's almost non-existent brain to mouth filter.

"He's doing fine, and you know good and well I can't tell you more."

Damned confidentiality laws. "Do you accept bribes?" Shit. Charlotte needed to get her ass in here and give an update.

"No, but maybe a family member might." Andy winked and sauntered out of the room.

"Asshole. I *am* family," came out on a closing door.

The door reopened. Bo strolled in at precisely five thirty, still dressed for work, the best thing Lucky'd seen all day.

"Hey, nice room! Bet you're glad to be out of ICU." Bo pressed his lips to Lucky's forehead. "How're you feeling?" The man sure filled out the SNB regulation slacks and golf shirt well. The bag he placed on the side table promised goodies of some form or other, though a good sniff didn't give away the contents.

And who cared if everyone who'd walked through the door asked the same question? Bo actually gave a shit about the answer. "If I whine and complain, will you kiss it and make it better? And while you're down there..." Lucky did his best to waggle his brows.

The tight set of Bo's mouth relaxed into a smile. "If you're wanting sex, you must be getting better."

"How can I get better when I've always been the best there is?" Winking he could manage. Brow waggling? Not so much. While Bo slipped the wedge pillow beneath his shoulders, he had the perfect opportunity to...

Bo jumped and grabbed his ass. "No pinching."

"Awww... Why not? I ain't got nothing else to look forward to all day." He'd never admit how badly he'd wanted Bo to show up. He hadn't died—yet—but staying in the hospital freaked him out. He'd been in many hospitals for various reasons without a flinch.

Suddenly realizing he could die and didn't want to made him open his mouth and say, "Ahh..." at the right times and not bitch too badly about blood pressure readings. He'd had a lot of fun messing with the oxygen reader thingy on his finger until the nurse took his new toy back for bad behavior.

"I brought you something." Bo reclined in the guest chair, snagged the bag off the table, and opened the sack to reveal—a disk?

"You brought me porn! You know I love you, right?" Lucky batted his eyes, moving the one unhurt part of body.

Bo swatted his shoulder. "No."

"Ow! Nurse! He's beating up a patient!"

Bo rolled his eyes upward. "Yup, you're definitely feeling better. But I'll save the porn for when you get home. I brought the next best thing." He slid the disk into the corner DVD player and turned the TV on.

Familiar music quickened Lucky's pulse. Yay! *South Bend Springs*! "Why don't you get up here with me to watch this?"

"Actually, I think I'll lay in the chair so we'll both be more comfortable."

I'd be more comfortable with you in my arms stayed in Lucky's brain. But any jostling, and he'd scream. And here he'd been worried about dying. He should've worried about the fucking pain. Why didn't someone tell him he'd hurt this much? He kept his mouth shut. Bo didn't need to worry too. Lucky managed enough for them both. "But I can't cop feels with you down there," came out of his mouth.

"I'll pull the chair closer."

Lucky gave Bo's cock a quick rub and yanked his hand back to avoid a swat.

"Behave," Bo growled, though his eyes twinkled. He wriggled a time or two but settled in before the show started.

An unfamiliar busty blond strolled into a hospital set. "Who's she?" Why did all soap operas seem to take place near hospitals? Get reality out of Lucky's show!

"She's a new actress playing Lila."

"Another one? They need to bring the first one back. No one did mean girl like she did." Good folks came a dime a dozen on this show, but the truly bad ones he loved to hate? Priceless. They never should have written off Dr. What's-his-name, the only man conniving enough to stand toe to toe with Lucky's favorite soap opera diva.

"She's not too bad."

Lucky cut his eyes Bo's way. "And how would you know? Have you been cheating and watching this without me?"

If Bo tried for an innocent look, he fell short. "I couldn't exactly bring the disk without checking first to make sure it recorded right, could I?"

"I coulda watched online if you'd let me bring my laptop."

"No, 'cause then you'd work. And I'm thinking you didn't miss any episodes during my last assignment."

"Well, what if you'd gotten a chance to call me and wanted to know what happened on the show? I couldn't say I didn't know, could I? Besides, placing orders for fake drugs so I can bust a few heads when I get outta here ain't working. It's more like... a hobby." Lucky folded his arms across his chest... gently.

"Then no hobbies until you get better. We'll watch TV the old-fashioned way. With a disk and a DVD player."

Lucky growled, but he'd save his comments for later. The blond stalked up to a taller redhead, poked a finger in her chest, and screamed. Oh? Maybe this Lila wouldn't be as dull as the last one.

"How many kids she got now? She's had at least three since she started on the show. All with different men."

Bo ticked off points on his fingers. "Well, it turns out the oldest two are Ross's, which started a fight with Tom who'd assumed he was Devon's dad. And they're still leading us on about the father of her last one."

"Still only three?"

"Yeah. There was a scare a few weeks ago. Turned out to be nothing." Bo opened a pack of jelly beans, popped a few into his mouth, and passed the bag to Lucky.

"Bo?"

"Yeah?"

"Stop with the spoilers." Oh, black jelly beans. Nice.

"Sorry."

But at least now Lucky wouldn't have to try to puzzle out the plot if the drugs knocked him out before the end of the episode. Not like the show wouldn't recap a half dozen times and only give ten minutes of new content. "You know what they say about the green ones, right?" He held up a green jelly bean.

"Wrong candy." Bo held out his hand for more.

The pain of Lucky's incision dulled to a low ache, though he'd probably be hollering for pain meds later, if the nurse hadn't installed a self-serve happy meds button, not to be used with Bo around, though. No telling how he'd react. Just because he never mentioned cravings didn't mean they weren't there.

Lying the closest to Bo he'd been in days, watching TV like they were at home, made everything all right. He placed the now-half empty jelly bean bag on his stomach and laced their fingers.

Who cared if a family who'd thrown him out of their lives gathered together a few doors down, celebrating his dad's recovery? Who cared if he'd never join them for Christmas or other holidays again? Who cared if his niece would never know him? Probably for the best anyway.

He had all he needed in Bo, even if his eyes stung and his throat burned, picturing the Lucklighter clan. Had his mother's light brown hair turned gray? Had Daytona ever filled out to the point where'd he'd lost the nickname, "Scarecrow?"

Bo glanced up. "You okay?"

Lucky hid a sniff. "Yeah. Getting' sleepy, I reckon."

"I can go if you're ready for bed."

Holding Bo's hand tighter might keep him from leaving. "Stay. We've only watched one episode."

"Lucky?"

"Yeah?"

"Ease up, you're about to crack bones."

"Oh. Sorry."

The credits rolled, the music played, and the next installment filled the TV screen. The redhead again, doing rich people things with her rich father. He'd been in enough fancy houses to know the bookcase didn't belong. Bo had the same one back at their place. Hard to imagine a millionaire corporate raider shopping at Ikea.

Blah, blah, blah, hot guy, fashion-model woman, another hot guy. But no Lila. Surely she'd appear in the bar scene.

Nope.

Man, he loved a good troublemaker.

The episode ended. "That's all? What happened to Lila?"

"This is Ernst's plot line. Maybe Lila is in the next one."

"She better be. The show's downright boring without her." Still no Lila. Lucky stroked a finger down Bo's neck. He might be talking a better game than he stood a chance of backing up, but it never hurt to remind Bo of the fun times. He reached for Bo's leg. Damned short-assed arms.

Oh! If they got creative... "We could jam the chair against the door and..."

Bo shook his head. "You have to recover. No fun and games."

Spoilsport. "The doctor didn't say not to." Bo didn't need to know that anything beyond a kiss was out of Lucky's possibilities right now.

"He probably assumed he didn't have to. I'm sure not many of his patients get frisky after surgery." Bo's words said no, but the cocked brow and smile on his lips said, *"You might be able to talk me into something."*

If Bo danced in his leather chaps now, Lucky would pop his stitches and staples. "Frisky? Did you say 'frisky'?"

Bo glared, but he didn't push Lucky's roving hand away, which equaled a great big "Yes!" in Lucky's book. Not that he'd be able to do much, but he wasn't dead yet.

Nurse and patient roleplaying? Hell yeah! As long as the nurse wasn't Andy the stalker.

Numbness spread out, making Lucky's eyelids droop. In moments like these, he understood why people got addicted to painkillers. Lovely things. But like many lovely things, also deadly if mishandled.

A knock on the open door jolted him awake.

"Mr. Harrison?" A woman stepped through the door. "I hope I'm not disturbing you. My daughter said she'd talk to you, but I wanted to come myself and tell you how grateful we are..." Every bit of color fled the woman's face. "Richmond?"

Oh shit! "Mama?"

CHAPTER FIFTEEN

Lucky grabbed the bed railings and tried to wriggle into a sitting position. "Ow! Hot damn! Motherfuck!" Jelly beans flew in all directions.

Bo leapt off the chair and caught Lucky's mother before she hit the floor.

Spots formed before Lucky's eyes. He yanked a pillow against his incision. "Motherfucker, motherfucker! Oh, sorry, Mama!"

"Lucky, are you okay?" Bo shifted Lucky's mother around until she lay on the chair.

Lucky lied and nodded, sucking in and pushing out air. He jammed his thumb down on the happy drug button. Gradually the stabbing in his belly lessened, but didn't stop. What he wouldn't give for a shot right now to knock his ass out.

But...

He twisted as much as the gnawing in his gut allowed. "Gah!"

Bo pressed a button and a wonderful nurse with the great meds shot into the room and rushed to the bedside. "What happened?"

Bo spoke. Lucky couldn't. "He tried to jump out of bed."

"Fuck, fuck, fuck, fuck, fuck!" Lucky clutched the bed railings tighter.

The nurse fiddled with something and set about checking Lucky's bandages.

Oh, sweet relief! Lucky sighed and settled back on the bed.

"What about her?" The nurse nodded toward the reclining chair.

Oh crap! "Mama?"

A moan. Bo holding out his arm. Fingers clutching Bo's hand.

And then...

The world faded to black.

"Why did he let us think he was dead?" The outrage in his mother's voice made pretending to be passed out his best option.

Adulthood hadn't dimmed Lucky's fear of Mama taking on "The Tone."

And Bo's voice held the proper amount of fear. "I should wait and let him tell you this..."

"You'll tell me right this minute!" Memory served up a mental image of Mama Lucklighter, hands on her hips, ripping one of her young'uns a new asshole about something or other they'd done.

She hadn't fussed nearly enough at her oldest.

But, oh hell. Time to spill the whole ugly truth or die for real.

On the one hand, Bo might tell the story better, leave out the parts Mama didn't need to know. On the other hand, even a coward couldn't make someone else deal with the family. Not a family of hotheads like the Lucklighters. And not someone Lucky loved.

"Mama?"

She jabbed a finger into Bo's chest, much like Lila did to the redhead. "That's my son! I have the right—" Oh, Lord. On a roll and no stopping her now. But Lucky'd try. "Mom!"

She-bears with cubs had nothing on Southern mothers in full protective mode. She stepped forward, rising on her toes to stare Bo down. "Who are you and what are you doing here? What's going on? Why did you keep my son from me?"

Bo stepped back and flattened himself against a wall. Trust him to be too polite to fight back. He should learn from dealing with Charlotte about fierce Lucklighter women.

Lucky braced his incision, took a deep breath, and bellowed, "Sheila Annette Lucklighter!" There. Nothing got a Southerner's attention better than all three names—a Southern mother's weapon of choice for generations.

Even if the effort nearly killed him.

Bo and Mama both whipped their heads toward Lucky, the "Oh thank God!" in Bo's eyes screaming louder than words.

The woman Lucky hadn't seen in way too many years bore down on him like an avenging angel and stopped mere inches from the bed. More wrinkles, strands of gray. Still Mom.

One by one, tears streaked down her face.

Oh damn. Now he'd gone and made her cry. "Mom, sit down, I can explain everything."

She grabbed him in a chokehold and held on. "My boy's alive. That's all I need to know."

Lucky screamed. His mom let go.

"Oh, I'm so sorry." She dropped down into the chair while Lucky struggled to keep most of his swearing inside his mouth. Dear God! Pain!

Breathe in, breathe out. Again. Again. There. Better.

"God, I've missed you." She dabbed at her eyes with the back of her hand. Bo handed her tissues and retreated to the far side of the room.

Smart man.

"I've missed you too." Even on pain meds, Lucky flinched at how hard Mom gripped his hand.

He wouldn't say so. He'd waited too long to have her hand in his. "I'm sorry for being such an as... jerk, all my life." He'd always be an asshole, it's what he did, but he could still be sorry for his mother's sake to have an asshole for a son.

Correction. Two assholes, counting Bristol.

"I..."

"Shhh..." She put a finger to his lips. "Don't talk. I know how much pain you're in, if your daddy is anything to go by."

Daddy. She had to mention Dad. "How is he?"

"He'll live." She paused before adding, "and he owes you

his life," holding his hand, stroking along the back. More quietly than before, she asked Bo, "Why don't you tell me what's going on?"

Bo connected his gaze to Lucky's, brows raised.

Ah hell. Lucky hadn't imagined this day coming, so couldn't form a plan. "Mama, I..."

She shushed him again. "If this young man is who I suspect he is, he'll be able to answer without you having to talk."

Lucky sighed. "Okay, you win."

Bo's brows rose higher. "Just like that? You're doing what she says without arguing?"

Yeah, yeah, rub it in.

Bo grinned. "Mrs. Lucklighter, when all this is said and done, can you teach me that trick? He always argues with me."

"It's not hard once you set your mind to it." Her smile fell. "Now start talking."

"Better do it," Lucky warned. "I'm pretty sure she has a concealed carry permit." And a house full of guns.

Bo dragged a hand through his hair. "I believe you remember the part about Lucky being arrested?"

Mama nodded.

"Well, two years into his sentence, he made a deal to cooperate with the Southeastern Narcotics Bureau while working off his time. He's one of the best agents we have."

She cocked her head to the side. "He still is? But his sentence should've ended."

Ah, and here Lucky thought his family didn't care enough to know any details about his life.

"It did," Lucky answered.

"And then we were told he died." She shot Lucky an accusing glare.

Bo came to Lucky's rescue. "Ma'am, with all due respect, your son put a lot of criminals in prison. They don't take too kindly to his testifying against them. The bureau faked his death and gave him a new identity for his own protection. He stayed on."

No need to tell Mama the real reason Lucky stayed with the bureau stood three feet from her, resting the finest ass this side of the Mississippi against the wall. He'd once been close with his mother, but some things he didn't need to share.

"I read about how he'd died saving another agent and all. Most of the family said there'd been a mistake, but I knew my boy." She wiped at her eyes again and sniffled.

Bo handed her another tissue from the box on the counter. "He got hurt pretty bad, spent time in the hospital. Hel... Um... Even I believed he'd died."

Slowly bewilderment turned to understanding on Mom's face. "Charlotte knew the truth."

"Not at first. But yeah, she figured it out." Bo left out the part about Charlotte pulling a gun on him, trying to protect Lucky.

Mama's sniffles became sobs. "She didn't tell me!"

Time for Lucky to step in and save Bo. Besides, narcotics dulled his self-preservation instincts. "I asked her not to."

"Why ever not! I'm your mother!"

"Y'all weren't speaking to me at the time, but also, there's some folks out there who might've used my family to get to me. I've made a lot of powerful enemies over the years." The orange blossoms in a vase on the side cart caught his attention. Some powerful friends, too, but still. "Being associated with me isn't exactly safe."

Bo snorted and coughed into his hand, "Understatement."

True.

What could Lucky possibly say to make things right?

Mama blew her nose.

Bo passed over the tissue box. "You'll be happy to know your son is the department's best undercover agent."

Just until Bo officially claimed the title, which would probably happen once he'd fully recovered from too much time spent in someone else's head.

Had the nurse given Lucky too many drugs or did Mom widen her eyes?

Lila's outraged face remained frozen on the TV screen. At some point Bo must have paused the show.

Mama followed Lucky's line of sight. "Is that *South Bend Springs*? You used to watch it with me when you were little, remember?"

Bo gave Lucky his best, *oh, really?* brow-lift and smirk combo.

Time to stop looking at Bo for a while. Lucky grabbed the remote off the side table and turned off the TV to say the words he'd longed to. "I'm making an honest living now. I did my time."

"He's now training leader." If they ever had kids, Bo would probably hang every single childish doodle on the refrigerator door. He got too proud of the littlest things.

"Really?" Mama didn't have to act so amazed.

He might only have her here for a few minutes. No telling what would happen once she walked out the door. She couldn't leave without knowing as much of the truth as Lucky did. "Did y'all really disown me 'cause you assumed I sent Daytona drugs?"

Mama's gasp nearly sucked all the air from the room. "Why would you do such a thing? You know how hard he struggled."

"I didn't."

"But the card came from you."

Bo stepped in. "By 'vice' Lucky meant a video game."

"A video game." Mama wobbled, face pale. If Lucky could've moved, he'd have inched closer to catch her if she fell again.

"Yes, Mama. I sent him a video game for his birthday, to the farm, since I didn't know he'd left for college yet, and figured it best if you and daddy knew what he was getting. Someone must've gotten the package, traded the game for drugs, and sent them to his dorm." And if Lucky ever found the sorry bastard who'd nearly killed Daytona...

"A video game." She sounded more convinced this time. "But who would do such a thing, and why?"

161

Lucky shrugged, about all the motion he could manage without agony. "Dunno. But I'm trying to find out."

The sobs began again. "All these years! All these years we haven't spoken to you, for something you didn't do."

"I still broke laws, got thrown into jail. What I did do was bad enough." And if he ever got charged for all his sins, he'd never be a free man again.

The edge returned to his mother's voice. "And you turned on Victor. He's dead. I might not have agreed with how he made his living, but he was good to you. He was good to the whole family."

True. And he'd turned a dumbass redneck into a slightly smarter dumbass redneck. "I can't tell you Victor's story, but I don't believe he's holding any grudges against me."

Her mouth opened and closed a few times before she managed to say, "Then he's still alive too?"

Damn. Bo wasn't the only one who should give spoiler alerts. "Forget you heard that. He'd dead. Deader than dead, and not working with international drug enforcement."

Mama glanced at Bo and back to Lucky.

It took Lucky three tries to say, "Old news. This here's..." His energy gave out.

Bo held out his hand. "I'm Bo, Lucky's partner. His off the job partner. Why don't we finish this conversation somewhere else and let Lu... Richmond get some rest? Can I buy you a cup of coffee?"

Twin kisses landed on Lucky's cheeks.

Lucky let his consciousness fade. Bo had this.

Maybe.

CHAPTER SIXTEEN

Lucky jerked awake. Crap. Someone here. And Bo's movements no longer disturbed his sleep. Not Bo. The hairs on the back of his neck stood on end. Why wasn't Moose growling? He slipped his hand over the side of the bed, inching toward the nightstand and his .38.

Rails. Bed rails. Oh. Hospital. Not home. Darn the luck. Dim lights didn't give him a clear view, but someone definitely stood over him.

No drug-induced hallucination either.

Playing asleep might be the best option. He scrunched his eyes closed. After an eternity, he cracked open one eye, to a dark silhouette. Too short for Bo. Too tall for Mom or Charlotte.

Just right for Nurse Andy. But the creeper had never been subtle.

And not a weapon at hand. The intruder had to hear the *bang, bang, bang* of his heart.

Ever so slowly, he worked his fingers toward the nurse call button. *Jab!*

A disembodied voice asked, "Can I help you?"

The silhouette shot out the door. Oh shit! Bright hallway lights! Darkness again.

Damn it! He didn't get a good look.

"Sir, is everything all right?" the voice asked.

"Um... Can I get a cup of decaf?" No way he'd go back to sleep now.

***

Nurse Andy whistled while taking Lucky's vitals.

In a moment of quiet, Lucky hummed The Police's *Every Breath You Take*, getting louder on the part about watching.

Four long-assed days of hell. Though the throbbing agony eased some, pain shot through Lucky each and every time the nurse made him walk.

Sadistic prick. Whenever Andy passed by the door, Lucky prepared for the worst. Sometimes the nurse glanced in and kept walking, sometimes he came in to fluff a pillow and otherwise freak Lucky out with too much attention, and other times he dogged the heels of anyone rambling out in the hallway.

Afraid someone might come in besides him? What'd he have? Bedpan envy? Didn't he get enough of staring holes through Lucky last night when he stood over the bed?

And there Andy came, this time shadowing Walter. Walter stepped through the open door. Andy kept on going.

Ah, to have the office betting pool handy. Several twenties might find their way into Lucky's pocket by wagering how long before Andy passed by again.

"You know my nurse is trying to kill me, right?" he told Walter.

Walter planted himself in the doorway, potted ivy in one hand and a Starbucks cup in the other.

Lucky nodded toward the open door where Nurse Nosy traipsed past. "I see you, you stalker."

"And good afternoon to you, too, Lucky."

Lucky held out his hand and took the cup. If Walter ever wanted him out of the way, all he had to do was poison the coffee, which at this point, Lucky might drink even knowing he'd die afterwards.

Lucky occupied himself with coffee to keep from getting all mushy. Ah, good and hot, filled with sugar, not stevia, but missing caffeine. Dammit. Even after being on decaf at Bo's insistence, Lucky missed his morning caffeine jolt, though he slept much better at night now.

But at least he still got to enjoy the taste. And sipping coffee passed the time while Walter found a place for the plant and settled himself into the chair with a sigh. "Attempts on your life aside, how are you feeling?"

"Worse than shit."

"Ah, an improvement then. When last we spoke you were, how did you phrase it? 'Worse than warmed-over shit.'"

Leave it to the boss to classify feeling like shit into levels. "How's things going?" Even though the pain kept him in bed most of the time, Lucky never idled well. He'd get up and do something—as soon as his guts stopped trying to kill him.

"Loretta is doing an admirable job with the trainees back in Atlanta, but I'm afraid Bo's made a huge mistake at the Richmond office."

"Not Bo!" Surely Mr. I-Love-Everybody hadn't taken Lucky's job of pissing people off.

"Yes, I'm afraid after less than a week they've already contacted me, asking to transfer him permanently to their office."

"And?" Hell, Lucky'd turned down a job with Nestor's international outfit, and now Bo got an offer? Would he turn this opportunity down? The moment came like a slap to the face. In the time he'd known Bo, the man had grown to be a superior agent. With his kind disposition, of course he'd be in demand.

When Lucky got out of here, he'd damned well keep the promise to be a better partner, lest he lose Bo to someone more thoughtful, like Walter might lose Bo if the Richmond office made a good enough offer.

No, not right. Lucky would be a better partner, not out of fear, but because Bo deserved to be treated right.

As soon as Lucky figured out how.

Walter spied the rather conspicuous flower arrangement worth more than Lucky's first car. "Did you get your answer?"

"Yup. Nestor Sauceda came sneaking in here, said I should know better than to have to ask." Though the details seemed a bit fuzzy. "I mean, if I didn't hallucinate the whole damned conversation." But hallucinations didn't bring very real flowers.

Walter nodded. "What else did he say?"

"He'd try to find out who did."

Again Walter nodded. "Who would do such a thing besides Victor?"

Lucky shrugged all his painful body allowed. "At the time I hadn't turned anyone in, so hadn't made the enemies I have today. I'd say Stephan Mangiardi, but the little asshole wouldn't spend his money on someone else." Or more accurately, he wouldn't have spent Victor's money on anyone else.

"How much does your family know about your... current arrangements?"

"My mother and sister know I'm still around, but they said they'd keep quiet until Dad's recovered. He doesn't need the shock right now, and my brothers can't keep secrets for shit."

Walter rose and rearranged the flowers on the table, placing his in front of Nestor's. Nothing happened by accident with Walter. "All the same, I'd like to interview your family members, with your permission. Maybe they'll recall something helpful. We won't reveal anything you object to."

"I appreciate it, but won't the powers that be have something to say about you nosing about for me?" While Lucky needed answers, the bureau didn't have a dog in this fight.

"The delivery of a large amount of heroin to a college campus is a legitimate case, worth investigating, no matter how long ago the crime took place." Walter removed his bifocals, rubbed the lenses on his shirt, held them up to the light, and plopped them back on his nose. "There. That's better."

"But statute of limitations and all." No one understood statutes like someone bound and determined to put time and distance between themselves and their past misdeeds.

"Someone dealing in heroin of those quantities wouldn't give up easy money. Perhaps they're still around and active."

The boss had spoken. Pity anyone who argued. If a way existed to make Daytona's supplier pay, they'd better watch out. Even the most powerful drug lords feared Walter Smith. "Can you check out the nurse for me? Something about him sets my alarms off. Andy something-or-other." Why couldn't Lucky remember the name?

"Lucky, I trust your instincts. If you have doubts about him, I'll have Loretta perform a background check."

"You could've brought my laptop or my work phone, and I'd be able to do the checking myself." Lucky's cheap personal phone couldn't surf the internet. But if he couldn't do the check himself, Loretta Johnson would be his next choice, after Bo.

Walter sighed. "How much rest would you get if you spent your days researching the entire hospital staff and looking up every prescription for possible counterfeits?"

Good point. "Okay, but I need you to get right on this. This nurse keeps slinking around. Last night I woke up and caught him standing over the bed watching me sleep."

"Are you sure it's not your medication talking?" But Walter's suddenly stiff backbone meant he'd gone into alert mode.

"I'm sure. He's passed by this room several times since you got here."

Right on cue, Nurse Andy paused outside the door, peered in, and took off when Lucky glared.

"See what I mean?"

Walter parked a hand on Lucky's shoulder. "I'll have him checked out. You have my word."

***

Walter reappeared later in the day. "I'm afraid your family didn't offer any additional information." He slurped from a coffee cup while handing Lucky another. "The oldest of your younger brothers..."

"Bristol."

"Ah, yes. Bristol. Excuse my saying so, but he's a bit—"

"Of an asshole," Lucky finished for his boss.

Walter smiled. "I might have used other words, but sometimes the simple terms are the best. Yes, I'm afraid your brother is an asshole." Asshole? The word sounded so strange coming from Walter's mouth. Of course, his vocabulary tended to head south around Lucky.

"The family used to say he got switched at birth. Ever since I remember, he's been acting like he's better than the rest of us, ashamed of being a tobacco farmer's son." Being a dumb redneck saved Lucky's life on occasion. And being underestimated gave him a big advantage over folks who imagined him too dumb to be a threat.

Serving twenty years in federal prison gave the ones who'd underestimated him plenty of time to see the error of their ways.

"Chances are, whoever it turns out to be is long dead or serving time." Lucky could hope.

"At any rate, it's still a crime to be solved." When Walter got an idea in his head, Hell and half of Georgia couldn't change the man's mind.

"But it's not a pharmaceutical crime." While the Southeastern Narcotics Bureau's Department of Diversion Prevention and Control investigated out of their area when necessary, they normally didn't handle street drugs—the DEA got those cases. Lucky them.

"No, it's not. But it is a crime." Walter might appear to be casually interested, but he took care of his own. And if he considered Lucky a son, Daytona came with the package.

May God have mercy on anyone who messed with Walter's family, for Walter wouldn't. Because Lucky had never heard of his boss killing someone and disposing of the body didn't mean he hadn't. Just that Walter hadn't gotten caught. Wouldn't get caught.

Lucky peered around his boss toward the open door. No Nurse Andy. Yet. "What did you find out about the nurse?"

"He's a relatively new addition to the staff, but has high credentials and not so much as a traffic ticket." Again with Walter's stiff pose.

Lucky scrutinized his boss. It wasn't like Walter not to snap to Lucky's attention, but he'd never endanger a part of his team. Something about his clenching and unclenching fists said the matter wasn't over, and Nurse Andy pinged Walter's felon instincts. No telling what Lucky'd find if he crawled inside the man's mind. No thanks. He'd enough demons living in his own head.

And an unnerving nurse to keep an eye on.

Damn, damn, ouch, ouch, oh holy fuck! Lucky doubled over, breathing through the worst of the pain. Thank God they'd unhooked his IV, or else he'd have to haul the damned apparatus down the hall.

Walter might be doing background work, but nothing beat good old-fashioned surveillance.

He peeked around the corner. There. Nurse Andy, speaking on a cellphone. His voice changed, reminding Lucky of O'Donoghue, who'd pick up and lose an accent at will.

Andy hissed into the phone, "How much longer? And what happens then? The hospital has already kept him longer than usual. Sooner or later, someone's bound to get suspicious." Oh, really? *I'm already suspicious, motherfucker.* Lucky flattened against the wall and slunk back down the hall. Well, he'd learned two things: he'd been here too long, and Andy really was out to get him.

A Starbucks cup sat on the side table. With any luck, Walter assumed Lucky sat downstairs having some test or other run. He'd better come back soon and hear all about what Lucky heard.

Ahhh... Coffee. Dark and sweet. Perfect. *Thanks, boss!*

Lucky swam to the surface of murky dreams and managed to open his blurry eyes. The chair beside the bed squeaked. Ah, a visitor. He lacked to energy to see who. What happened? Coffee and a bitter taste coated his tongue. "Wha...?"

"You should have stayed dead, asshole."

Okay, someone who wanted him dead narrowed down the possibilities to about two thousand. The Southern drawl reduced the number to a few hundred. The words chilled Lucky's blood.

"I hate you, you know that, right?"

Which upped the number into the thousands again.

"Why?" Lucky managed to ask. "Why in particular?" took too much energy. Why wouldn't his eyes stay open?

"You're an asshole." The chair squeaked and footsteps tapped away from the bed, only to return, along with the scent of overly-sweet cologne.

Common knowledge. Most people hated him for being a smartass or shoving their sorry drug-dealing asses into jail.

The voice and cologne weren't Nurse Andy's. Bed, pillow, lovely, lovely sleep called. The nurse might make his skin crawl, but right now he couldn't care. He'd gladly kiss the man for showing up. Why the hell hadn't he demanded his gun from Walter?

Okay. The dipstick visitor said his piece. Now get out and let a man rest.

The pacing stopped. A sharp bite in his hand forced Lucky's eyes open. Ow! He grabbed his offended hand and came away with damp fingers. Blood. "What are you doing?"

A man-shape shoved something into his pocket. "You're no good alive, but you had some use to me dead. Only... you being alive again might cause a few complications. You should've drank the whole cup of coffee and saved me the effort."

"What are you rambling on about?" Even with Lucky sedated, a can of whoop-ass began to open. He struggled to sit up. Stars danced before his eyes. What heavy weight pressed down on his chest?

The blur held up an empty syringe and grinned, face eerie in the room's greenish night light. "So long, motherfucker."

Shit! Air! Need air!

Black filled Lucky's vision.

CHAPTER SEVENTEEN

Oh! Coffee. Worth waking up for. Ouch! Bright lights! Lucky slitted his eyelids and tried again. Huh. Light blue walls, not white. And way too much fucking sunlight streaming in through a big-assed window. No humming machines. Out of his room now. But... This sure as hell wasn't a normal hospital room. A couple dozen or so hospitals, visited for various reasons, tended to turn a man into somewhat of an expert.

Walter sat in a chair beside the bed, holding a Starbucks cup. Would killing someone for the contents of one of those cups count as justifiable homicide?

But trusting coffee after his last cup being drugged might be a bit of a stretch.

"Where am I?" Good, enough brain cells survived their pharmaceutically-induced vacation to form words. Holy hell! Grabbing his head didn't squeeze out the pain. His temples pounded, and the ripped open parts of him now remembered they'd been cut open.

"Safe." Walter extended the cup toward Lucky. "And no longer in the hospital. It's not safe for you there."

More wince-inspiring words never existed.

Walter scowled. "Oh. Need something for pain? I'm afraid we're limited in our options at the moment. No opioids, but you can have ketorolac."Ketorolac. What they gave folks when opioids became a no-no. Lucky shifty-eyed the room. "Where's Bo? Where am I? And what the fuck ran me over?"

A woman Lucky didn't recognize hurried into the room

and fumbled with his IV tubing. Sweet relief followed. But...
an IV again?

"He's currently busy with a new case. Attempted murder."

"Say what?" Staring holes through the boss happening
in five, four, three... His headache fought a battle with really
good drugs and started winning.

"In hospital terms, you coded. Heart attack. I'm afraid you
died. Again." Walter tutted. "You seem to be making a habit
of this."

Lucky settled his head back on the pillow. Dead. Yeah.
He'd been there. He'd lie here until he woke up, the world
started making sense again, or someone tossed him into the
ground and piled on dirt. "Okay. Dead. Got it. Who am I waking up as?"

"I believe it's your decision." Walter placed the cup on a
bedside table. Lucky's arms were too heavy to move.

"Gonna stop stalling and tell me what's going on? If I'm
dead, what got me this time? I'm told I'm hard to kill so must
be something good." Had to be creepy-assed Nurse Andy.
But...

There'd been someone else too, right?

"The official story is a heart attack, brought on by the
stress of your organ donation. It seems the doctors missed
a heart defect in your pre-surgical screening." Walter met
Lucky's bleary gaze head on. "In reality, you suffered a near-
fatal overdose. Some form of narcotic, but the lab results so
far have been inconclusive." He leaned against the railing on
Lucky's bed. "How much do you remember?"

"Remember? You're shitting me, right? I'm so high I can't
keep my eyes open. How am I supposed to remember anything?" Shit! Yelling hurt!

"Try."

"Some really awful water someone dragged a piece of
chicken through for about five seconds and called it soup,
orange Jello. Pills in a cup. Walking down the hall..." Nurse
Andy, on a cell phone. "I overheard Stalker Nurse talking

about me, about me getting suspicious." Pain or no pain, Lucky struggled to sit. "There was a Starbucks cup in my room when I came back. I figured you'd brought me coffee, and I slurped it down."

A surprisingly strong hand held him in place. Walter's bushy eyebrows tried to meet over his nose. "Shhh... I can assure you, if I visited your room and you weren't there, I'd find out why. And no cup was found in your room. Do you remember anything else?"

Fear. Hate. Someone wanting him dead. Someone in his room, maybe? Being helpless sucked big time. "No."

"You don't remember a man coming into your room and putting a syringe in your hand?"

"No? Should I?" Someone came into his room and tried to kill him? Who? Why? Most of the folks who'd go through that trouble were all dead themselves. Still, vague notions of someone stabbing his hand lingered around the edges of his mind.

The spot beneath a circular bandage on his hand prickled.

And unless they were playing with Lucky, the two most dangerous men he'd ever met now considered themselves his guardian—somethings. Not angels.

"Did you ever find out anything more on Nurse Andy?" The sneaky-assed nurse needed interrogating.

"No. However, in light of the recent attempt on your life, we're not ruling out anyone with access to your room. All visitors for the last twenty-four hours will be questioned. And I brought you a present." Walter picked up Lucky's computer bag from the floor. "I'd brought it up with me, and merely waited for the right moment to allow you access. I believe the time has come."

Yay! "What did you tell my mother? My sister?" They didn't deserve to go through hell again on his account. "Were they told I'm dead? Again." Mama and Charlotte both might kick his ass this time, for lying.

"I'm not sure they believe me. Your sister said something about you having nine lives. Oh, by the way." Furrows formed

174

between Walter's brows. "What is a pine knot, and how tough is it, exactly?"

His laptop! Finally! But no gun stuck in the side pocket. Damn it! He'd rather be home than in wherever Walter stuck him.

Lucky typed in his password and began searching out every scrap of information available on James Andrew "Andy" Polatty.

Nothing. Squeaky clean. Too clean. Like Simon Harrison's records. Lucky might be out of the hospital now and in protective custody, but the asswipe with the silly grin still roamed the halls near Lucky's nearest and dearest.

Nothing. Not even a speeding ticket.

And Magnolia Manor Long-Term Care turned out to be a legitimate entity, though they might want to rethink their uncomfortable beds. Why did so many Southern care facilities insist on calling themselves "Magnolia" something or other?

Nothing but four walls to stare at and plenty of time. And no TV. Maybe Lucky could find *South Bend Springs* online.

But wait. In all the time he'd been outcast, and as many people as he'd dug up dirt on, he'd never checked on family. They didn't want him around? He'd give them their freedom.

But now?

Now he stood a chance of one day clearing his name and possibly being invited back into the fold.

Embarrassing Lucklighter histories? Come to Papa.

Damn. Things had really gone downhill for Daytona. Twelve stints in rehab, four arrests. Bad credit. The family farm listed for his last known address. Even though Victor paid for his college, he still hadn't finished.

Dallas hadn't wasted his education. Ran his own building contracting company. Modest house. Still married to his childhood sweetheart. Still had only the one daughter. Decent credit. Member of First Baptist Church of Greensboro.

Charlotte made the newspapers a few times for being a Boy Scout den mother and doing charity work. Hmmm... She'd started taking some online courses. Maybe she hadn't lost her dream of becoming a nurse after all.

Her boys seemed to be doing well in school. Ty played high school soccer and Todd ranked second on the tennis team. They'd both been in band.

Next, he searched for his Uncle Ned's obituary. He'd died of natural causes about midway between Lucky's arrest and conviction.

Natural causes, huh? Twelve or thirteen different substances could make a death appear natural, and be hard to find unless suspected. No wife. No kids. No telling who the old man left his measly belongings to, though five minutes plus his computer equaled answers.

Did Lucky really want to know about Bristol? The strangest Lucklighter had always been ashamed of the name, never brought friends to the farm.

Wow! Huge house. Decent job at a bank. Decent, but not enough to afford a house four times the size of Lucky and Bo's. And why such a pretentious place with only him living there?

Country club. Damn, what a car. And get a look at the beauty queens in pictures with him. Bristol always had been the one in the family out to prove himself. Seemed he'd overcome his redneck past after all.

And grew into a no-account asshole who wouldn't help his own father.

Nice article on him speaking to the Chamber of Commerce. Nothing but time on Lucky's hands. Why not click the video link?

"Blah, blah, blah, blah, blah." Some man in a suit droned on and on, singing someone's praises. Couldn't be Bristol's.

When the man stepped away from the podium, another took his place who shared features Lucky saw every morning in the mirror. "Good evening, ladies and gentlemen."

That voice!

Oh shit.

CHAPTER EIGHTEEN

The voices jumbled in his head, Nurse Andy's and Bristol's, both saying, "You should have stayed dead."

Victor's old home territory included Richmond. What if someone who'd dealt with him hadn't gotten the word about Victor still living and decided to get revenge?

Or a million other bastards out there might have it in for Lucky. *You should have stayed dead.*

Lucky last "died" during the Ryerson pill mill case. Surely Dr. Ryerson and her accomplices hadn't come after him. Would be his luck to survive the worst drug lords in the country to be taken out by a Southern belle with a ruthless streak. But one never could tell what people might do with their backs against the wall. Her trial got delayed yet again, and she walked relatively free for now.

Nurse Andy could be working for her. But Bristol's voice sent chills up his spine. Could be a holdover from their past, but might be more.

But what if Bristol had been in the room and knew Lucky still lived?

They might have called him Idiot Boy in younger days, yet he'd been the smartest of the bunch. Yet Bristol used to cry when getting a shot. Fainted at the sight of a needle.

The dial swung back to Nurse Andy. Lucky's gut told him either Nurse Andy or Bristol had tried to kill him, and his gut feelings weren't often wrong.

Or maybe he'd eaten way too much soft food lately and his stomach staged a rebellion to get a burger and fries. Whatever. Either one of those two assholes had access to Lucky's family.

Bristol had sense enough to figure out that if Lucky lived, Charlotte knew.

And Bristol hadn't wanted to help Dad. Claimed him dying was God's will. What if Bristol decided to play God?

Damn it all to hell! Until the meds cleared Lucky's system, every single thought could be real, or simply paranoia.

No use taking chances, then. He slid out of bed. He should have been going home today anyway. Ow, ow, ow, ow, ow. He crept out into the hallway with his IV pole. At least wearing loose sweat pants meant his bare ass wasn't shining out the back of a split-tailed hospital gown.

Gray walls, gray floor. Not a lot of people about. He stuck his head around a corner. An old man and woman sat in wheelchairs in the hallway. The smell of the hallway didn't scream "hospital in a can" like the place he'd left.

He should find some clothes. What about a car?

"Lucky? What are you doing?"

Damn. Busted. He turned a sheepish smile on Bo. Holding completely still kept his gut pain to a minimum. Still there, but bearable. The image of one good jab to his stitches and his remaining liver sliding out raced through his mind.

Bo grabbed him by the arm.

Lucky yelped and let himself be led back to his room. "We gotta get back to the hospital."

Bo tucked Lucky into bed, checked his IV, and folded his arms across his chest. "Why?"

"Because whoever tried to kill me is still there. With my family."

"We've got surveillance in place, and Keith's counterpart in the Richmond office is going over security videos to figure out who went into your room."

Not good enough. Lucky needed to be in the middle of the action. "I got a real good idea who tried to off me."

"Who?"

"Nurse Andy or Bristol Lucklighter."

Bo let out a long-suffering sigh. "Andrew Polatty? I searched, and found nothing on him."

"I checked him too. He checks out, all right. His record is almost a perfect match for Simon Harrison's. Which means it's fake."

Bo palmed his face. "Oh, shit. And you'd be able to find dirt on him if it existed, wouldn't you? I told Walter it was too soon to give you your laptop."

"Well, I don't have access to a few more records I need, but yeah."

The hand dropped, revealing Bo's wide eyes and open mouth. "Wait a damned minute. Bristol? You suspect your brother? Why?"

"There ain't a bit of love lost between us, I can tell you. He hated having a hick family. It must've stuck in his craw kinda bad to have a brother go to prison." Not much of a way Bristol could explain the arrest to the pack of rich kids he'd hung around with.

Bo tapped a finger against his chin. "You do realize narcotics and sedatives can induce paranoia, right?"

Yeah, they could. "Listen to me. This ain't drugs talking. We gotta get over there." Lucky struggled to get up. Bo kept him down with one hand on his chest.

"You're not going anywhere. If anything, I'll go. And I'll call Walter on the way. Tell him your suspicions. But not liking you isn't a motive for murder. If it was..."

No need saying how many times Lucky would have died by now if contempt killed. Too bad housekeeping came back for the knife he'd kept from his lunch tray, taking away his only defense from homicidal maniacs. "You don't believe me." Lucky stuck out his lip. Normally, Bo had his back.

"I didn't say that."

"You didn't have to."

"It won't hurt to question a few folks again." Damn, Bo had gotten good at imitating Walter's blank-face expression. Things worked better when every thought, good or bad, registered on his face.

"I need to go with you."

Bo crouched down, nose to nose with Lucky. "No. You've always wanted me to trust you. It's time for you to trust me. Now you stay here and behave yourself. I'll call if we find anything out."

Oh hell no. "No. I'm going with you."

"Are not." Bo lifted his chin, in full stubborn mode.

Nobody did stubborn like a Lucklighter. "Am too."

"Don't make me do this."

"Do what?"

Bo turned toward the door. "Josh?"

An armed guard stepped through the doorway. "Yes, Mr. Schollenberger?" Damn, what a pile of muscle.

"Make sure Mr. Harrison stays in his room. For his own good."

"I need to be there." Why couldn't the man see reason? A fight or running might be beyond Lucky's current abilities, but he'd take his chances. Bo, Mama, and Charlotte's lives depended on him.

"Okay, you win!" Bo threw his hands in the air. "But first go take a shower." He wrinkled his nose.

Shower, right. Lucky sat. Crap. IV.

"Go start washing. I'll get someone to take out your IV." Bo flapped a hand toward the bathroom. "Go! Time's a wasting."

Lucky gritted his teeth and climbed out of bed. No showing Bo how much he hurt. He shuffled into the bathroom wearing nothing but a T-shirt and worn sweatpants. Where was the nurse to get the damned needle out of his hand?

"Toss out your clothes. I'll pick you something to wear," Bo called through the door.

Oh, yeah. Clothes. One-handed, Lucky shucked off the pants. Hmmm... The shirt might be a problem. He'd have to wait until the nurse got there.

Lucky opened the door and tossed the pants out.

He waited.

And waited.

Finally, he wrapped a towel around his waist, opened the door, and stuck his head out. "Bo?"

Nothing. The dresser drawer stood open. And empty. What? Nothing in any drawer. No shoes. What the fuck?

"Josh!" Lucky yelled.

The hired muscle strode in. "Yes, sir?"

"Where're my clothes?"

"I was instructed to tell you if you asked that you don't need them. And that you'd get them back later."

Fuck.

Lucky awoke to Nurse Andy standing over his bed.

"I know who you are, Agent Harrison. Or should I say Lucklighter?"

Oh shit. What was the point of witness protection if every damned person on the planet knew Lucky's real identity? He eyed the rolling bedside table for a weapon. No help there. Not even a bedpan to clobber the asshole with.

Damn housekeeping for taking his knife. Lucky inched close enough to grab the nurse call button if needed.

But it wasn't himself he worried about. "How'd you get in here? Where's Bo and Walter?" If the bastard so much as ruffled a hair on their heads... Pain and agony. And the bastard's mangled corpse would never be found.

He'd work out details later on how to hurt the man without hurting himself.

What had Bo called the guard? "Josh? Josh!"

"I sent him home." The world's scariest nurse stuck his hand out. "Agent James Salters, Southeastern Narcotics Bureau, Division of Hospitals. Most folks call me Jimmy."

"We have a Division of Hospitals? Not in Atlanta, we don't."

"I'm out of the Virginia office."

"Prove it." Lucky measured the distance from the bed to the door. Cut in half, gimpy ankle. Yeah, he didn't stand a snowball's chance in hell of escape. Oh crap, and naked from the waist down. He pulled the bed covers tighter around his middle. He owed Bo big time for making off with his clothes.

181

Nurse Andy, Jimmy, or whoever pulled out his wallet and flashed a badge, very much like the one in Lucky's wallet.

"Anybody can forge a badge." Not well, but Lucky managed a passable copy to prove a point once.

The guy currently maintaining the upper hand pointed toward Lucky's computer case. "You got a laptop right there. Check me out."

Keeping a close eye on his visitor, Lucky followed the guy's advice, but only because he wanted to anyway. Jimmy told the truth. An agent with three years' time in. "Mind 'splaining what's going on?"

Nurse... Jimmy flipped a chair around backwards and dropped onto the wooden seat, arms folded on the back. "Probably all the better you don't recall."

"Why?"

Jimmy met and held Lucky's gaze. "What do you know about Bristol Lucklighter?"

Lucky suspecting Bristol might be a felon and hearing proof from someone else were two different things. "He's my brother, he's an asshole, and he hates me." Who didn't? "What about him?"

"He left your room, and we had to jolt you full of naloxone. A few seconds more might've been too late."

Good point. Lucky'd thank him later. Maybe. "What'd he give me?"

"Labs results came back an hour ago. Carfentanil. Thank God he'd over-diluted or nothing could have saved you."

Carfentanil? Jeezus! Scary stuff.

"Yup, about ten thousand times more powerful than morphine. Powerful enough to tranquilize an elephant. Or to kill a man with a nearly invisible dosage." For a moment Jimmy sounded like Bo, quoting a textbook. Newbies. "You're only alive because whoever it was didn't know what the hell they were doing."

How had Lucky's would-be killer gotten hold of something so powerful? "I still haven't ruled you out."

182

Jimmy brought his nose closer to Lucky's, close enough to reveal a tiny scar on his chin. "I studied chemistry. I wouldn't have made a mistake. But me knowing what the hell I'm doing, and being a 'stalker' as you said, saved your life. I was first on scene. It took five shots to get you stabilized, then I started naloxone in a drip."

Not a bad idea, especially since Bo owed his life to the stuff capable of reversing an opioid overdose. Not that Lucky would tell Nurse... Jimmy.

So now both Lucky and Bo owed their lives to naloxone. "If you suspected Bristol, why haven't you arrested him?" Bo would have mentioned Bristol being taken into custody, wouldn't he?

"Ah, come on. You train agents. You know the answer."

Duh. Yes, he did. All the meds must be cooking Lucky's brain. "Because you need to establish a motive or find out if he's working alone."

"Bingo. And we need to find out where he got the drug."

If Lucky's brain wasn't hurting so bad, he'd shake his head to knock loose the cobwebs. Too much info, too fast. "Wait a minute. Why were you watching me?"

Jimmy flashed a tense smile. "Wasn't you I was watching, though I must admit, my target being related to the famous drug trafficker-turned-agent Lucky Lucklighter did kinda make me wonder."

Lucky might as well tattoo his birth name on his forehead. "Bristol? What are you watching my brother for?"

"He's been linked to a major drug trafficker. Um... besides you. And with his father checking into the hospital, I got assigned."

Asswipe. But goody-two-shoes Bristol? "What you got so far? I checked him out earlier and couldn't find anything."

"You're not in the office, so you don't have full access, do you?" Oh, how Lucky itched to bitch slap the superior grin off Jimmy's face.

No. He didn't.

Jimmy took on an "all business" pose, face devoid of emotion, so much like Walter in interrogation mode. "Tell me about your brother. What kind of relationship do you have?"

To hell with this twenty questions shit. "I'm not telling you diddly squat. I answer to Walter Smith."

"Why else would I be here? Seems he's thorough, and he got around my alias. But I'd heard of his skills and yours. He contacted the office demanding answers, and here I am. So, stop stalling and talk. What about Bristol? What kind of relationship do you have?"

Hell, no. Not taking anyone's word without proof. Lucky held up a finger, grabbed his phone to text Walter, and found a waiting text: *Please cooperate with Agent Salters.*

Damn it. Cooperating. Not Lucky's strong suit. "We don't. My family disowned me ages ago. They were told I died."

"What were you two like before your arrest?"

Yeah, asshole. Remind me of my mistakes. "He pretty much hated me. Hated the whole family. Hated being poor." Wasn't much Bristol hadn't hated but wealth, power, and his own self.

"So he liked money."

"Yeah. The house. The car. High class girlfriends." The drugs had to be keeping Lucky's mind from working right. Oh, to have a clear head right now. "We need to check his financial records."

"No. *The bureau* needs to check his financial records. You need to go home for your own safety. You're on medical leave. This isn't your case. I just needed information."

Bristol. Damn, how he must've crowed the day the family shut the door on Lucky for good.

The day the family...

Oh shit.

"I need to talk to Walter. Now!" Lucky hit the call button on his phone.

"What did you remember?" Walter shuffled through the door about the time Jimmy got Lucky into a wheelchair for the long ride to freedom—courtesy of the faded blue sweat pants he'd paid another patient way too much for.

"Our... friends. They were checking on something for me. I need you to feed them the name Bristol Lucklighter. Where's Bo?" Bo should be here. Lucky needed him.

"He's still investigating a few leads."

"But I'm going home, right? Ain't he taking me?" Bo ought to be headed for home with Lucky.

Jimmy spoke up. "No. I'm driving you."

"Now hold on one damned minute." The guy hadn't earned Lucky's trust yet and likely never would.

Walter grabbed the back of Lucky's wheelchair and started pushing. "Lucky, for once in your life, take an order and don't question. James will escort you back home to Atlanta into Loretta Johnson's care."

"What the fuck?"

"Bristol has dangerous friends and may not be working alone, if indeed he's behind the attack. Until we determine exactly who's after you and why, you're a target. The farther away you are, the better." The boss managed to miss bumps better than the orderlies back at the hospital.

Looked like Lucky might get to know Jimmy better than he'd ever hoped to.

But at least Agent Jimmy beat Nurse Andy.

Or did he?

"Are you comfortable? Need another pillow?"

A growl backed Jimmy away from fluffing the pillow behind Lucky's head. "No and No." Lucky might never be comfortable again, and one more pillow would crowd him out of the passenger seat of Jimmy's car.

"Are you sure?" Jimmy shut up long enough to trot around the hood and get in the car. "We should be there in about..."

Blah, blah, blah. There went Lucky's hopes of a peaceful ride home. Just his luck to get stuck with an overly-eager talker.

"I owe you, you know." A bit of Nurse Andy's creepiness shone in Jimmy's fan-boy smile.

The last time someone had said those words, they'd tried to kill Lucky. "Owe me what?"

To his credit, Jimmy finally started the vehicle and eased out of the parking lot. Goodbye, Magnolia Manor! "I owe you my freedom."

"Your freedom."

"Yeah." Jimmy's voice softened. "Several years back I got busted for pot. Not much, mind you, but enough to get me into some serious trouble."

Of all the states to legalize weed, Virginia might be one of the last. "And?"

"And I nearly lost my nursing license. Then my current boss heard about the operations you pulled off in Georgia and gave me a chance to redeem myself. If it weren't for you, that might never have happened. Then, thanks to both you and Agent Schollenberger, I got offered a permanent position once I'd done my time. Been with SNB ever since."

Bo and Lucky paved the way for others? Who'd have thunk it?

"Anyway, I'd put in for undercover ops training with you down in Atlanta, but a slot hasn't come up yet. And then what do you know? Here you come up this way." Jimmy's grin threatened to split his face. He gave a sheepish shrug. "Watching Bristol's father kept me close enough to keep tabs on Bristol, though he didn't visit much. I had no idea at the time that Simon Harrison and Lucky Lucklighter were one and the same. When a request came in for protection for a new patient, we discovered your link to my target."

"A request? When? And whose request?"

"The day you checked in, and I don't know who asked. Since I was already assigned to the hospital, switching over to you benefitted my case, since you and his... your father... were on the same floor."

The day Lucky's checked into the hospital. When had Walter gotten in touch with Nestor? "Who..." Had to be Victor and Nestor. Walter only recently found out about Nurse Andy being Agent Jimmy, ruling the boss out. Maybe learning about Daytona being drugged put Nestor and Victor on alert. They'd promised to watch out for Lucky, after all. And they definitely had the pull to make arrangements for a baby sitter. "Don't make a lick of sense."

"Since me hovering over you like a mother hen means you're still breathing, I guess the request proved right."

Couldn't argue there. "Is that why Bo took my clothes so I couldn't go with him back to the hospital? I still owe him one."

Jimmy grin fell. "I've never worked with him, but my boss sings his praises. Bo's a pro, but with you around, he'd lose focus and not concentrate on work. You know what happens to agents who can't keep their minds on their work."

Yep. SNB memorial page. But still, someday soon, when Bo least expected... "What's happening at the hospital? What's Bo doing there?"

"Maybe I shouldn't be telling you this, but he's keeping an eye on the rest of your family."

"Not to sound ungrateful or anything, but why?" If someone kept an eye on Bristol, the rest of the family should be safe.

"Let's call it a hunch." Jimmy stopped at a red light and turned to Lucky. "I'm afraid we have a lead to follow up on."

Lucky's mind reeled, and not from painkillers. He eyed a Starbucks sign. Good news or bad news all went down better with coffee.

Someone along the way must've trained Jimmy well, because after a thumb jerk in the right direction, he pulled into the drive through. "Black decaf, lots of sugar," Jimmy ordered. "Make that two."

He pulled up to the window, retrieved two cups, and handed one to Lucky.

Umm... coffee. Lucky eyed the cup with suspicion. Hopefully, he'd get over worrying about drugged Starbucks cups. Something to take up with his therapist next appointment.

And nothing scary about Jimmy knowing how Lucky took his coffee, or rather, used to. No, nothing at all. Lucky eyed the parking lot. If he could only run.

But more questions needed answers before he could bail on his ride, and no running until his insides put themselves back together. He set his drink in the console cup holder. "What do my mother and sister know?" They'd gone through enough the last time he'd been declared dead. Not to mention a whole lotta tears and prayers during his lawless younger days.

"We can't share a lot at this point, but enough to keep 'em from worrying too much." Jimmy frowned. "Your sister doesn't have a concealed carry permit, does she?"

Her super heavy purse slapping against Lucky's back came to mind. "I'm not positive, but I'm pretty sure she does, at least in Washington. Why?"

"'Because she took a shot at me with her index finger."

Lucky laughed and grabbed his stomach. Holy fuck! After a minute or two of deep breathing and a whole lot of cussing, the pain subsided enough for him to talk again. "You better not lie to her. She threatened my partner with a shotgun when he went looking for me after the last time I died." *Last time I died.* Who said such things? Lucky wasn't in the habit of apologizing. The "Sorry" he slipped out must've been the drugs talking.

Jimmy grinned again. "I didn't notice a wedding ring on her finger. I like her spirit, and always had a thing for redheads When all this is over, you won't shoot me for asking her out, will you?"

Oh, hell no. No looking across the dinner table at a rabid fan with eyes for Charlotte. "No, but she might." The moment Lucky got a chance, he'd ask his sister to change her hair color from the auburn she currently wore.

"She strikes me as the kind of woman who can take care of herself. I like that." Jimmy put his serious face back on. "Now, you sure you don't know why your brother wanted you dead? Have you come up with anything else to tell me about him?"

"He's a money grubbing sonofabitch who wouldn't even get tested to donate a hunk of liver and save Dad's life. And like I said, up till a few hours ago, he believed I was already dead." Charlotte had warned him Bristol might try to fight Bo for assets if he thought otherwise.

Assets. "Wait a damned minute."

"You remember something?"

You're no good alive, but you had some use to me dead. Whoa! "Yeah. Have someone check records from about three years ago. And if he took out life insurance on Dad." If Lucky was right... the bastard! If he was wrong... Hell, Bristol still might've tried to kill him.

"What am I looking for from three years ago?"

"If he came into some money about the time Richmond Eugene Lucklighter died."

Lucky jolted out of a doze. "Owww!" What the fuck? When had the sun gone down?

Jimmy shook Lucky's shoulder. "We got company."

The side mirror showed a shiny silver BMW. "How long?" He'd seen a silver Bimmer recently in pictures.

"Since we left Virginia."

Judging by the road signs, they were nearing Charlotte, North Carolina. Lucky's famous instincts twisted his gut into knots. "My brother owns a silver BMW. That's him, isn't it?"

"Yeah. We've run the plates. It's registered to Bristol Lucklighter." Jimmy held the steering wheel with a two-handed grip.

"So, he doesn't believe I'm dead."

"Nope. Your boss let something slip."

Walter didn't let information pass his lips by accident. "You asswipes are using me as bait!" Ow, ow, ow... Was he ever going to quit hurting?

"I'm following orders and taking you home." Jimmy glanced into the rearview mirror, watched the road a minute, and checked behind them again.

"Has he figured out who you are?"

"No. More than likely, he figures I'm your boyfriend." Jimmy gritted his teeth. Could be a smile, but maybe not.

"What's the plan?"

"Bathroom break."

He had to go and say that, didn't he? Lucky hadn't had to piss until Jimmy made the suggestion. Bastard.

They pulled off the interstate at a truck stop. The BMW followed.

And so did a familiar chicken shit green Malibu. And a black jeep. And a Kia.

Jimmy led his caravan of tails into the relatively empty parking lot of a fast food restaurant. *How about some subtlety, y'all?*

"I'm going to go in first and leave you in the car." Jimmy handed Lucky a 9mm Glock that fit into his hand almost as good as his dick did. "Use it if you have to, but try not to have to. I've been assured you won't. Smile, you're on camera, and you might not want to say anything bad about your boss. I've got a mic in here strong enough to pick up things you haven't even said yet."

Lucky kept his eyes on the BMW in the side mirror.

The car parked right behind Jimmy's Ford Escape.

Same sandy blond hair, same swagger. Couldn't be nobody else but a Lucklighter. Lucky kept his eyes on the driver's approach and tightened his grip on the Glock.

Please, God, don't make me have to shoot my brother. Mama will never forgive me.

The Malibu flanked them, and the Jeep cut off any possible escape. Where was Jimmy?

Lucky's heart pounded. He'd faced down many a drug dealer, but he'd never had to take down family before.

The seconds ticked away, Lucky's target grew closer. He readied the gun and let the window down. Footsteps padded toward the car. Closer. Closer.

They stopped. Lucky swallowed hard and turned to face his fate. "Bris..." His mouth dropped open. "What the fuck are you doing here?"

CHAPTER NINETEEN

The man standing at Lucky's window reached into his jacket. Who wore a jacket in this heat? The haunting scent from the hospital teased Lucky's nose. The same guy. Had to be.

Lucky raised his gun, heart pounding. "I don't wanna pull this trigger, but if you so much as flinch I will." And may God have mercy on his soul.

"Is that any way to talk to your brother?"

"Those are the first words you've spoken to me in twelve years." Lucky chanced a glance in the side mirror.

Jimmy waited a few yards away, gun at the ready. Behind the car, Johnson flexed her arms. Lucky didn't see a weapon, but that didn't mean she wasn't armed to the teeth. And being out after dark and not being home with her kid made "pissed off" her most dangerous weapon.

"Why are you holding a gun on me? I just want to talk." But the man kept his hand in his jacket.

"Then talk. I'm listening." With the Glock's safety off, but still listening.

"I wanna ask you..." The man pulled his hand from his jacket. "Yaaah!"

One moment, familiar eyes stared Lucky down, the next minute his stalker simply wasn't there—plowed down by a freight train. Never even had time to run.

Johnson pinned the guy flat, face in the pavement, and her knee in his back. She wasn't gentle about hauling his arms behind him, and if she pinched his flesh snapping the cuffs, she didn't look sorry.

Lucky was braced for more hatred, more fury. His social climbing brother never had a good word for him when he stood at Victor's side, enjoying the lush life. Not when Lucky had what his brother wanted so badly. And now, Lucky stood free and his brother wore cuffs.

Johnson hauled her prey to his feet. And maybe dislocated his shoulder.

But it wasn't Bristol.

Blue flashing lights lit up the parking lot. The crowd of gawkers gave up, pocketed their cell phones, and wandered back to their cars.

Show's over, folks. Nothing to see here.

Static crackled over a nearby police radio. Lucky watched a squad car pull away with his brother inside. Most honest folk were tucked in bed and snoozing by this late hour. No one ever accused Lucky of being honest. Not enough to totally blow his rep anyway.

Jimmy slapped Lucky's shoulder. "I believe I'm leaving you in good hands." He eyed Rett and tipped an imaginary hat. "Ma'am."

"You didn't just 'ma'am' me." Rett's scowl would've sent a smarter man hauling ass, though Jimmy's quick scamper might count. She threw an arm around Lucky's shoulder. "C'mon. Let me get you home."

Lucky staggered to the front passenger door.

"Nope, no need for that. I've made things nice and cozy for you in the back." She opened the rear door and gestured Lucky inside.

Pillows, blankets, and a sleeping bag sat piled on the backseat. "You don't do nothin' halfway, do ya?"

Rett lifted a blanket for Lucky to crawl under. "If it's worth doing, it's worth overdoing. Now get your ass settled, and I'll get our butts back to Atlanta."

"I'm not an invalid." Wow. She'd managed to make Lucky a fairly comfortable makeshift bed.

"Didn't say you were. You okay?" Johnson drove slowly out of the parking lot and had the decency not to hit any potholes.

"Are we there yet?" Lucky hollered.

"Don't make me come back there."

Strapped in the back seat of Johnson's Jeep, nestled in enough padding to shield him from direct impact with an eighteen-wheeler, high on two fucking amazing pills. If and when he stopped hurting, he might need to check into rehab.

"No, really, how far are we?" His bladder ached.

At least the ache in his bladder and side dulled the ache in his head and heart. Poor Mama. And Dad. And neither in any shape to deal with their kids' shit.

"Rett?"

"We're a half mile closer than the last time you asked."

"That's not what I intended to ask. Can you find out what they plan to do with my brother?" Had Daytona really intended to kill him? Did he have two brothers after his sorry ass, or just Day? He and Bristol favored each other enough to be mistaken on a video.

"They found a gun under the BMW's seat, but not on him, so they're taking him in for questioning."

"Where they taking him?"

"Greensboro."

Greensboro. Fuck. "Turn this thing around. I want to be there when they question him." Regardless of what he'd tried to do, the kid was still Daytona. He needed family, even family he wanted to kill.

Johnson glanced up at Lucky in the rearview mirror. "Walter said to take you home. I'm considering his words to be an order from a superior."

"I'm your superior, and I said we're going to Greensboro."

"Are you asking, telling, or ordering?"

"Whatever it takes."

Johnson did a U-turn in the middle of the road.

***

Man, returning to the Greensboro police department gave Lucky the screaming shivers. He could've gone his whole life without setting foot on the floors he'd last trod wearing handcuffs. Same lobby, same desk sergeant. Same gray walls.

A young lieutenant approached. "Right this way, Agent Harrison." At least he came as a guest this time, and not a new resident.No need for directions. The interrogation room where he'd spilled his guts about Victor hadn't moved.

Essence of Old Spice added a note of comfort to an otherwise nerve-wracking situation. Old Spice meant one thing, even without a visual: the boss. Lucky's escort opened a door and confirmed his suspicions. Walter. With Bo as a bonus.

"Are you sure you want to do this?" Walter stared through the two-way glass into the very interrogation room where Lucky once lost a game of Twenty Questions. He couldn't go back in time and change a damned thing. Normally Walter sat behind his desk. Today, he remained standing and nodded for Lucky to take the chair next to Bo.

"No. I don't want to, but I reckon I better anyway." Lucky clasped Bo's hand out of sight between the two chairs. Bo sat next to him, but not close enough. So much for Lucky's hard-assed demeanor. Seemed like someone got underneath his prickly exterior.

Three men sat at a table on the other side of the glass. Two he'd met in passing, one he knew. Or sort of did.

The years of hard living showed on Daytona's face. The youngest Lucklighter appeared older than Lucky and might pass for Lucky or Bristol at a distance. Same dirty blond hair. Same height, or lack thereof.

"He fucked me over," Daytona said, staring at his hands. "I was doing good, getting my life back on track." He clenched his hands together on the table. "Then he had to go and send me shit. He knew I wasn't strong enough to refuse."

Flat, emotionless words. The tone of a defeated man.

God, but Lucky's chest ached. It'd been Bristol in his room trying to kill him, right? But drug-addled as he'd been, maybe it could've been Day.

Damn, now his head hurt.

"I nearly died, got kicked out of college, lost my girlfriend. And campus security found the shit I hadn't used. Know how hard it is to get back on your feet after being busted and having possession on your record?" Daytona paused to take a sip of water from a plastic cup. "I hated him for it. Wanted to go after his sorry ass. But then he went to jail and that kinda evened things, ya know?"

The detectives said nothing. Daytona continued purging his anger. "Then he up and died. Seemed he'd straightened his ass out and worked with the Feds or something. Died a motherfucking hero." He buried his face in his hands. "I hated him for what he did, but he was still my brother."

Lucky didn't even realize he'd been squeezing Bo's hand with a death grip until Bo squeezed back.

"Mr. Lucklighter," one of the detectives prodded after too much dead air. "How did you find out Richmond still lived?"

"My brother Bristol told me. Said he'd seen the sonofabitch in the hospital bed. I went to find out for myself."

Shit. So the video showed Daytona.

"Where did you get the carfentanil?"

Daytona's head shot up. "Carfentanil? What's carfentanil?"

"The drug you injected into Richmond in a saline solution."

Lucky couldn't miss Daytona's trembling even through the glass and fifteen feet away. "I don't know what you're talking about. I went looking for Rich, wanted to talk to him, but he wasn't there."

The detectives glanced at each other. The talkier of the two asked, "What? You were observed going into his room."

"Wasn't me, I tell you. I got as far as the door, but he wasn't there. Someone said something about him dying, but I figured he'd lied once, he'd lie again. Then Bristol told me where they took him. I followed."

"Why did you follow your brother?"

"I done told you, I needed to talk to him. Needed to find out why. How could he do that to me?" The pure misery on Daytona's face tugged at heartstrings Lucky didn't often use.

All these years, the kid believed Lucky'd been the reason for his downfall.

"And you planned payback? You intended to murder him." Damn. Detectives at this precinct hadn't mellowed since Lucky's interrogation.

"What?" Daytona shot out of the chair. "Murder? I wasn't gonna kill him."

"We found a loaded .38 under the driver's seat of your car. That makes you a felon in possession of a gun."

"I don't know nothing about no gun." Years of dealing with professional liars, not to mention formal training in reading body language, taught a man a thing or two. Daytona spoke the truth—or his own version of truth.

"Mr. Lucklighter, do you realize why you're here?"

"For stealing Bristol's car, right?"

The two-way glass might stop Daytona from seeing him, but did nothing to shield Lucky's heart. He turned to Walter. "I want to speak to him."

Shuffling into the room bought Lucky some time, but not nearly enough. His mind still reeled when he came face to face with his youngest brother.

Daytona's eyes grew wide and he clutched the back of a chair when he saw Lucky. "Rich? Bristol said you were alive, but he's a lying son-of-a-bitch half the time. I can't believe it's really you! You're alive! Oh my God!"

"It..." Clearing his throat didn't dislodge the boulder cutting off Lucky's air. "It's me."

Daytona launched himself too quickly, and the detectives weren't fast enough to stop the redneck missile hell bent on a bear hug.

"Holy shit!" Lucky screamed. Direct hit to the gut! Bo and the detectives yanked Daytona back.

"Rich? What's going on?"

Lucky held his middle and stayed still until the stars stopped dancing behind his eyelids. Bo's arm around his waist helped him remain upright. Shit! That hurt!

"Why don't we all sit down?" Bo led Lucky to a chair.

Daytona froze in place, gaze riveted on Lucky. "Rich? Bro? You okay?"

Bo answered, saving Lucky the breath. "He gave your dad half his liver. He's still recovering."

"Oh. Oh!" Daytona's eyes went wide again. "It was you! That's what you were doing in the hospital."

"Yeah, it was me." Lucky tried not to fall into the chair. He grunted when his ass hit the seat.

"Mama said they found somebody." An angry glint came to Daytona's eyes. "Did she know all along you were alive?"

"No. Someone else contacted me." He'd never throw Charlotte under the bus. At least not until he figured out where Daytona stood.

Daytona took a step forward. Bo and the detectives stiffened. "I want to hug my brother, okay? I promise not to hurt him."

The detectives turned as one toward Lucky.

Lucky nodded. "Let him." Daytona couldn't have tried to kill him. No way, no how. No signs of guilt, no signs of lying.

The detectives backed off. Bo stayed. Daytona ignored them, squatted down, and wrapped his arms around Lucky. "God, Rich, I'm so glad you ain't dead." He cut off Lucky's air with the force of his embrace. Sobs wracked his body.

What now? Lucky raised a hand. Should he rub his brother's back? Pat? Oh, to hell with indecision and any pain. Damn, but he'd missed this little twerp—who'd grown up a lot. He tuned out both the ache in his middle and the ache in his heart and held on for dear life. The chance to be this close to Daytona might never happen again.

"Rich," Daytona blurted out, only to start bawling again.

"Sh... It's all right, brother. It's all right. Everything'll be okay." Lucky gazed over his brother's head. Bo shuffled close enough to place a comforting hand on Lucky's back.

For long moments they stayed in place, the only sounds Daytona's squalls. Gradually he quieted down enough for Lucky to make out his words. "I love you, bro. I hated you, or said I hated you, for years. But you're still my big brother. Now will you tell me why? I'd been clean for weeks."

Lucky lifted Daytona's chin with one finger and waited until they were eye to eye to answer. "I didn't. I only found out about the heroin when you told Charlotte on the phone a few weeks ago." And there he went, throwing her under the bus anyway.

"But it came from you. Your handwriting was on the card."

Lucky's throat burned. The guilty would pay dearly. "Day, why would I do such a thing?"

"He bought you a video game." Bo crouched to be on Daytona's level. "That's what he meant about your vice. Video games. Someone must've switched the package."

Daytona remained still. Eyes wide. Good. At least he listened.

Time for Lucky to make his case. "I sent my gift to you at the farm, not your dorm. Hell, at the time, I didn't know you'd already moved into your dorm."

Daytona crumpled. "Well, who else could it have been?"

Who else indeed? Bo rested one hand on Lucky's knee. God, the amount of support in one simple gesture. "While I'm all for getting to the bottom of this, we have a more pressing matter. Who tried to kill Lucky?"

"I forgot about that." Daytona shot to his feet. "The cops who brought me mentioned a video. Can... Can I watch?"

Bo nodded. "I'll see if it can be arranged."

Twenty minutes later, they sat in front of a laptop.

Lucky's over-wracked brain didn't shake out any more clues. The video started, showing Daytona in the hallway, pacing back and forth before poking his head into a room—presumably Lucky's hospital room. He stalked back down the hall.

The next clip, taken hours earlier by the time stamp, showed the same man entering the room. No, wait. Not the same man.

Daytona spoke for them all. "Aw, hell."

CHAPTER TWENTY

Lucky's heart battered his ribs. Until seeing the proof with his own eyes, he'd held out hope for a mistake or someone else from his past finally catching up. No one deserved this shit. Though the figure's face stayed hidden in shadows, the camera captured enough detail to make out the identity of the man who'd paid Lucky a visit.

Daytona staggered to his feet. Bo caught him and eased him down on a chair.

A bit of wriggling pulled Lucky's chair closer. He joined Bo in putting an arm around Day. Poor guy had to be wrung out.

"Why...? Why would Bristol do something like that? Why isn't he glad you're still alive?"

How in the world had Daytona endured so much crap in his life and remained naïve? Now wasn't the time to share hard facts about another Lucklighter. The kid had been through enough for one day. Lucky addressed the detectives. "The guy you're looking for is Bristol Lucklighter, like we suspected." To Daytona he said, "How is it you got ahold of Bristol's car?" It wasn't like the asshole to share his toys.

"He... he gave me the keys and asked me to pull it around to the hospital entrance."

"Had he ever let you drive his car before?" Not likely.

"Well... No." The Lucklighter crease appeared between Daytona's brows. "Used to say he'd kill me if I so much as looked at it, when he talked to me at all."

"And you weren't suspicious when he gave you the keys?"

"I assumed maybe he was being nice, Daddy being sick and all, and me finding out about you."

201

No one ever accused the Lucklighter boys of being too smart. "He set you up. Even pointed you in the right direction, didn't he?"

Daytona's silence spoke for him.

One of the detectives took charge. "I'm going to need a statement from you both."

Lucky clasped his brother's shoulder. "Sure."

The best view in the world might be the Greensboro Police Department's parking lot, which meant freedom. Stars overhead in a clear sky. Damn. Staying up late again. Exhaustion pressed down on him, leaving Lucky disoriented, or maybe it was a combination of exhaustion and painkillers.

Jimmy's Ford Escape easily blended with a dozen other cars, but his bright-as-morning-sun hair positively glowed from a street light's glare.

Bo kept pace two feet behind Lucky, offering quiet comfort.

"What happens now?" Daytona rammed his hands into his pockets, looking small and lost next to Jimmy.

"He takes you home." Lucky nodded toward the man he still wanted to call Nurse Andy. "But you can't say a word about any of this. Understand?"

Daytona sniffled and nodded.

One more hug, and Lucky sent his brother on his way. "We'll catch up later, I promise."

Daytona clung for a moment and shuffled off.

"I'll take good care of him." Jimmy patted Lucky's shoulder and gave him a half smile. "Give my regards to your sister." He slid beneath the steering wheel and slammed the door.

As if.

Daytona climbed in the other side of the SUV and waved when Jimmy drove them out of the parking lot.

Johnson leaned against her Jeep. "You ready to go? You know I hate not being home to tuck my kid in, but not being there to send him off to school sucks canal water." She might be there in time to make him an after-school snack.

"What about you?" Lucky stepped close enough to feel Bo's body heat.

"I gotta get back," Bo said. "You go on home with Loretta. I'm still working a case."

Oh. "So much for going home and showing you my scar. Tell me a die-hard biker like you finds scars sexy."

Bo nuzzled Lucky's nose. "I find your scars sexy. In fact, I find every single inch of you sexy." The quick brush of lips didn't come close to the kiss Lucky wanted, but...

"Hey, guys. I'm standing right here." Johnson tapped the toe of her shoe.

"And?" Lucky growled.

"And you don't want me telling you how cute you are, do you?"

Lucky didn't give a rat's ass who saw, or even if Johnson said the "c" word. He kissed his man. Might be the last time for a while.

"If I can't keep an eye on you..." Bo dug in his pocket and pulled out the dragon key ring.

Lucky clung to his talisman all the way home.

"We're here." Johnson pulled up outside the gate to Lucky's neighborhood, rolled down the window, and punched on the keys. The gate slid open.

"How the hell'd you get the code?"

Johnson managed a weary grin over her shoulder. "I learned from a hard-assed motherfucker who never let gates stand in his way."

Yes, she had. Damn.

She helped Lucky into the house and settled him on his bed. He'd never been this tired in his life. "Want me to strip you, or can you do it?"

The loose T-shirt and sweat pants ought to slide off easily enough, if Lucky didn't mind Johnson glimpsing his junk.

"You ain't got nothing I ain't seen before," she said, hands on hips.

"How do you know? Maybe I got a third nut or something."

"Oh! Call Guinness! Three balls, world's shortest dick." Johnson rolled her eyes toward the heavens and started whistling.

Okay, maybe he wouldn't be showing her anything new. But still... She'd never seen *his* junk before and wasn't going to. "I'm all right." And world's smallest dick, hell!

"Good." She trotted out of the room and returned a few minutes later with a glass of water and a bottle of pills. "Take one and get some rest. I'll be out in the living room if you need me."

Like he'd need her. He tried to take off his shirt. Ow! Okay, take the pill first, then tackle his clothes. On second thought, they weren't bothering him too much. A blanket would be nice. But impossible without help.

Ah, home in his own bed. Alone. With too much time to blame himself.

He took the pill. He'd hunker down in guilt later.

No matter how he tried, he couldn't get comfortable.

Johnson wanted to be friends? What use were friends if he didn't intend to use them? "Hey, Jo... Rett! I could use some help here!"

The woman who'd waltzed into his life, too stubborn to leave, came charging in. "What you need?"

"Help getting undressed, just don't stare at my junk, okay?"

Her lips twitched. "I'll do my best to restrain myself."

True to her word, she didn't linger and worked with efficient motions. She didn't even gasp at the Steri-Strip covered incision—much. "When do those come off?"

"When they fall off." Like hell would Lucky try to peel the damned things off again. Holy crap! Felt like being ripped back open.

"What did the doctor say?" Trust Johnson to go all Mom on him.

"The internal sutures dissolve on their own. Leave the Steri-Strip at least seven days. The operative words there are 'at least.'"

Rett stepped back, palms out. "Okay, okay. I get it. Don't touch your ouchie."

"Damn straight."

She pulled the covers up to Lucky's chin. "Tuck, tuck, tuck."

"What the hell?"

"It's what I tell Tyrone when I tuck him in at night. Makes him giggle. You settled now?"

"Yeah. But you go on home to your kid. I don't need any more help."

"Says the man who couldn't get his shirt off. Look, they cut you open a week ago. I can stick around for a few hours. Granny has Tyrone." She strode toward the door. "I'll be on the couch whether you like it or not."

"Rett?"

"Now I done told you—"

"The guest room is made up. Might as well get what sleep you can."

She nodded and turned out the light. The door snicked shut.

In a bed, all by himself, without even Moose and Cat Lucky for company, and no telling when Bo might get to come home.

But Lucky wasn't by himself. Not really. He had Bo, Rett, and Walter.

And also Mom, Charlotte, and Daytona.

He could live without Bristol.

Lucky sat at the kitchen table. Again. Alone. The neighbor's lawnmower buzzed next door—for the third time this week.

Maybe some kind of code for, *"Dude, what grass you have needs cutting."*

No grass cutting for Lucky for a few more weeks. Maybe he should get Charlotte to bring him a few goats. That'd make the neighbors talk.

His phone chimed with a text midway through his second cup of coffee: *At SNB Atlanta. Be home later—B.*

Bo? Home? Hallelujah! Lucky's definition of hell included the week since he'd kissed Bo goodbye and came home to lie in bed, watch TV, and fend off Johnson's hovering whenever she came to check on him.

Dishes sat piled in the sink, empty dog food bags hung half out of the trashcan, and the four chairs clustered under the table. Might be a good idea to spruce the place up.

He gave himself a sniff. Yeah, he could stand a trip through the shower too, because, hello! Sex! Finally! With more than his right hand. And this time he wouldn't fall asleep in the middle like yesterday after taking his meds.

Coming home to a messy house meant Bo cleaning and not getting naked.

Lucky straightened up, showered, and shaved. Still too many hours left before Bo got home, and he'd hear lectures from both Walter and Bo if he showed up at work.

He could wait until evening to get reacquainted with his man. Yes, he really could. Maybe he should get a few things at the grocery store for dinner.

The car cranked on the first try, so unlike a few months ago before Bo had the Camaro overhauled and painted for Lucky's Christmas present. The dragon dangling from his keyring swayed in time to the music on the radio and Lucky's off-key warbling.

Hmmmm... How'd he get to Peachtree Street? Must've taken a wrong turn. Well...since he was here...

Lucky parked in his usual spot, and took the elevator to the floor housing the Southeastern Narcotics Bureau. The door opened, and he peered around the corner. No Lisa. Good.

But also no Bo. Not in their shared cube, the break-room, or Walter's office. And also no Walter. Lisa emerged from the conference room and traipsed back to the reception desk.

So that's where everybody went. The conference room. Lucky eased inside the partially opened door. All heads were bent over laptops. Maybe they wouldn't notice...

Walter glanced up from a pile of papers in front of him with a scowl. "Have you been cleared to return to work?"

Bo popped his head up. "No. Now get your ass back home where you belong. You've only been back a week."

Seven long, torturous days, with nothing to do but worry, and wait for some word from his family. Calling Mom, Charlotte, or Daytona might jeopardize Bo's case.

"I belong here." Lucky leaned against the wall, out of Bo's swatting range.

Bo drummed his fingers on the table. "No, you don't."

"Yes, I do."

"No. You belong at home resting and getting better."

"And how am I supposed to rest knowing someone's out to kill me?" Ha! *Answer that one, Mr. I-know-better-what's-good-for-you-than-you-do.*

Walter waved a dismissive hand. "Stay, but as an observer."

"Now wait a da—"

"You'll abide by my rules or go home." Walter going all boss wasn't a good sign.

"Oh, all right." Lucky inched up the table to Bo. Bo flipped his laptop screen closed. Two rookies sat at the far end. Oh, the young ones. So easy to intimidate. Lucky eased into a chair between them. "What ya got?"

The first one made eye contact with Walter. Damn, a smart one.

The dumber of the two blurted, "Bristol Lucklighter's financial records."

They had a suspect, now they needed a motive. As though being an unrepentant asshole wasn't reason enough.Walter's glare dried up Lucky's only lead in the room. "Why won't you let me help?" he demanded.

"Because, I don't want to involve you until we have to, once we've gotten a better feel for the events. Remember, you're not supposed to be here." Walter heaved out a sigh. "Besides, this is your family, you're too close."

Yeah. The doctor put him out of work for six weeks, contingent on his checkups. He'd been cut open two weeks ago. Still hurt, but he'd been through worse. Lucky left the rookies and parked himself by Walter.

Walter said nothing, but didn't truly try to hide his reading material. Lucky lifted a sheet and read. Nothing out of the ordinary. Their suspect—best not to acknowledge him as "brother" right now—paid his bills, made a decent living, but didn't manage to save a dime.

Damn. He sure paid for a lot of insurance. Lucky jabbed a finger at the page. "What's this?"

"We already have someone chasing down leads." Walter snatched the paper back.

Bo glanced at Lucky and turned his attention to Walter. "I believe we might have found something. I'm e-mailing."

Walter opened his laptop, pushed a few buttons, and read the message. "I see. Keep looking."

Like hell would they exclude Lucky from his own attempted murder case. "What are you looking for?"

Did Walter growl?

"Okay, okay, I'm going!" Lucky stepped out into the hallway. More than one way to skin a cat. He ambled down to his cube and opened the laptop someone brought back home. The insurance records weren't hard to find. Hard to explain, but not hard to find. Why pay so much to insure a car? The man hadn't even owned a house at the time.

Lucky pecked away on the keyboard, sifting through data for something relevant. Interesting, not so interesting. *What have we here?*

Lucky'd nearly put his findings together when Bo stepped into the cube. "Thought I'd find you here. Boss wants you."

Maybe he'd found something, maybe he planned to make good on his threat to toss Lucky out of the building.

Bo stopped before the closed conference room door. He said nothing, merely took Lucky into his arms and held him close.

Spending a week in Bo's arms would make one hellacious vacation, but Lucky had questions, and the answers might be on the other side of the door. He'd take a raincheck on the holding.

He pushed open the door to his doom, heart skipping a beat. "You sent for me."

"Sit down." Walter shoved his fingers under his glasses and rubbed his eyes.

Lucky took a seat next to his boss.

"How much do you know about your brother in recent years?" Dark circles underscored the boss's eyes.

"He's a no-account asshole."

"From what I've seen," Walter waved at the pile of papers, "I'm inclined to agree. What else?"

"He liked to live high on the hog, as my grandparents might say. Why?"

Walter traded a look with Bo, who moved behind Lucky's chair and massaged Lucky's shoulders. Oh shit. Must be awful.

"Lucky, it seems Bristol Lucklighter loved his family very much," Walter began.

"What? Bristol? Bristol never cared about anyone but Bristol." Maybe Walter had the wrong Bristol Lucklighter.

"He did. He cared so much, in fact, that he carried a life insurance policy on each of you."

"He did what?" Lucky sprung out of his chair. Oh fuck! Ouch! He held his incision.

"It seems he even carried a policy on you, as sole beneficiary. When you died, he collected a half million dollars." The document on Walter's computer screen showed one hell of a lot of zeros.

"Sonofabitch." Lucky clutched his head to keep a sudden brilliant flash of the obvious from exploding his brain. "And he had one on Dad, too, didn't he?"

Walter punched a few keys and another form appeared. "Yes."

"'Sonofabitch' doesn't quite cover this one." Instead of

helping Dad, the bastard hoped the man would die so he could line his pockets.

"Now we have our motive. Your being alive makes things inconvenient for a man who'd cashed in your life insurance policy. Especially when he appears to be broke."

The big house, the fancy car. All paid for by a dead brother. But... "Go back farther."

"Already on it," one of the rookies spoke from down the table. "Here it is. A policy for Daytona Lucklighter, taken out fifteen years ago."

About the time the kid started messing with drugs. "He tried to kill Daytona and pin it on me."

Walter nodded. "A decent theory."

"Not only did he want Daytona's insurance money, he'd always wanted to be the oldest son. He couldn't stand me being the oldest." Twisted little bastard.

"But how do we prove he gave Daytona the drugs?" Bo went back to massaging Lucky's shoulders.

Walter frowned at his empty coffee cup. "We need to interview Daytona Lucklighter again."

Lucky waited at the house, pacing the living room. At long last, Bo pulled into the drive. Good. He started the tea maker for Bo's green tea and pulled a casserole dish out of the microwave. Chinese takeout, but still, Lucky did put dinner on the table.

He'd even gone to Mrs. Griggs and the Smiths' to get the pets and put Moose in the backyard until after they ate.

The day took its toll. Lucky sagged down into a chair.

Any minute Bo would come in, they'd have dinner, and he'd reacquaint himself with every inch of his lover's body.

And then grill him about the case.

Yeah, sounded like a plan.

"Lucky? Lucky!"

"Huh?" Lucky raised his head. How'd he gotten his face into a plateful of chow mein?

"Lucky, you're dead tired. Go to bed." Bo mopped at Lucky's face with a paper towel.

"What?"

"You fell asleep in your food. Go to bed."

"Don't wanna. Not without you." He still owed Bo one for stealing his clothes, and oh the creative ways he'd take his payback. When he worked up enough energy.

"Come on, then, I'll go with you." Bo guided Lucky to the bedroom, eased him down on the bed, and proceeded to strip him.

"Oh! Getting me naked so you can have your way with me, right?" Lucky's dick tried to rally but didn't get very far.

"Yeah. I'm going to take advantage of a man too exhausted to eat."

"Give me a minute, I'll be okay." And he would be too, especially with Bo stretched out beside him. "You're wearing too many clothes."

"Are you sure you're up to this?" Bo examined the Steri-Strip over Lucky's incision.

"Yup, I'm sure." Oh, hell, yeah!

Bo stood, wearing a playful smile and fewer clothes by the minute. What a body. What a cock. What a...

Lucky woke up with the sun streaming through the window, an empty bed, and a note: *Walter called me in. Said it was important. I'll let you know what time I'm coming home.*

Damn it!

Lucky tiptoed by the SNB reception desk even though Lisa wasn't there to question his being at work, and hauled ass for the SNB conference room. Bo, Walter, the rookies, Jimmy, and Daytona occupied chairs around the central rectangular table.

Daytona? Here?

"Oh, Lucky. Right on time." Trust Walter to pretend nothing happened by accident.

Lucky nodded and planted his ass halfway between Bo and Daytona. They played questions and answers, Lucky keeping his mouth shut at a narrow-eyed glower from Bo. Yeah, observer. Not his case.

During a break, Daytona asked, "So, it really wasn't you?" He appeared more his old self, less haggard, less pressed down by the weight of the world.

"To be honest, I'm kinda put out you ever believed I'd tempt you, after all you'd gone through. Come on, would I spend that kind of money on a twerp like you?" How easy old habits came back. Lucky teased Daytona, but gently. The kid used to run to Mama quicker'n shit.

Daytona chuckled and smiled for the first time since their recent reunion. "Nah. You wouldn't. I'm glad. I've missed you."

Lucky fought the flinch when his brother grabbed him too tightly.

When Daytona pulled back, his eyes glistened.

More time to catch up later. Right now they had a case to build. "We got a problem to figure out," Lucky said.

"What?"

"I didn't send you the drugs, but who did?" No need telling the kid about Bristol's penchant for insuring relatives.

Daytona squared his shoulders. "Easy enough. And I should've figured this out too."

"What?"

"Bristol sent me a birthday present the same year you did, the only one he ever gave me." Daytona tapped his fingertips on the table.

Walter ambled down to their end of the table. "What did he give you?"

"The video game I'd been wanting."

Sunlight gave way to shadows in the conference room when Walter finally called it a day, amid empty soda cans, coffee cups, and pizza boxes. Lucky pitied housekeeping.

"Are you sure you can't stay?" Even not at his best, he'd put on a burst of energy for his kid brother. "We got an extra room."

Daytona hung his head. "I'm afraid I can't."

Jimmy rose from his chair and rounded the table to join Lucky and Daytona. "It's imperative to our case that Bristol finds out nothing. Daytona returned his car and said he couldn't find you. Even so, long absences might get attention."

"In the meantime, Lucky, you'll continue to be watched." Walter made his presence known, his glare warning Lucky against arguing.

Lucky never had been one to heed warnings. "Not the rookie from IT again." Nothing subtle about Keith's latest protégé. "Bo'll be there. Why can't he watch me?"

Bo stayed silent.

Oh, hell. "You won't be here."

"I have to be back to Richmond first thing Monday morning, so I need to head out Sunday." Bo finally glanced up, lips pursed and lines showing around his mouth. Damn, but now would be a fine time for an appearance of The Dimple, and, *"Just kidding! I never have to leave you again!"*

No brother, no lover. Alone with the pets.

"Take care of yourself, bro." Day gave Lucky an enthusiastic hug and traipsed along after Jimmy out of the room.

"I'll be in my office if you need me." Walter gave the rookies his well-practiced, over-the-top-of-his-glasses glare. "You may continue working in your cubes." Wow. Nicest "get the hell out of here" Lucky'd ever heard. The rookies shot out the door.

Walter closed the door behind him, leaving Lucky alone with Bo. Lucky strolled over to the window slowly, listening for Bo's footsteps. In the distance, Stone Mountain kept watch over the city of Atlanta.

Once he'd walked up behind Bo here, put his arms around his man as Bo did now to Lucky. Lucky leaned back into the embrace.

"Hell of a time for you to have to leave. Can't they reassign you back down here?" Tonight, Lucky wouldn't fall asleep too soon. He might not be ready to run marathons, but he could... do something. Needed something. Before he exploded from lack of sex.

Bo brushed his lips against Lucky's temple. "I have to. Gotta finish what we started. Then I'll be home."

And forevermore one of them would leave, and the other stay, tossing and turning at night and worrying, visualizing their lover's face on the SNB memorial page.

"I don't like you being gone all the time. Or me neither." They'd done very little living together since deciding to live together.

"I know. But it's only for a little while."

"You can't know that. Little whiles have a way of turning into big whiles." Or really big whiles.

Bo ruffled Lucky's hair with his sigh. "What can I do? I have a job. A case. You better than anyone should understand."

"I understand and don't like it. Is this how the rest of our lives will be? Always apart for some case or other." Not the vision of picket-fence domestic bliss Bo claimed to want.

"We've done our time. Nothing's making us stay here." They could find other jobs. Do something not requiring being shot at, or shot up.

"We're good at what we do, and do we even know how to do anything else?"

Lucky did—mostly illegal stuff. "You got a college degree."

"I could never go back into a pharmacy. You know that. And pharma companies wouldn't be a good bet, either."

No, they wouldn't. Not with all the temptation they'd offer a recovering addict. "Just the same. I don't like you being gone. I don't like the dangerous work you do."

Bo snorted. "And your work isn't dangerous?"

"Not anymore, unless some overexcited rookie misses a target and shoots me. And being raised redneck taught me how to duck." Bo wanted kids. Maybe Lucky did too. Wouldn't be fair to bring a child into their unstable lives.

Bo answered with kisses on the back of Lucky's neck.

Lucky turned. Rising on his toes might hurt, so he stayed still, summoning Bo down to his height.

Bo opened his mouth for Lucky's tongue, moaning when they connected. The scent of him, the feel of him in Lucky's arms—oh God, he needed Bo now.

Anyone might walk in, but getting caught during an intimate moment didn't matter. Lucky ran his fingers up Bo's arms, resting his hands on Bo's broad shoulders. So familiar, yet so new at the same time. Their moans mingled, vibrating through their joined tongues.

Lucky traced Bo's jawline with his fingertips, the slightly crooked nose, a day's worth of stubble adding interest. He stepped close enough to rub his cock against Bo's leg through their pants.

Bo clutched him tighter, just shy of painful. A moment later pain couldn't reach him, only Bo's hand, climbing up under his shirt, knuckles teasing Lucky's nipples.

The meeting of tongues and bodies continued. They shouldn't be doing this here, but right now Lucky couldn't remember why.

Bo pulled back, a bit breathless. "Let's go home. It's been too long."

"I don't know how much good I'll be." For Bo, Lucky would crawl through broken glass.

"All you gotta do is be there."

Worked for Lucky.

He didn't even have to stop by the cube to get his laptop, but he waited while Bo got his. Leaving his computer here gave him reason to sneak back into the office if needed. Together Lucky and Bo trudged down the hall to the elevator.

Lisa winked from behind the reception desk. "Good to have you back, guys."

Bo nodded. Lucky lacked energy for words.

They stepped onto the elevator. The moment the doors slid shut, Bo attacked, much like Lucky's ambushes during Bo's rookie year.

Mouth, neck, chin, forehead: Bo caressed them all in an open-mouthed kiss, one hand on Lucky's back burning a hole through his shirt, the other cupping Lucky's hardness through too-damned-in-the-way pants.

Without looking, Bo slapped the panel behind him. The elevator stopped. No telling what kind of cameras the IT geeks installed.

Let 'em watch.

Lucky wound up with his back against the wall. He let out a grunt.

"Oh, God. I'm so sorry. Did I hurt you?" Concern filled Bo's eyes.

"Nope. And tell me you'll pick this up at home." No condoms! Hallelujah! No condoms!

The Dimple appeared. "Let's try not to break any speed limits."

Despite Bo's warning, they got home in record time. Speeding? Gunning the Camaro through yellow lights? Well... Maybe.

But risking a ticket might be worth the lip lock Bo laid on him right inside the front door. He nearly jerked the blinds off the windows getting them closed, and slowed down when helping Lucky strip.

As reverent as a worshipper, Bo removed Lucky's shirt and urged him down on the couch. Lucky gripped the arm to keep the couch from flipping backwards as it'd done before.

On his knees, Bo wriggled off first one of Lucky's shoes, then the other, brought Lucky's feet to his mouth, and placed a kiss on the instep of each. Slowly, so slowly, he removed both socks, his grin promising so many bad, wicked, totally amazing things.

He reared back, rolling his shirt up over the lean muscles of his chest, yanked the cotton knit over his head, and tossed the SNB uniform shirt to the floor.

Somehow he managed to unbutton and unzip his pants, and have them off in two seconds flat. No professional

216

strip-tease, just the unveiling of all his glorious flesh. Boxers, socks, shoes... all discarded in a pile on the floor.

Who was this man, and what had he done with Lucky's neat-freak lover?

Bo lowered his head and trailed gentle kisses around Lucky's incision. "There. All better, right?"

Nope, but wrap those lips around Lucky's cock, and give him a distraction.

Lucky ran his fingers up tight abs and around Bo's side, drawing him close enough to bathe Bo's warm skin with his tongue, and caress his erection.

"Up!" Lucky motioned with his hand. *Up! Up!*

Bo stood again, and Lucky swiped his tongue over the head of Bo's cock, lingering over the tasty drops of pre-come. Hot damn. The scent, taste, feel, all brought Lucky too close to the edge for someone barely getting started.

Bo straddled Lucky's thighs and ground his wonderfully round ass onto Lucky's so-hard-it-ached cock. He could lap dance on Lucky any damned time.

Perfect.

Bo turned and knelt. Mouth to mouth, cock to cock, sliding, gliding, thrusting... A helluva reunion.

Somebody should be inside someone else, but damned if having Bo against him didn't feel too good to move. Lucky wedged his hand between their bodies and captured both of their cocks. Bo joined the task, and they stroked together, skimming their tongues against each other's in time with their humping.

Smooth skin, coarse hair, bunching muscles, part and parcel of Bo. Harder, faster...

"I'm gonna blow," Lucky muttered against Bo's lips.

"Do it."

Lucky let go, falling over the edge of ecstasy and taking Bo with him.

Oh my God! Lucky gritted his teeth and clutched his middle. OW!

Bo kissed away the hurt.
And then some.

CHAPTER TWENTY-ONE

The doorbell yanked Lucky out of his post-sex stupor. Moose barked from the backyard. The sun shone in through the sliding glass doors.

Damn! They'd slept all night on the couch? "Fuck! We didn't feed Moose and the cat!"

Bo, lying half on the couch and half off, cracked open one eye. "I did. And... umm... cleaned us both up a bit." He jumped up, tugged on yesterday's pants, helped Lucky into his T-shirt and jeans, and kicked their boxers, shoes and socks under the couch.

Really? Bo pulling a *"Lucky's method of cleaning?"*

The doorbell rang again.

"Coming!" Bo shouted.

Lucky snorted. "Not at the moment, but you will. Later." Oh, yes, Lucky was back. Maybe. Sorta.

Bo scowled, stalked towards the entry, and flung the door open.

Walter filled the doorframe. "I hope I'm not interrupting. I came to update you."

Bo stepped aside. Walter crossed the floor in a few long strides and sank into a chair across from the couch.

Oh, dear God. Someone kill Lucky now. Couch sex followed by an appearance of the boss might haunt his dreams.

Moose whined and scratched his paws again the glass doors. Walter smiled indulgently at the furry beast.

The traitorous dog beelined straight for Walter, tongue lolling, the moment Bo opened the door.

"I'll go make coffee." Bo disappeared into the kitchen.

219

Coward.

Walter idly rubbed Moose's head. When he stopped scratching, Moose head-butted his hand. Demanding cuss. Boss had probably spoiled the critter while pet sitting. "We have the reports, the video of your brother entering your room, and the evidence the Richmond office sought on his associates. An arrest warrant has been issued."

Bristol? About to be arrested? Lucky chewed his lower lip. "I want to be there."

His boss scowled. "You're off duty, and this is a job for local law enforcement."

"But what if they screw up and he gets away?" All this time Lucky had been the black sheep, rotting away in prison when Mr. Goody-Two-Shoes deserved to be there too. But he'd better pay the piper now, and stay the hell away from Lucky's nearest and dearest.

"Have some faith."

Moose rolled over for a tummy rub.

Bo strode into the living room, loaded down with coffee cups. The man still waited on Lucky hand and foot.

Time for Lucky to work on being a better partner. "Thanks," he said, prompting a double-take from Bo.

"Excuse me?"

"Thanks. Thanks for the coffee."

Bo kept suspicious eyes on Lucky. Yeah. Lucky had some groveling to do. Starting the moment he could move painlessly.

"Not that I'm not happy to see you, but why are you here? You could've called us." Bo handed Walter a cup and settled next to Lucky on the couch.

"One, to keep Lucky from finding a way to interfere with this case—"

"Hey! Wait a darned minute." It'd been Lucky's case. Well, sorta. Being the victim counted, right?

Bo glared Lucky's way. "What's two?"

"I'm expecting word that Bristol Lucklighter has been taken into custody, and I believed this news best shared in person. After all, he is Lucky's brother." Walter patted the only dog in the neighborhood built in perfect proportion to his mass. "I also wanted to visit Moose. My wife and I became quite attached while he stayed with us."Chiming sounded from the vicinity of Walter's pants pocket, and he dug his cell phone out. "Walter Smith. Yes." He eyed Lucky. Every bit of expression disappeared from his face. "Oh, I understand. No one else was involved?" Silence followed. "Yes, please do."

He hung up the phone, lips pursed. After a moment he rose, crossed the distance to the couch, and sank down beside Lucky.

"He got away, didn't he?" Lucky should've been there. Should've taken matters into his own hands.

Walter placed his hand on Lucky's. "No, he didn't."

"Then what?" Why all the dramatics to say Bristol got arrested?

"Officers knocked on his door to serve the warrant. There was no answer. They found the backdoor open, and your brother... well, they found your brother in the basement."

"And?"

"Lucky, I'm afraid your brother is dead."

What the hell? "How?" Surely Lucky hadn't woke up yet. This must be a dream. A horrible fucking dream. He didn't like Bristol, but he'd never wanted him dead.

"That's for the coroner to decide. Suicide hasn't been ruled out, nor has homicide. There are reasons to believe he didn't die of natural causes." Walter patted Lucky's shoulder. "I'm so sorry."

"Why? Why don't they think natural causes?" Bristol, three years younger than Lucky. Too young to die.

"I wasn't given full details. You heard a bit of the conversation."

Maybe boss told the truth, maybe he lied. Either way, nothing anyone said or did would change a thing.

***

221

Who smacked him upside the head with a two by four? Lucky's head spun. Mama. He should call Mama. And Charlotte. Make sure they were okay. But... They were home with Daddy, and Dad didn't know about Lucky living and breathing yet. And until the coroner's report came back, they might still be facing a homicide. Who'd want to kill Bristol? Was the rest of the family in danger? Fuck. Trust Walter to come in here, drop a bomb, then stroll back out. No, not fair. Boss man hadn't known about Bristol's death when he arrived.

"Look, Lucky. I'm sorry about your brother." Bo took the spot recently vacated by Walter and pulled Lucky toward him.

"I'm not sure if I am or not. This is so fucked up."

Bo nodded. "I know. And it's a lot to take in. But I'm here if you need to talk."

Talk. The last thing Lucky wanted right now. Maybe doing something normal might calm Lucky down. "C'mon, let's get a bath."

Bo secured Lucky in a tighter embrace. "I'm not dirty."

"I can fix that."

Bo's resigned sigh had to be a good thing, right? "Okay. A bath, nothing more."

Spoilsport.

Bo fished their underwear out from under the couch and stepped toward the hallway. Lucky stopped him. "I'll start the water."

Bo froze midmotion. "Why?"

"Why what?"

"Why are you doing it?"

"Because I can and I want to." *Because it gives me something to do to keep my mind off Bristol, and it's about time I started treating you right.*

But no. Bo ran when he most needed a hug, didn't let Lucky help shoulder the burden. He wouldn't do the same to Bo. "I'm worried. About you, the family. Gut instinct tells me we're dealing with something much bigger than we ever imagined."

Bristol tried to kill Lucky. Had Lucky's powerful friends played judge and jury?

"You know I'm not at liberty to give you details of my case, but yes, I agree with you." Bo stood by the couch, socks and boxers dangling from his hands.

Lucky steadied himself with a hand on Bo's arm and wriggled off the couch. "I don't want you going back there."

"I have to." Bo leaned down, pressing his forehead to Lucky's.

Lucky nodded. "I know you do. But I don't have to like it. And I can't stop worrying."

"I've gotten to know the crew at the Virginia office. They're good agents." One side of Bo's mouth quirked up in a half-smile. "Not as good as you, but they have my back, and I have theirs. Not only do I have a case to solve, I have teammates I can't let down."

Oh hell. "You're not planning on staying there after this is over, are you?" Surely Bo wouldn't take the offer to turn his temporary assignment into a permanent one, as Walter had mentioned.

"No. My life is here. With you. And I'm doing all I can to put the pieces together and come home. Where I belong." Bo sealed his words with his lips over Lucky's.

Lucky's throat burned. He blinked suddenly blurry eyes and ran his hand over Bo's lightly stubbled cheek. "I—" No, words wouldn't do. He'd have to show Bo how much he wanted him, needed him.

Loved him.

He rubbed his lips against Bo's and trudged into the bathroom. Bending to start the water wasn't too much of a problem, but lifting his arms over his head to remove his T-shirt still sent a twinge through the incision site.

"Here. Allow me." Bo rescued him from himself, making short work of the shirt. He'd already stripped off his own clothes, cheating Lucky out of the chance. No use grumbling. Not with a naked Bo around.

223

Lucky ran his hand over Bo's ass and laid his head on Bo's chest. The scent of him, the scratch of his chest hair against Lucky's face, the bunching of muscles beneath Lucky's fingertips. He'd never get enough of this man.

He turned the water off and arranged himself on the side of the tub—no getting his incision wet yet. Bo lowered himself into the water.

Lucky explored his lover's face with caresses and kisses. Sucked on an earlobe and the sensitive meeting point of Bo's shoulder and neck.

Bo moaned, but didn't stop him. Lucky carried on, nibbling on Bo's shoulders, working his way down to lightly bite the peaks of Bo's nipples. Lower, and lower still, but the parts he wanted remained out of reach.

"Sit on the side," Lucky urged.

Bo did as told without arguing.

Lucky turned off the water and got on his knees in the tub, with the water up to his thighs. He licked a path from Bo's knees to his groin, pausing to discreetly scrub a hair off his tongue. And still Bo didn't stop him. He tongued Bo's balls. Damn, what a cock, hard and full, just the way Lucky liked.

"You don't have to do any more," Bo murmured.

"Yes, I do." Lucky lowered Bo's foreskin and licked the head of his lover's cock. A single drop of fluid coated his tongue. Poor, neglected man. While Lucky had been in pain and unable to have sex, Bo had been healthy and doing without, with not a single word of complaint.

He didn't hurry, but took his time, pouring all he couldn't say into the careful reverence of Bo's erection, using his mouth, his hands, his breath.

Bo bit his lips and rocked, but didn't thrust, grasping the side of the tub in a white-knuckled grip.

Lucky swiped his tongue around the sensitive glans, down the side, leaving no part of Bo's flesh uncared for. Up and down he bobbed, the water sloshing around his thighs.

Bo fell back against the wall and gripped the towel bar above his head.

Lucky stroked himself.

Eyes closed, head thrown back, Bo released the bar to cradle the back of Lucky's head and silently urge him on.

Lucky put his all into loving Bo, expressing his appreciation for his man with every tongue stroke.

And increased the pace of his hand.

Bo lost the battle not to thrust. He arched up, muscles straining. "Ah... Ah..." The back of his head hit the wall the moment he let go, filling Lucky's mouth.

And damned if Bo's coming didn't tip Lucky over the edge.

Lucky tensed, any second now. Oh, one second more... He jerked, warm fluid coating his fingers as he came. And came. And came. So fucking good. He toppled onto Bo, totally winded, and buried his face in Bo's neck. Laughter escaped him.

"What's so funny?" Bo lifted Lucky's chin with two fingers.

"Nothing. Everything." How to explain the joy of life, of looking the grim reaper in the eye so many times and walking away? The total absurdity of the past few weeks. Too much to take.

The laugher grew harsher, more of a cry. Lucky held Bo, sobbing. Bristol. Why? He might have been an asshole, he might have tried to kill Lucky, but he'd been kin. Lucky's brother. God, it hurt.

"Shh..." Bo held him, wrapped Lucky in comfort he didn't deserve and never wanted to live without.

He cried for his parents, who'd lost a son, for his other brothers and sister. For his grandparents. They shunned him, sure. But they weren't bad people. And they'd lost one of their own. No telling how yet.

Bo ran a wet washcloth over Lucky's skin, staying away from his abdomen, washing him, caring for him. Lastly, he washed the salt and tears from Lucky's face, kissed him. Let him know without words, *I'm here for you.*

The water cooled. Lucky shivered.

"C'mon. Let's get out of here." Bo reached beneath Lucky's armpits and lifted.

They toweled off and wound up in the bedroom. Lucky sank down onto the bed.

Bo remained standing. "I need to get packed if I'm leaving tomorrow."

I don't need reminding. Lucky batted his eyes. "You keep telling me to rest, right? I'll sleep better with you beside me. We'll worry about the morning when it gets here."

"Oh, all right. But take your medicine."

Lucky lay on the bed, Bo in his arms. He woke up long enough to down a sandwich and watch a few episodes of *South Bend Springs* with Bo.

Today. He had today.

CHAPTER TWENTY-TWO

Lucky waited until Bo started snoring to wriggle out from under his arm and slip from the room. He settled on the back deck, Moose playing footstool, and texted: *Charlotte?*

I'm here. Barely.

How could he say this? *Are you okay? Are Mom and Dad okay?*

Lucky stared at his phone's screen. Seconds stretched into minutes. Too many minutes. Maybe Charlotte went to sleep.

Lucky nearly dropped his buzzing phone before managing to answer the call. "H... Hello?"

"We talk on the phone now, Rich. I'm numb, Mom's doing as well as can be expected and putting on a front 'because we haven't told Dad, Dallas, or Daytona about Bristol yet."

"I'm sorry."

"Why are you sorry? You didn't put a gun to Bristol's head and make him do illegal shit."

Anger. Loud and clear. Lucky's therapist once told him about the stages of grief: denial, anger, bargaining, depression, and acceptance. The venom in Charlotte's voice said she'd passed denial a few miles back.

"Still, I'm sorry. I've given y'all nothing but grief. At least you had a few good years with him."

"Bullshit. Do you have any idea how much my boys look up to you? You've accomplished more starting with less than anyone I know. Less support, less understanding. You've built yourself when no one ever even mentioned there were building blocks." More softly, she said, "Just knowing you're there and have my back is helping me get through this. Mom too."

227

"Reckon I should talk to her?"

"She's still in denial. The doctor prescribed sedatives for her. I'd wait a few days."

"I want her to know I love her. Daddy too. I'm here for them." Or as much as they'd let him be.

"She knows, Rich. She knows. But no mother should ever have to lose a kid. She's taking it hard, as she did when we got word about you."

Ouch. More deserved guilt. "Will you let me know if she needs anything? If you need anything?"

"You gave us Daddy, that's enough."

"Still, I wish I was there." If Bo and Walter let him he'd haul ass right now.

"Me too, Rich. I'm sure there's things I'm not allowed to know yet, but you'll get the whole story, won't you?"

"I'll do my damnedest."

"And your damnedest beats anyone else's. I love you, brother. I'm so glad I can say that out loud, and not in a text or e-mail."

"I love you too."

"Goodnight. Get some rest."

Lucky gazed up at the stars and breathed in the night air. Soon summer would bring heat and mosquitos. And hopefully, a day for reckoning for whoever supplied Bristol with carfentanil.

He couldn't be with his parents right now, or the rest of his family, but the family he'd chosen for himself lay asleep inside the house.

Too late to be a better son or brother. Not too late to be a good partner.

"What are you doing?" Did Bo realize how adorable he looked, partly covered by a sheet and rubbing sleep from his eyes?

"What does it look like I'm doing?" Lucky sat the tray on the nightstand. He'd gotten the toast a bit dark, but blackberry jam hid the worst of the burn.

"You made me breakfast?"

"Yep." Even if he'd gotten tea leaves all over the kitchen floor trying to shove them into one of those little tea ball thingies. Breakfast didn't require grilling outside and amounted to pretty much all Lucky'd learned to cook indoors.

"You didn't have to. You should be lying in bed with me taking care of you. How're you feeling?" Bo ran his fingers lightly up Lucky's T-shirt, over the spot where he'd been cut open.

Bo had The Dimple, Lucky had The Scar. "All right, I reckon. Now hush and eat, 'fore it gets cold."

Bo eyed the tray and then Lucky. "What did you do?"

"What do you mean?"

"Why're you trying to butter me up?"

Oh! What a great idea. Butter. Or cooking oil. He'd soak Bo until his skin gleamed...

"Lucky? Your mind plunged into the gutter, didn't it?"

Ever since he'd healed enough to consider sex, Lucky's mind stayed in the gutter. "But butter might be fun."

"Yeah, and hell to wash out of the sheets. So, if you don't have ulterior motives, I guess it's okay to eat this." Bo propped his back against the headboard, placed the tray on his knees, and took a bite of scrambled eggs. "Oh, this is good. Where's yours?"

"I ate mine while cooking." And to destroy the evidence of a few scorched eggs. Okay, more than a few, but nothing destroyed food evidence like their own personal four-legged garbage disposal. Thank God Lucky got the severely burnt toast out in the backyard without setting off the smoke alarm.

Bo tucking in did Lucky's heart good. How many times had Bo served him breakfast in bed, and yet this was the first time Bo got the same treatment?

Not anymore. Did the desire to please his partner mean Lucky had to be all sunshine and rainbows? No. And he'd never been anyone's idea of perfect—not even close. But he could try harder.

229

Bo moaned while munching the toast and jam, doing things to Lucky's insides.

And his outsides. One part in particular. If Bo licked his finger one more time...

He did, flashing a coy smile. Oh. The tease.

Lucky grabbed the tray and lobbed it toward the bedside table. They both winced at the crash when he missed. He'd worry about broken dishes later. About time they got rid of the "yours, mine, and ours" dinnerware anyway.

He crawled on top of Bo.

"Watch out for your incision."

Lucky slammed his mouth down on Bo's and stopped. No. This wasn't going to be some whiz, whirr, thank you, sir. He pulled back enough to connect his gaze to Bo's. He'd fallen into those brown eyes long ago, though he hadn't even realized at the time he'd never want to escape.

"Are you sure you're up for this? I mean, we went two rounds last night, and I need to head back to Richmond today." Bo stroked his knuckles along Lucky's jaw.

Don't go noble on me now, Bo. Lucky pasted on a grin and thrust his hardening cock against Bo's thigh. "What does the evidence tell you?"

Bo connected their lips again. "You're wearing too many clothes," he mumbled without breaking lip contact.

"So I am." And Lucky would try his damnedest to get his T-shirt up and cut-off blue jeans shorts down and off without ending the kiss.

The doorbell ringing broke them apart. Who could be here be at this hour? And how'd they get through the gate—though Walter certainly hadn't had a problem yesterday.

Couldn't be one of the neighbors. His forceful refusal of Miss Tupperware's plastic ware party invitation pretty much put an end to people stopping by unannounced.

"You stay here. I'll get it." Bo shimmied out from under Lucky.

Like hell he would. Bo wrapped himself in a robe and
230

Lucky pulled his shorts back on, complete with .38 hidden behind his back. They stood together when Bo opened the door.

Walter waited on the porch, dressed in a shirt, tie, and jacket. "May I come in?"

Bo stepped aside. No need asking how he'd gotten through the gate. He had his ways.

Bo and Lucky trailed Walter into the living room. If he stopped by this early on a Sunday morning, before church, whatever he had to say must be urgent.

Walter sat down in the chair he'd claimed as his own. Bo and Lucky took the couch, with Lucky sliding his gun down between two cushions. "What's this about, Boss?" Cat Lucky slunk into the room, gave Walter baleful eyes, and disappeared into the hallway out of sight.

"I received a full report from the Richmond office."

Lucky traded glances with Bo. "And?"

"And the initial toxicology report confirmed the cause of your brother's death. As many have suspected, he died of an opioid overdose."

Overdose. The same way he'd tried to kill Daytona—and Lucky. "Anything else?" Focusing on the case might keep Lucky from dwelling on the loss of his brother. Bristol was an asshole, true, but also a Lucklighter.

"Richmond police removed heroin, fentanyl, and carfentanil from his basement, along with scales, glassine packets, and other related items. We're also checking out reports of the overdose death of a young woman who might have purchased tainted heroin from him."

"Fuck." Lucky scrubbed a hand through his hair. "Bristol ran a full-scale packaging operation."

"I believe you're correct. And if you hadn't uncovered his secrets, they might never have been known." Moose ambled in and dropped his head down on Walter's lap. Walter fondled his ear. He'd be brushing dog hair off his clothes later. "You had an uncle named Edward Lucklighter?"

"Yeah. Uncle Ned."

"Were you close?"

"Not really." Not at all.

"It's seems your brother's plan to profit from the deaths of others didn't end after he tried to kill Daytona."

Oh God. What now? "What are you saying? His obituary said Uncle Ned died of natural causes."

"Only because no one felt the need to perform an autopsy. And since he was cremated, there's no body to exhume and test now." Walter's shoulders sagged, and shadows darkened the skin beneath his eyes. "Guess who benefitted from his life insurance policy?"

CHAPTER TWENTY-THREE

What a shitty couple of weeks. Brother tried to kill him, possibly killed an uncle for money, Bo packed and left without goodbye sex, Walter banished Lucky from the office until the doctor cleared him to return to work, and now this.

Lucky stared down at the back deck and a suspiciously squirrel-shaped bundle of fur. Moose's tongue lolled out of his mouth and if his tail wagged any harder the mutt might get whiplash.

"Did you do that?" Lucky pointed at Moose's kill.

Wag, wag, wag. Damn, hard to stay mad at a pooch with an "I saved you from a dangerous beast" vibe going on.

Lucky took care of the dead squirrel, let the unrepentant Moose in, and flopped down on the couch to watch some TV. Nothing on this channel. Nothing on the next either. Or the next.

Nope. Not one of those crime-solving shows. *Click.* Real surgeries? Oh, *hell* no.

He paced, cleaned the kitchen, took out the trash.

What kind of assignment had the Richmond office given Bo? Was he in danger?

Bo worked for the SNB. Of course he was in danger.

Undercover. No calls and no telling when they'd see each other again.

Lucky plopped down on the couch. Life couldn't get any worse.

The cat hopped up on the couch.

And dropped a dead mouse on Lucky's lap.

"How are you, Mama?" Lucky sat on the living room couch, staring out the sliding glass doors at a rainy June day.

"Doing as good as I can. Charlotte's boys are here now, helping out pretty good for two young'uns not raised in the country."

"If you need me to..."

"Richmond, you've gone above and beyond already, and just had surgery. Clarence is getting better slowly, and if you're going through the same thing, rest, get better."

"But I want to be there." If Lucky closed his eyes, his mother's kitchen filled his memory, and if he tried real hard he might catch a whiff of bacon or blackberry jam.

"I know you do, son." Mama held something back.

"You haven't told Daddy, have you?"

Silence, then, "The time isn't right yet. He's still recovering, and then what with Bristol and all, and the cops keeping us quiet about his death."

Calling home didn't soothe Lucky's soul like he'd hoped. "Mama, I want to see him again."

"And you will. Give it more time."

At this rate, Lucky might never truly have his family back. But if things didn't start going better soon, he might go crazy and take the rest of the world with him.

Lucky flipped through a magazine, without reading, keeping an eye on the receptionist. The waiting room hadn't changed in all the time he'd been coming to counseling. He'd missed a few appointments while having his insides carved out and growing new organs.

Soft music played, to go with the soft lighting. Soothing, designed to calm patients and get them ready to offer up details of their lives they'd sworn to never tell.

The door behind the reception desk opened. "Mr. Harrison?" Dr. Libby Drake waited for him to join her before taking her usual chair.

Lucky settled on the same ugly-assed couch where he'd confessed his deepest, darkest secrets to her on too many occasions. He'd been told confession was good for the soul, but his confessions probably kept Dr. Libby up at night.

A trace of cinnamon air freshener reminded him of Mom's apple pie. Damn, now he'd have to stop by a diner on the way home.

"Look, doctor. I'll be honest. I need you to clear me to return to work."

"Lucky, I'm a psychologist, not your medical doctor." Dr. Drake crossed her legs, a sure sign she'd never budge. She'd learned many things about him these past few months.

He'd also learned about her. "But you're still a doctor. Says so on your door."

Dr. Drake sighed. "I'm not clearing you to return to work after a mere four weeks. You'll have to ask your medical doctor."

Lucky'd been afraid of that. Might as well make use of the hour his insurance paid for. "I need to talk to you about my brother..."

Too bright lights. Antiseptic smell. Crowded waiting room. If the guy sitting next to Lucky made one more damned phone call...

"Mr. Harrison?" A nurse, not the doctor, called him back to an examining room. "Make yourself comfortable. The doctor will be here in a few minutes."

Yeah, right. Lucky lay back on the table. Might as well take a nap while he waited. Dr. Libby could've saved him a lot of trouble by signing the damn form.

"No pain?"

Lucky hid a wince and pulled his T-shirt back on. "Nothing to speak of." He'd lie his ass off if it meant doing more than sitting at home, brooding. Puttering around the house didn't help.

"Your blood pressure is normal, and all tests are within normal limits. But still, it's rare to send a patient back to work four weeks after major surgery." The doctor tapped away on his tablet computer. "What type of work will you be doing?"

Lucky waved a dismissive hand. "Desk duty for the next month, part time, nothing strenuous." Well, he did have a desk, so not a complete lie.

The doctor tapped some more.

Oh, for the love of... "Please, doc. My physical health don't mean nothing if I lose my f... ever-loving mind."

The doctor studied Lucky, bushy black eyebrows nearly meeting when he frowned. "Have you discussed the matter with your employer?"

"I have. If I get tired, I go home." He pasted on a smile. *Please, please, please, please, please.*

The doctor relaxed his scowl. "If you're certain. But I'm giving you a list of instructions to be followed to the letter, understand?"

Lucky strolled out of the office with his ticket back into the game. If he couldn't be with Bo, he'd at least be in a position to keep up with whatever went on.

Ah, cube, sweet cube. Lucky eased down into the chair from hell and counted, "One, two, three, four..."

Johnson showed up at the count of eight. Lisa must've tipped her off to Lucky's return.

"Good to have you back." She slapped Lucky's back, not nearly as hard as usual. When would folks stop treating him like an invalid?

"I would say it's good to be back, but I wouldn't want to lie," he lied. Lucky barely looked up from his desk. The sooner folks stopped singling him out, the sooner he'd get back to work. He'd pissed away too much time taking things easy. Time to go kick some drug dealer ass.

With no warning, Johnson swooped in and probably made a sticky red mess on his cheek. "In case I haven't told you before, you're a good guy."

He'd done one good deed and shot his reputation to hell. "Don't you dare tell people stories about me."

"Your secret is safe with me. Now, boss man wants you."

What now? He closed his laptop and followed the familiar path to Walter's door, tapped once and entered without waiting for an invite. "If this is about me coming back to work, the doctor released me." Sort of. He needed the Bureau's resources to track down how Bristol got a hold of carfentanil. And keep tabs on Bo? Nah.

But the tracker he'd stuck on Bo's Durango wasn't going to download its own data.

"Sit."

Oh, shit. Walter in boss mode and not in the role of favorite uncle. Ready the shit to hit the fan.

"What'd I do now?"

"I wouldn't even hazard a guess. You're quite creative." All said without cracking a smile. Walter emitted a sigh. "I have to ask you something. Feel free to say no." He sighed again. "Our mutual friends with the limitless budget have gotten involved in your case, as it has multi-country implications."

"And?" Lucky's heart sped. Nestor, he could handle, but the possibility of meeting Victor again fried his nerves. Sure, they'd been lovers once, and Victor went out of his way to look out for Lucky from the sidelines, but Lucky's new life had no room for exes. Nothing good could come of him revisiting his past.

"We've kept your brother's death quiet for the time being. And spoke with a girlfriend. She claims he kept the basement door locked and never allowed her to enter."

Whoever she was, she'd never stand toe to toe with the Lucklighters if she let a little thing like a door lock stop her.

"So, what do you want from me?" Please let it not be coming face to face with this woman. Lucky didn't know her, but more than likely she'd been poisoned to the Lucklighter black sheep, and might even blame Lucky for Bristol's death—if she wasn't involved in his little drug operation.

"She's told us all she knows, and has been most forthcoming with his e-mails and cell phone." Walter waved at a pile of papers. When would he stop killing the rainforest and get his reports online instead of paper form?

Strange how cooperative people got when trying to avoid being implicated. And Lucky didn't rule anyone out until they'd proven their innocence. "What have you found?"

"Your brother regularly met someone at the Greensboro Airport, which Jimmy confirmed from his own surveillance. The girlfriend mentioned he made the trip every few months. He'd go to the airport, pick someone up and take them to an undisclosed location." Walter tapped an ink pen against his desk blotter. "Agents from the Virginia office followed him on three separate occasions."

"How did he explain that away?" Bristol had never been a good liar. And as long as he kept bringing in the big bucks and giving her new cars to drive, likely the woman never questioned.

"He said his meetings were job related for the bank where he worked. His employer is unaware of any such arrangements."

Mystery woman must own one hell of a set of blinders. "What's the plan? You got someone watching the airport?"

"Yes. But we also need to make contact. From what we've gathered and observed for ourselves, you and your brothers look remarkably alike."

"Except for Dov... Dallas." No need to be childish around the boss. "He took after Mom's side of the family."

"All the same, your help is needed to play the role of your brother and keep the next meeting." He pinned Lucky in place with a tremor-inducing gaze hot enough to cut through steel.

"You do realize I wouldn't have asked this of you without directions from higher up. It's too soon, and they shouldn't even suggest such a thing to an agent. Feel free to say no."

Too soon. A million years from now would still be too soon to step into Bristol's shoes. Lucky barely bit off "Oh hell no!" Work. This was work. His job. He'd gone undercover too many times to count. Just another assignment—that might bring him closer to Bo, and the answers he needed about Bristol. "When?"

"Thursday, but only if you feel able and are willing." Walter's searching gaze bore into Lucky's. "I'll not risk you."

Fuck. "Who's going to be with me?"

"Don't worry. You'll have adequate backup from the Richmond office. I won't expose you to any more danger than I have to."

Sometimes the world went to hell anyway.

Was it safe to touch anything? Marble, marble everywhere. Marble countertops, marble dresser tops, real wood floors gleaming in the sun's last rays.

Nothing seemed out of place. It shouldn't be, with maid service twice per week. Bristol spared no expense in creating the life he'd always wanted.

"How do I look?" Pretty stupid, if you asked Lucky. The mirror before him likely cost more than the down payment on his house.

"Hold still." Jimmy untied Lucky's noose of death and slithered the material over itself like a snake. He ended by pulling the tie way too tight. "Your brother favored a Windsor knot."

Windsor? Lucky yanked at the tie.

Jimmy slapped his hand away. "You want to look the part of a successful banker, don't you?"

Not really. Bikers, drug dealers, even homeless drug addicts were all familiar parts to play. Big wheel pricks who spent more than they made? Not so much. "Where is Bo?"

Jimmy glanced away, lips pursed.

Walter disengaged himself from the wall and strode up to Lucky's side. "He's in place. Your paths likely won't cross, but he's there."

For Walter's ears only, Lucky asked, "He's okay?"

"You trained him well. Trust him."

Trusting Bo wasn't the problem. The other folks involved in this big mess? Not a snowball's chance in Hell.

Walter rested his hands on Lucky's shoulders. "Focus, Lucky. You better than any know the dangers of distractions."

The vest hidden under Bristol's expensive monkey suit chafed a bit. No wonder his brother was broke if he'd thrown all his money away on a fancy house, fancy clothes, and fancy cars.

"Yeah." He glanced down at the Rolex on his wrist. "It's almost show time."

Photos lined the dresser: Bristol and a gorgeous blonde woman on a cruise ship, in front of the Eiffel Tower, in Times Square... All appeared to have been taken close together, as the two in the pictures didn't change much. Even Victor, with his bottomless wallet, didn't toss money about like Bristol.

And not a single picture of any other Lucklighters anywhere.

An officer stepped forward and clipped a nearly invisible microphone to Lucky's tie, designed like a tie tack in the shape of a tennis racket. "Testing, testing," she said.

The two-way radio on her belt squawked. "Coming through loud and clear."

She stepped back with a satisfied smile.

"Now," Jimmy told him, removing the arm he'd slung around Lucky's shoulders at Lucky's growl. "Surveillance video shows your brother's car pulling in front of a hangar at the back of the airport. His car is on camera at least six times, so they'll be looking for the BMW. He pulls in the gate and waits. After a while a man will come out of the hangar, get into the backseat, and the car drives away."

"Who?"

"It could be one of six or seven men."

Lucky scowled at his reflection. "They'll never believe I'm him."

Jimmy straightened Lucky's lapels, reminding Lucky of "Nurse Andy's" constant fussing and pillow fluffing. "We've covered all the bases, kept Bristol's death out of the news. The bank has him listed as on vacation. Only your family and the girlfriend knows the truth. The girlfriend is under surveillance, and you trust your family, right? Your contacts have no reason to suspect anything's wrong. You got the intel and studied the videos, right?"

Lucky nodded. "Where am I driving to after pickup?"

"Let him tell you." Jimmy frowned and adjusted the tie again. Obsessive-compulsive much?

"Not the kind of plan I'm used to."

"Based on your brother's phone records, you could go to any of the three locations we showed you on the map. Your brother remained with the car while his passenger went inside and stayed about twenty minutes. Then Bristol took them back to the airport." Jimmy handed Lucky a phone. "He was just a flunky, and didn't seem to interact much with his passenger. Just take your contact wherever he wants to go, and the team will step in from there. Here's his phone. Can you sound like him if you need to?"

"Kinda late to be asking now, ain't it?"

Jimmy scowled.

Lucky rolled his eyes. "All right." He pulled in a deep breath, let it out slowly, and tried to imitate Walter's words in a Southern accent. "Hardly the time to ask such a thing, is it not?"

Jimmy winced. "I'll check the bookcase for family videos."

Walter kneaded Lucky's shoulders. "Are you sure you're up to going through with this?"

Lucky stared at himself—not himself—in the mirror his brother had probably used every morning. Hair parted and slicked into submission. Topped off with the too-sweet scent he'd noticed in the hospital. Add a bit of a sneer and damned if he couldn't pass for the guy in the photos. Just a driver. No real danger of being made if he stayed beneath notice. "I need to find out how deep in the shit Bristol was."

Not to mention put a stop to whoever brought carfentanil into the country. As if the US didn't already have enough drug problems. But truthfully? Lucky missed his job. Being in the action. What a hypocrite. One moment he worried about winding up dead, the next he nursed an adrenaline rush.

Jimmy stepped back into the bedroom, stuck a disk into a DVD player, and turned on a wall-sized TV.

Bristol's face appeared. Despite the circumstances, Lucky's heart lurched. Maybe if he hadn't been so hard on the guy as kids...

Onscreen, Bristol asked, "How do you want your steak cooked?" Someone off camera must have spoken. Bristol nodded. "Rare it is."

Jimmy paused the video.

A cookout. With people Lucky didn't know and who hadn't been a part of his life. Another felon to portray. Nothing personal. Nothing at all. "How you want your steak cooked?"

Walter cringed and didn't bother to hide his reaction.

Still needed work. "How do you want your steak cooked?"

Jimmy sighed. "Let's try another clip." He fast-forwarded and tried again.

Bristol pulled his lips back in a lazy smile. "You're sexy dressed like that."

An image came to Lucky's mind of Bo in his damned hot assless chaps. "You're sexy dressed like that."

Walter smiled, possibly for more than one reason. "Better. Try again."

"Wow! He looks so much like you. And your other brother," Jimmy commented, gazing at the video. "If he'd been wearing a hospital gown the day I saw him go into your room,

I'd have fussed at him to get back in bed. I've seen plenty of videos and pictures, but seeing him here, now, with you for comparison..."

After fifteen minutes of watching, Lucky did a perfect imitation, "Hi, I'm Bristol Lucklighter." He even managed the same oily smile.

"I have something for you." Jimmy grabbed a box off the bed, crouched down, and lifted Lucky's pant leg. "You can't be too careful. How's that feel?"

Lucky tested the weight of the leg holster and gun. "Works."

Walter searched Lucky's soul through his eyes. "How are you doing? Feeling all right? Remember, I trust your gut instincts more than any intel. Say the word, and this operation stops here. No one will fault you."

The incision seemed hell bent and determined to be a pain in the side for of all eternity, not to mention the wood chipper ripping Lucky's heart out piece by piece. Yet he'd never abandon tonight's effort and pass up a chance to learn the truth. "I'm tougher'n a pine knot, as my sister says."

"I'm sure you are."

Jimmy slapped Lucky's shoulder. "Nine o'clock. Show time."

Hey, that was Lucky's line.

If Lucky's heart pounded any harder, it'd fly out of his chest and beat him to the airport. He hummed *Achy Breaky Heart* into his microphone, sending Bo a message, if Bo happened to be within hearing.

At one time the silver BMW might have been Lucky's dream car. Now, surrounded by his brother's things, wearing his brother's clothes, it made his stomach churn. Mama always said to respect the dead.

Hard to do when the dead tried to kill him.

Lucky pulled the car into the gate and parked near the hangar, like he'd watched his brother do before on videos. Bristol had been a lackey, with nothing much expected of him.

All the same, Lucky ran his hand under the seat and caressed his .38.

After a few moments, his target emerged from the hangar, stepping straight into a floodlight's glow. "Six feet, about two-hundred pounds," Lucky murmured to his tie tack. "Forty-ish. Dark blue golf shirt, khaki pants. Bulged out backpack."

The guy got into the back seat, set the bag aside, and closed the door. "Did you take care of that matter we spoke of last time?"

What matter? Killing Lucky, maybe? "Yes." Lucky added a "sir".

"Good."

He sat idling. What now?

After a few moments of nerve-wracking quiet, the man said, "Take me to the warehouse. And be quick about it. I need to be in Toronto by morning."

Lovely when suspects spilled information. Soon the SNB would have a complete list of all passengers bound for Toronto within the next sixteen hours. Lucky drove the car out of the gate, toward a warehouse off I-95, one of the routes he'd memorized.

The man spent the entire ride on his cell phone. Lucky strained to hear the words. With any luck, the mic caught everything.

Somewhere at the end of this whole ordeal, maybe he could get on with his life. He pulled into the warehouse gate Jimmy said normally stayed locked.

Unlocked and opened. They were expected. A lone streetlight barely chased back shadows. Shadows. Good to hide in.

Lucky stopped the car.

His passenger slipped a packet over the front seat, the size of a deck of playing cards.

Gloves. The man wore plastic gloves. And Lucky didn't have any. No way would he touch the wrapper when a touch might kill him, even though he'd brought along naloxone, the magic elixir, in case—in handy little inhalers. No needle required.

The man chuckled. "I've forgotten how fastidious you are." He placed the pack on the console. "A gift."

Lucky made no move to touch the package.

"Come with me."

Wait! What? "You want me to..."

"Yes. Come with me. And leave your gun under the seat."

Oh fuck.

CHAPTER TWENTY-FOUR

Lucky stayed two steps behind the man who suddenly made his world scarier. In over a decade with the SNB, he'd never been burnt while undercover.

He'd keep his perfect record, thank you very much. The fact he walked behind gave some comfort. No one in their right mind turned their back on an enemy.

The ankle holster offered some comfort—not much—but better than nothing.

He followed the man up a set of steps to a loading dock and into a darkened building. Darkness, his one true friend in this situation. Outside, other agents better be regrouping, rethinking original plans and figuring out how to cover a man inside.

Their footsteps echoed in a cavernous room, empty except for a few metal racks, illuminated only by emergency exit lighting marking doors, and a light up ahead. Lucky mentally marked exits. If worst case scenario became reality, he'd learned to duck and run.

Only, his gimpy assed-leg didn't allow for much running, nor did his partial recovery from surgery. He donned Bristol's sneer, pulled himself up his full five-feet-six inch-height, and squared his shoulders. He'd make use of something he'd learned in training—from Bo.

For the next few hours, Lucky Lucklighter, Simon Harrison, and any of Lucky's other personas didn't exist. Bristol Lucklighter. That's who he'd be. The high-living, low morals, money hungry sonofabitch who profited from loved ones' deaths and wouldn't help his own father.

Nope. Not the way to get into Bristol's head. Not loved ones' deaths if you didn't have anyone you loved more than yourself.

Money. Power. Possessions. And being more than a tobacco farmer's second son. In his own head, Bristol had overcome his past, deserved to look down on lesser beings like his family. He'd made something of himself.And Bristol hated his older brother, a man who hadn't gone to college, hadn't scratched and scraped his way up the ladder, but still managed to live the life Bristol wanted, thanks to a wealthy and powerful lover.

If his parents had tried harder, they could have provided a better life, a life Bristol didn't have to hide from the popular kids he'd tried to impress in school. And he wouldn't have had to depend on his brother's rich lover to pay his way through college.

Screw them. Screw them all. The asshole walking in front of him provided a means to an end. Nothing more than a bug smear on the bottom of Bristol's expensive Italian loafer. Without trying hard, he'd own these guys, run the whole show.

By the time they approached the hallway light, smug aloofness replaced any fear.

The backpack he'd been staring at for the past few minutes held the key to all a man like Bristol wanted.

His escort opened a door and entered a dimly-lit room, not even bothering to glance over his shoulder to make sure his flunky followed. Bristol's heartbeat raced, but not from fear. Pure adrenaline shot through his veins.

No windows, only one door. Standing behind Backpack Guy kept him somewhat concealed, both by shadows and the man's body, and close to the exit. He swept his gaze over a scene he'd witnessed many times: the drug deal. From tiny casual buys to massive trafficking operations, he'd seen them all.

The stacks of bills spread out before him on a table in what must have once been a conference room rivaled any single buys he'd participated in.

Two men stood on the opposite side of the table. One exuded authority, the other held a semi-automatic weapon.

Don't leave home without the hired muscle. For a moment, Lucky's facade wavered. He knew the muscle. Every single inch, from the dark, tousled hair to the freckles across the nose and on down to the assets hidden beneath jeans and a tight T-shirt.

No recognition shone in Bo's eyes, other than a quick once-over. No. Not Bo. Rent-a-Thug, who didn't know Bristol Lucklighter. *Bristol Lucklighter. I am Bristol Lucklighter.*

Lucky had been told to leave his gun behind, so he wasn't supposed to be an open threat, but he was definitely backup and possibly a witness. Whoever Backpack Guy was, he didn't trust his partners in crime, or he wanted to exert a little authority himself. And judging from the bulge in his light jacket, he'd come prepared.

Why not have Lucky armed too? Oh. Right. Bristol never could shoot worth a shit. Maybe as a sign of faith too. Honor among thieves and all. Either way, dumbass move on Backpack Guy's part. Never, ever, let the buyer have the upper hand.

The buyer bore a striking resemblance to one of Lila's baby-daddies on *South Bend Springs*—information to be filed away for later use in descriptions.

The man he'd brought to the party flung the backpack onto the table. "It's all there."

The one he pegged as the boss kept a steely-eyed glint on the supplier and opened the backpack with gloved hands. Packets fell out onto the table and floor. The buyer trained his beady, hard-edged gaze onto the dozen or so escaped packets.

Oh, dude, you never bring that much money to a buy, screamed through the part of Bristol's brain still owned by Lucky. *You've given up your leverage. One squeeze of the trigger and we get the money and the drugs.*

Sloppy.

The seller nodded but didn't reach for the money. "Bristol, get the cash."

On a first name basis. If the guy turned around and got a good look...

"You're not going anywhere." The buyer stiffened, took a step back, and nodded to his thug. The gunman aimed his weapon straight at Lucky. Oh shit.

Backpack Guy shouted, "What? Why not? We had a deal."

The man with excellent peripheral vision replied, "We did, but that's not Bristol Lucklighter. I had him killed."

Fucking hell.

All three men honed their sights on Lucky.

Lucky had transmitted a lot of evidence to the SNB. Killing him now only prolonged the inevitable.

All traces of Bristol fled.

And so did Lucky.

Outrunning healthy men wasn't happening, not with Lucky's beat-up body. Why hadn't he listened to Walter and Bo and taken things easier?

Because if push ever came to shove, he needed to be here, for himself, his family, his department, and even Bristol, learning firsthand how deep in the shit his brother had sunk.

He's done nothing you haven't done. Yes, he had. Lucky never tried to kill anyone or betray his family. And he didn't get the moral high ground often.

Being in unfamiliar territory left him with few choices. He could either limp through the warehouse where he made an easy target but knew the lay of the land, or find out what waited behind door number one.

He chose the door and hunkered down in a janitor's closet. Footsteps pounded by. "Get the little asshole!" the boss of the group shouted.

Lucky crouched, putting him in position to use the ankle-holstered gun he'd properly thank Jimmy for later.

He cracked open the door and peeped out, straining his ears in the silence.

Bap, bap, bap, bap, bap.

Oh shit. Gunfire. Never a good thing. And Bo out there, God knew where. The toy-sized gun with a thirteen-shot clip fit oddly in Lucky's hand, nothing like his .38.

Thirteen shots better be more than he needed. He eased out of the closet, his back to the wall and his gun at the ready. The room where they'd met to deal lay to the right, and the shots came from the left.

Right, then.

In times like these, his lack of height gave him a huge advantage, making him much harder to spot.

He paused long enough by the conference room door to snap and send a few pictures, and clue in the listeners-of-the-mic to his whereabouts. Too bad they couldn't tell him what the fuck the shots were about.

More footsteps, coming his way.

The empty office across the way made an excellent vantage point. The boss came back, huffing for breath, shoved some drugs and cash into the pack, and shot down the hall to the right, one hand pressed to his side.

He'd left behind quite a haul. Desperate, then.

Lucky counted to ten, murmured his intent to his tie tack, and silently stalked his prey. Dark spots glistened wetly on dingy, industrial-gray carpeting. Ahead several light fixtures lacked bulbs, giving both predator and prey darkness for hiding.

The asshole who said he'd had Bristol killed would answer to a pissed off Lucklighter.

The blood trail led straight down the hallway and veered off once or twice, into windowless rooms. The wounded man sought a way out, and didn't appear totally familiar with the building. Worked for Lucky.

According to the plans Lucky reviewed earlier, the warehouse lay that way, conference room, offices with no windows. The hall eventually led to an exit with a chained metal door and metal grids on all windows.

Both he and his quarry worked their way into a dead end.

He observed but didn't try to apprehend. Not without backup.

Walter's lessons finally hit home. Boss would be so proud.

The hallway came to a T intersection. Movement caught his eye and he fused his back with the wall. The blood marked a turn. Someone—and not the one he sought—lingered in the hall to his left. They stopped, so might suspect his presence.

Not good. He counted to three, gripped the gun in both hands, and popped out of his hiding place.

And stared down a gun barrel.

He froze a scant second before his brain screamed, *Shoot!*

Bo's wide eyes met his. Relief whooshed out of him. If choosing one person to run into at a time like this, Bo ranked number one.

Bo ranked number one anytime. Lucky pointed toward where the dealer dripped blood, down an unlit hallway.

Bo nodded.

He'd kiss the guy later. Lucky took point, darting down the hall and squeezing himself into a recessed doorway. He bounced from doorway to doorway, Bo taking each shelter he vacated.

A breeze brushed Lucky's face, and he glanced around a ledge to an outside door standing partially open. Oops. Jimmy gave him bad intel about chained exits.

He'd chew the asshole out later.

Stooping, he dashed to one side of the door and put his back against the wall. Bo took the other side.

Not a sound came from outside, save the distant shrill of sirens, growing closer by the second.

Open gate. Parking lot. For the office workers, most likely, back before the place was abandoned.

Lucky eased up to see around the doorframe. Squinting didn't help his night vision. His side pained him some, about five on a scale from one to shot. He'd live.

Tires squalled and three carloads of Greensboro's finest came barreling through the gate, followed by a black SUV.

Judging from muffled sirens, more cars surrounded the back of the warehouse.

An officer hopped from the first car, gun aimed and ready for business. "Step out with your hands on your head."

Idiot. At this angle Lucky could take him out easily. Good thing Lucky only played a felon for the job.

Now.

Hearing his boss's voice in his head, he swung the door wide and did as told. The officer kept the gun trained on him. "Pat him down."

Another officer approached, took his gun, and began going through the motions of a search.

"Those aren't drugs in my pocket," Lucky growled. "I've just got a really big..."

Bap, bap, bap, bap. Lucky dropped to the ground and crawled on his belly to the nearest police car. Fuck, that hurt! The cops were gone. Probably sheltering behind their own cars.

Where was Bo?"

There came a time when a man got too old for this shit, and a clock ticked away in Lucky's head.

A black van approached. Oh, cool. SWAT team. Dark shapes hopped out of the van, fully geared, scuttled into the shadows and, one by one, entered the building. Let 'em. Lucky'd stay right here.

Steps sounded behind him. The farther he kept away, the better. Realizing his sorry ass really could die changed his way of thinking.

The officer crept up to him, gun aimed.

Lucky kept his voice low. "I'm Agent Lu... Harrison, Southeastern Narcotics Bureau. And I'm wired."

The man nodded, but kept his gun at the ready. Gee. Suspicious much?

"My partner, Agent Schollenberger, was right behind me coming out." And dear Lord let him not have been in the path of one of those shots. Better clue in the new arrivals. "There's packets in a conference room. Tell your men not to touch the shit without gloves, you got me?"

The officer nodded but continued to hold his gun on Lucky. "Hands on your head."

Lucky grabbed hold of the car door and climbed to his feet.

Moments passed at a snail's pace. The occasional sweep of a flashlight shining from a warehouse window pierced the darkness. Sure was creepy out here at night.

"Wouldn't we be better off waiting in your car?" Standing here made them easy targets. If the guy fought him, he'd pull rank.

The officer nodded. The other officers fanned out around the parking lot. They'd brought one hell of a lot of firepower. Someone hadn't given him all the details.

A shot rang out, and another, and another. Inside the building.

Then outside.

Lucky sprung and knocked the officer off his feet. "Fuck! Fuck! Fuckety fuck!" Damn, but that hurt! With any luck, Lucky hadn't torn anything open. The cop struggled beneath him, still not realizing he'd been saved by one of the good guys.

Over a month after surgery. When would the shit quit hurting?

Pop, pop, pop. The shots came slower now, like the last few kernels in a bag of microwave popcorn.

A flurry of activity, then, "Man down! Man down!"

Oh, God. Please not Bo.

Jimmy bolted out of the SUV. An ambulance arrived mere seconds later. Must've been on standby at a safe distance.

Night turned to day, and Lucky shielded his eyes from the glare of a half-dozen floodlights.

He let the wiggling cop go. The guy pointed his gun at Lucky again.

"Have you ever known a suspect to try to save your sorry hide?" Jeez, when would the guy get with the program? Then again, Lucky wasn't much of a trusting soul, either.

The agent in him yearned to sprint inside, be in the middle of the action. The man who wanted to be alive come the weekend told the agent to shut the fuck up. Not his case. He'd done his part. Time to let someone else earn their keep.

Except... Where was Bo?

Paramedics hauled a gurney out, loaded with a body fully covered by a sheet. Two SWAT team members followed them, dragging two men Lucky hadn't seen before in handcuffs. Damn. How much backup had money man brought?

More emerged. How many people were in there? All around him radios crackled, offering up bits and pieces of information. Two dead from the warehouse, one officer down.

Shit. Two dead. Please, please, please. Not Bo.

A man nearly as large as Walter, with the same, you'd-better-do-as-I-said bark reached down a hand. "Would you mind pointing your gun in some other direction?" The cop lowered his gun and backed away.

Lucky struggled to his feet.

"Agent Harrison?" The man kept his grip on Lucky's hand.

"Some days."

"Yeah, I know what you mean. Special Agent Gaskins, DEA."

"My partner..."

"All our men are accounted for. One casualty—one of our own. I lost a good man tonight."

"There were two suspects involved directly in the drug deal."

"Can you identify them?" Agent Gaskins towered over Lucky but kept his voice low.

Lucky nodded. "Yeah."

"Come with me."

Lucky followed Gaskins into the building, past the conference room full of blue uniforms into the warehouse. Two cops stood guard over a body.

A semi-automatic lay on the floor next to the deceased. Bo's.

"That's the man I brought here, the supplier." Lucky nodded to the body. "The buyer was bleeding last I saw him, and exited the building right before your men arrived."

"We've got him on camera, and we're looking for him now."

"Good. Can you tell me what went down at the airport?"

"Arrested four, and found a pallet of unmarked boxes. We backed off to let the lab handle cleanup." Gaskins rubbed a hand over his head. "They know better what we're dealing with. I hate the shit these assholes are bringing into this country."

Right now, assholes, the shit they sold, and even Mr. DEA didn't matter. Lucky trudged through the building as fast as his beat-up body allowed.

He strained to make out voices, recognize a familiar face in shadowy rooms, heart falling with each, *Nope, not him.*

Finally, a familiar drawl yanked Lucky toward the conference room, followed by Mr. DEA. Bo made eye contact while deep in discussion with an officer. Hallelujah! Closing his eyes, Lucky blew out a breath. Alive. Still alive.

If not for the roomful of people, he would happily check Bo head to toe for injuries.

"Umm... Harrison? You all right?"

Lucky opened his eyes to find Special Agent Gaskins staring down at him.

"Yeah. Just tired. It's been a rough few hours."

"I'll bet." Gaskins tugged on rubber gloves from a box on the table, lifted a packet from the floor, and dropped the instrument of death into a zip-close bag. "I can't understand why people do this horror."

"Some assholes mix stronger stuff into heroin." Made the heroin more potent, but in the end shot the dealers in the foot by killing their clientele. Which might have happened to the woman Bristol allegedly sold to.

The guy nodded. "First started coming into this area about four months ago. We've had twelve overdoses since then. I'd love to believe this operation supplied them all, but I've never been much of an optimist. What say we get out of here?" said the first DEA man Lucky'd met in a long time who didn't insult him.

"I'm game."

"Thought you might be. Care to drive the BMW back to the station?"

His brother's BMW. Bought with ill-gotten gains, though Lucky had yet to figure out how much profit Bristol made and for what. So far all he'd seen tonight was enough drugs for minor deals, and acting as a cab driver. Flunky work alone didn't finance Bristol's lifestyle. And he'd supplied his basement operation somehow. "I'd really rather not."

"Don't blame you. I'll get one of my men. You can ride with me."

Lucky followed behind the man, too tired to argue, with a dull throbbing around his heart—and in his side.

Gaskins opened the car door for Lucky. "I can't tell you how much we appreciate your help. And if it's any consolation, I'm sorry about your brother."

"Yeah, me too." And not just Bristol. The whole situation likely fucked with Daytona's head, not to mention the hell Mama went through. Or Charlotte.

Breath whooshed out of Lucky when Bo stood silhouetted on the loading dock. Safe. Still safe. Bo nodded once and returned inside the building.

Right. Still on a case. Lucky'd done his task.

He needed his family, now more than ever, with every fiber of his being. "After we finish the formalities, can I get a ride up to my parents' farm?"

"It can be arranged."

Time to officially reenter the Lucklighter clan.

CHAPTER TWENTY-FIVE

Few cars sat in the police station parking lot at barely past sunrise. The pink horizon gave way to blue skies, dotted with a cloud or two, the day shaping up to be a warm one.

With any luck, Lucky would soon be snug in a bed, and not alone, sleeping and loving his way through the heat. But no, he couldn't lose himself in the wonders of sex and block out all the painful shit in his life.

No need to keep secrets anymore. The whole family would soon know what happened to Bristol. The whole fucked up story.

His perch by Bo's Durango, parked near the door, gave him clear view of anyone coming or leaving. No chance of Bo getting away without saying goodbye.

A uniformed officer nodded on his way to the steps leading to the station's front door, a fast food bag in his hand wafting the drool-inducing scent of sausage. Probably a biscuit, nice and fluffy, like Mom used to make, slathered with butter and filled with meat, eggs, and cheese.

Lucky's rumbling belly protested until another officer, reeking of cigarette smoke, trotted by slightly out of breath. Shift change, and he'd been here most of the night, except for a brief visit to an all-night urgent care clinic to check any damage he might have done.

Scrapes. Bruises. Soreness. He'd live.

Cigarette Man climbed the steps and held the door while Bo strolled out and made a beeline for Lucky. Bo. Finally. And alone.

After a quick left to right perusal, Lucky grabbed the man he'd been within reach of for the last few hours but unable to touch.

257

"Aaaak!" Bo struggled all of three seconds.

Nothing shut the man up quicker than a tongue to the mouth. After a moment, Bo answered passion with passion, slamming Lucky against the side of his Durango.

Oh, hell yes. Lucky ground against his man. Five minutes, all he needed—or less. Nights like last night made him want to hold on and never let go. But he had to. "What's your plans for the next few hours?" he stepped back enough to ask.

"I heard you needed a ride to your parents' house." Bo jutted his chin out. "I'm driving you."

Stubborn looked good on the man. Lucky ought to argue, put his foot down. Bo had to be worn completely out and in need of a few hours' sleep. He couldn't be up to a visit to Redneckville. Being bone-weary himself took the fight out of Lucky. Maybe he should sleep first, but no, he needed to be with his family. If they'd have him.

And he needed to be with Bo. Bo acting as driver also meant no more undercover—for now.

Damned if giving statements didn't become more time consuming each time. Seven fucking A.M. Not the hour of day to come calling unannounced.

"Okay. You win." Arguing with a smart man like Bo used up energy Lucky'd rather keep.

The Dimple peeked out of Bo's cheek and disappeared. Yup, probably too tired to pull off a megawatt smile. "What? You're giving in so easily? I didn't even have to employ any of your mother's techniques to pull you into line."

Double-teamed. He'd keep an eye on his partner around his mother. Charlotte too. "Just remember, there's more Lucklighters where we're going. Lots of 'em."

"I'll take my chances. Now get in the truck." Bo jogged around the hood and got in the driver's side.

Lucky crawled into the passenger seat, buckled himself in, and called his Mom's cell phone. "Mama. I need to see you. Can I come by?" *Please say yes! Please say yes!*Silence. Not good. Finally, his mother answered, "Yes, I suppose I've kept things from your father long enough. Charlotte's been begging me to let her talk to him. I reckon it's time."

"Okay, see you soon." Lucky ended the call. "Here's the address, or close enough." He punched a store near the farm into Bo's navigation system. Even satellites couldn't find the Lucklighter farm.

Bo gave Lucky's hand a squeeze and pulled out onto the road. "I heard you went to urgent care last night. Everything okay?"

"Yep. Just banged up a little."

"Good. Seeing you hit the ground like to have made my heart stop, let me tell you. It was all I could do not to say 'fuck the case' and come running out to check on you."

"Same happened to me when I heard shots." And envisioned Bo lying in a pool of blood. The no-fraternization rule at work made more and more sense. Distracted agents became liabilities, or worse, dead agents.

One side of Bo's mouth quirked up. "Aren't we a pair?"

"A pair of what?"

They passed a club Lucky used to haunt with Victor. No need pointing out such a landmark to Bo. Twenty minutes later stores and office buildings gave way to green fields and black barns of tobacco farms.

With each mile Lucky's heart pounded harder. Almost home.

And then the surroundings grew more and more familiar. "That's where I went to high school," he pointed out. Nothing like the massive school buildings in Atlanta. Might as well give his partner the grand tour. "And over there's the feed and seed. I went there a lot with my dad when I was a kid." The twinge in Lucky's chest had nothing to do with his surgery. The post office and a handful of businesses rounded out the wide spot in the road Lucky used to dream of leaving.

He rolled down his window, letting fresh air wake him. "We don't have Starbucks, but stop at the convenience store, m'kay?" Coffee. Even decaf, might make him feel human again.

Not one damned thing seemed to have changed since Lucky last came home over twelve years ago. He left, and life continued without him at the same molasses pace.

Birds chirped in the trees when he got out of the car, and he caught a slight whiff of honeysuckle and freshly-mown hay. Home. He'd come home.

"You all right?" Bo placed a hand on Lucky's shoulder, snapping him out of his daze.

"Just tired, I reckon. You?"

"Same. But not too tired to be here when you need me."

No, Bo would never be too tired, too busy, too sick, to have Lucky's back. He made a great partner, both on and off the job. Would asking Bo to marry him here and now count as being under duress?

The words sat on Lucky's tongue, but Bo deserved hearts and flowers and some grand romantic gesture.

"C'mon. Let's get you some coffee." Bo ushered Lucky into the store, holding onto Lucky's arm, but Lucky lacked the energy to say anything about being treated like an invalid.

He dawdled at the coffee pot, excitement and fear pouring through him in equal measure. Mama accepted Lucky back, but Dad? Stubborn didn't begin to describe him. When he dug his heels in, nothing changed his mind. And Mama wouldn't go against Daddy.

"You're stalling, aren't you?" Bo didn't accuse, merely pointed out the obvious. "I'm here with you. No matter what. But things never turn out as bad as we fear."

Yeah. Lucky'd remember to say those words when they ventured to Arkansas to reconnect with Bo's folks.

He plodded back to the car on autopilot, buckled himself into the passenger seat, and sipped coffee while pointing out rights and lefts. "There's where I wrecked my four-wheeler, and across the road I used to go fishing with my dad."

The Lucklighter kids once waited at the end of the driveway for the school bus. "Turn off the paved road here." Lucky pointed to a "blink and you'll miss it" dirt road.

Packed red clay and gravel crunched under their tires. Pecan trees came into view. Many an afternoon, the Lucklighter clan gathered pecans to sell to a local farmer's market.

The garden where he'd spent summer days weeding and picking beans, squash, and other vegetables now hid beneath tangled overgrowth. Twelve years hadn't done the barn any favors.

White goats with red heads dotted the landscape, interspersed with white shaggy bodies, Moose's ilk, keeping watch over the herd.

No rolls of hay stood curing in the fields. No one kept the place up with Daddy sick. Guilt overcame anxiety. What a piss-poor son he'd been. His sorry ass should be out on a tractor, cutting the field or plowing the earth for the garden.

Bo stopped his Durango before the house came into sight, lifted Lucky's chin with his hand, and connected their lips.

Lucky latched on like a dying man, the last few hours slamming home: grief, guilt, terror of Bo being hurt, and for the next few hours he'd cling tightly to denial regarding the new facts he'd learned about Bristol.

He soaked in the comfort of Bo cradling his skull in one hand, the love surrounding the man who put up with all his bullshit. When the kiss ended, he rested his forehead against his partner's.

For good, bad, better, and worse, this man would always be a part of him. And in return, Lucky had given away something of himself he'd never get back. Didn't want back.

"You ready?" Bo asked one thousand years too soon.

"As I'll ever be."

In true Southern fashion, Bo smiled and replied, "I heard that."

Fate awaited.

So did the Lucklighters.

The old swing Lucky and Charlotte used to sit in as kids still hung from the front porch. Roses scented the air.

The old frame two-story farmhouse flaked white paint. Brilliant red geraniums bloomed on either side of the steps. The same blue curtains hung in the window of Lucky's old up-stairs bedroom—a room conveniently located close to a mas-sive oak tree.

So many times he'd slipped out the window, shimmied down the tree, and got into a little late-night mischief. If the hayloft could talk...

Two tabby cats met Lucky on the path up to the front door. "Mroow?" One stropped against his leg and he bent to scratch a furry ear, his incision halting him in mid-motion. Bending. Not a good idea.

Barely out of kittenhood, neither of these critters knew him, though the gray tabby lying on the front porch might. "Don't tell Cat Lucky I cheated on him and tried to give his scritches to other cats, okay?" Lucky muttered.

Bo stood off to the side, saying nothing about Lucky's cow-ardly attempt to buy time. Sooner or later, he'd have to knock on the door and face whatever came his way.

The entryway seemed so much bigger from the porch, the old timey screen door in bad need of new screen. The moment of truth. He sucked in a deep breath. Sweat trickled down his face, due to more than a sweltering summer day.

Bo sidled closer and gave Lucky a smile.

With Bo at his side, he'd face down a hundred drug lords. Or family.

Lucky opened the screen and rapped on the front door. The scent of coffee teased his nose. Once more he knocked. His pounding heart kept time with the beat.

Bo clutched his hand, an anchor to hold fast to.

Curtains fluttered in the living room window. The door screeched open a few seconds later.

Lucky stared into eyes so much like his own. Folks called him the spitting image of his father, but his eyes? He'd gotten those from Mom.

Her worn apron spoke of the many meals she'd cooked,

and the scent of bacon clung to her like a living advertisement for breakfast.

She launched herself in his direction. Lucky wrapped his arms around her, steadied her trembling. "Oh God, Richmond. My son. My son." Her back and forward swaying took him with her.

This woman gave him life, raised him, loved him, tucked him in at night, punished him when necessary—not nearly enough—and though she went silent for a while, eventually accepted the prospect of Lucky never bringing home a wife.

Home. He'd finally come home.

"I'm so sorry for... so many things," she choked out.

A hand too large to be his mother's found the middle of Lucky's back. He absorbed support from his lover and tears from his mother. As long as she stayed, he'd hug her, whisper, "It's okay, Mama. I'm here now. Everything'll be just fine."

All too soon, his mother stepped back, wiping her face with her apron. "Look at me, keeping y'all on the front porch. Come in, come in." She held the door open.

Taking a deep breath, Lucky entered a house he'd never dared hope to set foot in again. Family pictures lined the walls in the foyer, many of him and his siblings as kids. His Mama and Daddy's wedding photo no longer hung in the same place it'd been for all of his time here.

And there, instead, hogging a wall by itself...

Oh, dear God!

An eleven by twenty-inch picture frame, the largest on the walls, displayed a photo of him, along with the newspaper write-up of how he'd died saving a fellow agent.

His knees buckled. Bo's arm around his waist kept him standing.

Mom stood at his other side. "We're so proud of you for turning your life around. And deeply ashamed of ourselves." She stared at a worn spot on the throw rug at her feet.

Lucky nodded toward the picture. "You can take that down now. I'm not dead."

His mother raised her head, but didn't meet his eyes. "But you did save a man's life."

Words lodged in Lucky's throat.

Bo answered for him. "Yes, he did. Mine."

Strange being back here. Lucky never noticed the distinct smell of the old home place before, a combination of lemon-scented wood cleaner and an underlying hint of old house. And over all... bacon.

But something wasn't quite right. His Mama shouldn't be looking so guilty.

The acrid scent of something burnt hit his nose. "Mama? You got something on the stove?"

"Oh, Lord!" Mama threw her hands up and darted to the left, through the living room, and into the kitchen.

The closed door on the other side of the foyer caught Lucky's attention. His parents' room. More than likely, one oak panel separated him from his father, the same way a thin curtain had in the hospital.

He might prove to be a nasty surprise if Charlotte hadn't talked to the old man yet. Lucky'd often stomped up the stairs to his room, but today he put his hand on Bo's back and urged him toward the kitchen, stepping lightly. "Welcome to the farm."

"You still like your coffee black and sweet, right?" Mama shoved a mug nearly as old as Lucky into his hand the moment he entered the kitchen.

"Yes, ma'am, but I drink decaf now, with stevia." Though a cup of sugary-sweet full-caf might keep him going a while longer.

"I'm afraid we don't have decaf. Or stevia." She took the mug back. "Can I get you something else? Sweet tea?"

Lucky wouldn't mention tea being caffeinated and full of sugar too. "Tell you what. Got any fresh milk? The store-bought stuff ain't the real thing."

His mother gave a sniff and smiled. "Sure do. Old Elsie gave us a gallon this morning."

Mom named every milk cow they'd ever owned "Elsie." This current milker must be Elsie the fifteenth or sixteenth.

"How about you?" Mama turned her watery eyes Bo's way.

"Milk sounds good to me."

Probably the lesser of the evils. And Bo's manners didn't allow him asking for anything else, or turning down the offer completely. Southern mamas fed people as an instinct. Better to eat than be asked every five minutes, "Are you sure I can't get you something?"

Mama darted between the cabinet, the refrigerator, and back, with a glass of milk in each hand.

Not even completely cold yet. Milk didn't come any fresher, or with traces of cream floating on top. The refrigerator and stove were new, and somewhere along the line Mama finally got her wish of a dishwasher, but Granddaddy's handmade white cabinet still took up one wall, and a table big enough to fit all seven Lucklighters showed the marks of time—and a few scratches from the pocketknife Lucky used to carry.

Had Mama ever found the "REL" he'd carved underneath?

A tablet computer, a new addition, sat on the counter, a recipe showing on the screen.

Traces of coffee, bacon, and vanilla taunted his nose, along with the ghostly cinnamon of a million apple pies. Sweetest smell in the world.

"You boys want some bacon?" Mama tossed out a few burned bacon strips and started over cooking more.

Mmmmm... Bacon.

"Nah, that's all right." Lucky's stomach roared, calling him a liar.

Mama set her spatula on a nearby spoon rest, hanging her head. With an unfamiliar chill in her tone, she said, "I didn't know how to tell your Daddy about you and Bristol. Charlotte's in with him now, trying to explain. I thought it best if she talks to him."

Really? Mama and Daddy had always told each other everything.

265

"I hope this ain't a bad time, but I needed to check on how y'all are doing." And deep down inside, the little boy in Lucky needed his parents.

Mama sniffled. "As well as can be expected, I reckon. I keep wondering where I went wrong, like I did with..." She shot Lucky an eyeful of guilt.

Lucky placed his hands on her thin shoulders. "You didn't do one thing wrong, Mama. You raised us right. Not your fault we went our own way."

"That's what your sister keeps telling me. I'd never have made it these past few months without her." She sighed. "And now you're back. I'd always dreamed of having all my young'uns here again. Now..." Silent sobs racked her body. "After you... after they told us... oh, God, how it hurt. I'd lost you twice, the first time because of stubbornness, and then..."

Once more Lucky offered all the comfort he could. He'd shed his tears for lost years later. For now, he'd be strong. For Mama.

She rolled wet-lashed eyes upward. "Tell me. Did Bristol commit suicide? Reverend Hildebrand says suicides can't go to Heaven."

The sobbing began anew. Charlotte appeared in the doorway. "I done told you, Mama, it don't say that nowhere in the Bible that I've seen." She gave Lucky a one-armed hug and eased their mother from Lucky's arms into hers. "'Sides, we have to wait for the coroner's report."

A world of hurt in his sister's eyes hit Lucky so hard he staggered. He wouldn't tell them how Bristol died. Not now. Not the time.

Charlotte made a shooing motion with her hand. "Daddy's waiting. Go talk to him. Bo, would you mind helping me with Mama?"

Tiptoeing down the hall like he'd done when he'd stayed out late and snuck in after curfew came way too close to the anxiety-ridden trek he'd made from free man to jail cell.

Lucky stood in front of the bedroom door. Breathe in/breathe out.

He put one of his counselor's calming exercises to use:

Name five things you hear. His own panicked breathing, a rooster crowing in the yard, his sister crooning in the kitchen, a clank like a spoon in a cup, the creak of the board beneath his feet—the same one he'd fallen victim to in his youth.

Name five things you see. Cracks in the plaster on the foyer wall, the unpainted oak of his parents' bedroom door, the antique glass doorknob, the metal skeleton key Daytona jammed into the lock about twenty years ago and couldn't get out. The photos hanging on the wall.

Name five things you feel. His wildly thudding heart, his fist clenched tight, the beginnings of a stress headache, the ever so slight pull from his healing incision, sweat beads sliding down his face. He wiped them away with the back of his hand. No, not sweat. Tears.

The voice he never dared dream to hear again shouted, "Well, you planning on staying out there forever or getting your ass in here?"

Oh shit. Show time.

CHAPTER TWENTY-SIX

Lucky turned the knob, eased the oak door open, and stepped inside. No hiding the tremor in his hands and legs.

A patchwork quilt covered the iron-framed bed, and the lamp sported a lop-sided, hand-crocheted shade—one of Charlotte's earlier works.

Great-grandfather's clock sat on the mantel, likely placed there by the man himself after he'd built the house. The faint hint of tobacco lingered—not from smoking, but from a man who'd spent his whole life planting and harvesting the stuff.

His father cleared his throat.

The man seated in a chair by the window appeared older than his years. His illness had taken a toll. The same furrow often found on Lucky's face formed a permanent trench between his father's eyes, and hair once the same color as Lucky's bore a smattering of white.

Daddy gripped the arms of the rocking chair, fingers stained and work worn. "Your sister says I wouldn't be sitting here now if it wasn't for you."

Lucky stayed quiet. So far so good, and talking might break the winning streak.

"Why?" How'd Daddy manage to pour so much suspicion into one word?

"Why what?"

Curious eyes met Lucky's own. "Why did you let them cut you open? For me."

"You're my Daddy. I couldn't let you die."

"Nice to know family still means something to you."

What? Daddy turned his back, not Lucky. "It always did.

I don't know what it means to you, but I talked to a lot of dial tones." He hadn't really expected open arms, but he hadn't expected hostility either.

"And my son let me believe he died."

"I spent the last twelve plus years eating Christmas dinner alone." And the last one he'd eaten in a greasy spoon restaurant, but not alone. Never alone again. Not with Bo in his life.

"And there was an empty chair around the family table."

"I'd of been in that chair if you'd've let me." Ah, hell. Lucky never should have come here. What did he expect from a man who'd turned his back? Stubborn mule never admitted to being wrong or even listened to another's point of view.

Bo might comment about the apple not falling far from the tree.

What now?

Neither said a word, sizing each other up from a few feet and a thousand miles away. His father spoke first. "You look pretty good for a dead man."

Lucky flushed all the way up to his ears. "I'm sorry 'bout that, but honestly, at the time, I didn't figure you'd care."

"What kind of father do you take me for?"

Lucky clenched and unclenched his fist. "That kind who hangs up whenever his son calls. Every time I called, you slammed the phone down. Victor dead, me facing years in prison. I needed you."

"I thought you'd hurt Daytona."

"And you never bothered to even ask? At least I got a trial with the law. With you I got condemned and sentenced without saying one damned word." Maybe Lucky should leave and pretend this conversation never happened.

Daddy stared out the window. "I drove down to Durham for your trial."

"I didn't see you." Lucky leaned against the wall and folded his arms over his chest.

"I stayed in the truck. Couldn't bring myself to go in. I was mad. And yes, at the time, I thought you were where you belonged."

Ouch. "It wasn't only you. Mama, Grandma and Grandpa, my brothers. The only one in this whole family who stood by me was Charlotte."

If Lucky hadn't known the man so well, he might have missed the wince. "I told them about you, how you made your living, you being more than Victor's employee. I didn't tell anybody but your mama about you sending drugs to Daytona, just said to leave you alone."

The man might never know the amount of pain he'd handed down. He'd forfeited any right to make Lucky watch his mouth. "They could have told you to fuck off."

Daddy nodded. "I made sure they didn't."

Anger and pain ripped at Lucky's insides. "Then I'm not sure we have anything left to say to each other." He turned and reached for the doorknob.

So quietly Lucky barely heard, his father said, "Please don't go. I'm sorry, I'm screwing this up. Sit. I need to talk to you." He gestured toward the bed. Lucky stayed put.

Daddy sighed. "Your mama did what I told her, even though she didn't want to. I warned her not to see you, call you, or answer your calls." He met Lucky's eyes. "Do you remember how we used to be? Me and your mother? When my friends told me stories about their wives cheating, spending too much, or drinking, I remembered how blessed I was. We loved each other dearly."

His parents' affection gave Lucky a model to work toward with Bo. But, "Loved?"

"Ever since I put my foot down, things have been tense, her resentment growing every day. Then... Then we got word you died. She came to me, said, 'You cost me my son. You don't get to tell me anything anymore." Daddy wiped at his eyes with his fingers. "She moved upstairs to Bristol's old room, hung that picture of you on the wall right outside the door, and dared me to say anything. I believe if I hadn't gotten so sick, she would've left me outright." Holy hell."

"Charlotte didn't know?"

Daddy shook his head. "No, we didn't talk about our personal problems to our kids, but we didn't talk to each other anymore either. Daytona found out when he moved back home, as Charlotte did when she came to stay."

Of all of Lucky's feared homecoming scenarios, he'd never imagined anything like this. "I don't know what you want me to say."

"You don't have to say anything yet. But my stubbornness is coming home to roost. My parents took your Mama's side, now they're not speaking to me either. And all because I judged my son."

Hard to feel sorry for the man, under the circumstances. "I know I've done my share of terrible things, but you never gave me a chance."

"And I'm paying the price. I just found out my living son is dead, and my dead son's still living. And is the reason I'm still breathing. Thank you for that, by the way. 'Specially under the circumstances." Dad drew in a harsh breath. "That had to be a hard decision."

"Not at all." Lucky parked his ass on the edge of his father's bed, much as he'd done years ago during heart-to-heart talks with this man. "How much did Charlotte tell you?"

"That it wasn't you sent Daytona drugs. Most likely Bristol done it." Daddy stared out the window. If he didn't already know about the life insurance policies, Lucky wasn't telling. Not the time or the place.

Broken. He'd expected pride, stubbornness, anything but his idol fallen from a pedestal and smashed in pieces on the ground. Must be Bo's influence, the sudden bout of compassion. "I... I missed you, old man."

"Wasn't a day gone by I didn't miss you." The man Lucky still wanted to admire lifted his head, gave a sniff, and blinked hard. "I hear you're some kind of cop now."

"I'm a senior agent with the Southeastern Narcotics Bureau. I put away guys like me." Oh crap? Had Lucky actually straightened and held his head higher?

"Guys like you used to be. Charlotte also said you done bought a house and built a nice life for yourself."

"Yeah, Daddy, I did."

"You've turned into one hell of a man. A better man than me." Again with the staring out the window.

Silence lasted long enough to make Lucky worry if he should leave.

"Are you a good enough man to forgive me for being a stiff-necked fool who turned his back on his own son?"

Wait! What? "What did you say?"

Pain shone in Daddy's glistening eyes when he turned Lucky's way. "What I did, there's no excuse for, no matter what reason I thought I had. But if you can't forgive me, hate me all you need to, but please don't hold my stupidity against the rest of the family."

"You mean that? You're really sorry?" And all these years Lucky'd simmered in self-hate for having deserved his shunning.

"I've never been sorrier."

"Look—"

Daddy held up a hand. "I know I'll never be able to say or do anything to make it up to you, but if you'll let me, I'll try."

For years Lucky had clung to guilt for Victor's death, and the certainty he'd lost his parents by his own actions. "I'm a stubborn ass myself, but there's a man out in the kitchen with Mama who'd have a few choice words for me if I said no."

"Then he must be a good man too."

"None better." For a one-time consummate liar, the truth fell so easily from Lucky's tongue these days. But Daddy? Sorry? "You have no idea how bad your turning your back hurt me. Especially when I had no idea what all you blamed me for. I thought it was because I got arrested and I deserved to lose my family."

Daddy shook his shaggy head. "I'm learning. I'm getting a dose of my own medicine. It don't taste none too good."

272

Outside a goat cried out. When Lucky lived here, he'd be making sure the critter hadn't gotten its fool head stuck in a fence.

Weathered skin and recovering health aged Clarence Lucklighter, his arms permanently browned by countless hours spent working in the sun. "You should know that when the doctor told me I didn't have long if I couldn't get a transplant, a part of me wanted to call it quits. I'm glad I didn't. Even if you never speak to me again, and I'd understand if you didn't, it's good to see you again, son."

Son. A sliver of ice chipped off Lucky's innards. "It's weird being back."

Dad scrutinized Lucky long enough to make Lucky squirm. "I'm glad to have you back. Even if…"

Even if he had to lose Bristol. Lucky kept his mouth shut.

"And all this time I was convinced you'd sent Daytona drugs when he'd just gotten out of rehab."

"I didn't, and I wouldn't." How could his own family believe he'd supply his brother's habit for even a moment?

"Seems you've done well for yourself." Nice to hear pride in the man's voice. No matter what happened between them over the years, the little boy in Lucky still wanted his father's approval.

But the grown man in him, the one who no longer crawled, needed to punch the crap out of something in a boxing ring. "I have." With Bo and Walter's help.

The skin around his father's eyes crinkled. "You do understand I'll have to give this man of yours hell, see if he's good enough for my boy, right? It's the Lucklighter way."

Maybe now, but where was this protectiveness when Charlotte married the undisputed prince of assholes? Dad could have saved her a lot of beatings and a cross country move to escape. Victor came to her rescue, not their father.

Bo was a better man than Lucky could have dreamed of, no matter what Dad thought.

"Bo's a good man. The best. Take that as a given. Besides, he won't give you a chance to not like him." He'd have Daddy

273

Lucklighter eating out of his hand in no time. Mama probably already was. Stress from the last twenty-four hours pressed down. Lucky needed sleep, and didn't want to consider his father's words until more of his brain worked.

Daddy flapped a hand. "Now, go on and get out of here. I'm sure the rest of the family wants time with you."

Lucky stood. "Aren't you coming?"

"Probably best I don't. They're not very happy with me right now, and I don't want to meet your man if I'm never going to get to see him again. Maybe later, under better circumstances." Dad rose and gripped Lucky in a hug. "I love you, son. I want you to know I never stopped loving you, though I know I had a piss poor way of showing it." He gave a final squeeze and let go.

"I know, Daddy. I know." Saying the words right now seemed shallow, a kneejerk response to Dad's own declaration. Not that he didn't, but... His thoughts churned, making too little sense at the moment. An anchor. He needed his anchor. Lucky stood at the door, watching the man who'd once been his hero—might still be his hero—shuffle to the window and gaze outside. He might be down, but not out. Lucklighter stubbornness came in handy at times.

Lucky followed voices into the kitchen, rich with the scents of bacon and fresh baked biscuits. May Bo forgive him for the food sins of the next ten minutes.

Dallas and Bo stood by the sink. They stopped talking when Lucky walked in. Dallas opened and closed his mouth a few times. Nothing emerged.

Words needed saying, but maybe not today. "Well, lookie here," Lucky said. "If it ain't Little Dover Lucklighter, all growed up."

"Don't call me that." Just like always. Dallas's grin called his gruff tone a lie.

They studied each other, Lucky tilting his head back to get a good look at the lone tall Lucklighter. Maybe he'd save calling the guy the mailman's kid for when Mama wasn't around.

The moment stretched. Dallas moved first, wrapping Lucky in a bear hug. "I'm sorry, man. I'm so, so sorry."

Lucky wriggled enough to breathe again. "For what?"

"For believing the worst about you."

"Brother, I got convicted and sentenced to ten years. I'm not exactly an angel with a bright shiny halo." How dull would sainthood be? Besides, Lucky couldn't take another person beating themselves up like Daddy just did.

"I know. But still…"

What could Lucky do to dry the tears in Dallas's eyes?

As quick as he'd been twenty years ago—at least in Lucky's mind—he grabbed his brother in a headlock and scraped his knuckles against Dallas's scalp in a noogie.

"If you boys are gonna wrestle, take it out to the barn," Mama said, echoing what she'd uttered many times over the years. She opened the oven and removed a pan of biscuits, nice and brown on the top.

Folks always said everything changed. Thank God, some things stayed the same.

"Let's sit, shall we?" Mama bustled around the table. "Bo, sure you don't want some bacon?"

Out of habit, Lucky and Dallas took their old places at the table. Bo took the spot normally reserved for Daytona. No one so much as glanced at Daddy's place at the head chair.

"I'm sure. But I will have a biscuit or two." Bo raised his brow at the meat Mama piled on Lucky's plate. Lucky shrugged. Couldn't let Mama down, could he? He tucked in, avoiding Bo's eyes.

"Richmond, Bo here tells me his Mama died when he was a young'un." Mama dropped the biggest biscuit onto Bo's plate. "Tell me, Bo, are you any relation to the Chapel Hill Schollenbergers?"

"No, ma'am. Not that I'm aware of. I'm closer to my mama's family than my daddy's. They're Cleggs. My Aunt Janie raised me and my brother." Bo spooned strawberry jam onto his biscuit. One taste of Mama's jam and he might rethink his stance on sugar.

"Any kin to—"

"He's from Arkansas, Mama," Lucky said. Good Lord. Why did Southerners have to play Six Degrees of Separation with everyone they met?

Mama passed around a bowl of scrambled eggs. Lucky grabbed another slice of bacon.

"What part of Arkansas?" Leave it to Mama Lucklighter to search and search until she found someone she and Bo knew in common.

Bo swallowed a mouthful of biscuit. "Pine Bluff."

"Oh! Then do you know—"

Lucky and Dallas both blurted, "Mom!"

"I was just curious." Their scolding kept her quiet all of a minute. "The Stevensons. They used to run a hardware store there."

"I'm afraid I don't, ma'am." Bo shot Lucky wide "Help me!" eyes.

A car engine rumbled ever closer up the driveway. Mama stiffened, then relaxed. The engine sputtered and quieted, a door slammed, and Lucky tracked footsteps across the front porch.

Mama, Bo, and Dallas jumped up and busied themselves cleaning the kitchen. Uh-oh. What did they know that Lucky didn't?

The front door slammed. Daytona strolled in and claimed the last biscuit.

Lucky's youngest brother dropped into a chair next to Lucky and took a bite of biscuit, keeping his eyes focused on his food. "I figured you might be here when I saw that Durango out front." He ripped the biscuit into tiny pieces, raining crumbs onto the table. "I know it ain't right of me, but I need some time, okay?" He raised his eyes then. "I've spent so many years hating you, blaming you. Yeah, Bristol egged me on a bit, but I should've known you wouldn't do me like that."

Lucky stayed quiet.

"Anyway, I'm sorry, but I need to figure things out. Everything I believed turned out to be lies." He shook his head. "Now Bristol's dead. I gotta think. You always did say I wasn't the sharpest tool in the shed." His forced grin wouldn't fool anyone. "So, anyway, I'm going to my room. Maybe next time you come visit we can talk."

Daytona dashed out the door, his footsteps pounding like thunder on the stairs.

Lucky'd gotten his family back, but maybe not all. "Day, wait..."

Mama murmured, "Let him go."

Dallas put a hand on Lucky's arm. "He'll come around. He always does. He's just a little slow about it at times. After all the things he's said about you over the years, he's carrying around a load of guilt." More quietly, he added, "We all are."

"Shouldn't I go talk to him?" Lucky started toward the stairs.

"I'll go." Charlotte disappeared out the door.

Lucky carried his plate to the sink. His family stayed quiet, probably straining to hear anything from Daytona's bedroom, directly above the kitchen.

Footfalls tapped down the stairs. Mama and Dallas sprang into action, rushing around the kitchen and trying way too hard to look like they hadn't been concerned.

Charlotte entered the room. "He's on the phone with his sponsor. He'll be okay."

Maybe Lucky had been selfish to come here and disrupt lives so used to not having him around. "As long as he don't start using again, he can take all the time in the world." Damn. The years had not been kind to the Lucklighter clan.

Still so much needed saying. And Lucky might never tell his folks about Bristol taking out life insurance on Dad. Nothing good would come of him implicating Bristol in Uncle Ned's death. He'd work with Charlotte to settle his brother's affairs and keep the details to a minimum.

They'd been through enough already. Lucky rinsed his coffee cup. "Mama, me and Bo got to get back."

"What? You just got here. I planned to make up your old room."

He exchanged a glance with Bo. "We got work to do." And thoughts to sort out.

One more hug couldn't hurt. If he woke to find he'd dreamed this reunion, he'd at least have something to remember. Damn, but having his mother's arms around him felt good.

She'd changed. Hard to imagine her and Daddy no longer being an unbreakable team.

Her eyes glistened when she stepped back. She latched onto Bo. "Now, don't be a stranger. And keep Richmond in line, okay?"

Bo grinned his most evil. "I'll do my best, ma'am."

"You are coming to the funeral, right?" A tear spilled down Mama's cheek.

"If I can." Lucky hugged her one more time.

Time to go. But one day soon he'd be back. When he could stay longer. And under better circumstances.

Lucky took his place in the Durango, watching his family retreat into the house.

Bo put the truck into gear and started turning around.

Movement in the side mirror caught Lucky's eye. "Bo! Stop!"

Bo slammed on the brakes. Lucky hopped out of the truck, hiding a wince when he hit the ground a bit too hard.

His dad hit equally hard, clutching Lucky in a death grip, his blubbering mangling his words. "I'm sorry. I'm so, so sorry."

Daddy's tears mingled with Mama's on Lucky's shirt collar.

His father hugged him from the front and Bo from the back. Together, they might've exerted enough force to fuse the long-broken pieces of Lucky's heart.

"I hope you'll come back and see us soon," his father said.

"I will, Daddy, I will." Maybe after Lucky worked some shit out in his head.

His father shuffled back toward the house. Lucky watched him leave, leaning into his wife for support.

"Let's go." He climbed back into the Durango.

At the end of the driveway Bo's phone rang. "Schollenberger. Oh shit. Really?" He let out a sigh. "Okay. I'll be there."

He hung up the phone and pulled the truck onto the road. "I'm so sorry, Lucky. That was Jimmy. I gotta drop you off and get back to work. But I promise, come hell or high water, I'll be there for the funeral."

Fuck.

CHAPTER TWENTY-SEVEN

The old wooden church hadn't changed much. Same plank flooring and massive ceiling fans. They'd added a sound system and a TV monitor, but the table at the front might have been the same one from when Mama dragged Lucky and his siblings to church.

For the first time in years, Lucky sat with his family, Charlotte on one side, Bo on the other, Dallas and Daytona supporting Mama on the pew in front of him. Todd and Ty sat behind their mother. As many times as Lucky'd dreamed of being with them all again, the reason sucked.

Grandma and Grandpa Lucklighter sat on the same row as his mother, surrounded by various family members, many Lucky hadn't seen in twenty years.

Daddy sat alone, off to the side. Lucky crossed the distance and led him back into the fold. He took a place next to Charlotte. No one complained. Lucklighters stuck together, no matter what. Bo nodded his approval.

Bristol's girlfriend wasn't there, nor friends, if he had any. Nothing left of Bristol either but a box full of ashes. Charlotte sniffled. Lucky tightened his arm around her back, and met his Dad's arm embracing her from the other side.

The preacher said a few words, and one by one the family passed by the box holding Bristol's remains.

Lucky hugged Charlotte, he hugged Mama, and he hugged his Daddy. He hugged his two remaining brothers, his nephews, and his grandparents. Now wasn't the time for a lengthy conversation, but one day soon.

The truth might have set him free, but it brought none of the relief and peace the preacher used to promise. His brother. Dead.

Because of him. No, not because of him. Bristol made his own choices; a fact the ever-patient Dr. Drake might need to repeat a few dozen times before the fact sank through Lucky's incredibly thick skull.

Lucky plodded out of the church into the adjoining cemetery, filled with Lucklighters past. He roamed the grounds, clearing his head and paying respects to his great-grandparents. A relatively new headstone caught his eyes: Richmond Eugene Lucklighter: Beloved Son.

And damned if the tears he'd been holding back didn't fall like rain.

He never questioned the arms around him. Familiarity told him who comforted him. That and the scent of Bo's cologne. Bo held him while he cried—for Bristol, for Daytona, Mama, Daddy, Charlotte, Dallas, and finally, for himself and a lot of wasted years.

Lucky lazed on the grassy hill where he'd spent so much time as a kid. And like most times before, his sister stretched out beside him. His lover lay on his other side. The partner he'd never expected way back when.

Bo joined his hand with Lucky's. "You've got a great family. I really like 'em."

Poor guy. He'd gotten the shit end of the stick, familywise. Yeah, Lucky'd been, well, lucky.

"They're okay, I reckon, 'cept for Dover and Talladega." Years ago the family stopped talking about Lucky. Now no one spoke Bristol's name. Let them have their silence for now, but sooner or later they needed to work everything out.

"Hey!" Charlotte shouted. "Just 'cause we're supposed to be adults don't mean I can't still kick your ass."

"Can n—"

Bo placed a restraining hand on his arm. "Remember her heavy purse? She's armed."

Yes, she was. Lucky'd let her threat go for now, but when she least expected, she'd find a rubber snake in her bed. He owed her.

And he'd yet to pay Bo back for stealing his clothes.

A few feet away, two teenaged boys wrestled in the grass. How strange to answer to "Uncle Richie" again.

Lucky said, "If there's anything we can do to help, let us know." Helping Mama and Daddy might put Bo and Lucky back some, but they'd manage. More medical bills rolled in each day.

Charlotte sat up. "Which reminds me! I started one of those online contribution things to help raise money to cover Daddy's expenses. With everything going on, I haven't checked donations lately."

She punched a few buttons on her cell phone, then punched a few more. Her face went white. "Rich, would you make sure I'm not hallucinating?"

Lucky scrolled through her iPhone. Mr. and Mrs. Smith from Atlanta contributed two thousand dollars. Dayum! "Mr. Tibbles, ten bucks, Twinkles, ten bucks, Patches, ten bucks. Oh. Mrs. Griggs, fifty." Trust the woman to make donations in her cats' names. More contributors filled the list, this or that cousin or other relative, folks from Mama's church, with the occasional neighbor pitching in, a donation from Loretta Johnson, and...

"Bo?" Lucky handed the phone off like Charlotte had, mouth suddenly dry.

The last entry read, "Anonymous, Nice, France. One hundred thousand dollars."

Anonymous, hell.

The color came back to Charlotte's grinning face. "You know that'll pay off the rest of Dad's bills and yours, and keep him and Mama going till he gets back on his feet, right?"

Just enough, and not too much more. Trust Lucky's mentors to take care of things, like they always had.

But they better not expect any favors in return. And he'd probably never find a trace of who really sent the money, no matter how hard he looked. He'd always considered himself the best, but lately he'd found a few better.

Not by much, but better.

"Victor donated the money, didn't he?" Charlotte blurted.

Time to have a talk with his sister about mentioning Victor's name around Bo. The past was the past, but still... Bo didn't need to hear about Lucky's ex. "Nice, France. He's got a sister there." And she'd never trouble herself with Lucky's family. So had to be Victor. Or more likely, Victor and Nestor.

Charlotte kept going. "You know he made a college fund for the boys, right?"

"Yeah. He said he did."

"Todd's decided on Clemson. We'll be down in a few weeks to move him into his dorm." She fixed her gaze on Lucky. "Okay if we stay with you a few days? Now you're back, I don't intend to let you get away again."

Charlotte and her boys? In Lucky and Bo's house? The noise, the running around?

Oh, hell yeah. "Sure. We can put you up for a few days. I'll start getting things ready as soon as we get home." Though leaving the farm tomorrow might kill him. Only, with Mama in the next room, Bo still on assignment, and no time to sneak out to the barn, Lucky might die from lack of sex. "Um... Okay with you, Bo?"

"You even have to ask?"

No, reckon not. "You've been off work a few weeks already. Will your boss give you more time?" Sooner or later, Charlotte would have to return to Spokane. Damn it.

Charlotte reclined on her arms, turning her face to the sun. "Um... That's something else I need to talk to you about. I'm quitting my job and enrolling in nursing school. I've been taking classes online already."

"Why now?"

"Well, with Todd in college, and Ty planning on joining the Navy when he graduates, I reckon I need something else to focus on when my babies are gone."

"How will you handle Todd being so far from you?"

"I'm not sure. But I'm a Lucklighter. I'll manage somehow." Charlotte winked.

Lucklighter-speak for *I'll find someone else's life to meddle in.*

Oh hell.

Lucky laid his head back on the passenger seat headrest and closed his eyes, unwilling to watch his old home growing smaller in the side mirror. Easier to ignore his mother standing on the front porch, in the exact spot where she'd watched him leave over twelve years ago.

"Hey, you okay?" Bo said, resting his hand on Lucky's knee. Brown eyes, full of concern, wrinkles etched between his brows.

"Have I ever been?"

For one moment, The Dimple appeared in Bo's cheek, gone in a heartbeat. "Okay enough for me."

Lucky's tired laugh came out more of a chuckle. "Dude, you need to raise your standards."

"They're high enough, thank you very much. Now, take a nap. I'll wake you up when we get back to Richmond."

"What about you?" Bo had to be running on fumes too.

"If I get too tired, I'll pull over and take a nap."

"We both need some rest."

"Oh yeah?" Bo's high-wattage smile belied the weariness in his eyes and dark circles underneath.

"Yeah. You're here. I'm here. The most annoying agent on the face of the earth isn't."

"You mean Keith? Why would he be here?"

"As hard as this is to believe, Jimmy is worse. Keith's an asshole, Jimmy's more like an overly friendly puppy who won't give us five minutes alone together." The man took cock block-ing to new heights, always calling or showing up whenever they wrangled some time alone.

"I'll tell you what. Let's go test the mattress in my rental It's been lonely there sleeping without you." Bo leered and waggled his brows. "Nap first, bounce test second?"

Oh, God, yes! Lucky's cock began to stiffen despite his ex-haustion. "Sounds fine to me." He closed his eyes, a smile on his face. Finally! He'd get Bo naked. The things they'd do.

He woke to Jimmy peering through his window. "Sorry, Lucky. I'm afraid we need your partner. And Walter Smith has asked you to return to Atlanta."

Fuck! He'd never wanted to kick the shit out of someone so badly.

Lucky glanced over at Bo. They both heaved a sigh. Someone forgot to mention sexual deprivation in their job descriptions.

CHAPTER TWENTY-EIGHT

Lucky rubbed his fingers over his bleary eyes and sank down in his usual chair in front of the boss's desk. One hell of a long ride home, Jimmy chattering nonstop all the way, and an entire day of fitful sleep hadn't restored his mood.

At least he'd had a relatively good night. Until his phone rang.

And rang. About every five minutes. He loved his family, welcomed the lot of them back into his life with open arms, but damn! Did they really have to know his whereabouts all the time?

"And you're sure you're okay?" Walter leaned forward in his chair, resting his clasped hands on the desk.

"I have it on good authority that I'm not any nicer."

The boss chuckled. "If you were, I'd worry." The humor fled his face. "I mean it, Lucky. You've been through a lot. Despite any animosity between you, you lost a close family member."

"I'll spill my guts to my counselor later." He'd rather talk to Bo. "Is that why you sent for me?"

"That and the need to get things back to normal here. I've been missing my two best agents, and I want them back." Walter stared at something over Lucky's head. "The Virginia office has been hinting at keeping you both. I needed to put my foot down."

Put his foot right up their collective asses, more than likely. Nobody messed with Walter's team.

"Jameson's latest class ends tomorrow, but I'd like you to drop by the session this morning and allow him to make introductions. After Fourth of July weekend, they're all yours, though I've asked Loretta Johnson to assist."

"I work alone."

Walter didn't have to smile so indulgently. "Of course you do. So much so that I assume you have no interest at all in Agent Schollenberger's recall to this office."

Oh crap! Hallelujah! "None at all." Lucky barely reeled in his excitement. Finally! "Say I was to be interested, any idea when he'll get back? Just so I can clean my empty coffee cups off his desk. He gets irritated about me taking over the whole cube."

"I believe he said he'd arrive around six thirty this evening."

"Boss, I'll attend the training this morning, but I need the afternoon off. Got something I gotta take care of."

Walter fought a grin and shuffled the ever-present paper pile on his desk. Oh look! If Lucky twisted his neck the right way, he'd catch a glimpse of the wood beneath.

"As long as you've completed your reports, I have no problem with you taking a half day."

"Um... If you see Bo before I do, tell him you had me run an errand or something."

Walter raised one of his bushy eyebrows. "Are you planning something that might make me regret covering for you?"

"Nah. I promise." Lucky nearly skipped out of Walter's office and down the hallway. Oops. Time to paste on a scowl.

Keith stood by Lisa's desk. "But it'll only take about a half hour," he whined.

Lisa shifted her attention from Keith to Lucky, *Please help me!* in her eyes.

"Oh, Lisa. Great. I caught you when you weren't busy." He gave Keith a pointed stare and grinned his most evil. "Do you like green drugs and spam? Are you an asshole, Keith, my man?"

The color drained from Keith's face. "You!"

"Yup, me. And interfering with another employee's work is a write-up offense. But I don't do write-ups." Oh, how priceless the fear on Keith's face. "I prefer to settle things in a boxing ring."

Keith relaxed his rigid stance and gave away his stupidity with a chuckle. "You're in no shape to box."

"But I am." Johnson flexed on up to the desk, short sleeves straining over her biceps. "And as Agent Harrison's second-in-command, I'll happily teach you a lesson you won't soon forget. Just say when." She led the relieved-looking receptionist away from the desk. "C'mon, Lisa. Let's go get some coffee."

Lucky whistled and swaggered away toward his cube, leaving Keith fuming alone.

Now... Forget Charlotte's shunning of e-mails. Lucky needed her help, and couldn't write as fast as she talked. Why write, when she'd write for him?

He pecked out an e-mail. *"Hey, woman. Bo's coming home, and I want to make it special. If you don't help me, I'll screw it all up, and Bo won't speak to either one of us for six months."*

There.

Knowing Bo waited at the end of the day made getting through a roomful of rookies—and Jameson O'Donoghue—more tolerable. Lucky tapped his foot, earning more than one scowl from the trainer.

Screw him. Or rather, no. Lucky counted the minutes until noon. At twelve o'clock he marched to his cube, printed his sister's reply, and trudged down the hall, shoulders slumped, like he'd noticed zombies do on a late-night TV show.

"Oh, you poor man," Lisa remarked. "You must be exhausted."

"I am. Gonna go get some rest." The moment the elevator doors closed, the dead returned to life. So much to do, so little time.

And worth every minute.

With him and Bo away for the better part of the last week, the chores piled up. Johnson swung by the house to feed the animals, but she drew the line at cleaning up. Lucky stopped by the grocery store, the hardware store, a housewares place, and the post office, to claim a package requiring his signature.

After unpacking his bags at home, he pulled Charlotte's list out of his pocket. First things first: let the dog and cat into the backyard to keep them out from underfoot. Next, he loaded the washing machine per his sister's instructions. Why he couldn't throw whites in with darks he'd never understand. It'd worked so far in his life.

Vacuuming took too much time, him having to stop repeatedly and wriggle free of the cord. Next, he did what he should've done months ago and fixed the garage door once and for all by replacing the motor and all parts even remotely suspected of causing grief.

He'd save painting the bedroom ceiling for the weekend. He washed the sheets, remade the bed, and located Bo's never-ending candle supply.

Unpacking the new dishes they'd been eyeing for a while took some time, as did running them through the dishwasher. Lucky packed the old stuff up for Goodwill.

One hour left. Not enough time to suddenly become an excellent cook. Takeout would have to do. Bo loved eggplant parmesan. He'd get what he loved. Lucky made the call.

Twenty minutes until time to go get dinner, Lucky sat down and opened the mailer he'd signed for.

The picture didn't compare to the sheer beauty of Bo's ring. The mountains stood out in dark gray against a lighter background. Inside the ring, Lucky had nearly given in and repeated the words he'd used the first time: "I love you, asshole." Hey, they'd worked before.

Charlotte never had to know.

In the end, he'd settled for mushy sentiment. "Love always, T-Rex." The old cheap rings found their way into the Goodwill box.

He picked up dinner and had everything ready when Bo got home.

Bo turned around and around in the living room. "Wow! Look at this place. What smells so good?"

"Your favorite." Without giving him a chance to answer, Lucky cut off any replies the best way possible—mouth to mouth.

Bo came up for air first. "Are you sure you're Lucky?"

Ouch. But not undeserved. "C'mon. Get cleaned up and eat before dinner gets cold." He patted Bo's ass on the way to the kitchen.

"Wow! When did you get the dishes? I've been meaning to, but with being up in the Virginia office and all..."

Oh shit. "These were the ones you wanted, right?" Please let Lucky not have screwed up.

"Yeah." Bo squeezed Lucky's hand under the dinner table. Wine, candlelight, although the sunlight still pouring in the windows at seven o'clock ruined the effect. May and June had whizzed past in a blur. Time for things to slow down.

All through dinner, Bo kept suspicious eyes trained on Lucky. Who could blame him? Lucky didn't often go out of his way to please his man.

But tonight wouldn't be the last time. He even managed to keep his mouth shut and not make innuendo about Bo biting into a baby carrot—a carrot he'd resisted temptation to carve into a penis.

Bo rose and picked up his plate at the end of the meal. "Thanks for an amazing dinner."

Lucky took the plate from his hand. "Go, sit down. I got this."

"Are you sure?"

Not really. "Yeah." Lucky had to rearrange the dishes three times before he could close the dishwasher door. He'd have to get Bo to teach him the correct way to stack dishes. Another time.

Oh! He dashed to the laundry room, removed the clothes from the washer, and put them in the dryer.

Bo sat in the living room, reclined on one end of a couch with his laptop on his knees.

Lucky moved the computer to the coffee table. "Enough with work. You're home now." He settled on the floor, removed Bo's shoes, and rubbed his feet. Oh, how nice to be able to move freely, without his middle threatening to rip open.

Bo moaned. "Not that I'm complaining or anything, but what are you up to?"

"Can't I do nice things for no particular reason?" The ring might be burning a hole in his pocket, but he'd wait until the right moment. No more getting turned down.

"Yes, but it's a bit out of character for you, isn't it?"

Not anymore. Lucky stopped his task long enough to click on the stereo with the remote. Soft music filled the room, some band he'd never heard of. He'd found the disk among Bo's CDs.

Lucky pressed his thumbs against the arch of Bo's feet, earning another moan. Bo laid his head back and closed his eyes. "I'll give you an hour to stop that."

"Can I take a half-hour and then you come with me somewhere?"

Bo snapped his eyes open, one brow raised. "What do you have in mind?"

"You'll see."

Late night department stores had their uses. Bo and Lucky didn't run into many other customers on their way to the yard and garden section.

Bo trudged along after Lucky. "What are we looking for again?"

"I'll know when I find it."

"Couldn't this wait until tomorrow?"

"No!" It couldn't. No way, no how. This needed doing.

They wound their way around patio furniture, umbrellas... Bo stopped. "This set would look real nice—Ack!"

Lucky dragged Bo by the arm past the furniture. "Later." After they'd completed their mission.

Finally they arrived at the display he'd sought. Oh shit. Four models to choose from.

"Eenie, meenie, minee, moe," he muttered under his breath. Metal? Stone? Chimney?

Bo edged closer. "Mind telling what we're doing here?"

"I think the backyard needs a fire pit, don't you? Which one do you like? I like that one." He pointed to the biggest. Bigger had to be better, right?

"Hmmm... while I can't understand why we have to do this now, I like this one too. Just think, we can sit outside, light a fire..."

"Let's get it and go." Choice made. Now to put plans into action. He would have already made arrangements, but he'd learned to let Bo help him pick things out for the house. Yes, he could be taught.

Bo smacked Lucky's hand and inserted himself between Lucky and the prize. "If you even get a notion about lifting so much weight, I'll cuff you and haul your ass outta here." He called a sales clerk over for help.

As long as they didn't take all night. Next, shopping for accessories, then getting out of the store and loading the truck.

Bo hunched his shoulders and leaned against the loaded Durango. Three young men barely out of high school wrangled their purchase into the vehicle. "I don't understand why we couldn't do this tomorrow. What's so all fired important about tonight?"

"You'll see." Fourth of July weekend. Three days of nothing to do.

Yeah, they'd find something to do, all right. Lucky held his hand out for the keys. His mission. He'd do the driving, even though his car's tiny trunk would have laughed at what he'd bought.

"It's my SUV. You could let me drive." Trust Bo to be stubborn.

"Could, yeah. Am I? No." Bo drove too slow and stopped for yellow lights. Lucky cruised right on through and got them home in five minutes flat. Hey! A new record.

Bo made of show of peeling his fingers away from the dashboard. "Planning a second career as an Indy car driver?"

Oh, the horrors! "Bite your tongue, man. We both know NASCAR is the only race worth watching." At least in his father's eyes—the reason he named his kids after NASCAR tracks.

Redneck, through and through.

Bo jumped out of the Durango before Lucky and beat him to the back of the vehicle. "Let me get this. You're not supposed to lift anything heavy."

"You can't carry it alone." One man couldn't lift the damned thing by himself, let alone lug the monstrosity to the backyard. Of course, they could try tying the box to Moose and using him for a pack animal.

"Y'all need some help?"

Lucky jumped. How did the guy from next door always know when they needed something? First thing tomorrow, he'd check the yard for cameras.

Bo gave Lucky a triumphant grin and turned toward the neighbor. "Please, if you don't mind. Lucky here had surgery recently and can't lift. Can you help me get this out of the truck?"

Recently? A month and a half. Ancient history.

Lucky tuned out the introductions beyond, "I don't think I've ever properly introduced myself. I'm Stanley Taylor." Like the guy had to say so. Lucky'd taken his name off the mailbox and planned to run a full background check the moment he found time.

His ears perked when Stanley invited them over for dinner and Bo promised to take him up on the offer. Meet the neighbors? Go into their house? Eat with them?

Bo probably needed two years more therapy after meeting the Lucklighters.

Lucky didn't exactly run the man off the moment they'd finished their task.

Bo elbowed him all the same. "He's our neighbor, being neighborly, did you have to scowl at him?"

"I wasn't scowling." Actually, he'd been going for more of a glare. Glares got folks' feet moving quick most times.

Bo stared at Lucky's gotta-have-it-now fire pit, hands on his hips. "Anyway, it's here, it's in the ground, what now?"

"Now we start a fire." Oh, yeah. Lucky planned some burning.

"Now?"

"Got something better to do?"

"A few things, actually." Bo swayed and ran his hands up and down his body, stripper style.

Oh, hell. Lucky's cock took notice. "Later."

Bo's mouth dropped open. "Later! Later, he says. I'm offering sex, and he says later."

Lucky hoped his gaze pierced Bo's soul, like Bo's so often pierced Lucky's. He nodded. "Oh yeah."

Bo's Adam's apple bobbed. "Oh. Alrighty, then. Let's get this fire started."

Using fallen twigs and branches gleaned from the backyard, Lucky fanned the flames of a cheery blaze five minutes later.

"Now." He looked Bo straight in the eyes. "I want every single damned condom out here in this pit. Now!"

Bo froze. And then grinned. "Yes, sir!" He darted through the backyard and up the steps, doing a gazelle-worthy leap over their couch-sized dog.

He returned a few moments later and skidded to a halt a few feet from Lucky. "You wanna do the honors, or you want me to?"

"I don't care, as long as those suckers burn." And the sooner the better. No more condoms for Lucky ever again.

Bo tossed in a handful. Then a whole unopened box.

Ah, what a pretty sight, the hints of color the rubbers added to the flames. Smelled like hell, but still pretty. Lucky stood watching the flames destroy them, arm around Bo's waist. "You get them all?"

"I think so."

"Bathroom? Bedside table?"

"Yes and yes."

"Your wallet, the couch cushions, the glovebox? The Harley's saddlebags?"

"Oh. Be right back." Bo took off like a shot, Moose chasing behind him. Damn if the mutt's barking didn't sound like laughter.

"What 'cha doin' over there?" the neighbor called from his side of their shared fence.

Oh shit. One introduction and now they'd never get rid of the guy. "I could tell you, but trust me, it'd be too much information." There. Let him chew on that.

Bo came back and dug packets out of all his pockets. How many condoms did they own?

As long as the answer from here on out was none, who cared?

Bo dragged two lounge chairs up near the fire. They sat in the chairs, holding hands, watching the flames getting smaller and smaller.

"Happy now?" Bo brought their joined hands up to his mouth and kissed Lucky's knuckles.

"Not there yet, but close."

Bo's eyes shone by the light of the dying embers and the security light Lucky installed before they moved in. Nice out here this time of evening. He'd take Bo back to the store and grin and nod while he picked out some patio furniture.

Later.

Bo forced his tongue between two of Lucky's fingers.

Much later.

If he'd been made a bit taller, a bit stockier—with longer arms—he'd have Bo over his shoulder in a fireman's carry and hauling ass for the bedroom. Hell, he could get Bo over his shoulder, but Bo's height meant he'd drag.But then someone had to go and whack a hole in Lucky's side, putting his dragging men days on hold for a while. Racing wasn't happening. Lucky settled for a fast shuffle.

Bo paused long enough to put out the fire and still beat Lucky into the house and got bathwater running. Lucky let Moose and Cat Lucky in, fed them, and locked up for the night.

A hot bath and a little one-on-one time... Lucky ambled down the hall and strode into the bedroom, a single thing on his mind.

Bo met him at the bathroom door.

Suddenly the candles he'd laid out and scented oils he'd bought to give Bo a massage fell down on Lucky's priority list.

Bo said, "I'm glad you're feeling bet—"

Lucky body-slammed his lover against the nearest wall and proceeded to squeeze any air out from between their bodies.

Breathing. Highly overrated.

Lucky sealed his mouth to Bo's, cutting off his protest by deepening the kiss. No doctor's orders, no worries about "Is it too soon?" or anything else would stop him or even slow him down. Hands up the front of Bo's shirt, Lucky ran his fingers through a light covering of chest hair and swallowed Bo's gasp of surprise.

Carefully, so as not to make Bo feel trapped or restrained, he raised their hands over his head, skimmed his fingers down Bo's arms, and broke the kiss long enough to yank Bo's shirt up and off. The heat in Bo's eyes might melt him, but what a way to go.

Bo got with the program, returning the favor, shirt-wise. They both toed off their shoes. Hands. Everywhere at once. Removing jeans, palming a butt cheek, running up firm abs, or in Lucky's case, Bo running a gentle finger near Lucky's scar, not getting too close.

Lucky turned Bo around to stand spread-eagled. Damn, but he looked good against a wall. Lucky rose on his toes, softly biting the spot where shoulder and neck came together. Bo moaned. One of many lustful sounds he'd make tonight.

Working his way down Bo's back, kneading, licking, biting, sucking, Lucky reacquainted himself with the hottest man he'd ever met. Bo's running showed in his muscles, firm and cut enough to stand out, stopping short of being bulky.

Lucky kissed every freckle and ended up on his knees, fondling the wonderful fullness of Bo's glutes, biting, stroking. He reached lower to play with Bo's balls and ran a hand upward. Oh yeah. Fully hard.

His probing finger met little resistance and a whole lot of ready to go. Wow, Bo'd prepped fast! Lucky groaned, resting his head on Bo's ass. Bo. Ready. Now. Maybe he'd missed their loving as much as Lucky had.

Bo bucked back, rocking Lucky's head, jarring him from his fight for control.

Lucky rose, rubbing his hand where he'd rested his head. Bo spread his legs wider, bringing him down to the perfect height.

Lucky positioned himself and slid inside, imagining Bo's preparations. Lube. The toy from the bedside drawer. Oh, man. And he hadn't gotten to watch.

But this beat any toy: slick, hot, home. Bo pushed back, establishing a rhythm. No barriers between them now or ever again. Lucky kissed Bo's back, sliding in and out, reaching around to work Bo's cock to the rhythm of their thrusts.

Nothing existed but the two of them, the scent of Bo and sex, their breathing, the slap of flesh against flesh. But no. Too hard. Too fast.

Withdrawing nearly killed him.

"Wha..." Bo glanced back over his shoulder.

Lucky turned Bo and locked their lips together for a slow shuffle across the floor, the closest thing to dancing they'd done in a while. Dancing. Give him a few weeks, and he'd take Bo out dancing. To dinner. Whatever the man wanted.

But for now, he guided them both across the floor to their bed.

Their bed. Their home. Their lives.

And nothing to fear after all. How had he lived before Bo?

Bo shoved Lucky backward on the bed. Forceful, huh? Oh, hell yeah! Lucky lay back, hypnotized by the play of light over Bo's muscles while Bo settled himself on top, closed his eyes, and let out a breathy sigh when he slid down Lucky's cock.

Bo splayed his hands on Lucky's chest, rising and falling, his gaze fused to Lucky's. He stopped and bent to join their mouths and tongues.

Palming whatever parts he got his hands on, Lucky urged the action on, thrusting upward to meet Bo's coming down. Hot, sweaty, man on man. Grunts, groans, and bed squeaks all became the sweetest music.

Every stroke, every so-damned-good-it-nearly-hurt stroke, brought Lucky closer and closer. To climax, to Bo, to shattering into a million pieces.

Those pieces would come back together as a better man.

Bo bent for another kiss, stoking his cock, his movements jerky and erratic.

Lucky grabbed Bo's ass and held on through the tremors, releasing his hold on his own control. Together they rocked through the earthquake, clinging to each other.

Bo collapsed beside him, pure joy bursting out of him on a laugh.

Running a lazy hand down Bo's side, Lucky put all other thoughts out of his mind. He'd live in the moment.

In the distance, his phone rang. Too comfortable to move, he remained still, catching his breath, Bo's come cooling on his belly.

When their breathing slowed, they shifted enough for him to place his head on Bo's chest, taking comfort in Bo's throbbing heartbeat. Why had he ever been afraid of commitment? Of loving the best thing to ever happen to him? Like hell would he ever let go.

Forever. He wanted forever. The rings lay in his pocket on the floor. Getting up to find them took energy. He'd get them later.

"Bo, would you—"

Bo's soft snores ended the moment.

Later. He'd ask again later.

He lay for a moment, trailing his fingers over Bo's chest. Where was the splashing noise coming from?

Oh, dear God!

Lucky shot out of the bed, tripped over Cat Lucky, and crawled into the bathroom on his knees in time to witness a white, furry butt disappear over the rim of the tub. Water sloshed onto the floor.

"Moose!" Lucky lunged for the running faucet. Ow! Had to remember not to stretch too far.

Moose, tongue lolling out the side of his mouth, lunged too, splashing more water and chasing Lucky's hand.

Ewww... Wet dog. Huge mess.

Not the way the night should've ended.

But it ended with Bo in Lucky's bed, their shared roof over their heads, Lucky's family calling every five minutes simply to say hello, and all right in the world.

Not a bad deal.

He checked his phone:

Richie, me and the boys are coming down, since it's a long weekend and Daddy's doing fine. You'll be home, right?

Yup. All right in the world.

CHAPTER TWENTY-NINE

Bo sat in the living room, wearing blue jeans and no shirt, laptop on his lap. "I wanted to show you this last night, but we got... um... distracted."

Lucky dropped down to stare at the screen—a hard thing to do with his lover's bare chest competing for his attention.

Holy crap. Bank records. Carefully planned deposits under one company name, all large but under ten grand so as not to draw too much attention or trigger an inquiry from the Internal Revenue Service.

Lucky checked out the entity. A front. The company's webpage showed buyer-guy's picture from the warehouse and little else.

"Curtis Allison, or one of his many aliases," Bo said. "The guy I was assigned to."

And the scum never realized where Bo's true loyalties lay. But then again, Bo excelled at undercover work. "They catch him?"

"Not yet, but he's joined the DEA's most wanted list. Only a matter of time, especially since we've got a recorded admission to having your brother killed, and I saw him shoot the supplier."

Hmm... Maybe a friendly note to Lucky's guardian devils might be in order.

Bo slid a finger over the touch-screen, scrolling down to more bank records. "See these deposits?"

Lucky studied the amounts, the dates, the... "Well, I'll be damned."

"Not if I can help it." Bo kissed his nose. "Bristol used his bank job to arrange these payments, laundering money for Allison and others in the organization." He called up Bristol's

300

personal account information. "The payments spiked here. He got greedy and tried to extort money from people he shouldn't have messed with."

"And they killed him."

Bo nodded. "I'm sorry. If I'd been in place in time..."

"Wasn't your fault."

"Still, he was as good as my brother-in-law." Bo took Lucky's hand.

Brother-in-law meant marriage. Now might not be the best time, but... "Bo, I..."

The doorbell rang. Damn it!

Bo closed his laptop. "I do believe my sister-in-law and nephews are here."

Five minutes too soon.

Lucky sat next to Bo at a round corner booth, with Charlotte beside him and the two boys next to Bo. Man, they'd grown up. They were still a bit gawky, and Ty carried some extra weight around his middle, but he'd burn the excess off with his next growth spurt.

Both boys piled their plates high with pizza from the buffet. So far, Bo hadn't said anything about Lucky's four slices of meat lover's. But he'd better watch out or he'd put on a few pounds before the doctor cleared him for intense workouts.

Ty stuck to the veggie and cheese pizzas and sat really close to Bo.

Served Lucky right for not being there. Now the kid sucked up any male attention.

But wait. Did they have their phones out?

Heh. Opportunities like this didn't come along every day. "Um... Bo, don't you always tell me it's rude to have your phone out at the table?"

"What?" Bo paused with a pizza slice halfway to his mouth, a lovely flush filling his cheeks. "Oh, yeah. Sorry. I was just showing Ty something."

Ty slipped his phone beneath the table and traded guilty looks with Bo.

"Seems like old times," Charlotte said, toasting Lucky and Bo with a glass of sweet tea. "Bo, did Richie here tell you that whenever he came to visit, the first thing we'd do is go out for pizza?"

Uh-oh. Bo's evil half-smile didn't bode well for Lucky. "No, *Richie* didn't."

"Yeah, Vic..." Her smile fell. "Crap. Me and my big mouth. Sorry, y'all."

Bo reached across the table and took her hand. "It's okay. I know all about Lucky and Victor Mangiardi."

She cut her eyes toward Bo and back to Lucky.

"Really. It's okay. Please, finish what you were saying." Bo leaned in. His ears might start flapping any minute now.

Charlotte waited, a question in her eyes. Good for her. After all this time she still had her brother's back. Lucky nodded. While he didn't flaunt his past in front of his present and future, it was a bit late to start hiding.

With his permission, Charlotte took off and ran. "Victor liked restaurants with valet parking, if you get my meaning. He didn't like throwing back pizza and beer with us rednecks."

Funny. Someone recently sent Lucky a photo of Victor and Walter, of all people, munching pizza.

Bo leaned in some more. "You don't say." Any farther and he'd topple over into Charlotte's lap.

"You've met me, right?" Lucky tossed in. "Then you know I'm redneck."

The waiter strolled by with a pitcher of tea. Everyone but Bo held up their glasses for more. "Thank you, hon," Charlotte said.

Bo wasn't finished digging up embarrassing facts about Lucky. "Charlotte, if you don't mind my asking, you've been living up north for years, and L... Richie's never lived out of the south. So how come your Southern accent is thicker than his?"

If looks could kill, Bo would be dialing 9-1-1. Just wait until they got home.

"Well... there's two reasons, really." She waited for Lucky's nod again. "Being around Victor exposed him to high falutin' rich folks. They kinda rubbed off."

What? "Did not!" He did *not* sound like Victor or his rich-assed friends.

"Did too!" Charlotte stuck out her tongue.

Strange how whenever they got together, they still acted like kids.

Bo broke up the fight. "You said two reasons. What's the other?'

Charlotte smiled, so much like the devious girl she'd once been. "'Cause I talk like this on girl's night out at the club and never pay for a single drink."

"Mom!" Todd shouted.

"What?" She raised a brow in her oldest son's direction. "You're grown and practically out of the house now. I don't have to pretend I'm perfect no more."

"You'll always be perfect to me," Ty said, batting his eyes.

"No, you're not getting a new truck, so stop buttering me up. You'll drive my car to get your license like your brother did." Damn, she did sound more Southern than Lucky.

Ty wilted. "Yes, ma'am."

She kept the truth to herself, but Lucky didn't have to be a genius to figure out her secret. Weekly calls to the parents probably left her talking like she'd left the farm only yester-day. And no rubbing Lucky's nose in the painful truth.

Hell, in a year or so, Lucky might revert to his old speech patterns. Who knew?

"What we doing the rest of the day?" Charlotte asked.

"I dunno. What you got in mind?" Lucky's recovery left hiking Stone Mountain out of a list of possibilities.

She flashed her wicked smile again. "You ain't tried to out-shoot me lately. Reckon you still can?"

He'd love to, but running off to the range wouldn't be fair to... What was with the phones? Bo, Todd, and Ty all had their heads together and their phones out again, fingers racing lightning quick across the keyboards.

"What are y'all doing?" Charlotte cocked her head to the side, angling for a view of the phones.

Three phones fell, three guilty looks rose.

With a series of exchanged glances, the trio apparently nominated Bo as spokesman. He placed his phone on the table. "It's this game. We all three play and, well, there's lots of stuff to collect around here."

A game? Oh! A game! "I'll bet there's lots of pookies or puffballs or whatever hiding all around Atlanta. Why don't you drive the boys around a bit? I'm sure they're getting bored hearing me and Charlotte talk about old times."

"You sure you don't mind?"

Chances to be the good guy didn't often fall in Lucky's lap. "Sure. Drop me and Char off at the house. We'll watch a movie or something. Give you fellas some bonding time."

Bo flicked a suspicious gaze between Lucky and Charlotte. "Well, if you're sure."

"We're sure," Lucky and his sister replied together.

The moment Bo let them out of the car at the house, Lucky asked, "You don't have your gun on you, do you?"

"Nah, gotta get it outta the house."

They waited in the driveway for Bo to leave with the boys before they grabbed Char's gun, Lucky's .38, climbed into Lucky's Camaro, and headed to the shooting range. No way she'd match him. He'd scored top marksman in the department three years running.

Only a handful of people filled the range. Lucky strolled down to the end, slipped on earmuffs, and handed a pair to Charlotte. "Ladies first."

His sister let out a snort. "If you think I'm a lady, you obviously don't remember all the times I kicked your ass."

She still had perfect stance, even if the last time they'd shot together had been beer bottles off fence posts. She tore the hell out of the center of a paper man-shaped target.

When they left the range, most of the men who'd ogled her on the way in gave her wide berth. Smart fellas.

Lucky kept the target to send to Jimmy up in Virginia, lest he get any ideas about following through on his interest in Charlotte.

"You didn't beat me." Lucky hadn't won by much though.

"Nah, but since I don't shoot at people for a living..." Charlotte patted her heavy purse.

"You're still good. Not rusty a bit. You practice?"

Again with the grin of a villain on *South Bend Springs*. "Every now and then some good-old-boy wannabe shows up at the hospital, talking shit about hunting and how good he is. I take him down a peg or two, and if they ain't cheap, I walk away a few hundred dollars richer." She huffed on her fingernails and brushed them against her collar. "Makes me real popular with some folks at the hospital too. They know where to put their money."

Sounded like Lucky teaching newbies the pecking order in a boxing ring, and the office betting pool profiting from the outcome.

Lucky stared at her target, her shots concentrated near dead center. She'd have beaten most guys in the department. He let out a low whistle. "Ever consider giving up on being a nurse and going into drug enforcement instead?" He wouldn't let her risk her life, but damn could the woman shoot.

"Not a chance, brother. I tell you what. When you send 'em to the emergency room, somebody's got to patch 'em up."

And if a shooter ever entered the hospital, they'd get taken out by the harmless-looking nurse with a Texas-sized handbag and a North Carolina accent.

Lucky flipped a veggie burger over on the part of the grill set off as the no meat zone. Moose whined, licked his chops, and returned to Todd and Ty's game of Keep Away with the football. Critter would sleep good tonight.

Lucky's cell phone rang. He checked the screen before answering. This made four times today. "Hi, Mama. Yes,

I'm fine. He's doing fine too." Like the last three times she'd called. "We've been busy with work, but we'll come visit you soon. Yeah, she's here with her boys. We're having a cookout. No, Mama. Okay. I understand. I love you too."

Maybe someday she'd stop calling to ensure he lived. But still, nice to be wanted, though she never mentioned his father, and Lucky never dared call his old man directly. Too many dial tones still haunted his memories. Maybe one day.

Charlotte ambled out the back door, arms loaded down with plates, forks, and spoons, which she dropped onto the picnic table Lucky'd sworn they'd never use the day they'd loaded the thing into Bo's vehicle at the hardware store. "Mama again?"

"Yeah."

"You'll get used to it. It helps if you text her first so she doesn't have to call."

Words to remember.

Charlotte strolled over to the grill, a glass of tea in each hand. "Looks like you've done well for yourself, big brother, even if you did try hard to be the black sheep of the family."

"Yeah. Who'd a thunk it'd turn out to be goodie-two-shoes Bristol?" He'd been welcomed back into the fold, but he wouldn't cut his brother out of his memory. Wouldn't stop using the name like the family stopped using his after his fuckup.

"It's hard not to hate him, ain't it?" Charlotte handed Lucky a glass of tea.

Lucky swilled down half the drink. "I'm not so sure I don't." He put an arm around his sister. "He took my family from me, tried to kill me, turned his back when Daddy needed him most, and damned near killed Daytona." Not to mention the jury still being out on what happened to Uncle Ned.

Charlotte, ever the voice of reason, snorted. "Don't. It's a waste of time. Besides, would you have the good life you have now if not for Bristol?"

306

Would he? Would Lucky have wound up with Bo if he'd not been hurt and so damned lonely? "That's what Bo tells me."

"Smart man. You should listen to him." She pursed her lips, crinkles forming the corners of her eyes. "But he couldn't have been too smart if he showed up at the door of a North Carolina redneck asking about her brother."

"Glad you didn't shoot him." And she hadn't given Bo any information, either, protecting Lucky with all the fierceness of a mother bear.

"Me too. He's good people." Her lips rose at the corners and fell again. "Things between Mama and Daddy might never be right again."

"Nope." If his parents hadn't been able to make their relationship work, what chance in hell did Lucky have of hanging on to Bo?

"And things might not ever be right between you and Daddy either."

"I always thought he could do no wrong, and blamed myself for him cutting me out of the family." Damn, how he'd beaten himself up over the years.

Charlotte stared up into Lucky's eyes. "I don't want to take sides, but as a parent, I can speak from experience. Parenting is hard. Lord knows I've made mistakes. And I'll make more, but I love my boys. Nothing, I mean abso-fucking-lutely nothing could make me turn my back on them.

"But what's done is done, there's no going back. The relationship you and Daddy had is over. It's up to you to decide if you'd like to have another, and what form it'll take." She stared off toward her boys. "Just remember, unconditional love goes both ways, and shutting off even a tiny piece of your heart affects every other relationship you have. Whatever you decide to do, make sure you've studied all the angles." She planted a kiss on Lucky's cheek and wandered off to set the table while Lucky turned back to grilling and mulling over her words. Occasionally she and Bo brought out buns, chips, lettuce, and such.

His wise-beyond-her-years sister left him with plenty to think on. No, he'd never again be the kid who idolized and believed his father could do no wrong. But he could be a man who respected another man, accepted his apology, and learned to love him again, flaws and all.

The way Bo loved Lucky despite his flaws.

Lucky's neighbor waved one hand through a hole in the plank fencing, flipping a burger with the other, while his kids played in the yard nearby and his wife set stuff on their picnic table.

Lucky'd better replace the faulty boards in the privacy fence if he planned on getting any privacy.

Ty shrieked in laughter, tussling on the ground with Moose, while Todd sat in a lounge chair, Cat Lucky in his lap.

Hell, Lucky had gone and got domesticated.

And he didn't give a flying fuck. Maybe he'd been wrong all those years to call a nine-to-five life and a house in the suburbs pure hell.

Nah. Couldn't be. Lucky was never wrong. Well, not often. Okay, not all the time.

Bo wrapped his arms around Lucky, while Charlotte snapped a picture with her cell phone. She grinned. "Aww... y'all are so danged cute together."

Lucky shot a glance at the neighbors to get their reaction. They'd better not be homophobes, or Lucky might be tempted to install a ten-foot tall privacy fence. Topped with barbed wire.

The man saluted with his spatula. His wife waved.

Okay. Lucky wouldn't put out search warrants on them today to see if they kept a stash of pot in the house for recreational use. He had bigger fish to fry, or rather, burgers to cook.

He had the partner, but the kids were borrowed. Sooner or later they'd leave with their mother.

And the house would be quiet again.

Somewhere along the way he'd learned to hate quiet.

***

Lucky sat at the kitchen table, watching the sunrise. He'd let Bo sleep for a while. Poor guy spent the better part of the night driving Todd and Ty around Atlanta hunting for poofballs, or snipe or what the hell ever on their cellphones. And tonight?

Tonight they'd stay indoors, watch movies on the big screen TV—the louder and funnier the better, and ignore the fireworks going off at neighbors' houses. Bo hadn't had a PTSD episode in a while now.

Lucky would do his damnedest to ensure he didn't tonight.

Strange, though. At one time, an act of God or Congress couldn't get Lucky out of bed before nine.

Charlotte came in and poured herself a cup of coffee. "Can I join you? I want to talk to you about something." The dark circles under her eyes said she hadn't slept well.

What now? "It's a free country," he said, but he meant *You're always welcome with me.* And she was.

"I been thinking..." She sat down beside him and took a sip of plain black coffee. Brrr... How'd she drink the shit without sugar?

"What you got on your mind?" He sipped coffee and pretended not to worry too much. For her to beat around the bush, this must be something bad.

"Nobody asked me about the house and the boys' college funds after Victor's arrest, and I sure as shit wasn't going to say anything."

Funny how she never seemed to swear in front of her kids, acting the perfect Mom and scolding them if they cussed, but whenever she and Lucky got together, time turned back and they were as comfortable together as they'd always been.

God, how he'd missed her.

"Anyway, with Todd starting school down here, Ty's a bit jealous his brother'll get to hang out with Uncle Ric... I mean, Uncle Lucky." Charlotte set her cup on the table with a clink.

"He can come visit when school's out. That is, if I'm not on assignment. They both can." It'd be nice having the young 'uns around from time to time. Not to mention how well they'd bonded with Bo.

"The boys think you're totally cool." She propped her arm on the table and rested her head on her hand. "Ty's changed his mind about joining the Navy. Been talking about following in your footsteps after graduation."

"Oh no!" Easy for a kid to hero-worship a living-in-the-fast-lane felon, but the kid would follow in his lawless foot-steps over Lucky's dead body. Which, if he waited long enough, might happen two or three more times before Lucky finally wound up with a headstone in a graveyard for real.

"I don't mean the drug running part. I meant law enforcement."

Oh hell. "No. Too dangerous." Lucky wouldn't wish the ugliness of the streets on anyone, especially blood kin.

"You worried about him?"

"Aren't you?"

Charlotte grabbed Lucky's chin and yanked him around eye to eye with her. "I've worried about you every single day since you left home. Didn't you know? You've given me quite a few heart attacks over the years. And here you are, the same ole cocky banty rooster, hell bent and determined to fight. It may have taken you a while to get your head out of your ass, but I'm told you're a pretty good narcotics agent. If that's what my son wants to do, yeah, I'll worry for him. But if he's deter-mined, you know as well as I do it's damned near impossible to change a Lucklighter's mind."

Yup. Lucky did.

"And having someone around who knows a thing or two you can't learn in a textbook can only be a plus." Charlotte let go of his face. Lucky missed the heat of her hand. "Anyway, I been considering my options. There're a few small towns be-tween here and Clemson where a decent house costs about a third of what mine would sell for."

Lucky's heart slammed against his ribs. "What are you saying?"

"I'm saying I miss my brother, my kids miss my brother, and we've wasted enough time. I won't get all underfoot and in your way, promise. You know I'm not like that. But I want you and Bo in my life. Besides, I never been away from my babies." She paused to sip her coffee. "I'd like to be close enough to see Todd when I want to. And you know how I always wanted to be a nurse?"

"Yeah."

"There's several places down here where I can transfer my online credits and go to nursing school a whole lot cheaper than in Spokane. So, I'm kicking around the idea of selling the house, moving down here, and maybe taking a part time job while I study nursing."

What? Charlotte living close? Close enough for him to be Uncle Richie to her boys again? Close enough to visit often? Finally follow through on her life-long dream?

Oh, hell yeah!

"Besides, your fur kids might need to stay with Auntie Charlotte sometime while you're on assignment." Her grin brought to mind her ten-year-old self, planning mischief.

"I'm afraid they might be the only nephews you get outta me."

"Why? Don't you want kids? Growing up you used to say you'd never get married, but at the time I didn't realize why. The world has changed. Nothing's stopping you now."

"Unless he keeps telling me no." Of course, Lucky hadn't gotten the words out the other night before Charlotte showed up. Maybe if he asked again...

"Give him time. Keep asking." Charlotte squeezed Lucky's hand. "Pour on the Lucklighter charm. And if he still says no, you can hog tie him and haul him off to the preacher."

"I might have to." Unless he wore Bo down.

"But it's not like parents have to be legally married or nothing." Charlotte swirled a fingertip around the rim of her cup. "Half the folks we went to school with ain't married. Didn't stop them from having a passel of young 'uns."

Lucky somehow managed to raise a single brow. "It's not like me and Bo can have kids. And nobody in their right mind is about to give a child to a man with my criminal record."

"Wasn't your record expunged when you got a new name?"

"Yeah." Still, the adoption people might not like giving a kid to a gay couple.

"Do you not want kids?"

No need blustering and lying. She'd see right through him. She always had. Confession time. "Yeah. So does Bo. But I'm not getting his hopes up to see 'em crushed. He's had enough disappointment in his life already."

Her grin turned wicked. "You and Bo might not be able to have a kid of your own, but I know the next best thing."

"What?"

She sighed and stared at her coffee cup. Okay, here came the part where she finally got to what was eating at her. "I've got two wonderful boys, but I don't want to raise any more kids."

"And what's that got to do with me having any?"

She locked her determined gaze to his. "Don't answer until you've had a chance to really consider my proposal and discuss the matter with Bo, but... even though I don't want to be a mom again, all my parts still work. I'd be a pretty awesome Auntie Charlotte, don't you think?"

If Lucky's heart somersaulted any harder, he'd be doing cartwheels. "Do what? What the hell are you saying?" Surely she wasn't implying...

Charlotte clasped Lucky's hand in a death grip. "I'm saying, when the time comes and you and Bo are ready to start a family, me having Bo's baby is the closest thing you'll get to your own. The kid might even look like a Lucklighter."

No. Any kids needed to look like Bo. A little girl with Bo's dark hair and freckles, or a boy with a dimple in his cheek. And boy or girl, they'd have a Grandma and Grandpa. Uncles and an aunt. Cousins...

"But what kind of father could I possibly be?" The things he'd done...

"A good one. Who makes mistakes. Who's human, and who loves his child dearly, is always there no matter what. And who understands when the child is human too."

Could Lucky be a good father? "I... I don't know what to say."

"Give it some thought." The weariness left her face. "Now, why don't you take your man breakfast in bed while I haul the boys out to the nearest Shoney's? I'll talk to them about relocating while you have a nice little chat with my future brother-in-law."

Those were some good drugs they'd given Lucky in the hospital. Was he still knocked out and dreaming? Or had Bristol succeeded in killing him, and all those years of his mother's prayers gotten him into Heaven?

He sat at the table while Charlotte roused the boys and left the house, then he rose and let the fur kids out to avoid fighting them away from the stove. On autopilot, he made pancakes and heated some wish-it-was-real-bacon. He'd even eat some of the soy meat substitute without complaining this morning. Topping the meal off with a cup of decaf green tea sweetened with stevia ought to earn him some points.

Or a blowjob.

No, this wasn't about Lucky getting off. Even he'd had enough of his selfish ways.

Bo still slept, letting out the occasional snore when Lucky strolled into their room and placed a breakfast-laden tray on the nightstand—next to a dragon keychain.

Lucky drank his fill of sleep-tousled hair and tanned skin, a far different look than the shaved body, highlighted hair, and buffed nails of the rookie who strode into his life three years ago, quoting textbooks and replacing bad eating habits and caffeine with healthier options.

Same bubble butt. Hallelujah.

Back then he'd tried so hard to be perfect, while Lucky put the same amount of effort into being an asshole. He might never come close to Bo's goodness, but somewhere over time

Bo's influence helped shave off a few of Lucky's rough edges and they'd come closer to meeting in the middle.

Had anyone dared suggest he'd want the rookie in his life permanently, Lucky would've hauled their lying asses to the gym and kicked butt in a boxing ring.

Bo saw past all the bluster and the shit Lucky'd sooner forget, rode out the storm of bad moods and hard times. Made Lucky a better man.

And good Lord willing, he always would.

Lucky eased down on the edge of the bed, admiring the light splash of freckles across Bo's ever-so-slightly crooked nose. He'd always appeared young, but the past few years added a bit of character. Here and there a white strand peeked through his dark hair—hair now spread out in waves on a pillow instead of the every-hair-in-place style Bo wore when they'd first met.

Pieces fell into place. How hard Bo used to work at being perfect to make up for the past. Now he'd learned to relax, be himself. He rested so peacefully, sprawled out on the sheets, when once he'd spent nights on the couch, unable to lie in a bed without having nightmares and flashbacks.

Maybe, just maybe, Lucky helped Bo too.

Lucky tip-toed to a door they'd left closed pretty much since moving in and entered the unused room. Colorful cartoon animals graced the walls, and if he didn't study the images too hard, he could ignore the rough patch job he'd done on the goose. Of course, the blurring in his eyes helped.

They'd put the crib over there...

ABOUT THE AUTHOR

You will know Eden Winters by her distinctive white plumage and exuberant cry of "Hey, y'all!" in a Southern US drawl so thick it renders even the simplest of words unrecognizable. Watch out, she hugs!

Driven by insatiable curiosity, she possibly holds the world's record for curriculum changes to the point that she's never quite earned a degree but is a force to be reckoned with at Trivial Pursuit.

She's trudged down hallways with police detectives, learned to disarm knife-wielding bad guys, and witnessed the correct way to blow doors off buildings. Her e-mail contains various snippets of forensic wisdom, such as "What would a dead body left in a Mexican drug tunnel look like after six months?" In the process of her adventures she has written fourteen m/m romance novels, has won several Rainbow Awards, was a Lambda Awards Finalist, and lives in terror of authorities showing up at her door to question her Internet searches.

When not putting characters in dangerous situations she's a mild-mannered business executive, mother, grandmother, vegetarian, and PFLAG activist.

Her natural habitats are airports, coffee shops, and on the backs of motorcycles.

For more information about Eden, please visit her website at www.edenwinters.com.

.

MORE FROM EDEN WINTERS

Other novels:

There are good guys, bad guys, and then there's Lucky.

Former drug trafficker Richmond "Lucky" Lucklighter flaunts his past like a badge of honor. He speaks his mind, doesn't play nice, and flirts with disaster while working off his sentence with the Southeastern Narcotics Bureau. If he can keep out of trouble a while longer he'll be a free man—after he trains his replacement.

Textbook-quoting, by the book Bo Schollenberger is everything Lucky isn't. Lucky slurps coffee, Bo lives caffeine free. Lucky worships bacon, Bo eats tofu. Lucky trusts no one, Bo calls suspects by first name. Yet when the chips are down on their shared case of breaking up a drug diversion ring, they may have more in common than they believe.

Two men. Close quarters. Friction results in heat. But Lucky scoffs at partnerships, no matter how thrilling the roller-coaster. Bo has two months to break down Lucky's defenses... and seconds are ticking by.

Dead men can't love.

Former drug trafficker Richmond "Lucky" Lucklighter "died" in the line of duty while working off a ten-year sentence in service to the Southeastern Narcotics Bureau, only to be reborn as Simon "Lucky" Harrison. The newbie he trained, former Marine Bo Schollenberger, is now his partner on (and maybe off) the job. It's hard to tell when Lucky doesn't understand relationships or have a clue what any sane human is doing in his bed. Bo's nice to have around, sure, but there's none of that picking-out-china-together crap for Lucky.

While fighting PTSD, memories of a horrid childhood, and a prescription drug addiction, Bo is paying for his mistakes. Using his pharmacy license for the good guys provides the sort of education he never got in school. Undercover with his hard-headed partner, Bo learns that not everything is as it seems in the world of pharmaceuticals.

When a prescription drug shortage jeopardizes the patients at Rosario Children's Cancer Center, it not only pits Bo and Lucky against predatory opportunists, but also each other. How can they tell who the villains are? The bad guys don't wear black hats, but they might wear white coats.

Winner 2014 Rainbow Awards Best Gay Mystery / Thriller

Renegade biker. Drug runner. Recovering addict. Wanted by the Southeastern Narcotics Bureau. But he isn't a crook, he's the law.

SNB Agent Bo Schollenberger's solved his cases using his brains and not a gun, and with his partner, not alone. Now he's handed a tough new case involving designer drugs that turn users violent. One false move could end his life as he immerses himself into a motorcycle gang to locate the source. His fate depends on how well he can impersonate someone else. Someone named Cyrus Cooper.

Cyrus is everything Bo Schollenberger isn't, including the badass enforcer for a smuggling ring. He establishes pecking order with his fists and doesn't take shit from anybody, not even the undercover agent who comes to help his case.

Simon "Lucky" Harrison's always been the best, whichever side of the law he was on. Former trafficker turned SNB agent, he damned well ought to be undercover in this motorcycle gang, instead of hanging around the office going crazy with new policies, new people, and "inter-departmental cooperation" that sticks him in a classroom. Yet he's passed over for the SNB's biggest case in decades in favor of the rookie who shares his bed. A man Lucky thought he knew.

When survival depends on a web of tangled lies, lines blur, worlds collide, and a high stakes game turns friend to foe. Lucky knows the difference between Bo the agent and Cyrus the outlaw, but does Bo?

Also in the series:

More from Rocky Ridge Books

Pro cyclist Luca Biondi lives for the race. For the star of Team Antano-Clark, victory lies within his grasp—if he can outdistance 200 other hopefuls, avoid suspicion from race officials, and keep his lieutenant more friend than foe. Luca also has secrets, and eyes for amateur cyclist and journalist Christopher Nye.

Christopher understands Luca's need to keep their relationship under wraps, but chafes at hiding in the shadows of his lover's career. He's ready to cheer Luca's victories, but he knows too well how triumph can turn to tears. While Christopher's heart sees Luca the man, his inner journalist—and his editor—sees the cycling world's biggest scoop.

From the jagged curves of the Colorado Rockies to the viciously steep Belgian hills, Luca can ride out any bumps—except rumors.

A few words in the wrong ear could crash everything. With miles between them, hints of scandal, and Luca's fierce need to guard his reputation, a journalist might have to let go of the biggest story of his career or risk forcing his lover to abandon the race. Christopher and Luca face a path more treacherous than any road to the summit.

The lights go down and stage lights up. The Dark Angels have arrived. With his come-hither voice and body made for sin, lead singer Angel Luv draws lovers like a magnet. And when he caresses and taunts shy guitarist Darius Stone on stage, well...it's an act, right? But every touch lights a fire, and every flirtatious glance chips away at Dare's certainty that he's straight. No one else has so captured his imagination.

Temptation beckons. It's hard not to notice the want in Dare's eyes, the way he stares when he thinks Angel's not watching. One wrong move might scare him away, but a work trip to exotic Bali might be the perfect place to let Dare explore his sexuality, with none to be the wiser. But their "friends with benefits" pact has an expiration date, that just might sour their friendship.

Also in the Dark Angels series:
    Tied Together
    Finally Fallen
    Happy Holidays